BLOOD

"I knew you were going to be trouble the minute I saw you," he murmured, his low voice brushing over her skin like a caress.

Serra frowned, glaring into Fane's hard, starkly beautiful face. Hell. He was supposed to be the aloof, untouchable Sentinel. The distant warrior she'd sworn had rejected her for the last time.

She couldn't possibly fight her aching need when he wasn't playing by the rules.

"You don't even remember our first meeting," she accused, her treacherous fingers lingering on his surprisingly sensuous lips.

His hands smoothed down her back and she shivered as he cupped her ass with an intimacy that made her breath tangle in her throat.

"I remember every second of our first meeting," he informed her, the movement of his lips beneath her fingers oddly erotic.

"You were the most beautiful man I'd ever seen."

He arched a brow. "Beautiful?"

"You are."

His hands skimmed up her hips to slide beneath the edge of her sweater.

She hissed in shock, but he held his searching gaze even as she shuddered at the feel of his hands on her bare skin. . . .

Books by Alexandra Ivy

Guardians of Eternity
WHEN DARKNESS COMES
EMBRACE THE DARKNESS
DARKNESS EVERLASTING
DARKNESS REVEALED
DARKNESS UNLEASHED
BEYOND THE DARKNESS
DEVOURED BY DARKNESS
BOUND BY DARKNESS
FEAR THE DARKNESS
DARKNESS AVENGED
HUNT THE DARKNESS

The Immortal Rogues
MY LORD VAMPIRE
MY LORD ETERNITY
MY LORD IMMORTALITY

The Sentinels
BORN IN BLOOD
BLOOD ASSASSIN

Historical Romance
SOME LIKE IT WICKED
SOME LIKE IT SINFUL
SOME LIKE IT BRAZEN

And don't miss these Guardians of Eternity novellas
TAKEN BY DARKNESS in YOURS FOR ETERNITY
DARKNESS ETERNAL in SUPERNATURAL
WHERE DARKNESS LIVES in THE REAL
WEREWIVES OF VAMPIRE COUNTY
LEVET (eBook only)
A VERY LEVET CHRISTMAS (eBook only)

And look for this Sentinel novella
OUT OF CONTROL in PREDATORY

Published by Kensington Publishing Corporation

BLOOD
ASSASSIN

ALEXANDRA IVY

ZEBRA BOOKS
KENSINGTON PUBLISHING CORP.
http://www.kensingtonbooks.com

ZEBRA BOOKS are published by

Kensington Publishing Corp.
119 West 40th Street
New York, NY 10018

All Kensington titles, imprints, and distributed lines are
available at special quantity discounts for bulk purchases for
sales promotion, premiums, fund-raising, educational, or institutional use.

Special book excerpts or customized printings can also be
created to fit specific needs. For details, write or phone the
office of the Kensington Special Sales Manager: Attn. Special
Sales Department. Kensington Publishing Corp., 119 West
40th Street, New York, NY 10018. Phone: 1-800-221-2647.

Zebra and the Z logo Reg. U.S. Pat. & TM Off.

First Printing: January 2015
ISBN-13: 978-1-4201-2516-0
ISBN-10: 1-4201-2516-8

First Electronic Edition: January 2015
eISBN-13: 978-1-4201-3737-8
eISBN-10: 1-4201-3737-9

10 9 8 7 6 5 4 3 2 1

Printed in the United States of America

Sentinels

The history of the Sentinels was mysterious even among the high-bloods.

Most people knew that there were two sects of the dangerous warriors. The guardian Sentinels who possessed innate magic. They were heavily tattooed to protect themselves from magical attacks, as well as any mind control, and were used to protect those high-bloods who were vulnerable when they were forced to travel away from the safety of Valhalla.

And then there were the hunter Sentinels. They had no magic, but they were equally lethal. Hunters were used to enforce the laws of Valhalla, and since they were able to "pass" as human and capable of moving through the world undetected, they were used to track down high-bloods who might be a danger to themselves or others.

It was also well known that both sects of Sentinels were stronger and faster than humans, with an endurance that was off the charts. And both were trained by monks to kill with their hands as well as with most known weapons.

But that was as far as public knowledge went.

How they were chosen and how they'd become the protectors of the high-bloods were closely guarded secrets.

No one but the Sentinels knew what happened behind the thick walls of the monasteries where they were trained.

Chapter One

One glance into the private gym would send most humans fleeing in humiliation.

What normal male would want to lift weights next to a dozen Sentinels?

Not only were the warriors six foot plus of pure chiseled muscles and bad attitudes, but the very air reeked of aggression and testosterone-fueled competition.

Hardly a place for the weekend jock trying to battle the bulge.

It was, however, the perfect place for the Sentinels to work off a little steam.

The vast fitness center was filled with mats, punching bags, and treadmills. And, at the back of the room, there was a row of weight machines where the baddest of the badasses was currently bench-pressing enough weight to crush a mortal.

Fane looked like he'd been sculpted from stone. A six foot three behemoth, he had the strength of an ox and the speed of a cheetah. A result of the natural talents that came from being born a Sentinel, and the fact he'd been honed from his youth to become a weapon.

He was also covered from the top of his shaved head to

the tips of his toes in intricate tattoos that protected him from all magic.

The monks who'd taken him in as a young child had trained him in all the known martial arts, as well as the most sophisticated weapons.

He was walking, talking death.

Which meant very few bothered to notice the dark eyes that held a razor-sharp intelligence or the starkly beautiful features beneath the elegant markings.

Something that rarely bothered Fane. For the past decade he'd been a guardian to Callie Brown. All people needed to know about him was that he would kill them the second they threatened the young diviner.

Now, he . . .

Fane blew out a sigh, replacing the weights on the bar so he could wipe the sweat from his naked chest.

Three months ago Callie had nearly died when they'd battled the powerful necromancer Lord Zakhar, and during the battle she'd fallen in love with a human policeman. Or at least Duncan O'Conner had been passing as human. Turned out he had the extra powers of a Sentinel as well as being a soul-gazer, which meant he could read the souls of others. He was perfectly suited to take over the protection of Callie.

Fane's hand absently touched the center of his chest where he'd once felt the constant connection to Callie. They'd transferred the bond last week, but he still felt the strange void that was wearing on his nerves.

He needed a distraction.

The thought had barely passed through his mind when a shadow fell over him and he glanced up to discover a tall, lean man with copper-tinted skin and ebony eyes. Wolfe, the current Tagos (leader of all Sentinels) had a proud, hawkish nose, with heavy brows and prominent cheekbones that all combined to give him the appearance of an ancient Egyptian deity.

It was a face that spoke of power and fierce masculinity. The sort of face that intimidated men and made women wonder if he was as dangerous as he looked.

He was.

Just as arresting was the shoulder-length black hair that had a startling streak of gray that started at his right temple. There were whispers that when Wolfe was a babe he'd been touched by the devil.

Something Fane fully believed.

Swallowing a curse, Fane tossed aside his sweaty towel. Damn. This wasn't the distraction he'd been wanting.

Wolfe was dressed in jeans and a loose cotton shirt with the sleeves rolled up to his elbows. He had his arms folded over his chest and was studying Fane with an expression that warned he wasn't pleased.

Around them the gym went silent as the other Sentinels pretended they weren't straining to overhear the potential confrontation.

"I heard through the grapevine you've taken a position as a trainer," he said. That was Wolfe. Always straight to the point.

Fane scowled. It'd been less than twenty-four hours since he'd made the decision to seek a position as trainer in a monastery halfway around the world. How the hell had word spread so fast?

"The grapevine should mind its own business."

The ebony eyes narrowed. "And I shouldn't have to listen to gossip to learn when one of my Sentinels is leaving Valhalla."

Fane met his Tagos glare for glare. "I have no direct duties here, at least not anymore. I'm allowed to return to the monastery without clearing it with you."

The air heated. Sentinels' body temperature ran hotter than humans, and when their emotions were provoked they could actually warm the air around them.

"Don't be an ass. This isn't about duties, I'm worried about you."

Oh hell.

This was exactly what Fane didn't want.

He'd rather be shot in the head than have someone fussing over him.

"There's nothing to worry about. You know that I was a trainer for years before coming to Valhalla. I'm simply returning to my brothers in Tibet."

"You've just endured the removal of a long-standing bond. A traumatic experience for any guardian," the older man ruthlessly pressed. "And *we're* your brothers, you thankless son-of-a-bitch."

Fane gave an impatient shake of his head. Wolfe was a hunter Sentinel, not a guardian, which meant he could never understand the truth of the bond.

"I know what you're thinking, but you're wrong."

Wolfe slowly arched a brow. There weren't many who had the chutzpah to stand up to him.

"What am I thinking?"

"Callie and I never had a sexual relationship."

"Did you want one?"

"No," Fane growled. "Jesus Christ. She was like a sister to me. She still is."

The dark gaze never wavered. "And it doesn't bother you that she's with Duncan?"

"Not so long as he treats her right." Fane allowed a humorless smile to touch his lips. "If he doesn't . . . I'll rip out his heart with my bare hands."

Wolfe nodded. They both understood it wasn't an empty threat.

"Good," the Tagos said. "But that wasn't my concern."

Fane surged to his feet, his tattoos deepening in response to his rising temper. It was barely past noon, but it'd already been a long day.

"Does this conversation have an end in sight?"

Wolfe stood his ground.

No shocker.

The man *always* stood his ground.

"This past decade has been dedicated to protecting Callie. Now you're going to have a void where the bond used to be. It's going to make you . . ." He paused, as if sorting through his brain for the right word. "Twitchy."

"Twitchy?"

Wolfe shrugged. "I was going to say as mean as a viper, but that would be an insult to the viper."

There was a snicker from the front of the room. Fane sent a glare that instantly had the younger Sentinel scurrying from the gym.

He returned his attention to his leader, his gaze narrowed. "And fuck you too."

"I'm serious, Fane." Wolfe insisted, standing with the calm of a born predator who could explode into violence in the blink of an eye. "You need to take time to adjust."

Fane grimaced. "Don't tell me your door is always open so we can chat about our feelings?"

"Hell, no." Wolfe shuddered. "But I'm always available if you need a partner who isn't terrified to spar with you."

"Ah, so you're offering to kick my ass?"

A hint of a smile softened Wolfe's austere features. "And to offer you a place at Valhalla. I'm in constant need of good warriors." The smile faded. "Especially after our battle with the necromancer. We lost too many."

Fane ground his teeth at the sharp stab of loss that pierced his heart. During the battle against the necromancer they'd lost far too many Sentinels. Many of them brothers that Fane had served with for decades.

And while the threat of death was a constant companion for warriors, they had rarely lost so many at one time.

It had left them dangerously weakened.

"All the more reason for me to train the next generation," he pointed out.

Wolfe refused to budge. Stubborn bastard.

"Someone else can handle the training. These are dangerous times. I need experienced warriors."

Smart enough to avoid ramming his head into a brick wall, Fane instead changed the topic of conversation.

"Did you find any information on the Brotherhood?"

Wolfe muttered a curse at the mention of the secret society of humans who had been discovered three months ago. Like many norms they held a profound hatred toward "mutants," but they were far more organized than most. And more troubling, they possessed a dangerous ability to sense high-bloods merely by being in their presence.

They were a new, unexpected complication.

The zealots might be nothing more than a pain in the ass. Or they might be . . . genocidal.

"Nothing useful," Wolfe admitted, his tone revealing his barely leashed desire to pound the truth out of the bastards.

"I can do some digging at the monastery if you want," Fane offered. "Their library is the most extensive in the world. If there's information on the secret society, it will be there."

"Actually I have Arel working on gathering intel."

Wolfe nodded his head toward a young hunter Sentinel who was running on a treadmill. The overhead lights picked up the honey highlights in Arel's light brown hair and turned his eyes to molten gold. He looked like an angel unless you took time to notice the honed muscles and the merciless strength that simmered deep in the stunning eyes.

He also had the kind of charm that made women buzz around him like besotted bees.

Including one woman in particular for a short period of time.

His hands unconsciously clenched.

"Arel?" he ground out.

Wolfe made a sad attempt at looking innocent. "Is that a problem?"

"He's young." Fane forced his hands to relax, his expression stoic. He'd lost his right to make a claim on any woman years before. "And he has no magic," he continued.

Wolfe deliberately allowed his gaze to roam over Fane's distinctive tattoos. "Which means he has a shot at infiltrating the group if we decide they're going to be a danger in the future. Something that would be impossible for most of us."

Fane couldn't argue.

Although guardian Sentinels had the benefit of magic, as well as the protection of their tattooing to avoid spells and psychic attacks, they did tend to stand out in a crowd.

Understatement of the year.

Arel, on the other hand, looked like a kid fresh out of college.

"It's risky," Fane at last muttered. "We don't know how powerful this Brotherhood is."

Wolfe lifted a shoulder. "He's a Sentinel."

"True." Fane tried to dismiss the problem from his mind. Soon enough he would be in the seclusion of the monastery and the dangers of the world would no longer be his concern. Right? "It sounds like you have it covered. I'll send you more warriors when they've completed their training."

"Dammit, Fane . . ." Wolfe bit off his words as the atmosphere in the gym abruptly changed.

Both men turned to discover what had happened.

Or rather . . . who . . . had happened.

"Shit," Fane breathed, a familiar ache settling in the center of his chest at the sight of the beautiful female who sashayed into the room.

Serra Vetrov had the habit of changing the atmosphere in rooms since she'd left the nursery.

Hell, he'd seen men walk into walls and drive cars off the road when she strolled past.

An elegantly tall woman with long, glossy black hair that contrasted with her pale, ivory skin, she had lush curves that she emphasized with her tight leather pants and matching vest that was cut to reveal a jaw-dropping amount of her generous breasts.

Her features were delicately carved. Her pale green eyes were thickly lashed, her nose narrow, and her lips so sensually full they gave the impression of a sex kitten.

Although anyone foolish enough to underestimate her was in for an unpleasant surprise.

Serra was not only a powerful psychic but she was also a rare telepath who could use objects to connect with the mind of the owner. Over the years, she'd used her talents more than once to find missing children or to track down violent offenders.

On the darker side, she could also use her skills to force humans, and those high-bloods without mental shields, to see illusions and could even implant memories in their more vulnerable minds.

Still, it wasn't her dangerous powers that made grown men scramble out of her path. Serra had a tongue that could flay at a hundred yards and she wasn't afraid to use it.

Wolfe sent Fane a mocking smile. "It appears I'm not the only one who listens to the grapevine. Good luck, amigo."

Turning, he strolled toward the cluster of Sentinels who

were watching Serra cross the gym like a pack of starving hounds.

Bastards.

Serra kept her head held high and a smile pinned to her lips as she marched past the gaping men. She was female enough to appreciate being noticed by the opposite sex. Why not? But today she barely noticed the audible groans as she took a direct path toward her prey.

She felt a tiny surge of amusement at the thought of Fane being anyone's prey.

The massive warrior was 250 pounds of pure muscle and raw male power. He was also one of the rare few who was completely impervious to her ability to poke around in his mind.

Which was a blessing and a curse.

A blessing because it was impossible for a psychic to completely block out an intimate partner, which was a distraction that would make any lover cringe. There was nothing quite so demeaning as being in the middle of sex and to realize your partner was picturing Angelina Jolie.

And a curse because Fane was about as chatty as a rock. His feelings were locked down so tight Serra feared that someday they would explode.

And not in a good way.

Or maybe it would be good, she silently told herself, gliding to a halt directly in front of his half-naked form.

There weren't many things worse than watching all emotions being stripped away as you approached the man you'd loved for the past two decades.

Especially when she was a seething mass of emotions.

She wanted to grab his beautiful face in her hands and

kiss him until he melted into a puddle of goo. No. She wanted to kick him in the nuts for being such a prick.

Maybe she'd kick him and then kiss it better.

To make matters worse she was on a lust-driven adrenaline high.

Just standing next to his half-naked body coated in sweat made her heart pump and her mouth dry.

God. She was so fucking pathetic.

Accepting that her companion wasn't going to break the awkward silence, she tilted her chin up another notch.

Any higher and she was going to be staring at the ceiling.

"Fane," she purred softly.

His dark gaze remained focused on her face, resisting any temptation to glance at her skimpy vest. Of course, if it hadn't been for the rare times she'd caught him casting covert glances at her body, she might suspect he hadn't yet realized she was a woman.

"Serra."

On the way to the gym she'd practiced what she was going to say. She was going to be cool. Composed. And in complete control.

Instead the fear lodged in the pit of her belly made her strike out like a petulant child.

"You're leaving?"

He gave a slow dip of his head. "I'm returning to Tibet."

The fear began to spread through her body, her hands clenching at her sides. "Did you ever intend to tell me?"

"Yes."

"When?" she snapped. "On your way out the door?"

"Does it matter?"

Oh yeah. He was definitely getting kicked in the nuts.

"Yes, it damned well matters."

He remained stoic. Unmoved by her anger. "What do you want from me?"

She lowered her voice. It wasn't that she gave a shit that they had an audience. Living in Valhalla meant that privacy was a rare commodity. But she had some pride, dammit. She didn't want them to hear her beg.

"You know what I want."

Something flared through the dark eyes. Something that sliced through her heart like a dagger.

"It's impossible," he rasped. "I'll always care for you, Serra, but not in the way you need."

She should walk away.

It's what any woman with an ounce of sense would do.

But when had she claimed any sense when it came to this man?

Instead she stepped forward, bringing them nose to nose. Well, they would be nose to nose if he didn't have six inches on her.

"Liar."

He frowned, the heat from his body brushing over her bare skin like a caress. Serra shuddered. Oh God. She'd wanted him for so long.

It was like a sickness.

"A Sentinel doesn't lie."

She snorted at the ridiculous claim. "Maybe not, but you can twist the truth until it screams. And the truth is that you've always used your duty to Callie as a shield between us."

His fists landed on his hips, his eyes narrowing at her accusation. "My duty was more than a shield."

Okay. He had a point.

His bond with Callie had been very real.

But that didn't mean he hadn't hidden behind his obligation as a guardian.

"Fine." She held his gaze. "And now that duty is done."

He was shaking his head before she finished speaking.

"My duty to Callie is done, but my duty to the Sentinels remains."

She clenched her teeth. It was true most Sentinels never married. But it wasn't against any rules.

Niko had just returned to Valhalla with a wife who promised to be a valuable healer, and Callie had recently married Duncan who'd lately become a Sentinel.

It might demand compromise and sacrifice on both sides, but it could be done.

So why was Fane so unwilling to even give it a try?

"I assume that's going to be your new excuse?" she forced between gritted teeth.

Without warning his expression softened and his fingers lightly brushed down her bare arm.

"Serra, I don't need an excuse," he said, the hint of regret in his eyes more alarming than his previous remoteness. She was used to him pretending to be indifferent to her. Now it felt like . . . good-bye. Shit. "I've never made promises I can't keep," he continued, his tone soft. "In fact, I've been very clear that you should find a man who can give you the happiness you deserve."

For one weak, tragic moment she allowed herself to savor the brief touch of his fingers. Then her pride came galloping to her rescue and she was jerking away with a brittle smile.

She would endure anything but his pity.

Hell no.

"Very generous of you."

He grimaced at her sarcastic tone. "I know you don't believe me, but all I've ever wanted was your happiness."

"And you assume I'll find it in the arms of another man?" She went straight for the jugular.

The hesitation was so fleeting she might have imagined it. "Yes."

She leaned forward, infuriated by her inability to read his mind. Dammit. Just when she needed her talents the most she was flying blind.

Was this how humans felt?

This maddening helplessness?

It sucked.

"It won't bother you at all to know that I belong to another?"

"I will be . . ." He took a beat to find the right word. "Content."

"Bullshit," she breathed, unable to accept he was actually prepared to walk away from her.

"Serra—"

"Look me in the eyes and tell me you don't want me."

He refused to be provoked. Worse, that pity continued to shimmer in his dark gaze. "I'm not going to play games with you."

"Because you can't do it," she snarled. "You want me. You're just too much of a coward to do anything about it."

"Find another, Serra," he warned, a muscle in his jaw bulging as he reached down to grab his towel and stepped around her. "Be happy."

Her heart screeched to a painful halt. "Where are you going?"

He hesitated, but he refused to turn around. "To pack."

She glared at the broad back covered in swirling tattoos. God. He was destroying her.

Did he ever care?

"When are you leaving?"

"In the morning."

Not giving her the opportunity for further discussion he simply walked away, his shoulders squared and his head held high.

"Bastard," she breathed.

Chapter Two

Serra left the gym and headed toward her private apartment three floors below.

Valhalla was the official home for many high-bloods, and by far the largest of all the various compounds that were based throughout the world. Including the monasteries where the Sentinels were raised, and where they were able to use the portals to travel from abbey to abbey.

Located in the Midwest, it was a vast community that had workshops, garages, and a large school spread over several thousand acres. There were also extensive vegetable gardens, a lake large enough to support a fishery, and heavily timbered hills that were home to protected wildlife.

In the center was a massive building constructed in the shape of a pentagon with a large inner courtyard.

There were few visitors who could claim to have ventured beyond the official offices on the main floor or the formal reception rooms, although they did have a few guest rooms for VIPs. Absolutely no one who wasn't a high-blood was allowed to explore the nine levels of private quarters and secret labs that were dug deep into the earth.

Leaving the gym, Serra took the elevator to the lower floors and stomped her way down the long corridor.

The thick-skulled, tattooed lummox.

He wanted to scurry back to his monastery and forget she existed?

Fine.

More power to him.

She hoped . . .

She hoped one of his students accidentally chopped off his dick during sword practice.

Then he could be a real eunuch and not just a man too scared to take on a real woman.

She grimaced, her steps slowing as she neared her door. Okay. She didn't want him to be castrated. Not even she was that vindictive. But she did hope he was miserable without her.

Jackass.

Reaching her apartment, she placed her hand on the touch screen, waiting for her prints to be scanned. The door was sliding open when she noticed the tiny, gift-wrapped box by the doorjamb.

She leaned down to pick it up, frowning as she stepped into her private rooms.

It wasn't her birthday. And Christmas was five months away. So who would be leaving her gifts?

A secret admirer? Yeah, right. More likely it was something her biological parents had sent.

When Serra had first displayed her psychic talents when she was barely five, her parents had wisely brought her to Valhalla where she could not only be trained, but where she would grow up surrounded by others like her. But despite not living beneath their roof, her parents had remained in close contact. Not only taking her home whenever she felt the need to bond with them, but often sending her little surprises just so she knew they were thinking about her.

She crossed her living room that was decorated in

shades of silver and plum. The furniture was sleek stainless steel with overstuffed cushions and a large mirrored coffee table in the center of the tiled floor. She had one wall that was covered from floor to ceiling with shelves to hold her collection of romance novels and in one corner a curio cabinet that held the exquisitely carved wooden figurines that Fane had given her over the years.

It'd never failed to astonish her that a man who was prized for his strength was capable of creating such delicate beauty.

Jerking her gaze away from the painful reminder of the man who'd just ripped out her heart and stomped on it, Serra tossed the box onto a table before heading into the kitchen.

She rarely drank since it affected her ability to shield out the psychic noises that constantly bombarded her, but she was in desperate need of something to wash away the bad taste in her mouth.

A shot of tequila might just do the trick.

She'd just entered the kitchen that echoed the rest of the rooms' sleek, minimalist style, when she heard the sound of her front door opening.

"Can I come in?"

Serra rolled her eyes. She didn't need her psychic ability to know who was intruding into her privacy.

Callie Brown . . . no, wait, she was O'Conner now . . . was more than just a friend.

They'd been raised together as foster sisters and were as close as any blood sisters despite the fact that it was Callie whom Fane had bonded himself to.

Today, however, Serra wasn't in the mood for company. She wanted to be alone so she could get shit-faced and forget the miserable day.

She was dusting off a shot glass her parents had sent her from Paris when Callie entered the room, looking gorgeous as usual with her red hair, cut short and spiky to emphasize her pale features, and her slender body, displayed in a lemon cotton sundress. But few people noticed anything about Callie once they caught a glance at her eyes.

They were the gemstone eyes of a necromancer. Perfectly faceted they shimmered with a pure sapphire glow. The beauty of those eyes was breathtaking, which was why she usually kept them hidden behind sunglasses when she left Valhalla.

Serra would have been jealous as hell of the younger woman if Callie weren't so impossibly sweet and utterly loyal.

"It's not really a good time," Serra said, pulling the bottle of tequila from the glass-paned cabinet.

Callie wrinkled her nose, moving to lean against the marble-topped counter. "I know, you've been leaking."

Serra clicked her tongue, pouring herself a shot. Because they'd grown up together they'd become connected on a psychic level. Which meant that Callie could sense the vibrations when Serra's thoughts were slipping past her mental walls.

"I told you not to call it that. You make me sound like I have a bladder dysfunction."

Callie smiled, but it didn't disguise her concern. "What's going on?"

Serra swallowed the tequila, savoring the fire as it slid down her throat. "Fane," she at last admitted, knowing there was no point in trying to keep it a secret.

By now all of Valhalla would have heard of her latest, embarrassing encounter with the aggravating Sentinel.

Callie's smile faded. "What's he done?"

"You haven't heard?"

"No."

Serra shrugged, pouring another shot. "It doesn't matter."

"He's still being an ass?"

Serra lifted her shot glass in a mock toast. "A grade-A, platinum-plated ass."

Cassie shook her head. "I don't know what's wrong with him."

"Join the crowd," Serra muttered before heaving a sigh. "Maybe I'm just deluding myself."

"About what?"

"Maybe he truly doesn't want me."

Callie gave a sharp shake of her head. "He wants you."

The tequila was spreading a warm glow through Serra. So why the hell was she shivering with cold?

"How can you possibly know?"

"I've seen how he stares at you when he thinks no one is watching. How he always waits until he knows you're in the dining hall before he goes to dinner. How he takes twice as long to carve the figurines he creates for you." Callie pushed away from the counter and crossed the short distance to gently remove the shot glass from Serra's hand. "He wants you bad."

"Then why the hell won't he do anything about it?" Serra snapped, fiercely holding back the tears. By God, she wasn't going to cry over the bastard. Not one tear. "I'm tired of being treated like I carry the plague."

Callie set the glass on the countertop, biting her lower lip before she tentatively made the suggestion that Serra had been dreading.

"Do you want me to talk to him?"

"No." She unconsciously pressed a hand to her heaving stomach.

Fane had not only been connected to Callie on a spiritual level, he'd also indulged her every whim.

God. The mere thought that he would force himself to show an interest in her to please Callie . . .

A low groan escaped her lips and Callie grabbed her hands to give them a gentle squeeze. "This can't go on, Serra."

Serra gave a sad smile. Callie was right.

This was it.

She'd tossed herself at Fane for the last time.

She wasn't wasting another day on something so stupid as unrequited love.

"I know," she admitted, a humorless smile twisting her lips.

Easily sensing Serra's sudden resolve, Callie regarded her with open concern.

Understandable.

Serra tended to act on impulse. Especially when her feelings were hurt.

"What are you going to do?"

Serra shrugged. "What I should have done a long time ago."

"I'm afraid to ask."

"I'm going to find a man who isn't afraid to love me."

It was a promise that Serra had made a dozen times before, but this time there was no mistaking the grim sincerity in her voice.

Callie gave a slow nod. "If you need me—"

"I know." It was Serra's turn to give her friend's fingers a comforting squeeze. "I've always known."

"Good." Callie took a step back, continuing to keep a worried gaze on Serra's face. "Come to dinner tonight."

Serra forced a teasing smile to her lips. "And watch you make goo-goo eyes at Duncan? No thanks."

"Goo-goo eyes?"

Serra gave a dramatic shudder. "It's sickening."

"Okay, okay." Callie gave a small chuckle, then her smile slowly faded. "Serra, I don't want you to be alone."

"I won't. At least not for long," she swore, abruptly deciding she needed more than tequila to improve her dark mood. "I have a new pair of Fendi boots that are just dying to go out dancing. I intend to oblige them."

Callie hesitated, as if weighing her chances at insisting that Serra spend the evening in the protective custody of her and her new husband. It took only one glance at Serra's stubborn expression for her to accept defeat.

"Arel's here," she instead murmured.

Serra's smile became genuine.

Despite her pitiful love for a man who barely noticed her, Serra had occasionally sought out a partner who could help to ease her aching loneliness. Why not? It wasn't as if Fane gave a shit what she did.

And Arel had been her favorite.

The hunter Sentinel was not only a charming companion, but he was a lover who understood exactly how to please a woman.

"Yes, I saw him earlier," Serra said, recalling a brief glimpse of Arel as she'd entered the gym. He was looking as fine as ever. "This might be his lucky night."

"Good." Callie brushed a quick kiss over Serra's cheek before she was heading out of the kitchen. "Just remember, my door is always open."

Serra waited until her friend had left the apartment before she aimlessly returned to the living room.

If she truly intended to go out for the evening she needed a shower and some quality time spent on her mani-pedi, but she found it nearly impossible to stir up the necessary enthusiasm.

With a grimace, she instead reached to pluck the forgotten package off the table. Maybe her parents' gift would lift her drooping spirits.

Untying the bow, she made swift work of the wrapping paper to find a flat jewelry box. She smiled. Her mother knew how she loved her bling.

Almost as much as she loved designer footwear.

Flipping off the lid, she felt an odd chill inch down her spine as she reached for the silver locket that was snuggled in a square of cotton.

A frown touched her brow. The simple heart-shaped necklace wasn't really her style, which was strange, considering her mother usually knew her so well.

She pulled the locket from the box and studied it in confusion. Maybe it was a family heirloom, she at last decided, running a finger over the edge of the locket to search for the latch that would open it. Didn't lockets usually have pictures inside? There. She felt the tiny lever and pressed it. But instead of popping open, the stupid thing poked a hole through her skin.

With a hiss she stuck her finger into her mouth, sucking the drop of blood that welled from the tiny wound.

Damn. Heirloom or not, she didn't want anything to do with the locket.

Debating the best place to hide the thing until she had to wear it when her parents came for their next visit, Serra was distracted when she abruptly sensed the approach of an unexpected visitor.

Fane.

What the hell?

She was in no mood for another round of "good-byes."

Especially when a clammy sweat was suddenly coating her skin and a distracting buzz was beginning to fill her mind.

Damn tequila.

For a frantic moment she considered the possibility of scurrying into her shower. Fane had the superior senses of a Sentinel; he would hear the water and know she was unavailable.

Then she squared her shoulders and told herself to stop being a coward.

In a few hours he would be gone. Surely she could pretend she didn't give a damn until then?

Licking her dry lips, Serra pulled open the door and confronted the current pain-in-her-neck.

He'd showered and changed since she'd last seen him. The scent of his clean male skin teased at her senses, while the tight muscle shirt that was tucked into his green khakis emphasized the beauty of his sculpted muscles.

She had a sudden vision of licking her way over the swirling tattoos exposed by his shirt before the buzzing in her head overrode the treacherous thought.

"Fane, what do you want?" she muttered, pressing her fingers to her temple.

"I didn't like how we left things."

She shrugged, holding on to the door as a dizzy spell nearly sent her to her knees. Damn. How much had she had to drink?

"If you want me to pretend I'm happy you're leaving then you're wasting your time," she muttered, the words coming out with an unexpected slur.

Fane frowned, studying her with a searching gaze. "Have you been drinking?"

"None of your damn business."

His jaw tightened, but his expression remained carved from granite. "Can I come in?"

She hesitated. It was more than a reluctance to spend time with Fane. The weird buzzing in her head was slowing to become a persistent murmur. As if someone was whispering directly in her mind.

Obviously she needed to spend some time working on the shields that protected her from random conversations that floated on the psychic plane.

Sensing Fane's growing concern, Serra heaved a sigh and stepped back, giving a mocking wave of her hand.

"Please . . . enter."

Stepping over the threshold, Fane glanced down at the locket that was still clutched in her fingers.

"What is that?"

"A gift."

Without thought Serra slid the chain over her head to allow the locket to nestle against her cleavage.

There was a burst of heat as Fane narrowed his gaze. Anger? Jealousy? Lust?

Impossible to say.

"From who?" he growled.

She took a sharp step back. "None of your business."

His lips parted, as if he intended to argue. Then, muttering a curse, he gave a regretful shake of his head.

"Serra, I'm sorry. I . . ." His words were cut off as she turned away, her fingers rubbing her temple as she struggled against persistent murmurs. "Are you okay?"

"I'm fine."

Of course he couldn't leave it there.

Fane might not allow her any place in his life, but he was happy enough to shove his handsome nose in hers.

"You seem distracted."

"You're not the only one who has a life and duties."

"Serra." He gently touched her shoulder. "Look at me."

She hissed at the pleasure that seared through her,

desperately wanting to turn and bury herself against his hard body. She didn't know what was wrong with her, but she was certain being in his arms would make it all better.

A dangerous illusion, she sharply reminded herself.

Fane didn't want her in his arms.

Not now. Not ever.

"Go away, Fane," she commanded, shrugging off his hand.

"You're in pain."

"I'm tired." She grimaced, not about to admit she was feeling increasingly queasy. "I want you to leave so I can lie down."

"Do you need a healer?"

"Oh for Christ's sake." She whirled back to stab him with a furious glare. Was he deliberately trying to piss her off? "Just go."

He studied her for a long moment. A romantic fool might think he was trying to preserve his last memory of her.

But she wasn't a romantic fool. Not anymore.

Perhaps sensing her fierce need to have him gone, Fane gave a slow, solemn dip of his head.

"Good-bye, Serra."

She didn't bother with good-bye as he turned and left her apartment.

They'd said everything that needed to be said.

At midafternoon the corridors of Valhalla were mostly empty. A good thing since Fane was in the mood to knock aside anyone stupid enough to get in his way.

Why had he gone to Serra?

He knew that she was hurting. And that he was the cause. But the memory of her wounded expression as he'd walked away from her earlier had haunted him until he'd been driven into seeking her out. As if he could somehow ease her pain.

Idiot.

Clearly his decision to leave Valhalla for Tibet was a good one.

All he'd done was make matters worse.

Taking the elevator down to the apartments reserved for Sentinels, he entered the sparse space and methodically began to pack his few belongings.

Unlike Serra who'd created a home that reflected her strong, unique personality, he kept his own apartment supplied with nothing more than the bare necessities. A bed, a couch, and a kitchen table. Except for his workroom. Everything in there had been handcrafted from the tools he used to sculpt his figurines to the workbench where he spent countless hours.

That was the one place he could go to find the peace denied to him in most of his life.

He'd packed his few clothes and was just placing the last of his tools in a heavy crate to take with him when a knock on his door interrupted the silence.

His first impulse was to ignore the visitor. Protracted good-byes weren't on his agenda. But catching a familiar scent, he realized this was one farewell he couldn't avoid.

Moving through the apartment, he pulled open the front door to reveal the small, red-haired necromancer who'd been in his care for the past decade.

His expression softened. "Callie."

She smiled, reaching up to touch his neck in a gesture that revealed the depth of their friendship.

"How are you?" she asked softly.

He grimaced. Only the two of them would ever comprehend the bond that had formed when he'd been chosen as her guardian. Or the wrenching sense of loss when the bond had been broken.

"Adjusting," he said.

She wrinkled her nose, moving her hand to lay it over her heart that now belonged to Duncan O'Conner.

"Yeah, me too."

Fane narrowed his gaze, suddenly wondering if there was more to this visit than a chance to say good-bye.

"The bastard is treating you right?"

She rolled her eyes. "He has a name. And he's treating me very right."

He hurriedly held up a hand. "No details, little one," he muttered.

It wasn't jealousy. But Callie was like a sister to him. He found it impossible to think of her with any man.

She flashed a teasing grin. "Deal."

"If you don't need me to beat Duncan to a bloody pulp, then what are you doing here?"

Her smile abruptly disappeared, concern darkening the sapphire of her eyes. "I was hoping that you knew where Serra is."

Fane froze, his instincts on full alert. "Why would I know?"

"Fane." Callie gave a chiding shake of her head. "You can fool most people, but not me."

His jaw clenched. He didn't share his feelings for Serra with anyone. Not even Callie.

"I spoke with her earlier. She said she was tired. Have you checked her rooms?"

"Of course."

Fane frowned. "Why are you concerned?"

"She told Arel she was going to meet him in the dining hall, but she never showed."

Jealousy ripped through Fane. The younger Sentinel

had been panting after Serra for years. He'd even managed to lure her into a brief affair that had tormented Fane. It was one thing to tell Serra he wanted her to find a man to love, and another to watch her being seduced by a male half his age.

He wasn't a damned saint.

"Maybe she changed her mind," he said, taking pleasure in the thought of the arrogant cub being stood up.

"She would have let him know," Callie insisted. Although cell phones didn't work, there were landlines placed throughout Valhalla that made communication easy. "Arel came to me when he searched Valhalla and couldn't find her."

Abruptly Fane remembered Serra's strange behavior when he'd last seen her.

At the time he'd put it down to anger and wounded pride. Now he had to wonder if there hadn't been something else wrong.

"You said that you tried her apartment?"

Callie nodded. "She didn't answer the door."

"She could be asleep."

"No, I have a key." Callie bit her bottom lip. "I went to check on her but she wasn't there. And—"

Fane ruthlessly crushed the fear that threatened to cloud his years of training.

If something had happened to Serra she needed a warrior, not the man who'd wanted her for longer than she would ever know.

"Tell me," he commanded.

"There was a mess in her bedroom."

Shit. He gripped the edge of the door, the wood cracking beneath the pressure.

"A mess?" he barked. "Like she'd been attacked?"

"No, her clothes were thrown around like she'd been packing in a hurry."

Oh. A portion of Fane's fear eased.

If she'd packed a bag then there was a chance this was nothing more than a misunderstanding.

"She has a home south of here," he pointed out. Most psychics had private homes in isolated areas where they could get away from the "psychic noise" caused by living in a crowded community. "Maybe she was going there."

"Without a word to anyone? I even called Inhera to see if Serra had been called away on an assignment."

Inhera was the leader of the psychics and was responsible for scheduling their duties.

Fane grimaced. "She might have felt a need to leave Valhalla that had nothing to do with her job."

Callie stabbed him with an accusing glare. "I know that she was upset, and why. But Serra has never just disappeared. She knows how worried I would be."

Fane gave a slow nod.

Callie was right.

Even if she was pissed as hell with him, Serra wouldn't leave without gaining approval from Inhera.

And more importantly, without saying something to Callie and her foster parents.

"Damn."

He spun on his heel to cross to the far side of his living room where he laid his hand on a scanner. It took only a second for his fingerprints to be accepted and for a panel in the wall to slide open to reveal a hidden room that was built into all the Sentinels' apartments.

"Fane?" Callie murmured in confusion, following him into the room and gazing at the high-tech equipment in fascination.

It couldn't compare to the command center at the lowest

level of Valhalla, but it was built with steel walls lined with powerful computers, which were linked to satellite feeds that kept track of government agencies. They also ran surveillance monitors.

Including surveillance for Valhalla.

Going to the nearest computer he tapped on the keys to bring up the camera that monitored the hallway outside Serra's apartment.

"I want to check the tapes," he muttered, clicking the rewind until he reached the point of Serra's first entering her apartment.

"Why?" Callie demanded.

"There was something bothering her."

He watched as she opened her door and then bent down to pick up something off the ground. What was it? He zoomed in. A gift-wrapped package. Was it the locket he'd seen her holding?

She entered the apartment and closed the door. He zoomed past Callie's visit and his own arrival and abrupt departure. After that there was . . . nothing.

No one entered the hallway. Not until Serra's door was opened and she walked away from her apartment with a suitcase clutched in her hand.

Once again he zoomed in, a cold trickle of sweat inching down his spine. There was no mistaking the pallor of her skin and the tightness of her features. Twice she reached up to rub her temple, as if she were in pain.

"Goddammit," he growled, clicking to another camera to watch her progress through Valhalla. "I should have insisted she tell me."

Callie swore beneath her breath. "Considering you were more than likely what was bothering her, I doubt she would have shared."

He accepted the familiar pang of guilt, he deserved it,

but he gave a shake of his head at the thought this was about his decision to leave.

Watching Serra take a tunnel to the outer garage and halting next to her personal SUV, Fane scowled in confusion.

She walked past a dozen friends who'd all tried to get her attention, her expression unfocused and her movements lacking her usual grace.

That wasn't like Serra.

Then she opened the back of the SUV and shoved in her vintage Louis Vuitton suitcase that had been a gift from her parents. Callie gasped in disbelief.

"Okay, that's it. There's something really, really wrong," she muttered. "Last year Serra nearly ripped off the head of a bellboy who tried to touch the handle of her bag without gloves on. She would never toss it around like a sack of garbage."

Fane was moving before he even realized he'd made his decision.

"I'll find her."

Chapter Three

The St. Louis penthouse office was exactly what was expected of a successful businessman.

Consuming the twentieth floor, the office had three walls that were decorated with priceless abstract paintings, high-tech computers, and a dozen flat-screen monitors tuned to the stock markets from around the world. The fourth wall was made entirely of glass and offered a stunning view of the Gateway Arch. The furnishings were a sleek black and steel design and arranged over the marble white floor.

It was polished. Discreet. Expensive.

A perfect setting for the elegant CEO of Cavrilo International.

A tall, slender man, Bas Cavrilo had pale, delicately carved features that might have been pretty if not for the hint of ruthlessness in the line of his jaw and the arrogant thrust of his narrow nose. His dark hair was cut short and brushed away from his lean face, emphasizing his light brown eyes and the lush curve of his lips.

Currently attired in a charcoal gray Armani suit, he stood near the window, gazing down at the streets that were nearly empty of traffic.

At five in the morning, most people were still snug in their beds.

At least most normal people were snug in their beds.

But Bas was about as far from normal as you could get.

A humorless smile stretched his lips. The world was slowly beginning to accept the presence of high-bloods. Valhalla could be thanked for that. After centuries of being reviled as monsters, they'd learned the value of a top-notch PR blitz. There was nothing like giving a gloss of exotic mystery to a group of people. And while there would always be people who considered them as "freaks" and "mutants" the humans no longer huddled in fear when they heard a high-blood was near.

Stupid humans.

Valhalla might have given them the image of harmless, law-abiding citizens, but the truth was far less innocent.

No matter how hard the Mave might try to tame them, there were always those high-bloods who refused to be neutered.

Men like him, and those who followed him.

They remained monsters. And were damned proud of the fact.

Of course, he'd learned from the Mave's success. People were laughably easy to fool. An expensive office, a closet filled with thousand-dollar suits, and a Lamborghini and they were happy to accept that he was just another human businessman.

Hiding in plain sight had proven to be far easier than skulking in the shadows.

Fucking amazing.

On this night, however, he wasn't savoring his latest success. Or sorting through his files to select a potential client.

He'd been warned his entire life that his sense of superiority would eventually bite him in the ass. And his entire life he'd laughed at the warning.

He wasn't laughing anymore.

The faint footstep in the outer lobby would have been undetectable to human ears, but Bas was already turned toward the door when it was pushed open and Kaede stepped into the office and crossed to stand directly in front of him.

A slender man with smooth black hair brushing his shoulders and dark eyes, Kaede was built along trim lines with the Asian features of his ancestors. Tonight he was wearing a black T-shirt and black jeans.

To the public he was Bas's administrative assistant. In truth, he was Bas's enforcer.

Despite his lack of bulging muscles, Kaede was one of the most lethal killers Bas had ever met.

Ironically, he also happened to be a damned fine administrative assistant.

Organized. Efficient.

Prompt.

"The psychic has reached the outskirts of the city," the younger man said, bringing the news that Bas had been waiting for. "Do you want her taken into custody?"

Not by the flicker of an eye did he allow his relief to show. He was a leader of thugs, outlaws, and misfits. The second they sniffed weakness he would be devoured by his own sect.

But he better than anyone knew the thousand things that could have gone wrong.

"No." He shook his head, his tone low but filled with the authority he'd earned over the past century. "We don't know if our people are being monitored. The less attention we attract to her arrival the better. Meet her in the underground parking lot and bring her up by the back elevator."

"You got it."

Without hesitation his companion began to turn back toward the open door, only to halt when Bas lightly touched his shoulder.

"Kaede."

The enforcer turned back to meet Bas's narrowed gaze. "What?"

"She was alone?"

"Yeah."

"Tell the watchers to make sure she wasn't followed."

Kaede arched a brow. "By who?"

Bas's humorless laugh bounced off the walls. "A good question, old friend. We seem to be gathering enemies at an alarming rate."

"No shit."

They shared a mutual grimace.

Until two days ago their small sect had managed to fly under the radar.

They had their selective clientele, but they went to extreme measures to make sure that they avoided any unwelcome attention.

Now he had his balls in a vise and they were being squeezed so tight he had no choice but to put a target on his back.

"I was referring to our guest's abrupt departure from Valhalla," he clarified. He'd done everything in his power to lure Serra from Valhalla without attracting attention, but no plan was perfect. Especially one that had been slapped together in less than an hour. He'd be an idiot not to be prepared for failure. "The Mave isn't stupid."

His companion frowned. "If she suspected something was wrong wouldn't she have stopped the psychic from leaving?"

"Not if she wanted to know who was tampering with her

people." He knew what he'd do. He would use the victim to track down the bastard responsible. "Make sure you scan the psychic and her car for any hidden bugs and disable the GPS."

Kaede touched the knife hidden beneath his shirt. The enforcer could filet a grown man in under three minutes.

"You're playing a dangerous game."

"Do I have a choice?"

Kaede moved toward the door. "I wish to God you did."

"So do I," Bas muttered, reaching into his pocket to pull out a small photo of a silvery blond-haired, bronze-eyed girl with a smile that could light the world. "I'm coming, Molly."

Beneath the fog that clouded her mind, Serra understood that something was terribly wrong.

She was supposed to be enjoying a night of mindless fun with Arel, wasn't she?

But even as she tried to clear her thoughts, she couldn't battle the overwhelming urge to get into her vehicle and speed through the night. She didn't know where she was going, or why she was going there. She just knew that she couldn't stop.

Her confusion only deepened as she hit the outskirts of St. Louis and drove straight downtown.

She'd visited the area before, but not enough to have navigated with such ease through narrow back streets until she was pulling into an underground parking lot. It was as if she was deliberately choosing a route that would throw off anyone trying to track her.

It was creepy as hell.

Pulling to a halt in the nearly empty lot, she crawled out of her SUV and stood as still as a mannequin until a slender, dark-haired man appeared from the shadows and led her toward an elevator hidden in a dark alcove.

Her teeth clenched, sweat beaded her forehead as she desperately struggled to organize her muddled thoughts. This wasn't right. She didn't know this man or why she was so easily allowing herself to be herded into the steel-lined elevator that whisked them toward the top floor, but her instincts were screaming in warning.

There was a faint shudder beneath her feet as the elevator came to a halt and the doors slid open. Then, while she struggled to breathe, the man beside her grasped her elbow and led her through a small reception room and into an elegant office.

If she'd been thinking clearly, she might have admired the minimalist vibe of the black and white room. And she most certainly would have been charmed by the impressive view of St. Louis revealed by the bank of windows.

Instead her restless gaze continued to scan the massive office until she was shoved onto a low, leather chair and a stranger was crouching down until they were face-to-face.

Her first thought was that he was handsome.

Dark hair slicked from a lean, clean-cut face. Light brown eyes and surprisingly full lips.

Her second thought was that there was a callous ruthlessness etched onto his pale features.

An icy fear trickled down her spine.

"Welcome, Ms. Vetrov," he murmured, his velvet tone disguising the power of his magic that wrapped around her. "Can you hear me?"

She gave a jerky nod. "Yes."

"Good girl." His voice soothed, even as it tightened something deep inside her. "I want you to think back."

"Okay."

"Do you remember leaving Valhalla?"

She frowned. The memory was fuzzy, but it was there. "Yes."

"Did you tell anyone you were going to come here?"

It took a second before she shook her head. "No."

"Did anyone try to stop you from leaving?"

"No."

"Excellent." He leaned forward, the scent of his expensive cologne teasing at her nose. "Did you speak to anyone after you left? Maybe on your cell phone?"

Had she? She had a vague suspicion that she'd heard her phone ring more than once, but she hadn't answered.

"I haven't spoken to anyone," she assured the stranger, reaching up to lightly touch the man's face. Was he real? Or was he just a part of an ongoing nightmare? "Do I know you?"

"I'm Bas."

Bas. She allowed the name to seep through her mind. When it didn't strike any bells of recognition she gave a shake of her head.

"I don't understand what I'm doing here," she muttered.

"All will be explained, but first." He turned to wave a hand toward the silent man standing a few feet away. "Leave us."

"You're sure?" the man demanded, making Serra wonder if he was some sort of security guard.

He didn't look very big, but she'd been around enough Sentinels to know that size rarely mattered.

"Make certain we're not interrupted," Bas commanded.

There was a tense silence before the man grudgingly left the room and shut the door, leaving Serra alone with the stranger.

Another tingle of fear inched down her spine as Bas lifted a slender hand and gently touched the side of her neck.

There was a weird *pop*, as if a bubble had just burst

inside her brain. And just like that . . . the fog that had been clogging her thought process was suddenly gone.

Serra blinked. And blinked again.

Then with a hiss of fury she was on her feet, glaring at the bastard who slowly straightened to watch the heat of embarrassment crawl beneath her cheeks.

She'd been mind-fucked.

Her.

Serra Vetrov.

One of the most powerful psychics in the world.

She didn't know whether to crawl into the corner and hide in shame or use her skill to crush the bastard's brains.

She knew which one she preferred.

Unfortunately, if she turned him into a babbling idiot she would never learn how he'd managed to ensnare her in his compulsion spell.

Which meant everyone in Valhalla would remain a potential victim.

Besides, the fog might be gone, but her psychic abilities remained on the fritz. Unless there was some other reason she couldn't penetrate his thoughts. Which meant she would have to find out what was going on the old-fashioned way.

Forcing herself to meet his steady gaze, she went on the attack. It was her default response when she felt threatened or afraid.

Hell, it was her default response . . . period.

"What the hell is going on?"

He smiled, giving the pretense of the perfect, urbane host. "Can I get you anything? Water? Tea."

She narrowed her gaze. "You didn't answer my question."

"What do you want to know?"

She allowed her glare to shift toward the office that could only have been designed by a high-priced interior decorator. It even smelled expensive. Cordoba leather. Venetian glass. Freshly cut flowers.

"You can start with telling me where I am."

"St. Louis." He waved a hand around the room. "The Cavrilo International Building to be precise."

Cavrilo International. She allowed the name to rattle around in her brain.

Nope. Nothing.

"How did I get here?"

He shrugged. "You drove."

"No shit." She clenched her hands. Maybe she couldn't squash his brains, but she could still punch his perfect nose. "*Why* would I drive to St. Louis?"

"I'll explain everything."

He moved to press a button on a wall, triggering a hidden panel that slid aside to reveal a small wet bar. Ignoring her impatience, not to mention the fact that once her powers came back online she could destroy his mind with one concentrated burst of energy, Bas poured an amber liquid into a balloon glass before turning and moving back to stand directly in front of her.

"Here. Drink this."

Serra took a step back. "Yeah right."

"It's harmless, I promise."

She made a sound of disgust. "And I should believe you why?"

With a nauseating calm, he lifted the glass to sip the liquor, a hint of mockery in his eyes.

"Obviously if I wanted to hurt you I could," he murmured. "I have no need to be subtle."

She refused to admit he had a point. "Fine. You said you would explain. So explain."

"I needed your . . . services." He took another sip of his

drink before setting the glass on a table next to the chair. "So I called for you."

She scowled. Called for her?

She didn't remember any call.

Of course, everything had started to go fuzzy after Callie had left.

Oh hell. Was that what he was talking about? Had he spiked her tequila? Or bespelled something in her apartment?

No. A hot ball of rage exploded in the pit of her stomach.

Not something in her apartment.

Something she'd stupidly taken inside her apartment.

"Dammit," she snarled. "It was the locket."

"Very good, Ms. . . . ." He paused to straighten a cuff of his jacket. "Can I call you Serra?"

She ground her teeth, sensing he was deliberately trying to annoy her. Logically she understood his tactic. If he could keep her emotions frazzled while he stayed in control, he would maintain the upper hand. But she didn't want to be logical. She wanted to be pissed off.

"Whatever."

His lips twitched. "Thank you."

"There was a compulsion spell on the locket?"

"Yes."

Her eyes narrowed as she realized the reason she couldn't force her way into his mind. Her powers weren't broken, he just had the ability to block her.

"You're a high-blood," she said, the words barely leaving her lips before he was allowing the illusion shrouded around him to fade.

Suddenly he was more than handsome, he was breathtakingly beautiful. His hair wasn't just dark, it was a rich, glossy ebony. His skin wasn't pale, it was a flawless ivory.

And his eyes. Oh God, they were gorgeous. Not brown, but a shimmering bronze with flecks of gold.

"Guilty as charged," he murmured softly.

He turned his head to the side, revealing the small emerald mark just below his ear. It wasn't large, but the eye shape proclaimed it more than just a birthmark or a tattoo.

"Witch," she hissed.

"You have a prejudice against witches?"

Of course she didn't. Her foster father had been a witch. A man she adored. But he'd lived by a strict code of ethics.

He would consider a compulsion spell no less than rape.

"I have a prejudice against people who use their magic to steal my free will and force me from my home," she snapped.

Bas was superbly indifferent to her outrage. "It was a simple, harmless spell."

Harmless? She had a vivid image of her fist connecting with his arrogant nose. Oh, it was going to feel so good.

"Yeah well, I doubt the Mave is going to consider it a simple, harmless spell," she warned. "She's not going to be pleased when she finds out what you've done."

A strange emotion flickered through the bronze eyes. "The Mave hasn't been pleased with me for several decades."

Serra was caught off guard by the warm familiarity in his tone. "You know her?"

"Our paths crossed years ago. It was . . . memorable."

Hmm. She'd trade her Ferragamo purse to hear that story. But later. After she knew what the hell she was doing in St. Louis.

And after she'd broken his nose. And made him spend a few days believing he was a mushroom.

"How did you get the locket past Valhalla's security system?" she instead demanded.

He shrugged. "I have a talent for becoming invisible when I want to."

He'd snuck into Valhalla? Was it even possible? Surely it would have taken a miracle to get past the magical layers that protected Valhalla, not to mention the high-tech alarms.

Or someone who had skills she'd never heard of.

"Who are you?"

"I told you, I'm Bas. A witch and businessman."

She shook her head. A mere witch couldn't have snared a powerful psychic with a compulsion spell. And he sure as hell couldn't have gotten into Valhalla unnoticed.

"Who are you really?"

His lips twisted. "It depends on who you ask. To most of the world I'm B. D. Cavrilo, a highly successful businessman."

"And to the rest?"

He hesitated, the beautiful features hardening to reveal the ruthless nature she'd already sensed.

"I'm the leader of a shadow society of high-bloods."

Serra frowned. Was he screwing with her?

"Sounds very James Bond," she taunted.

"Not really," he denied. "We're just trying to survive."

"Why in the shadows?"

"Because we don't play nice with others," he said, obviously proud of their outsider attitude. "Those who follow me have turned their back on Valhalla. Either by choice or necessity."

She wrinkled her nose, unimpressed. Long ago she might have been intrigued by a man who refused to play by the rules; now she just found them childish.

A true man understood that power came from protecting those weaker than himself, not flexing his muscles to prove he was a badass.

"You're criminals?"

"Some." He smiled at her blatant disapproval. "Others have an allergy to following the Mave's rules."

"But they'll follow yours?"

"*Follow* is a debatable term," he conceded. "They accept my protection in return for offering their services when I need them. Otherwise, I stay the hell out of their business."

She couldn't deny a curiosity. She'd met a few high-bloods who preferred to live as norms. And even a few who lived in complete isolation, far from Valhalla and civilization.

But she'd never met an entire community of high-bloods living in secret.

"What services?"

"It varies depending on their powers."

He was deliberately vague, but Serra abruptly realized what had been staring her in the face.

"You're mercenaries," she said in shock.

He shrugged away his lack of concern that he was breaking one of the high-bloods' most sacred laws. Since the formation of Valhalla it'd become illegal to peddle talents to the norms. Once high-bloods had bartered their services to survive. Gypsy fortune-telling, magical conjuring, and sideshow acts had been the most famous, but most weren't nearly so harmless. Sentinels had hired themselves out as warriors and bodyguards and trackers. Paid killers. Psychics had compelled norms to become little more than slaves. And witches had used magic so dark it had tainted entire swaths of land.

Now high-bloods were forbidden from using their gifts for financial or personal gain. They were dedicated to benefiting society.

Or at least, that was the goal for most high-bloods.

But not this man.

"A necessary evil," he said.

Yeah, right.

"Did you kidnap me to force me to become a part of your posse?"

He blinked, something that might have been amusement shimmering in the bronze eyes. "Posse?"

"Answer the question."

"Only a temporary member."

She rolled her eyes. He was delusional if he thought he could force her to turn against the Mave and work for him.

"And it didn't occur to you to pick up a phone and call me? I could have told you I wasn't interested and saved us all a lot of time and trouble."

"Which is precisely why I didn't bother calling." He held her gaze. "Your agreement to help me is nonnegotiable."

Oh, he didn't just give her an ultimatum, did he?

Her spine stiffened, her eyes narrowed. Only an idiot told a female she had no choice.

"You don't know me very well," she said in a low, dangerous tone.

His gaze slid suggestively down her rigid body. "Something I hope to change once our unpleasant business is concluded."

She slapped her hands on her hips. "So not only do you assume I'm too weak to decide who I offer my services to, but that after I've been kidnapped and manipulated to become your unwilling employee you think I'll still spread my legs for you?"

His gaze lifted to meet her furious glare. "I can be very persuasive."

"Not a chance in hell."

"We'll see."

"No. We won't." Whirling on her heel, Serra headed for

the door. She should have left the second the spell was broken. "I'm leaving."

There was the unmistakable sound of a lock sliding into place.

"I'm afraid we aren't finished, Serra."

She jerked back to glare at her captor. "What do you want from me?"

"I want you to find my daughter."

Fane stood at the edge of the small park hidden in the shadows of the trees as he studied the towering glass building across the street.

According to Serra's GPS she'd left her vehicle in the underground parking lot.

The question was why. . . .

Gritting his teeth, he ignored the screaming urgency to race across the street and rescue the female who'd claimed his heart years ago. He'd already gone to the trouble of circling the area a dozen times, making certain that he avoided the two cars that had followed her from the moment she'd hit the outskirts of town. He wasn't going to reveal his presence until he was certain there was no other choice.

Instead he pulled the cell phone from his pocket and punched his speed dial.

The Tagos answered on the second ring. "Go."

"Wolfe. I need information," he said, his voice a low growl.

"You have her?"

Wolfe hadn't been happy when Fane called to say what was happening. Hell, he'd nearly busted Fane's eardrum with his opinion of Sentinels who had shit for brains. They both knew Fane had waited until he was too far from

Valhalla for Wolfe to forbid him to chase after Serra without knowing what was wrong with her.

Now, however, Fane didn't doubt the Tagos would do everything in his power to make sure Fane completed his self-imposed mission.

"I've tracked her to an office building in St. Louis," he said, his gaze shifting to the smoke-glass doors that were stenciled in gold. "CAVRILO INTERNATIONAL."

"Hold on." There was the sound of tapping as Wolfe worked his magic on the computer. "Import/Export."

"Smuggling?"

More clicks.

"They're legit," Wolfe at last said, his tone distracted. "At least on the surface."

"But?" he prompted.

"It's too squeaky clean."

"What the hell is that supposed to mean?"

"Every company cuts a few corners when it comes to paperwork and regulations," Wolfe said. "Unless they have a reason for not wanting anyone poking around."

Fane studied the building, instinctively counting entrances, surveillance cameras, and the guards who were doing their best to lurk unnoticed in the shadows.

Even for a company worried about corporate espionage the security was over the top. Wolfe was right. This wasn't just an import/export business.

It was a place of secrets.

And Serra was inside.

"I intend to do more than poke."

"Fane," Wolfe snapped.

"What?"

"Now that we have a location, I'm sending backup. Wait for them."

It wouldn't take long for the backup. Now that they knew where Serra was, the Sentinels could use portals to travel from Valhalla to the local monastery. Still, it was an hour drive from the monastery to this spot.

An hour too long for Fane.

"No fucking way."

"Fane. Goddammit. You get yourself killed and I'll—"

In no mood to argue, Fane shut off the phone and shoved it into his pocket.

If Wolfe wanted to haul his ass over the coals when they returned to Valhalla . . . fine. Right now, nothing mattered but getting to Serra.

Chapter Four

Serra was still pissed.

No one screwed with her mind, forced her from her home, and terrified the life out of Serra without becoming her enemy.

But she couldn't deny the stark words had touched her heart.

Dammit. She'd always had a soft spot for kids. Yes, she pretended to be a kick-ass, take-charge kind of female who didn't have time for things like a family and a pack of brats. But beneath her brash image she was a huge sucker when it came to the precious munchkins, and she'd offered her services more than once to help the police locate a missing child.

"Your daughter is missing?" The words slid past her lips before she could stop them.

"Not missing." A murderous fury glowed in the bronze eyes. "She was kidnapped."

"I know the feeling," Serra muttered.

"She's four years old and a helpless norm," Bas chided,

his voice frigid. "I doubt very much you know how she's feeling."

Serra grimaced. The man was a jackass, but if he was telling the truth then she could understand his desperation.

What father wouldn't be distraught?

"You're right," she said. "But, if she really has been kidnapped then she's in danger. You need the police, not a psychic."

"No police."

"Fine." She shrugged. "Then pay the money and get her back."

He made a sound of irritation, the witch's mark on the side of his neck deepening in color. She frowned as she realized beneath the eye-shaped mark were several small horizontal lines tattooed into his skin, disappearing beneath the collar of his expensive shirt. They looked like a barcode.

An odd choice for a tattoo.

"You think I wouldn't give them every penny I could get my hands on to have Molly returned to me?" he rasped, offering a hint of the volcanic emotions that smoldered just below the surface.

Serra hesitated. So the kidnappers weren't demanding money? Unusual.

"Then what do they want?"

"It won't matter once you've found my daughter."

Serra shook her head. "No."

The muscles of his jaw knotted, his expression closing down as he studied her with a ruthless resolve.

"That wasn't a request."

She tilted her chin, refusing to be bullied. Better men than Bas Cavrilo had tried. And failed.

"Dammit, I'm not taking the responsibility for a young girl's life," she snarled. "Get someone else."

He leaned forward, holding her captive with the mesmerizing bronze of his eyes. "No one else has your talent for tracing."

Tracing was a rare gift that only a handful of psychics possessed, and even fewer could use with Serra's skill.

Some psychics could hold an object and catch a vague impression of who owned it and where it was from. Others could actually get a mental image of the owner. Serra, however, could touch an object and connect with the mind of the owner.

It was why the police had called her in when a child went missing.

"It's not magic," she told Bas, giving him the same speech she gave to everyone who came to her wanting miracles. "I don't touch an object and instantly connect with the person. Especially not if that person is a norm."

Expecting another death glare and warning that she had no option, Serra was startled when he gave a slow nod.

"I've been told it's a matter of proximity. Is that correct?"

She frowned. Told by whom?

"Yes."

"How close?"

"It depends on the person connected to the object." She gave a lift of her shoulder. "The greater their telepathic powers the easier it is for me to touch their mind."

"Give me a rough estimate."

Bossy bastard.

"For a norm I would need to be within a few hundred feet." She folded her arms over her chest. "Not that it matters. I've told you, I'm not doing this."

He abruptly turned to pace toward the glass wall, his brow furrowed. "So close," he muttered beneath his breath.

Released from the potent power of his gaze, Serra sucked in a deep breath. "Did you hear me?"

Abruptly he turned back, his impatience humming in the air. "We need a reason for you to be in St. Louis."

"You want a reason? I'll give you a perfect one," Serra assured him. "I'm here to haul your criminal ass back to Valhalla. The Mave has made it very clear she won't tolerate high-bloods pimping out their powers."

She didn't know why she was provoking him. Well, beyond the fact she was mad as hell that he'd kidnapped her and then tried to make her feel guilty for not rushing to rescue his daughter, despite the fact she quite likely would do more harm than good.

But her taunting words didn't piss him off as she'd hoped. Instead, a slow smile touched his lips.

"You're right," he breathed. "That's perfect. It might even buy me more time."

She threw her hands up in defeat. "Are you off your meds?"

"No, it is perfect," he assured her, the edge in his voice making her wonder which of them he was trying to convince. "Just think, if the Mave had heard rumors of high-bloods living outside her strangling reign of tyranny—"

"Strangling reign of tyranny?" she mocked.

"It's all a matter of perspective." He shrugged. "Then she most certainly would send someone to investigate. And who better than a psychic? I can claim that I need to lie low while you're in town. That should give you time to locate Molly."

"Okay, I'm done," she muttered.

She didn't know what the hell the man was babbling about, and she was quite certain she didn't want to. Not when it obviously concerned her. But even as she started to turn back toward the door and try to force it open, there was a discreet *beep* and Bas was turning toward one of the monitors mounted on the wall.

"Shit," he muttered.

She moved to stand at his side, instantly alarmed.

Did this have something to do with his daughter? The thought made her stomach queasy.

She refused to take responsibility for finding the little girl, but that didn't mean she wasn't horrified by the thought Molly might be hurt.

"What?"

"Sentinel."

Her fear converted to disbelief as her gaze focused on the tattooed warrior who was standing in the center of the outer lobby, his arms folded over his chest as he calmly studied Kaede who was blocking the door to the inner office.

A nuclear bomb waiting to explode.

"Fane," she breathed.

Fane had been taken into the monastery when he was ten years old. Before then he'd survived on the streets of Budapest, working as a pickpocket and thief until a monk had scooped him from the gutters.

Those days had taught him to ignore the obvious. It was never the knife you could see that cut you. And the largest man in the room was rarely the most dangerous.

Which meant that he wasn't fooled by the lack of bulging muscles on the dark-haired man currently standing between him and Serra.

Just a glance was enough to reveal the man's perfect balance as he surveyed Fane for any sign of weakness, and the hand that was inching toward his back where he no doubt had a handgun tucked.

A trained soldier.

Perhaps even a Sentinel, although his powers were too weak to set off Fane's natural ability to detect high-bloods.

Fane hid his annoyance behind his stoic expression.

He'd managed to slip into the building undetected and using his innate magic, he'd avoided the predictable security system. But once he had caught Serra's scent in the penthouse office he'd accepted that he wasn't going to be able to use stealth to enter.

It was going to take a more direct approach.

The man narrowed his dark eyes. "You must be Fane."

Fane stretched his lips into a humorless smile. "Have we met?"

"Your reputation precedes you."

Good. Fane was a guardian. He understood that any fight might leave him weakened and unable to protect those in his care. It was always better to avoid physical confrontations.

"Then you know you're going to have to kill me if you intend to keep me out of that office."

The threat was delivered in a flat tone. The sort of tone that warned he wasn't screwing around.

The man foolishly remained between Fane and the door. "How did you get into the building?"

Fane deliberately glanced down at the elaborate tattooing that covered his skin. The ancient symbols not only protected him from magic, but they also prevented psychic attacks and clairvoyants from messing with his mind.

"Spells can't keep me out," he said as he pointed out the obvious.

"And the electronic surveillance?"

Fane shrugged. "Technology has its glitches."

"You can disrupt the signal?" The man scowled, clearly

unaware that there were Sentinels capable of scrambling electronic devices. "Damn."

Fane took a warning step forward. "Stand aside."

The man spread his legs, his hand behind his back gripping the hidden weapon as he prepared for Fane's attack.

"I can't do that."

"Fine." Fane shrugged. "Then we do this the painful way."

Intent on each other, neither glanced at the door as it was pulled open. Not until a man with short dark hair and peculiar bronze eyes stepped into the office, closely followed by Serra.

"I'm disappointed Kaede," the man drawled, his voice edged with a punishing power that Fane could feel despite the powerful glyphs that were tattooed onto his skin. "This is the second occasion your security has failed us."

Kaede offered a low bow, his small flinch the only sign he was feeling the effects of the lash of power.

"I take full responsibility."

"Yes, you will. Your punishment, however, will have to wait."

Kaede straightened. "What do you want me to do with him?"

The bronze gaze settled on Fane. "A good question."

Fane studied the stranger, taking careful notice of the witch mark and the peculiar horizontal lines that ran the length of his neck.

The man didn't feel particularly strong in magic, but there was something . . .

Something dark and dangerous that lurked just below the surface.

Something Fane could sense, even if he couldn't pin it down.

He shifted so he could keep an eye on both men, allowing only a brief glance at Serra to make sure she wasn't hurt.

He couldn't allow his fear that she remained in danger to interfere with his training.

"Give me Serra."

The man frowned. "Does she belong to you?"

"Belong? Are you a freaking caveman?" Serra growled, typically displaying more courage than sense. "I don't belong to anyone. Not now, not ever."

Fane's attention remained on the elegantly dressed man. He was the more dangerous of the two.

"We're not bonded," he said, answering the question.

"If you're not her guardian, then how did you find her?"

"Because he's Fane," Serra retorted, the bite in her tone revealing she was still pissed at him. Obviously rushing to her rescue didn't earn him any brownie points. "Sentinel extraordinaire."

"Ah." The leader waved a hand toward his companion. "Kaede. Do a sweep to make sure he came alone."

Kaede hesitated. "Bas."

"I'll be fine."

Fane snorted. "I wouldn't count on it."

Kaede stepped toward his boss, his expression tight with frustration. "Dammit, Bas. Your arrogance is going to get you killed." He jerked his head toward Fane. "This isn't just another Sentinel."

Bas sent Fane a mocking glance. "You don't have to explain, Kaede, even I have heard of Fane."

"Then you know this is no time to screw around," the servant muttered.

The bronze eyes held an unnerving confidence. "Trust me, Fane is going to behave himself."

"If you believe that then whatever you heard about me is a lie," Fane assured him.

A cold smile stretched the man's lips. "No, I know that

you're one of the most feared warriors the monks ever trained."

Fane narrowed his eyes. "Then you know I won't hesitate to kill you, or anyone else who gets in my way."

"Not if this female's continued good health depends on your cooperation," Bas taunted, grasping Serra by her upper arm and dragging her to his side. "Go, Kaede."

Serra hissed in outrage, yanking her arm out of his grasp. "Get your hands off me."

Fane growled low in his throat, the air heating as his anger slipped its leash. "Do you have a death wish?"

"I am a man who is willing to use whatever methods are necessary." Bas grimaced, indifferent to the fact that Kaede had left the room and he was now alone with one of the most dangerous Sentinels in the world. "Unfortunately."

"Serra." Fane held out his hand, his teeth clenching when she hesitated. Goddammit. She was allowing her wounded pride to put her at risk. "Please."

"Fine." With an audible huff, she crossed to place her fingers in his hand. "I just want out of here."

"We're going," Fane assured her, his gaze trained on Bas as he took a step backward.

Bas folded his arms over his chest, making no effort to block their exit. "She leaves this building and she dies."

Fane hesitated. Goddammit. He didn't like the man's expression. It said that he knew something that Fane didn't.

"You can try to stop me," Fane bluffed.

"I won't have to." The bronze gaze rested on Serra's pale face. "The toxin is already in her system."

"Toxin?" Serra breathed. "What toxin?"

"It was injected into your system when you touched the locket."

Serra held up her hand, glaring at the pinprick wound visible on the tip of her finger. "Oh, shit."

Fane was moving with a blinding speed, grabbing Bas by the throat and lifting him three inches off the ground.

"You bastard," he rasped. "Give me the antidote."

"No."

Fane squeezed his fingers. "Then you'll die."

"Wait, Fane." Serra was abruptly at his side, her heart pounding so loud he could have heard it without his enhanced senses. "What's the toxin?"

Bas glanced toward her, his face expressionless despite Fane's crushing grip. "Belladonna."

Serra frowned. "That's it?"

They all knew the healers could easily cure her. Bas hissed as Fane's fingers dug even deeper into his flesh.

"The toxin doesn't matter," he choked out. "It's how it was delivered."

Fane felt as if he'd just been hit upside the head with a shovel.

Shit. He should have suspected the truth the minute he caught sight of the tattoo of lines on the man's neck.

Long ago they had represented a kill. Each line equaled one death.

"Assassin," he muttered, releasing his hold.

Choking the man wasn't going to force him to reverse his spell. And for now Fane needed the high-blood alive.

He would have to delay his pleasure in ripping out the son of a bitch's throat until he was certain Serra was out of danger.

"What does that mean?" Serra demanded, trying her best to hide her fear.

Fane moved to stand directly in front of her. It would be

easier to lie. To soothe her with a vague assurance that everything would be fine.

But Serra wasn't a woman who would appreciate his efforts to shield her. Hell, she would accuse him of patronizing her.

She would want the truth.

No matter how painful.

"The toxin has been enhanced by a spell. It's in your system, waiting for the caster to either release it into your bloodstream or to cleanse it from your body," he said. "It can't be removed by anyone but the bastard who cast the original spell."

Her lips parted, sheer horror darkening her eyes. "Oh my God. Who would use magic like that?"

Fane was one of the few who could answer the question. "Long ago the monks not only trained Sentinels, but they created a small, elite unit that had one purpose."

Bas smiled. "Death."

Chapter Five

Serra launched herself forward, slapping Bas's smug face.

A part of her knew that the blow landed only because he allowed her to hit him. He was bigger, faster, and stronger than she was. But it was still satisfying to feel her palm connecting against his cheek.

"You son of a bitch," she snarled. "Why?"

He met her accusing gaze. "You know why."

She did. His daughter had been kidnapped. And to get Molly back he'd been willing to compel her to St. Louis with a spell. And then to ensure her cooperation, he had filled her blood with a deadly toxin.

Fane stepped forward, his face as hard as granite. "Then tell me."

Bas took a discreet step back. Not out of fear, but simple self-preservation. Fane caused that reaction in most people.

"My daughter has been kidnapped," the assassin grudgingly confessed. "I want her back."

Serra tilted her chin. "Remove the toxin and I'll try."

"I've been alive a very long time, dear Serra," Bas drawled. "The toxin remains until Molly is back in the bed she was stolen from."

It's what Serra expected, but that didn't prevent the sharp chill of fear that pierced her heart.

She'd thought about death in a vague, far-in-the-distant-future sort of way.

Now she could measure her potential lifespan in every tick of the clock.

It was . . . horrifying.

"Who has her?" Fane rasped.

"First things first." Bas calmly adjusted his cuff, pretending he was indifferent to the furious Sentinel waiting for the opportunity to rip off his head. Literally. "Call Valhalla and assure them that you're with Serra and all is well."

Fane stood perfectly still, his lack of emotion a threat in itself. When Fane struck it would be without warning and with ruthless intent.

A killer with no mercy.

"They'll suspect I'm being coerced unless we return."

Bas gave a short laugh. "Oh, I have every faith you'll manage to convince them. You are, after all, the infamous Fane."

Fane shrugged. "I can't perform miracles."

Bas turned to send Serra a warning glare, clearly realizing Fane wasn't in the mood to be reasonable.

"Convince him," he commanded, heading back into his office. "I have a phone call to make."

A silence filled the small lobby as the door closed behind Bas and Serra fought back the panic that threatened to overwhelm her.

It wasn't like pounding her fists against the walls and screaming at the top of her lungs was going to change anything.

She would still be humiliated, trapped, and staring in the face of death.

Instead she turned to glance at the silent man standing in the center of the room.

The very last man in the world she would want to see her in such a vulnerable position.

"How did you find me?"

Fane frowned, clearly baffled why she was asking. "Callie came to me when you missed your dinner date. She was concerned."

Ah. She smiled. She adored Callie for loving her enough to be concerned, but Serra wished to God she'd chosen someone else to rush to the rescue.

"And?" she prompted.

"I watched the surveillance tapes and knew which vehicle you'd taken," Fane continued.

"You used the GPS to follow me."

"Yes."

That explained how he had found her. But not why. She impatiently brushed a stray curl behind her ear.

"Why you?"

"What?"

"I thought you were leaving for Tibet?"

His frown became a threatening scowl. "When you were in danger?"

Her gaze lowered to her fingers that were clenched together, her knuckles white as she struggled to hold her shit together.

"You couldn't have known I was in danger."

"I knew."

The soft, ruthless certainty in his voice sent a prickle of awareness over her skin. Dammit.

How did he do that?

"There are other Sentinels," she pointed out.

He hissed out an impatient breath. "Serra, it doesn't matter why I'm here."

With a grimace, she lifted her head to meet his unwavering gaze. There was no way in hell she was going to admit just how much it mattered. Not now.

"No, I suppose it doesn't."

Something moved in the back of his dark eyes. A glimpse of a powerful emotion that was swiftly masked.

"What do you know about the child that's been kidnapped?"

Serra sucked in a deep breath, wishing she possessed Fane's ability to crush her emotions so easily.

"She's a four-year-old norm," she said, proud when her voice came out steady. "And whatever the kidnapper is demanding from Bas it's more than he's willing to pay."

"Not money?"

"No."

Fane planted his fists on his hips, his brow furrowed as he considered the possibilities. "He's an assassin. It could be a demand for a hit."

"I can't see him hesitating over a death or two," Serra muttered. "His morals are obviously flexible."

"True." Fane glanced toward the inner office. "He didn't say anything about the kidnapper?"

She shivered. "No."

He stepped toward her, his fingers cupping the side of her neck in a gesture of comfort. "It's going to be okay, Serra."

She could count on one hand how many times Fane had deliberately touched her. She sucked in a sharp breath as the heat of his palm seared her skin.

"How is it going to be okay?" She licked her dry lips, nearly overwhelmed by the impulse to lean into his touch. "If I don't find Molly then I die."

His thumb stroked the tight line of her jaw. "Then we find her."

"We?"

"You aren't alone. I'm going to be with you every step of the way."

For a vulnerable second, Serra allowed herself to become lost in the dark promise of his gaze. Fane was a master at making everyone around him feel safe. As if nothing bad could ever happen when he was near.

No doubt it came with the job of guardian.

But even as she lifted a hand to touch the fingers that pressed against her neck, she was abruptly stiffening as she realized exactly why he was touching her . . . offering her the attention and tender care she'd so desperately desired over the years.

"Damsel in distress," she breathed.

Fane's jaw clenched as she sharply pulled from his touch. "What?"

She shook her head. Even on the verge of death she was an idiot.

Ugh.

"Tell me about the assassins," she said, fiercely latching on to the only thing that truly mattered. Finding a way to rid her body of the toxin flowing through it. "Why haven't I heard about them?"

Fane studied her rigid expression. He wasn't stupid. He had to sense her retreat. But thankfully, he knew better than to press her.

"They were the dirty little secret of the monks," he said as he instead answered her question.

The monks?

Serra shook her head. She shouldn't be surprised. They'd always been secretive, fiercely guarding their privacy. Who knew what went on behind the protected walls of their monasteries?

"Are they Sentinels?" she demanded.

"They're similar. They have the heightened senses of Sentinels, but they usually aren't as physically strong." Fane explained. "Their power is their magic."

Which explained the witch mark.

She shivered.

The thought of a powerful witch being trained as a Sentinel was enough to give anyone nightmares.

It was no wonder the monks kept them secret.

"Why aren't they tattooed?"

"They work and live in the shadows," Fane said, glancing down at the tattoos that protected him even as they revealed his position as a guardian Sentinel to the world. "They're very careful not to do anything that would attract attention."

Serra grimaced. "What else is hiding in the shadows?"

Fane looked grim. "I don't think any of us know for certain."

Bas sat at his desk, ruthlessly quelling his urge to fidget as he stared at the blank screen of his laptop.

During his years of training he'd been forced to sit completely still for hour after endless hour, ignoring whatever torture the monks had devised. At the time he'd hated the bastards; now he silently thanked them for the strength to remain impassive as he waited for the unknown kidnapper to respond to his attempt to contact him.

It was a risk.

Whoever had taken Molly was clearly insane. No rational person would deliberately provoke a group of mercenaries. And they certainly wouldn't give an assassin a reason to hunt them down and kill them as slowly and painfully as possible.

It was impossible to know how they would react to Bas's attempt to renegotiate the deal.

Concentrating on breathing in and out, Bas sensed he was being watched before there was a faint *click* and the outline of a shadowy form became visible on the screen.

"I'm running out of patience," the stranger immediately snapped. "I expected my prize to arrive by now."

Bas kept his expression bland. Emotions were the enemy.

"I told you it would take a few days to transport her to the location you demanded," he said smoothly. "Even in stasis she causes disruptions. And unfortunately there's been a new complication."

There was a low *hiss*, but with the sound being artificially manipulated it was impossible to know if it came from a man or a woman. Just as it was impossible to know from the shadowed outline anything about the kidnapper.

Bas was a master of illusion, which meant he could use the smallest detail to determine whatever he needed to know about his prey.

A wave of their hand could tell him if they were male or female no matter what their disguise; the set of their shoulders could tell him if they were tall or short even when they were seated; and even from behind Bas could guess a person's age within a few years.

The fact that he hadn't managed to discover anything useful about the kidnapper annoyed the hell out of him.

"Complication?" The voice was distorted, but there was no missing the edge of warning.

"A psychic and her Sentinel have arrived in town."

"What does that have to do with our deal?"

Bas chose each word with care. "They could be in town for their own business or it could be that the Mave sensed the disturbance created as we released your prize from her cell." He didn't have to fake his frustration. It was a constant, gnawing threat to his well-honed logic. "We need to lie low until we can find out if we're being investigated."

There was no visible change in the shadow, but Bas could sense a sudden fury. "This is a trick."

"You can find out for yourself, if you want," he informed the kidnapper. "They just checked into my hotel."

The shadow shifted, as if it were leaning forward. Bas's breath caught in his throat. There. That tilt of the head. A man.

Definitely a man.

"I warned you what would happen if you contacted Valhalla."

"Don't be a fool—"

"Careful, freak," the stranger interrupted. "I have your daughter."

"Which is exactly why I would never contact the Mave," Bas retorted. "Not only have I spent the past century deliberately avoiding her attention, but she has no connection to Molly. She would willingly sacrifice one little girl if she thought it was for the greater good. I won't let that happen."

There was a sharp silence, as the kidnapper studied his every expression. Then, obviously hearing the truth in Bas's voice, he made a sound of impatience.

"Then get rid of the psychic."

Bas held up a calming hand. "I intend to, but it will have to be discreet."

"People disappear all the time."

"Not when they have a guardian Sentinel as a bodyguard," he pointed out in dry tones. "Give me a few days. I'll find out if she's here because the Mave has sensed our secret or if her visit is just bad timing." He paused, biting the inside of his cheek until he could taste blood. The next few minutes would determine whether he was forced to choose between his daughter or the annihilation of thousands, perhaps millions of norms. "And until then we have to stop the transportation."

The weight of the man's gaze could be felt through the computer. Was the stranger a high-blood?

"If this is a trick—"

"No trick, but neither of us will get what we want if the Mave discovers our bargain," he soothed.

There was a long pause before the kidnapper muttered a harsh curse. "You have four days. After that . . . Molly dies."

Not by the flicker of an eyelash did Bas reveal his brutal relief. Christ. His gamble had worked.

He'd earned Molly a few days.

He would rip apart this city to find her.

Fane paced the lobby.

It's what a normal man did who was under enormous stress.

Only Fane wasn't a normal man. He was a trained Sentinel.

Which meant he didn't fidget. He didn't twitch. And he most certainly didn't pace.

Like any predator he understood the necessity of conserving his strength until it was time to strike.

Besides, pacing revealed a disordered mind.

Something that could get a guardian killed.

But for the first time in a very, very long time, Fane was battling emotions that refused to be leashed.

Serra was in desperate danger. Even now there was a toxin flowing through her blood.

And there wasn't a damned thing he could do to avert her death if the assassin didn't remove his spell.

He wanted to smash everything in the small lobby. He didn't doubt for a minute he could twist the fancy metal and leather furniture into a mound of pretzels. Or that he could hurl the desk through the window.

Then he wanted to wrap his hands around Bas's throat and squeeze until the life faded from his eyes.

Unfortunately, he wasn't going to get to do either.

And worse, Serra had made it clear she wasn't willing to accept the comfort he so desperately wanted to offer.

Not that he blamed her. He'd been the one to slam the door between them. Now he could hardly complain when she wasn't rushing into his arms.

It all combined to make him feel as if he was going to explode.

A faint *click* was the only warning the lock on the inner door had been released, but it was enough to urge Fane to come to a halt next to Serra, his body prepared to attack.

The door opened to reveal the assassin, his eyes narrowing as he sensed Fane was on a hair trigger.

"Have you contacted Valhalla?" Bas demanded.

Fane's jaw clenched. He'd reported to Wolfe that Serra was safe and that they would return to Valhalla in a few days. The leader of the Sentinels had agreed to call off the cavalry, but Fane knew that they would be lurking just out of sight. One signal from Fane and they would come charging to the rescue.

Until then, they would remain ghosts.

"Yes."

Bas's lips twisted. "A man of few words."

"You have no idea," Serra muttered, giving a toss of her head. "Let's get this over with."

Fane scowled, his gaze resting on the pallor of her skin and the bruises beneath her eyes. "You're tired," he said, not bothering to hide his anxiety. "You need to eat and rest before you collapse."

Her lips parted, her eyes sparking with anger. But before she could tell him what he could do with his concern, Bas was glancing toward the window where the city was beginning to stir with the promise of a new day.

"I agree." He reached beneath his jacket. "I've had rooms reserved for you at my hotel."

Serra made a sound of disgust. "Your hotel? Murder must pay well."

Bas smiled. "It depends on the contract." He pulled his hand from beneath his jacket, holding out a business card. Fane smoothly moved to take the card, not trusting himself not to snap if the man was stupid enough to touch Serra. "The address is on the card. I'll contact you later."

Fane lightly grasped Serra's arm, steering her toward the outer door. The fact that she didn't instantly pull away told him just how tired she truly was. But as he slammed his hand against the panel to open the elevator, she glanced over her shoulder.

"How long do I have?"

The assassin glanced at a gold Rolex strapped to his wrist. "You have a little over ninety-six hours."

Fane felt Serra sway in horror and his grip instinctively tightened as he tugged her closer. He studied Bas with an expression of cold purpose.

"I'm going to kill you."

The man tilted his chin, his eyes shimmering bronze in the muted lights. "Not until Molly has been returned home," he pointed out, his voice expressionless. "Nothing else matters."

The elevator door slid open and, urging Serra inside, Fane shifted so he blocked her from the view of the assassin.

"Wait." Bas was abruptly moving forward, ignoring

Fane's warning growl as he reached to shove something in Serra's hand. "Here."

Serra hissed in protest, grudgingly glancing down at the crumpled photo of a little girl clutched between her fingers.

"I don't want anything from you."

Bas stepped back, his face hard. "Hate me all you want, but Molly is innocent. She needs you."

The door closed and they were headed downward at a stomach-dropping speed. Fane closed his eyes, forcing his breath in and out at a measured pace. It was the only thing that prevented him from returning to the penthouse and beating the assassin to a bloody pulp.

Instead, he contented himself with the promise the day of retribution would come as his arm circled Serra's shoulders.

He was patient.

He would bide his time and then take full, glorious pleasure in destroying the son of a bitch.

The elevator came to a halt and they stepped into the dark underground parking lot. Fane led Serra to her vehicle, disturbed as she passively allowed him to help her into the passenger seat. She didn't even squawk when he climbed behind the steering wheel and fired the engine.

Shock.

He grimaced as he punched the address of the hotel into the GPS and shoved the vehicle into gear.

She'd been forced from her home, held captive by a man trained to kill, and informed she had ninety-six hours to save the life of a child or die.

It was nothing less than a miracle that she was still functioning.

Crushing the instinct to reach over and touch her too-pale cheek, Fane instead concentrated on following the directions that led him just a few blocks west of the office building.

He rolled his eyes as he pulled to a halt in front of the towering glass and steel building. What was it with the assassin and glass? Screw the view. The last thing he wanted for Serra was to feel exposed.

Tossing the keys to the uniformed valet, Fane kept Serra firmly at his side as he crossed the elegant lobby decorated in tones of blue and silver. Not surprisingly, the clerk was handing over the card key before Fane could open his mouth.

If Bas had been trained by the monks, then he would be meticulous, efficient, and compulsively organized.

And paranoid.

Taking the key card, he tugged Serra toward the elevators, ignoring the speculative glances from the housekeeping staff who were preparing for the day.

Thankfully Bas wasn't the only one trained by the monks.

Or paranoid.

Very, very paranoid.

Chapter Six

Serra felt like she'd been shoved back into the fog of confusion that had compelled her to drive from Valhalla to St. Louis. Only this time she wasn't completely oblivious to her surroundings.

She knew that she was in an upscale hotel a few blocks from Bas's office building. And that she was riding in a glass elevator up to the top floor. She even had a vague impression of the breaking dawn painting a beautiful pink glow over the nearby river. A sight that she might have appreciated any other morning.

But the only thing that seemed truly real was the feel of Fane's hand that was planted at her lower back, the heat of his touch a welcome assurance that she wasn't alone.

The elevator came to a halt and, following Fane to one of the two suites that composed the top floor, she waited for him to use the card key to push the door open.

With an effort she tried to shake off the strange sense of lethargy, glancing around the large sitting room with low, comfy furniture in browns and tans that were arranged to take advantage of the glass wall that offered a stunning view of St. Louis.

Against one wall was a fireplace with a large-screen TV

suspended over the mantel and on the other was a wet bar complete with a wine rack. There were doorways leading to two bedrooms and another that offered a glimpse of a bathroom as large as her entire apartment at Valhalla.

Serra forced a stiff smile to her lips. "I suppose there could be worse places to spend the last hours of my life—"

Her words were cut off as Fane placed his hand over her mouth, leaning down so he could speak directly into her ear. "Shh."

Serra frowned, effectively snapped out of her weird fog as the Sentinel scoured the room, pulling out two hidden transmitters that he crushed beneath his feet before lifting his hand toward the chandelier in the center of the room. There was an electric prickle in the air as he used his powers to disrupt any hidden cameras.

He sent her a searching gaze, as if trying to determine if she was going to do something stupid if he left her alone. Then, giving a nod at her fierce scowl, he jogged into the attached bedrooms to perform a similar sweep. The bathroom was last, and much to Serra's disgust he found two transmitters and a camera hidden in the overhead light.

She would have accused Bas of being a perv if she wasn't certain he was more interested in keeping track of his guests than seeing them naked.

Destroying the last of the expensive equipment, Fane returned to the sitting room, and headed directly toward her.

"Happy now?" she asked.

"No, I'm damn well not happy," he growled, astonishingly wrapping his arms around her waist and yanking her against his chest.

"Fane." Serra tilted back her head. She couldn't have been more surprised if he'd sprouted wings and begun flapping around the room. "What the hell?"

He lowered his head, burying his face in her tangle of dark hair. "I need to hold you," he muttered.

Oh.

Serra briefly allowed herself to savor the strength of his arms as they held her as if he was never, ever going to let her go.

God. It was . . . perfect.

Just as perfect as she'd always fantasized it would be.

His exotic, male scent that teased at her nose. The searing heat of his hands as they pressed against her lower back. The solid thud of his heart beneath her ear.

He was all man. And he made her very glad she was all woman.

The desperate urge to melt against him surged through her. To depend on him to support her, if only for a few minutes.

She released a small sigh. Her hands were already sliding up his chest when she remembered why she felt so damned vulnerable.

Bas, the assassin. Deadly toxin. Kidnapped a little girl.

"No," she breathed. With a sharp shove, she was out of Fane's arms, her chin tilted to a defiant angle.

Fane frowned. "What's wrong?"

"I won't be your damned damsel in distress."

His eyes narrowed, as if caught off guard by her defiant words. "Is that what you think?"

"It's not what I think, it's what I know," she corrected, wrapping her arms around her waist as her body trembled with an urgent desire to return to his embrace. "You were perfectly content to walk away when I was a capable, independent woman who could be a true partner."

Something that might have been regret tightened his stark, mesmerizingly beautiful features.

"You could've been my partner, but we both know I could never give you what you need."

"And what's that?"

"Time . . . attention." His dark, piercing gaze lowered to her lips before returning to meet her glare. "A life we could build together."

She snorted. Fane had been using that wearisome excuse to keep her at a distance for years.

"You're no longer bound to Callie."

"No, but I am bound to my job," he stubbornly countered. "It always comes first."

Serra understood what he was saying.

Many hunter Sentinels had long-term relationships. Some even married. But guardian Sentinels found it much more difficult. They were mystically bound to the highblood they were protecting with an intimacy that might not be sexual, but was just as intense.

Few partners could bear to see their lovers that closely connected to someone else.

Still, no relationship was perfect. And if she was willing to accept the inevitable strain of being with a guardian, what right did he have to try to convince her that she needed more?

She gave an aggravated shake of her head. What did it matter? That was all in the past.

Fane had made his choice.

Even if her current . . . hmm, her current what? Situation? Difficulties?

Near-death experience?

Whatever.

The fact she was in danger was stirring his need to play knight in shining armor.

"Your problem is that you have a hero complex."

His jaw tightened, but he met her gaze squarely. "It's my nature to protect."

"Well, I don't want to be your latest victim that needs to be rescued."

"Serra—"

"Okay, I'm not stupid," she interrupted his protest. "I know I need your help. But that's all I want from you."

His hand lifted, but he dropped it as Serra instinctively stiffened in rejection. "Serra, my decision to leave Valhalla was because I thought it would be better for both of us."

She pointed a finger directly into her face. "You know what? You don't get to decide what's good for me."

"Fine." Moving with a speed that she didn't have a hope in hell of avoiding, Fane lightly grasped her wrist, his thumb skimming over the pulse thundering beneath its skin. "Tell me how Bas managed to poison you."

Serra blinked, unprepared for his abrupt change of subject. Or maybe she was just so unbalanced by the light caress of his thumb that she couldn't force herself to knock it away.

"It was in the locket that was left in front of my door."

She could sense Fane's surprise. "It was hand-delivered?"

She nodded. "By Bas."

"He got into and out of Valhalla unnoticed?"

"So it would seem," she said dryly.

The dark eyes flashed with fury. "Damn. Wolfe needs to examine our security system."

Serra desperately tried to ignore the searing heat of his fingers as they stroked slowly up her bare forearm. Was he deliberately trying to set her blood on fire? Or was it just an unconscious desire to offer comfort?

Either way it was sending tiny jolts of renegade pleasure through her body.

She sucked in a deep breath, needing a distraction.

"Have you ever met an assassin?"

"When I was still in training." Seemingly unaware of her intense response to his touch, Fane allowed his fingers to drift back down to her wrist. "He was brought to the monastery when one of the monks was found dead in his bed."

She lifted her brows. The murder of a monk must have caused a shockwave through the high-blood community.

"The assassin tracked down his killer?"

"Yes." Fane's face hardened until it looked like it'd been carved from granite. Which meant he'd been emotionally attached to the dead monk. The deeper Fane's feelings, the harder he tried to hide them. "Two days after the assassin arrived, the cook was left on the altar minus his head."

Yikes.

Killing was one thing. Cutting off a head was another.

Of course, it did leave a potent message.

"Do you know why the cook had murdered the monk?"

"The documents left with the body proved the cook was selling info on the monastery to Emperor Franz Joseph of Austria-Hungary." There was an edge of his disgusted resignation in his words. Those in power had been trying to control, manipulate, abuse, or even eliminate high-bloods since the beginning of time. "The monk must've stumbled across his betrayal and the cook killed him to silence him."

Serra frowned. "A brutal way to die, but it was in the name of justice," she said. "Isn't that what hunter Sentinels do?"

Fane shook his head. "Hunters are trained to deal with high-bloods that prove to be dangerous." A barely leashed anger smoldered in his dark eyes. "They aren't stripped of their emotions and turned into cold-blooded killers who are willing to deal out death to whoever is their latest hit. And no hunter would ever take money to kill. Not ever."

"Cold-blooded." Serra grimaced, brutally reminded of

Bas's willingness to choose the threat of death as his first option. God forbid that he actually came to her and simply asked for her assistance. "Bas is certainly that. The snake."

Fane went rigid, his muscles bulging as he battled to maintain his composure. Serra knew it went beyond his anger that she was being threatened. Fane had a pathological need to be in control of events.

That's why he trained so hard, and why he constantly scoured the world for ancient knowledge or obscure spells that might give him the edge in a fight, and why he focused his entire life on his job.

If he was the biggest, baddest, smartest man around then he could always be in the superior position.

The fact that the toxin coursing through her body was beyond his ability to fix had to be making him nuts.

Of course, he wasn't about to admit his feeling of helplessness. Oh no. Not Fane.

He'd rather cut out his tongue.

"He does, however, care for his daughter," Fane said, his voice predictably calm. "We can use that to our advantage."

Serra frowned. At this point she was willing to latch on to any hope.

"How?"

"I don't know yet."

"Great." She rolled her eyes, heading toward the bathroom. "Until you do I want to have a hot shower."

"And breakfast," he informed her. "I'll order room service."

She halted, turning with a shake of her head. "Oh no. I'll order my own breakfast, thank you very much."

His brows snapped together. "Serra, we have to work together if you're going to survive."

"This has nothing to do with working together," she muttered, moving toward the phone set on a smoke glass table. "If I have ninety-six hours left to live I'm not eating horse food."

Fane looked genuinely confused. "Horse food?"

"Oatmeal, dry wheat toast, blah blah blah." She shuddered. Unlike Fane, she wasn't a follower of the philosophy "whole body/whole mind." Her mind needed chocolate. Lifting the receiver of the phone to her ear, she pressed the number for room service. With admirable speed she was being asked what she wanted. "Yes, could you send up a Denver omelet with extra cheese, a stack of blueberry pancakes with maple syrup, hash browns, and a side of bacon?" She sent Fane a taunting smile. "Oh, and a carrot muffin, no butter. Bill it to the room."

Fane shook his head as she replaced the receiver. "You never eat bacon."

"Today I'm eating bacon."

With a toss of her head, Serra turned and continued her trek into the bathroom, firmly closing the door behind her.

Fane was determined to give Serra the space she obviously needed.

As much as he might want to bully her into accepting his support, he knew that he risked driving an even greater wedge between them. He'd hurt her too many times and the female was stubborn enough to put herself in danger rather than lower her guard.

Which meant he'd have to respect her barriers until he'd earned back her trust.

He stood in the center of the room, silently repeating the stern warning as he heard the rush of water as Serra turned on the shower. He even managed to convince himself that the closed door between them wasn't making him twitch.

Then he heard a faint, barely perceptible sniffle and all his good intentions were forgotten.

He'd be damned if he was going to let Serra cry alone.

Pausing to remove the handgun holstered across his chest and the other hidden at his lower back, Fane wrenched off his boots. He was removing his T-shirt and khakis as he entered the bathroom and by the time he'd crossed the tiled floor he was completely naked. Stepping into the shower it took him a second to find Serra. The marble stall was large enough to fit a dozen Sentinels with room to spare. But once his gaze adjusted to the jasmine-scented fog, he spotted her leaning against the marble tiles, her shoulders bent as the hot water cascaded over her slender body.

Fane's heart clenched at the sight of her down-bent head and the hands that covered her face as she cried.

The realization that this magnificent female felt the need to hide in the shower to release her emotions tore him apart. Christ, had he forced her to this? He'd wanted to protect her. Not drive her away.

But even as he cursed his past arrogance, he couldn't deny a pang of relief that Serra at least had shaken off her shock.

Her stoic lethargy had been far more worrisome than her tears.

Knowing he was taking his life in his hands, Fane moved forward in silence, managing to haul her shivering body into his arms before she could realize she was no longer alone.

Instantly she stiffened, her head jerking back to glare at him in frustration. "Have you ever heard of privacy?"

His arms tightened, the warm water flowing over them. "You don't have to do this alone, Serra."

"Fane."

"Lean on me, you stubborn female." He cupped the back of her head, gently pressing her cheek to his chest. "Just for a minute. Then you can return to spitting fury."

"I'm not stubborn," she muttered, but to his intense relief she allowed her muscles to relax, pressing herself against him.

His fingers lightly skimmed up and down her spine, his head lowering so he could press his lips against her temple.

"Whatever you say."

There was a long silence as she permitted the last of her tears to stream down her damp face, allowing the crippling fear to flow through her before she determinedly regained command of her battered emotions.

Serra might not be a Sentinel, but she was a warrior.

She needed to release the anger and frustration, and outright terror, so she could consider her situation with a clear head.

Laying his cheek on the top of her head, he tugged her so they weren't directly beneath the deluge of water.

"Do you feel better?"

She gave a last, defiant sniffle. "Don't patronize me."

His lips followed her hairline before tracing the damp shell of her ear, his determination to offer her comfort swiftly transforming into something far more intoxicating. . . .

Dangerous.

"God forbid," he murmured, allowing his hands to slide back to her hips so he could urge her against his hardening erection.

She sucked in a startled breath, her hands lifting to grasp his shoulders. "And don't do that!"

He nipped the lobe of her ear, relishing the taste of her

warm satin skin. A groan was wrenched from his throat. How many nights had he tormented himself with thoughts of what she would taste like?

Now he knew. . . .

Chamomile.

Mmm. He could easily become addicted.

"Do what?" he asked.

She shivered, her nails digging into his skin. "Nibble at me."

The thickening thrust of his erection pressed into her lower stomach. This time she groaned.

"Is that what I'm doing?" he asked.

"You know it is."

He smiled as her words came out as a breathy whisper. "Actually that was nuzzling." To prove his point, Fane used his teeth to nip a path down her throat. "This is nibbling."

He actually felt the jump of her heart. "Fane."

Fane smiled, unable to resist the temptation of the warm, wet woman in his arms.

No . . . not just a woman.

Serra.

His precious, splendid, always forbidden female.

"This is fondling," he assured her, his hand gliding up her side, circling to cup one lush breast.

His breath abruptly hissed through clenched teeth. Holy shit. She fit perfectly in his hand. Soft, but firm with a dark nipple that was already furled with anticipation.

Pleasure exploded through his body.

He was barely touching her and he was already on the edge of climax.

What would happen if he actually bent down and sucked that tempting nipple between his lips? If he yanked her higher so he could wrap her impossibly long legs around his waist and leave her open and ready for the penetration of his rock-hard cock?

Desire, as sharp as a razor, sliced through him.

"I told you that you could help me." Serra's husky voice broke into his enticing fantasy, "but no . . ."

"Fondling?" he helpfully supplied, his thumb teasing the hardened tip of her nipple.

"Exactly."

Her breath brushed over his chest, making his teeth clench in actual pain. My God, this wanting, aching need . . .

"What about nuzzling?" he rasped, his lips following the sleek line of her shoulder.

She tilted her head back, her eyes darkened with passion. "You're just trying to distract me."

He gave a low, throaty chuckle. This was the most intensely erotic distraction he'd ever enjoyed.

"Is it working?"

She trembled, but always stubborn, she shook her head. "No."

With a slow, deliberate motion he lowered his head to lick the very tip of her nipple. "Are you sure?"

Her nails cut into the skin of his shoulder. "Oh, hell."

He groaned, allowing his tongue to explore the sensitive peak. The taste of her was addictive.

"It feels like it's working," he said softly.

"Fane," she breathed.

He very nearly missed the faint tremble in her voice. His acute senses were homed in on the feel of her slick satin wet skin, and the scent of chamomile that clouded his mind with the promise of sweet paradise.

But even as his fingers began to lower so he could cup her soft ass, he gave a low hiss and lifted his head.

What was he doing?

He'd come into the shower to offer her his strength. And more than that, to convince her that she wasn't in this alone.

Not to seduce her when she was weak and tired and at the mercy of her stressed emotions.

Pressing a rueful kiss on her forehead, Fane reached over to shut off the water. Serra shivered and he swiftly opened the shower door and grabbed a towel off the heated rail.

"Hold on, *milaya,*" he murmured.

Her brows lifted. "*Milaya?*"

He ignored her reaction to the Russian endearment. It's how he'd always thought of her in his mind even if he'd refused to allow the word to slip past his rigid guard.

"Let me help," he insisted, using the towel to dry off the droplets of water, before wrapping it around her damp hair. Then, taking her hand he urged her from the stall. "Come."

She allowed him to lead her out of the bathroom and into the nearest bedroom with a wary frown. Not that Fane was stupid enough to think for a second she'd accepted his driving need to become her guardian. No. Nothing could be that simple with Serra.

She was merely too weary to continue the fight.

Without him asking, she crawled beneath the covers of the king-size bed that was covered in a black and gold satin comforter, snuggling against the mound of pillows. Fane took just a second to appreciate the sight of her as she reached up to remove the towel around her head.

She was every man's fantasy with her satin fall of dark hair and pale, ivory skin. Her light green eyes shimmered with the wicked enticement of a vixen and the stubborn set of her chin dared a male to try and earn her elusive attention.

She was beauty and intelligence and a sexual challenge in one lush package.

It was no wonder that every male at Valhalla had tried at one time or another to earn their place at her side.

Pain sliced through his heart at the thought of her with another man. It was a familiar ache. One he'd endured for years. But today it was . . . unbearable.

Was it because he'd finally given in to his combustible need to touch her? Kiss her?

Or was it because for the first time ever he'd been forced to consider a world without her?

Whatever the explanation, he knew beyond a shadow of a doubt that no other man was ever going to try to take this woman away from him.

His hands balled into fists, the urgent need to crawl onto the bed and drag her into his arms pulsing through him.

Thankfully, his sensitive hearing picked up the sound of the elevator opening before he could give in to the impulse. He'd already discovered the danger of trying to offer comfort when they were both wet and naked.

She was never going to get the rest she needed if he touched her again.

With a low growl, he was crossing to the nearest closet to find a white robe and yanking it on. Then, unable to meet her wary gaze, he left the bedroom, picking up one of his handguns before moving to open the front door.

This was why most guardians tried to avoid becoming lovers with those they bonded with. It turned a highly trained, perfectly logical warrior into a seething mass of insanity.

Opening the door just far enough to reveal the muzzle of his gun, he pressed himself against the wall, allowing his senses to determine the threat.

He picked up the sound of approaching footsteps. The pace was light, quick. So a female. And she was pushing a cart. He heard the *squeak* of a wheel and caught the heavy scent of food.

There was no hiss of a blade being unsheathed, and no odor of gunpowder. Nothing to indicate she was armed, but Fane wasn't in the mood to take chances.

"Leave the cart and return to the elevator," he commanded.

There was a momentary silence, as if he'd caught the woman off guard. Then, with a last push to arrange the cart in front of the door, he heard the sound of her swiftly rushing back to the elevator.

He waited until the elevator closed before he inched open the door, glancing up and down the corridor before grabbing the cart and pulling it into the suite.

It wasn't fear for Serra that made him cautious. For now, Bas needed her. Besides, he'd already turned her into a ticking time bomb. The rat bastard.

But he didn't doubt that the assassin would be happy to get rid of anyone who would try to protect her from his manipulations.

And Bas damned sure understood that once the toxin had been removed from Serra's body, Fane was going to kill him.

Locking the door, Fane wheeled the cart into the bedroom, his lips twisting as he realized Serra had found a matching robe to slip on. A pity, but no doubt for the best.

His body remained hard and aching, his control on a hair trigger.

Another glimpse of her naked body and he wouldn't remember she was in desperate need of food and rest.

He'd have her flat on her back and finishing what he'd started in the shower.

Arranging the cart next to the bed, Fane stepped back to watch as she pulled the silver covers off the food and placed the tray on her lap.

He folded his arms over his chest, his brows rising as she poured the maple syrup over the huge stack of pancakes.

"Are you going to eat all of that?"

"I'm not only going to eat it, I'm going to savor every bite."

Cutting a huge bite of the pancakes, she shoved it into her mouth, licking the syrup off her lips with decadent pleasure. Fane swallowed a groan as he took another step backward. Shit. He could vividly imagine pouring that syrup over his body and letting her lick him clean.

Oh . . . Christ.

"Food should be fuel, not sludge," he said, keeping his tone light.

For now it was enough to tend to her most pressing needs. Everything else could wait.

She wrinkled her nose, pointing her fork toward the small plate with a carrot muffin.

"You eat your horse food and let me enjoy a real breakfast."

He rolled his eyes. "When we return to Valhalla I'm going to make you a healthy breakfast that will make your mouth water."

She lowered her gaze to the mound of food, her expression unbearably fragile. "*If* we return."

The words hit him like a blow to the gut, blasting the air from his lungs. Dammit. That fucking assassin had stolen something vital from this woman.

A belief in her own future.

He desperately wanted to smash his fist through the expensive wood of the headboard.

But leashing his surge of murderous fury toward Bas and the toxin flowing through her blood, he kept his expression unreadable. Serra needed him strong, in utter command. Not incapacitated by his emotions.

Just as the monks had taught him.

"There's not a doubt in my mind we'll be returning," he said with stark, unrelenting confidence. Moving forward, he bent down to press a tender kiss on the top of her head. "Finish your breakfast and rest, *milaya moya,* I'll keep watch."

Sensing Serra regretted revealing her inner fears, Fane turned to leave the bedroom. She would feel more comfortable eating without him standing guard over her. And besides, he had a small task to deal with before he could lie down for a few minutes' rest.

Crossing the sitting room, he held the handgun at his side and moved out of the suite in complete silence. He pulled shut the door, and turned as if he was headed toward the elevator. Then, with a speed few could match, he was across the hall and kicking open the door to the suite that took up the other half of the top floor.

There was a muffled curse as a man rose from the desk where he'd been keeping watch on a monitor, his hand reaching for the weapon holstered at his side.

"Don't," Fane warned, his gun already pointed between the man's eyes.

"Okay." The man lifted his hands, his expression wary. "Easy."

Fane studied the stranger, who would have gone unnoticed in a crowd. He was average height, average size, with short clipped brown hair and brown eyes set in an unremarkable face.

The sort of man who blended into the background.

Fane, however, easily sensed he wasn't just another man.

He was a high-blood.

And a powerful one.

Fane narrowed his gaze. There was no tingle of magic, so the man wasn't a witch. And his hesitation at reaching for his weapon revealed he hadn't been trained as a Sentinel. He could be a psychic or a healer, but Fane was betting on a telepath.

The best spies were always readers.

He gave a brief glance around the sitting room that had been stripped of furniture except for the heavy desk and the surveillance equipment that could rival those used by Valhalla. Bas clearly demanded the best. His gaze shifted toward the corner that had been converted to a utilitarian kitchen. On the counter were one coffee mug and one plate with the crumbs from recently eaten toast.

It indicated the man was alone in the suite unless there was someone sleeping in the bedroom.

Returning his attention to the stranger, he kept close enough to the open door so he could make a swift retreat.

"I have a message for your boss," he said, his cold voice filled with the promise of death.

"I don't know what you're talking about—"

"You have one opportunity to walk away from this alive, don't blow it," Fane interrupted.

The man instantly stiffened, accepting Fane wasn't bluffing. He would be dead if he didn't follow Fane's instructions. To. The. Letter.

"What's your message?"

"If anyone enters Serra's rooms without my permission, they'll die. If anyone tries to plant a listening or camera device in her room, they'll die. If anyone tries to separate me from her side, they'll die." His face was devoid of expression. "Do you have that?"

The man grimaced. "He isn't going to be happy."

"Trust me, he's going to be more than unhappy by the time I'm done with him."

"You wouldn't be the first to try."

A cold smile of anticipation curved Fane's lips. "No, but I'll be the first to succeed."

Chapter Seven

Bas brazenly strolled across the bustling lobby of his hotel, taking covert pleasure in the sleek, clean lines of the blue and silver furnishings and the efficiency of his staff as they dealt with the tedious never-ending demands of the very wealthy.

Not bad for a man born in the sewers of Ragusa, Italy, nearly three hundred years ago.

He wasn't worried about being recognized as B. D. Cavrilo, the illustrious owner who visited on a weekly schedule. Hell, his own mother wouldn't recognize him.

It was more than the starched, black chauffeur's uniform with matching hat he was currently wearing. Or even his practiced air of deference that made him practically invisible.

The training he had received as an assassin meant he could create a magical illusion that was impossible to penetrate.

Today the illusion included making him six inches shorter, fifty pounds heavier with a round face and pale blue eyes.

Heading straight for the elevators, he arranged the heavy garment bag over his arm and waited until he'd reached the top before pulling the card key from beneath his jacket. It wasn't until he stepped into the hall that he realized the key wasn't going to be necessary.

Instead, he pulled the gun from his pocket as he headed toward the door that had obviously been kicked off its hinges.

"Samuel?"

There was the sound of footsteps before his most trusted reader appeared in the empty doorjamb.

"I'm here."

Bas narrowed his gaze. The man looked unharmed, which meant he'd been caught by surprise.

A rare occurrence.

"Troubles?"

The man jerked his head toward the door across the hall. "The Sentinel already made me."

Bas swallowed a curse. Goddammit. Maybe his plan to force the psychic to St. Louis had been slapped together in haste, but he'd tried to eliminate as many complications as possible, hadn't he?

It's what made him such a successful leader.

And yet, for all his efforts, he now had a rabid, fully trained Sentinel howling for his blood.

Talk about complications . . .

He gave a slow shake of his head. "I suppose I shouldn't be surprised."

Samuel wasn't finished. "He also destroyed the surveillance equipment we planted in the room."

Bas rolled his eyes. Of course the bastard had destroyed equipment that had cost him a small fortune.

Not that it truly mattered. What they did inside the privacy of their suite didn't interest him.

"Did he or the woman leave the hotel?" he demanded.

The reader shook his head. "No."

"Any visitors?"

"None."

It was what Bas had expected. The Sentinel wasn't stupid. He knew he was being watched and that any attempt to contact Valhalla would put Serra in danger.

Something Fane wouldn't risk.

The two might not be bonded, but it was obvious they were emotionally entangled.

Which was the only reason Bas wasn't currently plotting the best means to kill the bastard.

"I want a watch kept on the room at all times," he informed Samuel. "If anyone so much as lingers in front of the door I want to know."

Samuel nodded. He was a strong enough telepath to reach Bas even if they were miles apart. Which was why Bas had chosen him to keep guard on the female who was his only hope of saving Molly.

"You got it."

Turning, Bas moved across the hall, not at all surprised when the door was pulled open before he could knock.

Fane would have sensed his presence the minute he got off the elevator.

He was, however, faintly startled when the tattooed Sentinel wearing nothing more than a white robe recognized him the moment he caught sight of him.

"It's Bas," Fane growled, clearly speaking to the woman who was out of sight. "Do you want to speak with him?"

"Do I have a choice?" the female voice demanded, stepping into view wearing a matching robe. She looked deliciously rumpled, as if she'd just crawled out of bed. Then, catching sight of him, her brows drew together. "What the hell?"

"Assassins are masters of illusion," Fane said, his gaze never wavering from Bas.

The exquisite green eyes narrowed. "And you can see through it?"

Fane nodded. "Yes."

The female made a sound of annoyance. "Why can't I?"

"He can block you on a psychic level," the Sentinel said.

Serra looked offended. Bas was willing to bet she rarely met anyone capable of screwing with her powerful talents.

She sent Fane a frown. "But not you?"

The Sentinel shrugged. "We've had the same training."

His explanation did nothing to ease her annoyance, but with a toss of her glossy raven hair, she turned her attention to Bas.

"What do you want?"

He held up the garment bag. "I brought your clothes."

Her lips curled in disgust. "I brought my own, thank you very much."

Ignoring the Sentinel whose very presence was a threat, Bas stepped into the room and crossed to lay the designer bag on the low settee. At the same time he discreetly pocketed the gun. There was enough violence sizzling in the air.

No need to amp it up.

The more willing Serra was to finding Molly, the better for all of them.

"You don't know what you'll need," he calmly pointed out.

"And you do?" Serra arched a brow. "How?"

"I suspect that the . . . person who has taken Molly is one of my former clients," he confessed. "It's the only way they could have so much info on me and my people."

Fane folded his arms over his chest. "It could be one of your psycho band of traitors."

Bas gave a sharp shake of his head. "No."

"How can you be so certain?" the Sentinel pressed.

"Because they were thoroughly questioned the second I realized Molly was missing."

Bas didn't need to explain that the questioning had not only involved an intrusion into their memories, but extreme torture when he suspected he wasn't getting the full truth.

"Fine," Serra muttered with a grimace. "What do you want from me?"

"I intend to have you cross paths with those clients I've met in the past month," he announced. "They won't travel far from where they're holding Molly."

Bas wasn't surprised when the psychic looked less than impressed. "That's your plan?"

He shrugged. "It's that or driving aimlessly around the city."

She gave a toss of her head, her hair gleaming like polished ebony in the afternoon sunlight.

"Both plans sound like a waste of time," she said.

Another time and another place, Bas would have been impressed by Serra Vetrov.

He liked aggressive, powerful women.

Now her refusal to be intimidated was a pain in the ass.

Goddammit. Did she think he needed the reminder that his plan was little more than a cross-his-fingers-and-hope-for-a-miracle sort of strategy?

"You'd better hope not," he growled. "Your time is limited."

There was a faint breeze, then the Sentinel was standing so close their noses were nearly touching.

"If you want to survive, you won't mention your spineless method of coercion again," Fane warned, his soft voice filled with a menace that would make grown men piss their pants.

"You're right." Bas forced himself to take a deep, cleansing breath, stepping away from the lethal warrior. Emotions were the enemy. "For now we are all working on the same team. It will be easier if we try to get along."

Serra's emerald eyes flashed with fury. "We're not now, and never will be, on the same team," she informed him in icy tones. "Just tell me where we're going."

"We're going to a brothel," Bas said, ignoring her pissy attitude. Who could blame her?

She blinked in shock. "Your client is a whore?"

"A madam." Bas had decided to start with his latest client first and work his way backward. It seemed the only logical method. "With a very upscale clientele."

The green eyes narrowed. "Did you kill someone for her?"

His hand lifted to touch the side of his neck where a mark of each of his kills was etched into his skin. His illusion might cover the physical evidence of his brutality, but each of the deaths was written on his soul.

"No, she discovered that one of her girls had the poor taste to set up a camera and was secretly blackmailing several of the customers." Bas currently had the photos locked in his safe. You never knew when you might need a picture of a local congressman having sex with a whore dressed like a nun. "As you can imagine it wasn't particularly good for business."

"What did you do?"

"I had my psychic spend a few hours at the brothel," he said, taking a wry pleasure in watching her eyes widen in disbelief. "It was quickly determined which of the girls were responsible."

"You have a psychic willing to sell her gifts for money?"

"*His* gifts and yes, he's quite happy to receive monetary rewards in exchange for his services." Bas held her accusing gaze. This female had been born a freak, but she'd spent her life surrounded by people who loved and protected her from the scorn of the world. She had no idea of the cruelty that many high-bloods were forced to endure. Or sacrifices they made just to survive. "There's nothing shameful in that."

She curled her lips in disdain. "According to you."

Bas gave a soft chuckle. How could he possibly resist tweaking her arrogant little nose?

"Of course, on this occasion he accepted a reward that was rather more personal than money," he murmured. "He returned home a very happy psychic."

A startling blush touched her cheeks and Bas felt a twinge of envy. For all Serra's sensuality, she was still an innocent at heart.

Bas was fairly certain he'd lost that kind of innocence before the age of ten.

"Whatever," she muttered.

Fane took a protective step closer to the psychic, his face as hard as granite. Clearly the Sentinel wasn't amused by their banter.

All the more reason to continue it.

"They'll be suspicious if Serra just shows up," Fane snapped.

Bas smiled. "I've thought of a cover."

Serra slapped her hands on her hips. "Don't even suggest that I pretend to be a prostitute."

"You could be looking for your guardian," Bas offered.

"No," Serra snarled.

"So fierce." Bas lifted a hand to halt her angry protest. "You can say you are looking for a runaway high-blood. If they believe you're here on official business no one will stand in your way."

The emerald eyes flared with the urge to tell him to shove his suggestion up his ass, but with an obvious effort, Serra pointed her finger toward the door.

"Go wait in the lobby, I have to change."

It'd been well over a century since anyone had been foolish enough to try to tell him what to do.

He gave the orders.

End of story.

But he needed this psychic. And if she wanted to pretend she had some control over him . . . hell, he'd let her hold on to the fantasy.

Until he had Molly.

After that there would be no doubt who was boss.

Serra ignored Fane's steady gaze as she took the garment bag into the bedroom and began pulling out the various clothes. She knew it was a stupid waste of energy to taunt Bas. The man had her flattened between a rock and a hard place and mouthing off was only going to get her squished tighter.

But she'd never been able to play the obedient soldier.

Callie had been the good girl. Never in trouble. Never causing waves.

Serra had been the wild child. The hell-raiser who never met a dare she wouldn't meet.

And keeping her mouth shut was about as likely as hell freezing over.

Tossing the clothes on the bed, she grimaced. She wasn't surprised that they were all obscenely expensive. A smug bastard like Bas was hardly going to shop at some cheap second-hand store. But how the hell had he known her size?

She shook her head, digging through the lacy underwear and bras, refusing to dwell on the realization that Bas had such intimate knowledge of her.

That was the least of her concern.

Tugging on a pair of designer jeans that melded perfectly to her lush curves, she matched them with a cream sleeveless sweater and Gucci leather sandals with a three-inch heel. Then, in deference to the steamy July day, she pulled her thick hair into a high ponytail.

She didn't know the dress code for a whorehouse, and she didn't really care. No one was going to give her a second glance with Fane at her side.

He commanded attention by just . . . being.

A fact that was reinforced when she returned to the sitting room to discover him standing near the glass wall, his gaze trained on the city below.

Her heart did its familiar stutter-stop-stutter routine at the sight of him outlined by the golden rays of summer sunlight. God. He looked like he'd been carved by the hand of an artist, the intricate tattoos only emphasizing the sheer power of his muscular form.

His beauty was almost too perfect to be real.

But it wasn't just his flawless features and buff body that made her heart jump and her knees weak.

He might be stern and aloof, and occasionally unsociable, but at his heart he was a champion.

One of the rare good guys who devoted his life to protecting the weak.

How was a poor woman supposed to resist?

Swallowing a sigh, she squared her shoulders and wiped the yearning from her face. She needed his help, but she'd be damned if she accepted his pity.

"I'm ready."

He turned with a slow purpose, his expression stark with concern. "Are you sure?"

She shrugged. "As ready as I'm going to be."

He stepped toward her, his movement fluid despite the

rigid tension of his body. "I could contact the Mave. She might—"

"No," she said, nipping the dangerous suggestion in the bud. Valhalla was still recovering from the disastrous battle against the crazed necromancer. "Bas wouldn't be satisfied just killing me if his daughter dies. I don't want to risk putting our people in danger so soon after we lost so many Sentinels."

His gaze dropped toward the front pocket of her jeans. It would be nice to think he was enthralled by the soft curve of her hips; it was why most men ogled her, after all. But she knew enough about Fane to realize he'd somehow guessed she had the picture of a silver-haired child with a magical smile tucked in her pocket.

"And you want to find the girl?"

She turned away, heading for the door. She hated that he could read her so easily while his thoughts remained a constant mystery.

"I want to be done with this."

With a dizzying speed he was standing directly in front of her, his hands lightly gripping her shoulders.

"Serra, don't let your tender heart overrule your common sense."

She snorted, meeting his piercing gaze. "What if it were you?"

"It's not."

"If it was, you'd find the girl."

"But it's you . . ." he growled, his fingers tightening on her shoulders. "And I'll destroy anyone or anything that threatens you."

The dark intensity in his voice sent a renegade thrill of pleasure inching down her spine. Worse, it made her want to collapse against that wide, powerful chest and allow him to wrap her in the comfort of his arms.

A weakness she couldn't afford.

With an effort she pulled away from his touch and continued toward the door. "We need to go."

"Stubborn." She heard him mutter from behind her.

They traveled down to the lobby in silence, joining Bas who led them to a black Mercedes with dark-tinted windows waiting in front of the hotel.

The silence continued as she crawled into the backseat, sinking into the plush leather as Fane settled beside her. Bas took his own place behind the steering wheel and allowed the illusion to fade, revealing his stunning male splendor.

Putting the car into gear, he swiftly had them headed north.

Serra tapped an impatient finger on her knee, trying to ignore the tension that throbbed in the air.

Not that she was successful.

Fane might look stoic, but his smoldering temper was choking the air with heat and Bas wasn't helping with his mocking glances in the rearview mirror. She wanted to leap out of the car and find the nearest bar to drown her sorrows.

"Where is this brothel?" she at last demanded, needing a distraction.

"It's not far," Bas murmured.

Serra rolled her eyes. Could the assassin ever give a straight answer?

Fane appeared equally annoyed by the lack of specifics. "Tell me about the security," he commanded.

Bas arched a brow, turning down a narrow side street. "Why? You don't have to sneak in."

Fane leaned forward, meeting Bas's gaze in the mirror. "I'm not letting Serra walk into a situation I can't get her out of. That's nonnegotiable."

Bas, visibly annoyed at being given an ultimatum, tightened his hands on the steering wheel. But clearly accustomed to dealing with Sentinels, he wasn't stupid enough to think that Fane was bluffing.

If Fane didn't think he could keep Serra safe, she wasn't going into the brothel.

End of story.

"There are guards on the front and back entrances," Bas grudgingly offered.

"Norms?"

"Yes, but they're armed."

Serra frowned. Armed guards at a brothel? Were they protecting the girls, or keeping them prisoner?

Fane remained laser-focused on the potential danger. "Video?"

"Yes, but it's controlled by Madame Wagner not the guards."

"The locks?"

"Garden variety."

Which meant that Fane could bust through them with his bare hands.

"A basement?" the Sentinel continued his interrogation.

Bas shook his head. "No, but I know there are secret passages and hidden rooms."

Fane leaned back, processing the information and formulating a plan of action. Serra, on the other hand, peered out the window, growing confused as they entered a gracefully aging neighborhood with well-tended homes surrounded by yards and picket fences.

Her confusion only deepened as Bas turned the car into a drive that circled a three-storied Victorian house with a covered porch complete with potted plants and rocking chairs. On the large pane-glass window was gold lettering:

LEWIS AND CLARK BED-AND-BREAKFAST

"Here?" she muttered, as they reached the back of the house and pulled to a halt in a parking lot surrounded by a high hedge.

"What did you expect?" Bas asked.

She studied the structure that was painted white with cheery yellow shutters and matching trim. There was a small cupola on top of the slanted roof that overlooked the nearby river and lacy curtains in the window.

"Not a bed-and-breakfast," she admitted.

Bas turned so he could study her dubious expression. "It's within easy driving distance of the business district, it's isolated from its neighbors, and the parking lot offers privacy for the guests."

"It also looks like my aunt Edith should be crocheting doilies on the front porch." She wrinkled her nose. She loved her aunt Edith, but the thought of the softly rounded, gray-haired woman being paid for sex was enough to turn her stomach. "Not very sexy."

A mysterious smile curved Bas's lips. "You'd be surprised what some men find sexy."

She grimaced. "Ew."

Fane was not amused. "Shut the fuck up."

Bas sent Fane a taunting glance. "Ah. That's one thing I don't miss. Sentinels and their sour temperament."

Violence prickled in the air and Serra heaved a sigh.

These pissing matches were going to get real old, real quick.

"I'll need an object connected to Molly," she said, interrupting the male glare-a-thon.

The mockery was instantly wiped from Bas's face as he screwed down his emotions so tight it was a wonder he didn't crack beneath the strain.

Reaching into the glove compartment, he pulled out a tattered stuffed animal, shoving it over the seat.

"Here."

Serra took the small hippo that was a faded green with flowers painted on the fur. One eye was missing and the tail was unraveled, but it was soft and squishy and just right for a young child to cuddle beneath the covers.

Instinctively she lifted it to her nose, breathing deep of the sweet scent of little girl. She couldn't use her sense of smell like a Sentinel to track, but it helped her to connect with the mind she was searching for.

Bas watched her with a gaze that held the soul-deep pain that burned deep inside him.

"Do you need to keep it with you?" he asked, his voice thick.

Serra carefully pulled the fragile ribbon from around the neck of the animal, tucking it in her pocket with the photo.

"This should do."

Bas reached beneath the jacket of his uniform and pulled out a gold bracelet with a small charm.

"Here."

Serra took the piece of jewelry with a lift of her brows. "What's this?"

"A panic button," he said. "If you need help just touch the charm—"

Fane plucked the bracelet from her fingers, shoving open the door to toss it into the nearby hedge.

"She won't."

Fane climbed out of the car, turning to help her crawl out before slamming shut the door and leading her toward the wide steps of the back terrace.

"And you call me stubborn?" she muttered.

"The bracelet wasn't just a panic button, it held a tracking device," he said, the tension in his body revealing the effort it cost him to allow her to walk into the brothel. Together they climbed the stairs, then as Serra reached to pull open the door, he laid a hand on her arm. "You concentrate on trying to connect with the girl. I'll deal with getting us in and out."

Chapter Eight

Fane slid easily into his role of guardian Sentinel.

It was more than what he was trained to do.

It was who he was.

But for once he wasn't able to detach his emotions as Fane angled himself in front of Serra, his hand resting at his lower back where Fane could grab the handgun tucked into the waistband of his camo pants.

This wasn't a job.

This was Serra.

And his world would end if anything happened to her.

Still, no one would be able to detect anything but grim purpose as they entered the lobby that looked like a Victorian sitting room.

There were low sofas with red velvet cushions and curlicue designs on the arms arranged around a floral rug. The walls were covered by a damask paper with a pattern of white flowers edged with gold and framed with crown molding. There were several small tables that held freshly cut flowers and tiny Dresden figurines.

Exactly what you would expect in a local B&B if you wandered in off the street.

Or if you worked in Vice and were searching for a whorehouse.

A clever disguise.

They'd reached the middle of the room when a door was opened and a young woman stepped inside dressed in a black skirt and white top, her blond hair pulled into a smooth bun at her nape.

She was either the receptionist or she serviced those men who had a schoolmarm fetish.

Probably both.

"Welcome." Her practiced smile faltered as she caught sight of Fane, her eyes widening in appreciation as she took in his hard body revealed by his muscle shirt. A blush of arousal stained her cheeks, her tongue peeking out to wet her too-puffy lips. "Do you have a reservation?"

Fane ignored Serra's sound of disgust at the female's reaction. His only interest in her blatant flirtation was the realization that she didn't recognize him as a Sentinel despite his tattoos. A pain in the ass.

Usually his reputation opened doors without him having to play the heavy.

"Call for your manager," he said, his voice flat.

"I'm afraid she's unavailable." Another lick of the chemically enhanced lips, her hand skimming down her skirt in invitation. "Perhaps, I can help?"

"The Mave sent us." He pulled out the figurative big guns. No need for real guns. Yet. "Stand in our path and you'll feel the wrath of Valhalla."

The blue eyes widened, her brain at last putting together his larger-than-normal size and the intricate markings that covered him from head to toe.

"Oh." She held up a hand as she hastily backed out of the lobby. "Wait here."

There was the sound of her scurrying footsteps, before Serra turned to send him a mocking smile.

"The wrath of Valhalla?"

"It's what the norms expect." He studied her distracted expression, knowing she was using her psychic powers to try to connect with the child. "Do you sense anything?"

She shook her head. "Not yet."

"Keep your thoughts open," he murmured, picking his words carefully in case the assassin had wired the place. They might be forced to play by Bas's rules for now, but Fane had every intention of gaining the upper hand. But to do that, he needed information. "Who knows what you might pick up while we're here."

Serra arched a brow, easily deciphering his hint to search the minds of the whores. Someone had to have some connection to Bas for them to seek his help.

"I know how to do my job, thank you very much," she said, the tart edge in her voice making him smile.

There was no one else in the world who could stand toe to toe with him. Except Wolfe. And the Tagos didn't count.

Not when his renegade thoughts were turning toward hot, erotic nights tangled in ivory arms and the scent of chamomile filling his senses.

The painfully vivid fantasy was abruptly interrupted as a tall, middle-aged woman with short brunette hair and shrewd brown eyes stepped into the lobby. She was wearing a tailored pantsuit in a slate gray that should have made her appear businesslike, but instead made him think of whips and chains and men on their knees in submission.

"I'm Madame Wagner," she said, her smile not quite hiding her unease as her gaze flitted toward Serra before returning to Fane. "Lily said you're here from Valhalla?"

Fane gave a dip of his head. "We are."

"How can I help?"

"We're searching for a missing high-blood."

Fane didn't have to be a psychic to read the woman's genuine confusion. "What does that have to do with me?"

"We received word that she was working here."

The madam was shaking her head before he finished speaking. "Impossible."

"How can you be so certain?"

"I would know if one of my staff were not—"

"Normal?" he helpfully supplied.

"Yes."

"How?" he pressed, deliberately attempting to lead her to thoughts of her interaction with Bas. "Have you had any contact with high-bloods?"

"No." The denial was too quick, too fierce to be genuine. "Why would I?"

"Then you won't object if we take a tour of your establishment?"

Her spine stiffened as she realized her highly profitable business might be in danger. "Of course I damn well care."

Fane folded his arms over his chest. "So you have something to hide?"

"I . . ." She bit her bottom lip, her gaze shifting to Serra. "Are you a psychic?"

"Yes."

"Then you already know this isn't a traditional B&B."

"We aren't here to investigate any illegal activities," Fane said, regaining command of the woman's attention. He wanted Serra free to concentrate on searching for the child. "Once we're certain that the high-blood we're searching for isn't here we'll leave."

Logic battled against greed as the woman glanced toward a door behind them where a guard was no doubt waiting for her order to have them escorted off the premises.

Logic won, but she remained determined to protect her cash cow.

"There's a matter of privacy," she said. "My customers expect discretion."

"I don't need to enter every room," Serra assured the woman. "Just take me to each floor."

Fane stepped forward as the madam gave another glance toward the unseen guard. "Is there a problem?" he growled. "Do you want to personally speak with the Mave?"

"There's no problem." Genuine horror touched the woman's face as she hastily turned on her heel and headed toward the inner door. The Mave had an even more ruthless reputation than he did. "Follow me."

Stepping out of the outer lobby they entered a long reception room that destroyed any hint of a cozy B&B.

Gone was chintz and wainscoting and in its place were mirrored walls that reflected the nearly naked young girls that sprawled on black leather sofas and the white fake fur rug. The light was muted, but Fane was easily able to determine that the females were all beautiful and all dangerously young. It was little wonder that Madame Wagner was able to lure an elite clientele.

Ignoring their curious gazes, the older woman led them toward the staircase that led to the upper floor. They stepped onto the landing and Fane glanced down the paneled hallway to make sure the doors were tightly closed.

He wasn't concerned about Serra's modesty. She might be an innocent in many ways, but she wasn't naive. Her gifts had been used to track children before and far too often it meant walking through the seedier parts of human nature.

No, he was worried one of the male patrons might be stupid enough to think she was available for their pleasure. One untimely grope and the male would be missing his arm.

He didn't particularly care if he hurt a norm, but the paperwork was always a bitch.

In silence they walked to the end of the hall, Serra instinctively pressing close to his side as she depended on him to keep her safe while she shut out the physical world to focus on the psychic clamor that filled her world.

"Anything?" he asked softly.

She shook her head. "Nothing."

Fane glanced toward the silent Madame Wagner, jerking his head toward the door at the end of the hall.

"Let's go."

With a sour frown, the older woman stiffly led them up the narrow steps and into the hallway above.

Once again they walked slowly down the corridor, Fane blocking out the sounds of moans and soft cries as they hit the end hallway.

Serra came out of her light trance, frowning as she realized they had run out of real estate. Fane put a protective arm around her shoulder as he studied their companion.

"This is all of the rooms?"

"Yes."

"No," Serra abruptly said. "There are rooms above us."

Fane shifted Serra behind him, his face hard with warning. "Do you think this is a game?"

The older woman swallowed the sudden lump in her throat, trying to stand her ground.

"The upper floor is for administrative offices."

In no mood to squabble, Fane brought an end to the argument by reaching behind his back and pulling out his gun.

"Show us."

Madame Wagner gave a small gasp of shock, her hands shaking as she pulled a key ring from her jacket pocket and moved toward a nearby door.

Shoving the key in the old-fashioned lock, the woman pulled open the door, glancing over her shoulder to reveal a face pale with fear.

"Please try to be—"

Fane lifted his brows, forcing her to say the word. "What?"

"Discreet," she muttered.

Serra gave a short laugh, meeting Fane's wry glance. He was many things. Ruthless, deadly, and utterly loyal to name a few. But under no circumstances was he discreet.

With a shrug, he followed the woman over the threshold, on full alert as they moved down the secret corridor that had chairs set next to the wall. He grimaced as they by-passed a man sitting in one of the chairs, peeking into a hole that had been drilled through the wall.

There were always those pervs who preferred to get off by watching others.

Angling his body to protect Serra from the john, he kept his arm tightly around her shoulders as they came to the end of the passageway and Madame Wagner used her keys to open a door that led to another staircase.

A few minutes later they were standing in a cramped attic that had been converted to an office complete with several monitors that were hastily shut down by the male guard as they entered the room.

No doubt they were surveillance cameras to keep track of their workers.

Which begged the question as to how one of the girls had managed to hide a camera in her room without anyone's knowledge.

Was one of the guards in on her scam?

It would be easy for the man to secretly record the action

and then convince one of the girls to act as a front to blackmail the men.

Fane gave a mental shrug. He didn't really give a shit. All that mattered was whether the child was being held in the house.

Madame Wagner matched his sentiment, her lips tight as she glared at Fane. "Are you satisfied?"

"Serra?" he prompted.

She shook her head. "Let's go."

Without waiting for their irritated escort, Fane grasped her elbow and swiftly retraced their steps. He kept the gun held loosely at his side. A redundant threat, of course. His grim expression was enough to make people scurry away in fear.

Stepping out the back door, he brought Serra to a halt in the shadows of the terrace, just out of sight of the parking lot.

"Well?" he asked softly.

Serra knew exactly what he was asking. "When we spoke of high-bloods Madame Wagner visualized a short, gray-haired man I assume was Bas wrapped in illusion. There was something . . ." She wrinkled her nose. "Familiar about him."

Fane nodded. The more she was exposed to Bas, the easier it would be for her to strip away the illusion.

"Was he alone?"

"No. Kaede was with him."

"Did you get anything new about him?"

"They met at a small office building," she said, proving just why she was so successful as a psychic. It wasn't just her power, but her perception that made her so dangerous. "There was something painted on the window."

"What?"

"Hall . . ." She faltered as she tried to recall the memory. "No wait, it was Hull. Hull and Sons Insurance Company."

She gave a small frown as he yanked out his phone and swiftly punched in a message. "What are you doing?"

"Sending a text to Wolfe to check out the company."

She instinctively glanced toward the trellis that hid them from Bas's watchful gaze. "How much does the Tagos know?"

"He's not stupid," Fane said, slipping the phone back into his pocket. "He knows something is wrong, but he'll wait for my signal before sending in the Sentinels he has spread throughout town."

Serra didn't know why she was surprised that there were Sentinels hidden throughout the city.

Once Fane had trailed her to the Cavrilo International Building he would instantly have sent word to Valhalla. Which meant Wolfe would have sent warriors by portal to the nearest monastery as soon as Fane called. The Tagos knew better than anyone that Fane would never ask for backup.

Still, she had to admit there was a sense of comfort in knowing her friends were out there keeping a watch on them.

Even if they couldn't actually help.

Wiping her face of all expression, she left the protection of the terrace and crossed toward the waiting Mercedes. Instantly Bas was out of the car to pull open the back door.

"Nothing?" he muttered as she settled on the seat.

"Molly isn't here."

His face tightened with disappointment, but ignoring Fane who pushed past him to join Serra, the assassin returned to the driver's seat and put the car in motion.

Bas was obviously a man who didn't waste time on regrets.

"You could have easily bypassed security and checked

for yourself," Fane said, as they left the parking lot and headed for the nearby Mississippi River.

"I couldn't sense Molly if she was being hidden in a secret room," Bas argued. "Besides, if the kidnapper suspects I'm searching for Molly . . ." He was forced to halt and clear his throat. "I'm not willing to take the risk."

Serra turned her head to watch the passing scenery. Not that she actually cared about the brick warehouses and rows of cargo trailers waiting to be loaded on the next available barge. She just didn't want to see Bas's fear for his daughter.

He was the enemy.

She wasn't about to feel sorry for the bastard.

"Now where?" she muttered, her frustration abruptly bubbling to the surface.

"The terminal."

She turned back to meet his glance in the rearview mirror, her eyes wide with a faux confusion.

"We're going to travel by bus?"

"The river terminal."

"Oh goodie. We're going to travel by boat?"

The bronze eyes narrowed. "Are you trying to piss me off?"

She smiled. Busted.

"I doubt it takes much effort to piss off a murderous bastard," she said sweetly.

"Not today," he agreed.

Fane reached to grasp her hand, giving her fingers a small squeeze of warning. She grimaced, but bit back her mocking response. He was right. Baiting Bas might give her a childish sense of satisfaction, but it was a waste of energy.

"Why the terminal?" she asked, trapping her raw emotions back behind her wall of brutal determination.

She was going to survive this.

Dammit.

"Two weeks ago my necro traveled there to read the memories of a recently murdered member of a prominent family," Bas said, his own face wiped smooth of his brief irritation.

His necro?

She resisted the urge to roll her eyes. Of course he had a diviner on the payroll. He seemed to have every other type of high-blood working for him.

"Why contact you?" she asked as they pulled into an empty parking lot between two large grain bins. "The police can call in diviners for murder victims without charging an enormous fee."

Bas took off his hat and tossed it into the seat beside him before turning to meet her suspicious gaze.

"Because this particular family prefers to take care of their own justice."

"What . . ." Serra stiffened. "They're mobsters?"

Bas shrugged. "Cartel."

She made no effort to disguise her disgust. Whores. Drug lords. Was there anyone this man wouldn't take money from?

"Nice."

He smiled, indifferent to her revulsion. "Does it make you feel better to know that my necro managed to discover the man was shot by his jealous wife instead of a rival gang? He prevented a bloody war that would no doubt have killed a dozen innocents."

"Does telling yourself that help you sleep at night?"

"I sleep just fine, Serra." The bronze gaze slid toward the silent Sentinel at her side. "But if you're truly concerned you can share my bed tonight—"

Fane exploded into motion so quickly Serra couldn't track his movement. One second he was sitting beside her and the next he had lunged forward and grabbed the assassin around the neck, his grasp threatening to crush the man's throat.

"My temper is on a hair trigger," he said, his soft voice more terrifying than any amount of screaming. "Neither of us wants me to be provoked into something we'll both regret."

Bas held himself motionless, smart enough to know that Fane might not kill him, but he could make him deeply regret his taunting.

"You've marked your territory, Sentinel," he said, waiting for Fane to remove his hands before turning his attention back to Serra. "Perhaps you should ask your guardian what darkness keeps him awake at night."

"You're a real prick," she snapped.

Bas abruptly laughed with a genuine amusement. "I'm not sure if I envy or pity you, Sentinel."

Serra shivered. There was way too much tension in too small a space. Grabbing the handle of the door she shoved it open and stepped onto the broken pavement. Instantly she was shrouded in a thick, humid heat that made her bra stick to her skin.

She rolled her stiff shoulders as Fane joined her, followed by Bas who had removed his chauffeur's jacket and was now wrapped in the illusion of a middle-aged businessman with thinning, silver hair and a pot belly beneath his white cotton shirt.

"Are you sure the drug lord is going to be there?" she demanded.

The assassin pulled a phone from his pocket and punched in a short message before he lifted his head to glance around the empty lot. There wasn't much to see. The grain bins, a pile of rotting railroad ties, and a huge mound of gravel that blocked their view of the river.

"I contacted him to meet me."

"Here?" Serra asked in confusion.

"At the terminal down the road."

Serra frowned. "You can't believe he would bring Molly with him?"

"No, but he's too smart to stash her at his house, or even the homes of his cartel."

"Why not?"

Bas smiled. "They're under constant government surveillance."

Oh. Of course. That's what happened when you lived the life of a criminal.

"So you think she might be hidden at the terminal?" she asked, baffled by why she'd been brought here if the drug lord didn't have Molly with him.

"No, but he has several secret safe houses not far away," Bas explained. "While I keep my client distracted, I want you to check out the area." He nodded toward the car. "The houses belonging to the cartel are marked in the GPS."

"How did you discover them if they're secret?"

"I have many ways of uncovering what people attempt to keep hidden," Bas assured her, adjusting his cuffs. "Secrets are a very profitable business."

Arrogant ass.

"And money is so important?" she asked in dry tones.

"It's a weapon. And for an assassin, that's a gift beyond price." He smiled, but Serra sensed he'd revealed a fundamental belief. He was obsessed with his need to be in power. "I will meet you back at this location in half an hour."

Serra snapped her teeth together. She hated being given orders. "What if I sense Molly?"

"Don't do anything," Bas immediately warned, the eyes that were now a pale blue flickering to bronze. "I don't want to find her and then get her killed because I rushed her rescue."

Serra shrugged. That was fine with her. She had no intention of risking her neck by sneaking into the lair of a drug lord.

Bas was walking away, when Fane stepped forward. "Wait."

The assassin muttered a curse as he turned back to glare at Fane. "What?"

"You're going to meet the leader of a drug cartel alone?"

"How sweet." He flashed a mocking smile. "Don't tell me you care?"

"If you die the toxin remains in Serra."

"True." Bas shrugged. "I die, she dies."

Serra's breath caught at his sheer callousness.

Fane was a little more . . . demonstrative in his reaction.

With three strides he was directly in front of the assassin, his hand once again around his throat.

"Then you don't do anything that puts you in danger."

"You're not giving the orders here, Sentinel," Bas growled, his eyes narrowing as Fane squeezed his fingers. "Christ. Kaede is waiting for me. It would look odd if I didn't have some muscle with me."

Fane slowly released his grip, indifferent to the slender stiletto Bas held in his hand. Serra didn't know where it had come from, but she didn't doubt for a second that the assassin knew how to use it.

She moved to stand next to Fane, lightly touching his arm as his gaze remained trained on the other male. It seemed they were destined to be driven to the brink of insanity by Bas Cavrilo. Thankfully they were together to pull each other back from the edge.

"What excuse did you use to call the meeting?" she asked Bas, more for a distraction than any interest in his meeting.

Bas gave a twist of his hand and the stiletto disappeared. "To warn the cartel there's a powerful psychic and her Sentinel in town," he said, his composure perfectly restored. "No criminal wants to accidentally cross paths with someone who can peek into their thoughts. I share the info and he's in my debt."

"Debt I suppose is another weapon?"

He sent her a mocking smile. "You begin to know me so well, lovely Serra."

Fane planted his fists on his hips. "Go. Away."

Chapter Nine

Fane grimaced.

The neighborhoods had grown increasingly grungy as they traveled north, with houses that had gone from shabby to downright dilapidated. Hell, many were missing windows or doors, and sprayed with gang graffiti. And the few stores that remained open had heavy bars across the windows, while the lone park was overgrown with weeds.

Worse, he was forced to a slow crawl as he navigated through the narrow street that was made nearly impassible by the abandoned cars and overflowing trash cans.

If he were human, he would be terrified of the unnatural silence that cloaked the area and the clumps of men who stood on the corner, watching him pass with a malevolent glare.

But he wasn't human and his only fear was the heavy cost this search was demanding from the vulnerable female at his side.

"Anything?" he asked as she pressed her fingers to her forehead, her shoulders tense with stress.

"The usual," she muttered. "Anger. Fear. Lust."

Most people distrusted psychics, even as they wished they could have the power.

Who didn't want to know what other people were thinking? Or use telepathy to communicate? Or even have the ability to twist the mind of an enemy until they went crazy?

What they didn't consider was the fact that Serra was constantly bombarded by unwelcome thoughts and emotions.

Her rigid training allowed her to block the intrusions when she was in the protection of Valhalla. But when she was surrounded by masses of bleak misery and desperate greed she became overwhelmed.

"Do you need to take a break?"

"There's no break," she said in weary tones. "Not as long as we're in such a congested area."

Keeping his gaze on the men clustered at the end of the block, Fane held his hand toward his companion.

"Here."

"What?"

"Take my hand."

He heard her breath catch. "I don't need your pity."

His hand remained outstretched. "That's not what I'm offering."

"Then what?"

He heaved a sigh. He might deserve her suspicion, but they wouldn't survive this if she didn't learn to trust him.

"Just take my hand, you stubborn female," he growled.

"Bossy."

She gave a sniff, but at last placed her palm against his so he could wrap his fingers around her hand.

Concentrating on the skin-to-skin contact, Fane opened himself to the bond that allowed him to share the sensory onslaught that was pounding against Serra. He grimaced. Holy shit. How did she stand it? Within a few seconds he felt as if his nerves were being scoured raw.

With an effort, he shoved aside the barrage of emotions,

using his training from the monks to center himself. Instinctively, he visualized himself in a cave high in the Alps. It was a cave where he'd spent nearly thirty years seeking the perfect balance between mind and body.

In the center of the cave was a deep pool of water. Slowly he entered the pool, the brisk water lapping at his ankles. He paused, allowing the sensation to fill his mind before he continued forward. The water hit his knees, then his waist, then his chest. Then with one last step he was underwater, floating in the chilled darkness.

Enveloped in peace, Fane tightened his grip on Serra's hand, allowing his tranquility to flow through their bond.

"Relax," he murmured.

She made a sound of surprise as her muscles eased beneath his soothing touch.

"What are you doing?"

"Do you feel better?"

She sucked in a deep breath. "Yes. I can still touch the minds, but the emotions are—"

"Muted?" He offered the word she was searching for.

He felt her gaze sear over his profile. "How?"

"It's a gift that Sentinels can share when they're bonded," he said. "Protection comes in many forms."

She hissed in surprise. "But we're not bonded."

His lips twisted at her ridiculous words. He might have done his best to pretend he hadn't given his heart and soul to this female, but he'd never truly fooled himself. Was there any greater bond than that?

Not that he was about to share the disturbing info. Right now she was determined to believe his every effort was made out of some idiotic hero complex.

Instead he gave her fingers another squeeze and gave her an answer she could accept.

"Not formally, but the vow I made to return you safely to Valhalla is just as binding."

There was a brief pause, as if she sensed he wasn't being completely honest. Thank God his magically enhanced glyphs prevented her from reading his mind.

"What will happen when you leave for Tibet?"

Foolish female. Did she truly believe he would ever leave her side again?

He shrugged. "Let's concentrate on getting through today."

She clicked her tongue, clearly annoyed by his hedging. "Do we have to be touching?"

Nope. Absolutely not.

"Yes," he said, lifting her hand to press her knuckles to his lips.

He felt her tremble, revealing her vulnerability to his touch as she was hastily trying to disguise her response behind a brisk determination.

"Okay," she muttered. "Let's finish this."

He kept a tight hold on her hand as she returned her attention to the passing houses, doing his best to dampen the impact of the ugly and desperate thoughts that were blasting into her brain.

Circling the block that was marked on the GPS, Fane muttered a curse as he watched the gang of thugs that had been loitering on the corner step into the street, deliberately blocking his path.

They varied in age from sixteen to twenty, dressed in tattered jeans with muscle shirts to show off their various tattoos.

Common street bullies who ruled the neighborhood with brute intimidation.

He could run them over.

Bas was a paranoid freak, which meant that the windows

of the car would be bulletproof and the frame reinforced for maximum impact.

Unfortunately even in this neighborhood the death of a half dozen men was bound to attract the notice of the authorities.

Something he preferred to avoid.

"I think we've been noticed."

Serra instantly jerked herself out of her shallow trance, her brows drawing together with concern. "Fane."

He pressed her fingers to his lips before releasing them and shoving open the car door. "Don't worry. They won't hurt me."

"I'm more worried about them."

Already stepping out of the car, he glanced back at her with a lift of his brows. "Them?"

"I've seen you fight," she said with a grimace. "I prefer not to witness their blood and guts being spread across the road."

He shrugged. "We're just going to have a little chat."

"A chat?" She rolled her eyes. "Yeah, right."

"I promise."

Shutting the door, he turned to walk down the middle of the street, watching the unease that tightened the young faces hardened by a life on the edge.

They might not recognize him as a Sentinel, but they most certainly sensed he was a predator.

Instinctively two of the thugs pulled their handguns and pointed them at Fane. A rookie mistake. The best weapon was the one unseen.

He ignored the blatant threat, instead continuing to walk forward as he watched the covert glances toward the man standing at the center of the road. Obviously the leader of the motley crew.

The lean man had dark hair shaved into a Mohawk and flat, black eyes and a badass attitude that was about to get a painful readjustment.

"Is there a problem?" Fane demanded, coming to a halt far enough away to allow the fools to believe he wasn't a danger.

The leader puffed out his narrow chest. A typical blowhard who thought a gun made him tough.

"This is our neighborhood."

"That's not something I would brag about," Fane taunted, glancing toward a pile of rotting trash. "It looks like a war zone."

The man placed a hand behind his back, revealing where he had his gun hidden. Exactly what Fane needed to know.

"We want to know what the hell you're doing scoping out our territory," he rasped.

His posture was relaxed, nonthreatening. "Just passing through."

"I don't think so. In fact, I—"

The man's words became a high-pitched squeal as Fane exploded into action, closing the space between them. In one motion he was standing behind the leader, one arm around the man's throat and his other hand yanking the handgun from the back of his jeans. Then, with a deliberate motion, he pressed the gun to the man's forehead.

"You scream like my five-year-old niece," he mocked, shifting the man so he was a human shield between him and the rest of the gangbangers. A bullet wouldn't kill him, but it would hurt like a bitch. "Tell them to stay back," he ordered.

The man muttered a foul curse, but he pointed toward his restless companions. "Listen to him."

They scowled, but none had the balls to challenge him.

It was easy to be the biggest bullies on the block when they were facing vulnerable females and children.

"Now this is what is going to happen," he informed the cowards. "You're going to put away your weapons and walk away. Then you're going to call your friends waiting around the corner and tell them to stay out of my way."

The leader stiffened, but he made no effort to fight Fane's hold. "My boss won't stop until he knows what you're doing here."

Fane glanced toward the idiots trying to hide behind a ramshackle fence. Dammit. It didn't matter if the goons belonged to the drug lord who was currently meeting with Bas, or not. The last thing he needed was one of the over-eager minions tracking them back to the hotel.

"My business is with Valhalla," he said, pulling out his trump card.

The stench of fear filled the air, the thugs dropping their weapons to the ground as they backed away.

Unable to retreat, the leader glanced warily over his shoulder. "You're a freak?"

"I am, but I'm not the one to worry about." Fane offered a cold smile, nodding his head toward the black Mercedes. "With one psychic blast, my companion can turn you all into drooling, babbling idiots who will spend the rest of your pathetic lives being spoon-fed mushed bananas."

"Fuck that, I'm outta here," one of the men muttered, turning to run toward the nearest house.

As if his retreat was a catalyst, the rest of the cowardly fools were bolting after him, leaving the leader to fend for himself.

"What business does Valhalla have around here?" the man asked, trying to act as if he wasn't on the verge of pissing his pants.

"Do you really want to know?"

"No."

"Good choice." Lowering the gun, Fane loosened his grip and stepped back. "Run."

The man did.

And at a pace that might have earned him a spot on the Olympic relay team if he hadn't been a pathetic putz.

Serra entered the private hotel suite with a sense of boiling frustration.

Who could blame her?

The clock was ticking toward her death, and Bas had her running in circles chasing after whores and a drug gang with nothing to show for her efforts but a headache.

But deep inside, she knew her frustration was caused as much by the silent man trailing behind her as the stress of potential death.

What the hell had he been thinking to confront six armed drug runners by himself?

Okay, she logically knew that he could have destroyed the humans. She'd even tried to pretend she was concerned they might end up bloody corpses. But inside she'd been a seething mass of terror that Fane would be injured.

Which for some reason pissed her off.

Was this why he'd always been so insistent that he couldn't make her a permanent part of his life? Had he known she would be tormenting herself every time he stepped into danger?

After all, it was one thing to be at Valhalla knowing he might be at risk, and another to be watching as he deliberately placed himself in the line of fire.

She'd been so angry for so long at his stubborn refusal

to believe she was capable of accepting his commitment to his duties. She assumed he thought she was too pampered, too sheltered to be the partner of a warrior.

Now she was forced to accept that he might have had a point.

Watching him . . . shit. She'd been a breath from stepping out of the car and blasting them with enough psychic force to knock them out for a week. Only the knowledge that Fane would put himself in even greater danger if she'd attracted the attention of the thugs had kept her in the car.

Not that the nerve-wracking afternoon had changed her feelings for the aggravating beast. She wasn't sure there was anything that could destroy her love. But it forced her to admit that her resentment toward Fane hadn't been entirely fair. And to acknowledge that being the lover of a Sentinel might involve more than she'd originally antici-pated.

She hated being in the wrong.

"Well that was a waste of a day," she muttered, pacing the sitting room.

Bas had dropped them off in front of the hotel, warning he was returning at eight. Of course he refused to say where they would be going, only insisting that she was to wear the formal gown.

The bastard.

Moving without a sound, Fane was standing directly in her path, his hands lightly gripping her shoulders.

"It's not too late, Serra."

Her heart skidded to a halt at his touch, her mouth going dry. She'd spent the entire day trying to ignore her acute awareness of this man. Now she was too damned tired to deny the thrill of excitement that raced through her.

"What do you mean?" she asked, her voice husky.

His expression remained grim, but his grip eased, allowing his fingers to lightly trace the line of her shoulders.

"I can contact the Mave."

"No."

He scowled. "Serra—"

She lifted her hand to press her fingers to his lips, halting his protest. "Not yet."

Without warning he nipped the tip of her finger, his eyes darkening with a blast of arousal he made no effort to hide.

"I knew you were going to be trouble the minute I saw you," he murmured, his low voice brushing over her skin like a caress.

She frowned, glaring into his hard, starkly beautiful face. Hell. He was supposed to be the aloof, untouchable Sentinel. The distant warrior she'd sworn had rejected her for the last time.

She couldn't possibly fight her aching need when he wasn't playing by the rules.

"You don't even remember our first meeting," she accused, her treacherous fingers lingering on his surprisingly sensuous lips.

His hands smoothed down her back, his caress heart-stoppingly tender.

It was something that had always fascinated her.

How such a strong, lethally trained Sentinel could possess a touch delicate enough to carve the exquisite wooden figurines that filled the nursery at Valhalla or make a woman melt in desire.

She shivered as he cupped her ass with an intimacy that made her breath tangle in her throat.

"I remember every second of our first meeting," he informed her, the movement of his lips beneath her fingers oddly erotic. "I'd been away from Valhalla for almost fifty years and I was anxious to return to my favorite fishing spot by the lake. But instead of the peace and quiet I was expecting I discovered a dark-haired, green-eyed vixen who was wearing a dangerously skimpy tank top and short-shorts." His gaze drifted down to the low cut of her neckline. "You looked like a wood sprite."

His low words vividly conjured the magic of the day.

She'd escaped from her training so she could finish her latest romance novel. It'd been a rare autumn day filled with sunshine and just a hint of frost in the air. The sort of day that begged a young woman to play hooky.

Knowing that Inhera, the leader of the psychics and clairvoyants, would send someone in search of her, Serra had hidden among the reeds that surrounded the lake, feeling deliciously rebellious.

And then . . . Fane had appeared.

"I glanced up from the book I was reading and I was dazzled," she told him, her fingers moving to stroke the exotic tattoo that wrapped around his thick neck. "You were the most beautiful man I'd ever seen."

He arched a brow. "Beautiful?"

"You are." She smiled with rueful resignation. "But then you grunted at me and before I could even say hi you were storming away in a huff."

"Because I felt like a perv," he muttered, a shocking heat staining his high cheekbones.

She blinked in confusion. "What?"

"You were so young." He shook his head. "Too young."

"I was over eighteen."

"Barely." His eyes lowered to the swell of her breasts, his eyes dilating with a hunger he couldn't disguise. "Christ, all I could think about was laying you back on the grass and peeling away that teeny tiny top." His hands skimmed up her hips to slide beneath the edge of her sweater.

She hissed in shock, but he held his searching gaze even as she shuddered at the feel of his hands on her bare skin.

They scalded. Tormented.

Aroused.

"Then you spent the next fifteen years pretending I didn't exist," she muttered.

He gave a short, humorless laugh, his hands moving up to cup the heavy weight of her breasts.

"That pretense is well and truly over."

Serra swallowed a groan, her senses sizzling with electric anticipation beneath his bold seduction. His fingers found the straining tips of her nipples, teasing them with a blissful skill.

Oh . . . God.

This was her fantasy. Her deepest dream made real.

But even as her back arched with blatant invitation, an annoying voice whispered in the back of her mind that at this precise moment he would be in Tibet if she hadn't been in danger.

"Shattered by the sword of Damocles that hangs over my head?" she rasped.

"Shattered by fate." He lowered his head to brush a light kiss on her mouth, his thumbs stroking her nipples with increasing urgency. White-hot excitement curled through the pit of her stomach. "A fate I'm tired of fighting."

"I'm not sure what that means," she breathed, her hands grabbing his shoulders. To push him away? Or yank him closer?

She hadn't decided.

He teased her with another brush of his mouth, lingering just long enough to make her ache for a deeper kiss.

"Neither do I," he admitted in rough tones. "I suppose we'll find out together."

"But—"

He gave her lower lip a punishing nip. "Are you always this chatty when a man's trying to get you naked?"

Chatty? She narrowed her gaze.

"Do you always have such trouble getting a woman naked?"

He lifted his head to reveal a smile that sent a tingle down her spine. That smile warned of all sorts of wicked pleasure.

"Ah. A challenge." With a strength only a Sentinel could claim, Fane had her tossed over his shoulder and was headed to the bedroom.

She gave a choked gasp of disbelief. "Caveman."

Entering the bedroom he lowered her onto the bed, gazing down at her with a searing intensity as he bent down to tug off his boots.

"No more talking," he warned.

Serra wrenched her gaze from the dark promise in his eyes, feeling her entire body melt beneath the potent heat of his desire.

What the hell were they doing?

Twenty-four hours ago he'd been determined to leave her behind. Now he was staring at her as if he wanted to devour her.

Shouldn't she be kicking some serious Sentinel ass, not considering how long it was going to take to trace every one of those exquisite tattoos with the tip of her tongue?

Of course, in her defense, she'd wanted Fane with a desperation that was painful.

She hadn't lied when she'd told him he was the most beautiful man she'd ever seen.

He was obscenely magnificent.

Not only his lean, savagely handsome face, but the

sculpted body he was swiftly revealing as he tugged off his camos to reveal his perfection.

His skin was silky smooth beneath the tattoos and stretched tight over the impressive muscles that moved with liquid ease. His chest was broad and tapered to a slender waist, his arms were massive, and his legs long and powerful.

Lethal power combined with the gentle touch of an artist.

A potent combination.

"Did you just tell me to shut up?" she demanded, her gaze sliding down to watch in fascination as his cock hardened, revealing he was as generously proportioned as she'd always suspected.

Oh . . . hell.

"I told you to stop talking." A slow, wicked smile curved his lips. "There are more satisfying ways of communicating."

"Telepathy?"

Holding her gaze, he placed a knee on the edge of the mattress and lowered himself to plant his hands on either side of her head. Then, he dipped down to nuzzle a spot just below her jaw, making Serra's heart slam against her ribs.

When had that particular spot become so unbearably erotic?

"I was thinking something more physical."

"You're Mr. Taciturn, remember? You don't want to . . ." Her provocative words were cut short as his seeking lips found another point of pleasure at the base of her throat. "Oh."

"You have no idea what I want," he growled, nipping her collarbone. "Or how many nights I've tormented myself with thoughts of having you in my bed . . . screaming my name as I enter you."

His dark, musky scent brushed over her, seeping into her

skin and clouding her senses. It had to be an aphrodisiac. Why else was she stroking her hands down the magnificent length of his back, trying to urge him downward?

"You think you can make me scream?" she muttered.

His soft laugh sent a prickle of excitement over her bare skin as he reached down to grasp the hem of her sweater and with one smooth motion had it tugged over her head and tossed across the room.

"Do you want a detailed explanation of how I intend to accomplish my goal?" he demanded, easily dealing with the clip of her bra so he could peal the lacy garment away.

Serra shivered. His dark gaze was a tangible caress as he studied the full globes of her breasts. Her back instinctively arched upward. Her nipples were hard, agonizingly sensitive as they yearned for his touch.

"Arrogant."

He tormented the pulse at the base of her throat as he slid down her pants, pausing to tug off her boots before he had them stripped away and tossed on the carpet. Only then did he settle his heavy weight between her legs that had instinctively widened.

"Determined," he corrected.

"Determined to what?" she rasped, shuddering as pleasure blasted through her. Oh, hell. This was so much better than she'd fantasized. The welcome hardness of his body as it pressed her into the mattress. The sizzling heat of his touch. The brush of his breath over her breasts. "Seduce me?"

His tongue flicked over her nipple, the rough stroke wrenching a moan from her throat.

"Is it working?"

She dug her nails into the smooth skin of his ass. "You've always known how badly I wanted you," she said with blunt honesty. "I've done everything but beg to get you in my bed."

He continued to tease her nipple, his hardening erection pressing with flawless precision against her clit. Oh . . . God. It felt good. Beyond good.

"If you hadn't meant so much to me I would have been in your bed a long time ago," he said, licking a path of wet heat between her breasts.

"Is that supposed to make sense?"

With a low growl, Fane surged upward to claim her lips in an openmouthed kiss that was hard with unrestrained hunger. Desire streaked through her, destroying any hope of resistance.

"I knew I could never be satisfied with sex," he confessed against her lips, rubbing his erection against her clit. "I wanted to possess you. Completely and utterly."

Her hips instinctively arched upward. Somewhere deep inside she desperately wanted to believe his low, husky words.

"And now?"

He chuckled, scorching a path of kisses down her throat. "Now I intend to start the possession. Starting from the top and working my way to the bottom. With plenty of stops in between."

She retained enough sense to remember that she didn't entirely trust this abrupt change of heart. It was one thing to give in to the potent hunger that thundered through her. She wanted this man with an intensity she couldn't deny.

But while she might give him her body, her heart wasn't up for grabs.

Not again.

"Don't think this changes anything, warrior," she warned, scoring her nails up his back. She reveled in his violent shudder of pleasure. "No one gets to possess me utterly and completely anymore."

"Serra," he breathed. "Haven't you learned the danger of challenging a Sentinel?"

"It was a warning, not a challenge."

"Warning . . . challenge. It's all the same to me," he rasped.

His hands skimmed over her body, his lips searing a path down the quivering plane of her stomach.

Serra nearly came off the bed when his tongue dipped into her belly button, a shocking blast of pleasure traveling straight between her legs.

Man, oh man. Fane's lovemaking was as intense and forceful as he was.

A male who didn't apologize for being male.

Closing her eyes she savored the soul-shattering sensations. The thorough, detailed exploration of his hands, the thrilling heat of his lips, the hard thrust of his erection that rubbed against the center of her pleasure.

It was like being in the middle of a thunderstorm, sensing the lightning was about to strike at any second.

"I don't want to be a challenge," she managed to mutter.

He lifted his head to regard her with a dark, searching intensity. "Then what do you want, Serra?"

"Just to be a woman wanted by a man."

Chapter Ten

Fane was way past the point of no return.

How many years had he tried to play the noble Sentinel? Too many.

He'd denied himself the female who had stolen a piece of his soul the minute she'd glanced at him with those enticing green eyes.

Now he was done with playing the role of hero.

At some point between leaving Valhalla and arriving in St. Louis his need for Serra had altered from *want* to *have to have*.

Claiming her as his own was as necessary as breathing.

Serra, unfortunately, wasn't nearly so ready to accept their inevitable fate.

Or maybe it wasn't so unfortunate, he abruptly realized, sliding his hands beneath her to cup her sumptuous ass in his hands.

Convincing her that she was now his, and his alone, offered a wide variety of opportunities to earn the love she'd once so lavishly offered.

And until then . . . well, he wasn't opposed to allowing her to believe she was just using him for his body.

With one smooth motion he was flipping onto his back

and settling Serra until she straddled his waist. She made a sound of shock, her startled gaze searching his deliberately unreadable expression.

"What are you doing?"

"Putting you in charge."

She licked her dry lips, the unconscious gesture making Fane's cock twitch in anticipation.

Christ, she looked like the very image of temptation as she perched on top of him, her eyes darkened to a mysterious emerald and her dark hair a cloud of ebony spilling over the lush ivory of her breasts.

"In charge of what?"

"If you won't let me possess you, then I'm going to let you possess me."

Another lick of those sensuous lips. "Utterly and completely?"

Fane groaned.

Oh. Hell, yes.

What warrior didn't want a woman to possess him?

Especially if that possessing included the use of his body that was primed and ready to please her.

Not that she seemed to be in any hurry to start.

Dammit.

Calling on the patience that had been learned over decades of brutal training, Fane allowed his hands to lightly skim up her bare thighs. Her skin was satin soft beneath his fingertips, but he refused to rush her as he caressed the slender indent of her waist before at last cupping the plush softness of her breasts.

His body might be on the wrong side of pain with his need to be buried deep inside her, but nothing was happening until she was ready.

"My Serra," he said thickly, his thumbs strumming her hardened nipples. "You are so fucking perfect."

Her breath caught at the unashamed awe in his voice, her hands bracing against his chest as she leaned down to kiss him with a rough passion that made him growl in pleasure. She tasted of chamomile and warm, sweet temptation.

Fane's hips jerked upward, rubbing his aching cock against her, silently cursing the satin panties that kept him from completing their union.

He needed to be in her.

He needed to slide into her damp heat. To drown himself in her scent. To be connected on the most basic level.

As if sensing his primitive instinct, Serra gave his lower lip a punishing nip.

"This is sex," she muttered. "Don't try to charm me."

"I can't help myself." His hands followed the curve of her waist, ripping off her satin panties. "I'm a charming guy."

She made a sound of disbelief at his claim.

"You're a pain in the ass, is what you are," she muttered. "But I can't seem to resist you."

Fane sucked in a sharp breath as Serra used the tip of her tongue to trace the tattoos that were etched over his chest, her hips rocking against his erection. Irresistible?

He was a taciturn Sentinel who knew fifty ways to kill a man, but zero ways to win friends and influence people.

But hell, if she wanted to think that he was irresistible, then he wasn't going to argue.

In this moment he would have agreed he was the fucking king of England if it would convince Serra to put him out of his misery.

"Serra."

His plea was cut short as she swirled her tongue around his sensitive nipples before exploring ever lower.

Fane clenched his teeth and clutched the comforter beneath him. This was clearly his punishment for having denied the hunger that raged between them.

Unaware of how close he was to the edge, or more likely relishing her power over him, Serra continued to torment him, her lips sending sparks of bliss through his body. Then without warning, her seeking mouth closed over the tip of his cock, the moist heat nearly making him come on impact.

"Holy shit." He reached to grasp her arms, yanking her upward to kiss her with savage force. "Do you want me to beg?"

She tossed her dark hair over one shoulder, her smile smug. "I thought Sentinels were trained to last for . . ." Her eyes widened with shock as Fane arched his hips upward and with one smooth motion had impaled himself in her damp heat. "Oh, God."

Grasping her hips, Fane sucked the tip of her breast between his lips, delighting in her shocked groan of pleasure. She was tight around him, clenching his cock like a glove. Trembling from the effort, he waited until she relaxed.

"Are you okay?" he rasped.

"I'll let you know later," she murmured, lifting herself on her knees so she could draw him out to the tip of his cock before slowly sinking back down, burying him deep inside her. "Much later."

Fane choked back a curse, his grip tightening on her hips as he battled back his looming orgasm.

Dammit. She was right. Sentinels were infamous for pleasuring a woman for hours before claiming their own release. But this wasn't a woman.

This was Serra.

His woman.

Holding her gaze, he allowed himself to become mesmerized by the beauty of her pale emerald eyes. For once they were unguarded, darkened with passion as she quickened her pace.

His hips lifted to meet her downward strokes, his moan

of pleasure echoing through the air as she planted her hands on his chest for better leverage.

The air was spiced with the erotic scent of sex, her slender body tensing above him as she closed her eyes and lost herself in the pleasure.

"More?" he demanded, bewitched by the soft flush staining her cheeks.

"Yes," she whispered, giving a moan of bliss, as Fane took command, pumping deep into her at a ruthless pace. "Don't stop."

"I'm yours to command, Serra," he swore, abruptly sitting up so he could grab the back of her head and claim her lips in a savage kiss. "Whatever you need from me."

Their tongues battled, their bodies moving together in perfect harmony. As if they were specifically created for this mating dance.

Then, as Fane felt the glorious rush toward his climax, Serra at last stiffened in completion, her cry of pleasure muffled against his lips.

Threading his fingers in her hair, Fane hissed as her pulsing orgasm milked his cock, his hips slamming upward, unleashing his desperate hunger.

Gasping in stunned pleasure, Fane felt his seed burst from his cock, the shock waves of pleasure radiating through his entire body.

Serra.

Valhalla

Nine levels beneath the public rooms of Valhalla were the headquarters of the Sentinels.

The long communal room was a stainless steel masterpiece filled with state of the art computer systems and monitors directly linked into their personal satellites as well as a few owned by the government. The heavy wooden furniture was spaced to give the techs a sense of privacy and yet allowed them to share information with ease.

Along one wall were several doors that were closed and heavily monitored to protect the weapons as well as the more sensitive secrets of Valhalla. And at the far end was the Office of the Tagos.

The private room reflected the current leader of the Sentinels.

The office was sparsely furnished with a large walnut desk and two black leather chairs. Its wooden floor was left bare and the ivory painted walls decorated with a collection of priceless samurai swords.

It was stark. Efficient. And uncompromisingly male.

Seated at his desk, Wolfe was sorting through a stack of bills when he sensed an approaching visitor. Oh, thank God. He tossed down his pen and rolled his stiff shoulders.

Shit. He hated paperwork.

Duty rotations. Inventory. Accounts.

He was supposed to be a warrior, not a damned pencil pusher.

But leadership wasn't just about giving orders. Keeping the Sentinels properly trained, armed with the latest high-tech weapons, and rotated throughout the world was as important as picking up a gun and fighting at their side.

That didn't mean, however, that he had to like it, he ruefully acknowledged, watching as the hunter Sentinel filled the doorway.

Arel was the current favorite of the young women of Valhalla. With features that were just a breath from pretty, he had honey highlights in his light brown hair and eyes that were the color of molten gold.

It was easy to dismiss him as a playboy with more charm than skill, but Wolfe was well aware Arel was a ruthless opponent who could kill without mercy.

His angelic beauty only made him more dangerous.

"What do you have for me?" he demanded.

Arel held up a file folder. "I've got the info on Hull Insurance."

The younger Sentinel was dressed like Wolfe in worn jeans and a casual tee, but while Wolfe preferred heavy boots that he could use to kick ass, Arel wore running shoes that allowed him to move in silence.

"Close the door." Wolfe waited for Arel to shut the door before pointing toward the chair nearest his heavy desk. He'd taken the younger Sentinel off his current research into the Brotherhood to investigate the St. Louis company. "Sit."

The Sentinel crossed to take the leather seat, tossing the file onto the desk.

"On the surface it's a legit company that's been in business for the past thirty years." Opening the folder, Arel pulled out a black and white photo of a middle-aged man who was only remarkable for being so unremarkable. "This is Hull. No one's seen any sons."

Wolfe frowned, baffled by Fane's text to investigate the business. "Any connection to Cavrilo International?"

"None. In fact they don't have a connection to anyone."

"Explain."

"Hull and Sons have all the necessary paperwork for their business and they even have a secretary who shows up every day at the office, but the home address listed for Mr. Hull is bogus as is his private telephone number."

Wolfe tapped his finger on the polished surface of the desk, sorting through Arel's succinct report.

"So it's a shell corporation?"

"Yes."

Shit. That meant unraveling the truth of Hull and Sons just became ten times more difficult.

"Have the offices watched."

Arel flashed a grin that had been melting female hearts since he was in his cradle. "Already on it."

Wolfe hid his burst of satisfaction. Arel was young, but already he showed the type of initiative that would one day make him a leader. Most warriors were happy to follow commands, which made them perfectly suited for the field. He needed men and women who could carry out his orders without question.

Arel was always thinking a step ahead, like a master chess player using strategy to stay ahead of the enemy.

Which was why Wolfe had already started the junior Sentinel's training.

Not that Arel realized he was being molded by a subtle hand. He was still young enough to relish the thrill of the battle. He would rebel at the mere suggestion that he should be anywhere but at the front line.

"And?" Wolfe pressed.

"And I had Marco follow the secretary home," Arel revealed with satisfaction.

"So at least one of them has a real home."

"Not really," Arel corrected as he leaned forward, shuffling through the file to pull out the photo of a three-story brick building surrounded by an acre of closely tended grass framed by a high fence. At one side of the building was a cement parking lot and on the other was a white grotto and marble fountain.

"What is this?"

Arel shrugged. "This is where she went."

Wolfe grabbed the photo, holding it close enough to decipher the sign posted on the locked gate.

"CENTURY LAB," he read out loud. Lifting his head, he met Arel's steady gaze. "What do you know?"

"The tax returns list it as a research facility."

"What kind of research?"

The younger man grimaced. "I'm checking, but Marco claims the place is locked down tighter than Valhalla."

Wolfe was on instant alert. There were only a handful of reasons a business would go to such an effort to protect their secrets.

Few of them good.

"A government facility?" he said, suggesting the one acceptable reason for high security.

Arel shook his head, his expression suddenly somber. "Marco suspects high-blood. He counted three Sentinels patrolling the grounds around the building and at least one telepath monitoring the entrance."

With a hiss Wolfe was swiveling toward his computer, typing in the name Century Lab. No surprise it wasn't listed in his database. Which meant any high-bloods working there had lied about their place of employment, since all high-bloods were supposed to keep Valhalla updated on their addresses and work history if they chose not to live at one of the numerous compounds spread around the world.

Or they were rogues.

Both possibilities pissed him off.

"An insurance company that's not an insurance company. An unsanctioned facility being guarded by high-bloods," he snarled. "What the hell is going on?"

Arel's expression tightened with an anticipation he couldn't disguise. "Send me to St. Louis and I'll find out."

"No." Wolfe nipped the suggestion in the bud. Arel would still have plenty of opportunities to risk his fool neck. Right now it was more important that he use his skill at sifting through puzzle pieces to see the full picture. "I need you working your magic on the computer."

Not surprisingly, Arel wasn't pleased. "You have an entire staff of geeks to work computer magic," he protested. "I'm a Sentinel, I need to be in the field."

"Not this time."

Arel clenched his teeth. "Why?"

Wolfe didn't have to make up an excuse. Even if he wasn't trying to train Arel to occasionally use his brain instead of his brawn, he wouldn't allow the young man anywhere near Serra.

"Because if you show up in St. Louis Fane will kill you."

Arel scowled at the blunt explanation. "He could try."

Wolfe resisted the urge to roll his eyes. Arel would someday make a great leader, but he was no match for Fane's brute strength. Hell, no one could match Fane in a head to head matchup.

And when it came to Serra being in danger . . .

He shuddered at the mere thought of anyone stupid enough to try to come between Fane and the woman who'd captured his heart years before.

"Don't press it," Wolfe warned.

Arel clenched his hands, refusing to let it drop. Understandable. The younger man had been Serra's lover in the past.

"Why not?" he demanded. "Fane was the one who walked away from Serra."

Wolfe flattened his lips. He was probably the only one who truly knew the price Fane had paid to try to do the right thing for the beautiful, unbearably young psychic.

"He had his reasons."

Arel narrowed his golden eyes. "She deserves better. Much better."

Wolfe stilled at the unexpected edge in the Sentinel's voice. Christ. Did Arel feel more than affection for his previous lover?

That was a ticking time bomb he didn't need.

It'd only been a matter of time before Fane gave in to his primal need to claim Serra as his own.

"You think you would be better for her?"

"I care about her, I always have," Arel said. "Which is more than Fane can say."

Wolfe released his breath. Arel was protective of Serra, but his feelings didn't seem to go deeper than affection.

"You couldn't be more wrong," Wolfe informed his companion. "I just hope he hasn't realized the truth when it's too late."

There was a faint prickle of electricity in the air before a hidden elevator door behind Wolfe's desk silently slid open.

"Too late for what?" a low, mesmerizing voice demanded.

Wolfe knew who would be standing in the doorway before he ever swiveled his chair around. Only one person could make Arel jump from his chair and stand at rigid attention.

And certainly only one person could make him feel as if he'd been struck by lightning just by stepping into the room.

Besides, there were only two keys to the private elevator. And he had one.

Bringing the chair to a halt, he watched as the current leader of the high-bloods stepped out of the elevator.

No one knew the precise age of the current Mave, but her classically beautiful face was unmarred by time and framed by a smooth curtain of black hair that was currently left free to spill over her shoulders. Her eyes were a stunning gray, not the placid dove gray of most people, but a stormy, gunmetal gray that was at complete odds with her dignified composure.

He hid a smile of self-derision as his gaze slid down her tall, slender body, perfectly revealed by her casual jeans and her jade green sweater, cut low enough to reveal the birthmark on the upper curve of her breast.

The small mark in the shape of an eye proved that she

was a born witch, and the brilliance of the shimmering emerald color revealed the thunderous depths of her powers.

The darker the color, the greater her magic.

Not that his gaze was lingering on the soft swell of her breasts because he was fascinated by her witch mark, he wryly acknowledged.

He'd long ago given up the effort to slam shut his awareness of this female.

She might be the Mave, his esteemed leader, but she was also an exquisite woman who called to him on a deep, primal level.

A damned shame since nothing could come of his fascination but frustrated nights and long, brutally cold showers.

The Mave was supposed to be a fair and impartial judge to her people. Which meant she avoided any intimate relationships, whether it was with family, friends, or lovers.

She'd even given up her own name, Lana Mayfield, to cut all ties with her past.

A lonely existence, but one she'd chosen with her eyes wide open.

And one he had no choice but to respect.

Of course, that didn't keep him from being plagued by a savage urge to pounce and devour her delectable body.

Potent need blasted through him, leaving him gutted in its wake.

He wanted her pressed against the wall, those impossibly long legs wrapped around his waist. Or spread over his desk, her hands threaded in his hair as he went to his knees and tasted her most intimate magic.

Those infuriating, unstoppable images were a constant source of annoyance, which might explain why he was more of an ass than usual when she was near.

Slowly he rose to his feet. "Mave."

"Am I interrupting?"

His lips twisted at the polite words. Unlike the previous Maves, this female preferred to lead with the pretense of civility. Not that anyone was fooled.

She would crush any opposition with a brutal swiftness. "Would it matter?"

She regarded him with a lift of her brows, cool as a fucking cucumber. "It's a simple question."

Wolfe glanced toward Arel who was inching backward, as if afraid of getting caught in the crossfire.

Smart Sentinel.

"Anything you wanted to add, Arel?"

"Nope. Nada. Not a thing," he muttered, glancing toward the Mave with obvious unease.

Wolfe gave a resigned shake of his head. "Get back to your research."

"Great." Arel heaved a relieved sigh, giving a small nod of his head. "Mave."

"Arel," she murmured, his name barely leaving her lips before Arel was headed out of the office and shutting the door firmly behind him.

Wolfe perched on the edge of his desk. "I've asked you not to terrify my warriors."

"If I could truly terrify one of your warriors I wouldn't have to come to you and beg for information on what the hell is going on."

He forced his lips into a smile even as his gut clenched at the erotic thought at having this female begging.

On her knees . . .

"Hmm. That's an intriguing possibility."

She frowned. "What's intriguing?"

"You." His gaze lowered to the soft curve of her lips. "Begging."

The flare of emotion in the gray eyes was so fleeting no one but Wolfe would have seen it.

And only then, because he'd trained himself to watch for it.

Petty, of course. But occasionally he felt the overwhelming need to force her to remember she was still Lana Mayfield, a flesh and blood woman, beneath her role of Mave.

She stiffened at his less than subtle teasing. "Are you going to tell me what's going on?"

He folded his arms over his chest, his gaze lingering on the lush mouth that promised paradise.

"I might. Given the right incentive."

"Wolfe."

A blast of desire made his gut clench at the thought of hearing her breathe his name in pleasure instead of frustration.

"Lana."

Her frown deepened as the heat from his body filled the office. Sentinels always ran hotter than norms, but he didn't usually allow his powers to brush over his companion like a physical caress.

"Would you just answer the question?" She tilted her chin, her voice nerve-scrapingly calm. "We're both too old for this nonsense."

His lips twisted into a humorless smile. "Are we?"

"Enough, Wolfe."

The edge in her voice warned Wolfe he was treading close to the edge of her patience. He swallowed a thwarted growl and forced himself into his role of the Tagos.

She was right.

He was too damned old to be acting like a hormonal-crazed idiot.

"I haven't come to you quite simply because I don't know what's going on," he admitted, his voice crisp.

Her expression remained impassive, but he could physically feel her relief.

Someday . . .

He grimaced.

But not today.

"Tell me what you do know."

"Last night Serra left Valhalla without a word to anyone, including Inhera."

"That's not like her," Lana said, concern turning her eyes to smoke. This female might be a hard-as-nails leader, but she genuinely cared about her people. "Serra is headstrong, but she would never cause unnecessary worry."

"Exactly. Fane was concerned and tracked her to St. Louis."

The Mave blinked in astonishment. Fane and Serra's— complicated—relationship wasn't a secret at Valhalla.

"You sent Fane after her?"

"He made the decision."

"Ah." She grimaced. "Is he with her?"

Wolfe resisted the urge to point out a nuclear bomb couldn't separate Fane from Serra.

"Yes, he sent word that they were together and everything was fine."

It was the carefully constructed answer he was giving to everyone who asked about Serra's abrupt departure.

But Lana Mayfield wasn't just everyone.

She studied him for a long minute, her clever mind instantly latching on to the pertinent question.

"If he's with Serra and everything is fine then why is Valhalla missing a half a dozen Sentinels?"

"Because he didn't tell me to withdraw the Sentinels."

"He knew that you sent them?"

"Yes. He called when he first tracked Serra to St. Louis. I told him then I was sending backup."

"Maybe he forgot."

Wolfe gave a sharp laugh. His most fearsome warrior had never forgotten a thing in his life.

All Sentinels were *more* than human. But Fane was *more* than most.

"Fane better than anyone realizes the price the Sentinels paid during our battle with the necromancer, he would never allow them to be away from more important duties unless he needed them," he assured his companion.

"But he hasn't made contact with them?"

"No, but after his call he sent me a text requesting information." He nodded toward the file spread across his desk. "I'm in the process of trying to untangle what the hell is going on."

He watched the gray gaze shift toward the desk, jerking in shock as she was abruptly lunging forward to snatch the picture at the top of the pile.

"What's this?"

Wolfe pushed off the edge of the desk, his brows snapping together at the sight of the soft flush that touched her pale cheeks.

What the hell?

He could count on one hand how many times he'd seen Lana rattled. And each time they'd been facing certain death.

"The owner of Hull and Sons Insurance in St. Louis," he said, his narrowed gaze taking in the tightening of her pale, beautiful features as she studied the photo.

"No. Not Hull," she said softly.

"You recognize him." It was a statement, not a question.

"Yes." She brushed a slender finger over the face of the man in the picture, her formidable composure cracking at the edges. "When I knew him, he went by the name of Bas." She slowly shook her head. "How is this possible?"

"I assume he's not an insurance salesman?"

"Insurance salesman?" She lifted her head, glancing at him in confusion.

"That's what he's pretending to be."

She shook her head. "He's an assassin."

"Shit," Wolfe muttered, a cold chill inching down his spine. The secretive sect of Sentinels had been disbanded by the time he'd taken his position as Tagos, but there were whispers that their training had not only turned them into ruthless killing machines, but it had also stripped them of all human emotions. Which was why he kept close track of those who had been forced into retirement. Not all of them were . . . stable. "Why don't I know about him?"

"He disappeared over a hundred years ago." With a sharp gesture she tossed the picture back onto the desk, her eyes darkened with an emotion he couldn't read. "I thought he was dead."

Wolfe stilled, his instincts on full alert.

Lana had more than just a passing acquaintance with the assassin.

They shared a history.

One that had involved her emotions.

His hands unconsciously curled into tight fists, something dark and dangerous spreading through his blood at the thought of this woman being intimately connected to another man.

It didn't matter if it'd been a hundred years ago.

Or that he hadn't even known her then.

His inner caveman was convinced this female belonged to him, whether she shared his bed or not.

Any challenge to his claim was going to end in death.

"Unless the necromancer returned him from the grave he appears to be very much alive," he said in grim tones.

Lana made a belated attempt to disguise her intense reaction. "So I see."

Wolfe stepped close enough to breath in the light scent of vanilla that clung to the glossy black satin of her hair. It'd always struck him as incongruous that such a powerful female would choose such a light, feminine scent.

Now, it only served to intensify his possessive instincts.

With an effort, he forced himself to focus on the threat the bastard might pose to Fane and Serra.

Right now that's all that mattered.

"What do you know about him?"

She hesitated, as if debating precisely what she was willing to share.

"He was trained by the monks to be a warrior," she at last confessed. "But his true strength is his magic."

"A born witch?"

She nodded. Many high-bloods had some affinity to magic, including guardian Sentinels like Fane, but they couldn't conjure the same spells as a born witch.

"A powerful one. He also has some telepathy skills, but they're limited."

Wolfe grimaced. Lana's definition of "limited telepathy" was skewed. Her own skills were off the charts.

"Anything else?"

Her lips thinned, the shadows of a painful memory darkening her eyes. "He doesn't play by the rules."

Wolfe hid a feral smile. Good. When people broke the rules it gave him license to use whatever means necessary to do his job.

Including beating the shit out of the bastard.

"Why would he be interested in Serra?"

"I don't have a clue," she said slowly. "I could try to contact him—"

"No."

A dangerous expression settled on her pale, beautiful

features. No one interrupted the Mave. And certainly they didn't tell her no.

"What did you say?"

The air was thick with the choking force of her personality, but Wolfe refused to back down.

"Fane has kept his communication extremely limited and written in code as if he is afraid someone is monitoring his phone. I'm assuming he doesn't want to spook this . . ." It took an effort to force the name past his lips. "Bas. We can't allow anyone to know we suspect anything is wrong."

Her lips thinned, but she gave a grudging nod, accepting that Wolfe might have a point. She might be a hard-ass, but she was always ready to listen to her advisors.

"What can I do?"

Wolfe hesitated. He should let it go. Tell her that they had it under control.

But of course that would imply he could be rational when dealing with this female.

Not. Gonna. Happen.

"How close were you and the assassin?"

She met his searching gaze without flinching. "Does it matter?"

"It might help us figure out what's going on."

"I can't help." Her words were final. Uncompromising. "The man I knew is dead."

Wolfe felt a stab of fury. Was she willing to protect this assassin?

"Can't or won't?" he growled.

Ignoring the question, the Mave turned to step back into the elevator. "Keep me updated."

"Lana."

Her expression had returned to the calm, inscrutable mask that made him want to punch something.

"Yes?"

"Why were you so certain that Bas was dead?"

The doors of the elevator slid shut, but that didn't halt his heightened senses from picking up her soft confession.

"Because I killed him."

Chapter Eleven

Serra felt as if she were being blasted by a furnace.

Who knew that one Sentinel could create such heat?

Granted, he was a very large Sentinel. And he was cradled tightly behind her as they spooned in the center of the massive bed.

But still . . .

Telling herself it was the heat, not absolute terror, that made her try to scoot away, she hissed in frustration when his arm tightened around her waist.

"Where are you going?" he whispered, his breath brushing her bare shoulder.

She shuddered, arcs of pleasure shooting through her body.

Okay. It wasn't the heat that was edging her toward panic.

It was the way she savored the scent of Fane that clung to her skin. And how her heart leapt at even his most casual touch. And how she was already besieged by the need to cuddle against his strength and beg him never to leave her.

Dammit.

It was supposed to be sex.

Red hot, mind-blowing, uncomplicated sex.

Not a messy, emotionally charged joining that would leave her broken.

"I need to shower," she said, her voice ridiculously husky.

He chuckled, nuzzling her neck. "We have time."

She grimaced at his soft words, her thoughts effectively diverted from her fear of an eventual heartache, to a more basic fear.

Survival.

"Do we?"

His arm instinctively hauled her back until her back was pressed tight against his chest.

"All the time in the world," he rasped. "That I promise."

Her lips twisted in a wry smile. Arrogant man.

"You can't promise."

He nipped the lobe of her ear. "I just did."

"So certain of your own powers," she muttered.

"No, I'm certain of you." His hand lifted to brush the hair from her still-flushed cheek, his lips brushing the sensitive skin of her neck. "If Molly is in St. Louis you'll find her."

She pretended her heart didn't swell beneath his un-wavering confidence in her abilities.

Fane's belief in her had been a primary reason she'd pressed so hard to hone her skills. Idiot that she was, she couldn't have endured the thought he would be disap-pointed in her.

"That poor child." She sternly snapped her thoughts back to the only thing that mattered. Finding Molly before the toxin in her bloodstream put her in the grave. "Why the hell doesn't Bas just give the kidnappers what they want?"

"That's the question, isn't it?" Fane smoothed her hair behind her ear, his voice suspiciously bland. "It has to be something that threatens him more than the loss of his daughter."

Serra frowned. "Unless he fears the kidnapper intends to kill Molly the minute they get what they want."

"A reasonable hypothesis," he readily agreed.

She glanced over her shoulder, meeting his unreadable gaze. "Are you patronizing me?"

"You know better than that," he softly chided.

And she did.

He could be an infuriating bastard, but he always treated her as an equal.

"But you are hinting at something?"

He gazed deep into her eyes. "You're a psychic."

Just for a minute she threatened to drown in the dark, penetrating gaze. This close she could see the exquisite details of the tattooing that emphasized the man's stark beauty. He was exotic, lethal, and shatteringly male.

Her heart clenched with a dangerous emotion before she was abruptly turning her head back to stare at the opposite wall.

"Yeah, I've figured that out, thank you."

His fingers lightly stroked the line of her stubborn jaw. "What do you think his motives are?"

"How should I know?" She trembled beneath his soft caress. "I can't read him."

"He has trained to block your powers, but no shield is impenetrable."

Serra paused, considering his words. "You think I can penetrate his defenses?"

His thumb rested on the pulse that raced just below her ear. "I think you've already learned more than you suspect."

She jerked in surprise. Dammit. Did he think she hadn't tried to tap into the mind of the kidnapper?

"Then you think wrong."

"Easy, Serra," he murmured, his big, powerful hand splayed on her lower stomach. "Just relax and allow yourself to remember."

Relax? She stifled a humorless laugh. She was being scorched by his touch, her entire body shimmering with anticipation.

Closing her eyes, she created an empty room in her head and slammed the door on the world around her.

Then, counting backward, she slipped into a light trance. It was the only way to truly concentrate.

"Remember what?" she demanded.

"What did Bas feel when he spoke of Molly?"

Slowly, methodically, she reconstructed the image of Bas in the empty room in her head.

The pale, ivory skin. The short black hair. His bronze eyes.

She even added the witch mark on the side of his neck with the tattoos that tallied his kills.

Every detail helped to re-create the memory.

Next she added herself, stripping away her emotions as she replayed the conversation, word for word.

With no ability to read his mind, Serra instead concentrated on the expressions that touched his painfully beautiful face. Most of them were so fleeting it was no wonder she'd missed them the first time around.

Bas was a master of hiding his emotions.

Of course, she'd just come out of a compulsion spell and had been reeling from shock at the time.

Not exactly at the top of her game.

"Fear," she at last said. "Regret."

"And when he spoke of the kidnapper?"

That one was easier.

"Fury."

"But not fear?"

"No." She hesitated, biting her bottom lip. "I don't think so."

Fane pressed a kiss against the side of her neck, the searing sensation penetrating her self-imposed trance.

Oddly, the feel of Fane's touch wasn't an intrusion. It offered comfort rather than distraction.

As if Fane was capable of sharing his strength with her on a psychic plane.

A thought that should have been terrifying, not soothing.

"Trust your instincts," he urged.

Steadied by his solid presence, Serra allowed herself to trust what her senses were telling her.

"He fears the cost demanded by the kidnapper, but he'll pay it to rescue his daughter," she said with absolute certainty. "That's why he's so anxious for me to find her first. He doesn't want to be responsible for what happens if he gives the kidnapper what he wants."

"So what could frighten a man like Bas?"

Deconstructing the room in her mind, Serra snapped out of her trance and opened her eyes.

"Does it matter?"

"I have a feeling it might matter very much," Fane said, but suddenly his tone was distracted, and his hand was skimming up the flat plane of her stomach to cup her bare breast.

She hissed in pleasure, all thought destroyed as his thumb strummed the tip of her nipple. How could any woman think when his fingers were doing such lovely, wicked things to her body?

"Fane," she muttered.

"Hmm?"

Her heart stuttered, a perilous warmth exploding in the center of her heart as his lips stroked along the line of her shoulder.

Oh . . . shit.

It was madness. Complete and utter madness.

Hadn't she just been fretting and stewing over her intense reaction to Fane's touch? Hadn't she realized that she could never have "just sex" with this man?

"I told you, I need a shower," she breathed.

"It can wait."

"Wait for what?"

"This." He tugged at her extended nipple, chuckling at her low moan of pleasure. "And this."

She shivered as his other hand reached down to grasp her knee, tugging it upward so he could slide his muscular thigh between her legs.

"It's a formal event."

His lips continued to wreak havoc as thcy trailed back up her shoulder and found a highly erotic spot at the base of her nape.

"And?"

And? She struggled to keep track of her protest. Not an easy task when he pressed the impressive length of his arousal against her lower back.

Sensual anticipation flowed through her veins like warm honey, his heat no longer a trap to escape, but an invitation to paradise.

Not that she was ready to concede defeat.

Was she?

"And it takes more effort to get ready," she tried to bluff.

"Serra, you are the most breathtaking woman I have ever seen," he growled, his large thigh moving upward to press against her moist core. "You could throw on a rag and outshine every woman in St. Louis."

She made a strangled sound of shock.

For a man who could rarely string more than two words together, Fane seemed to know exactly what to say.

Impossible, aggravating, bewitching male.

Bewitching. Yeah. That just about summed him up, Serra acknowledged, vividly aware of the slide of his big hand over the curve of her hip that only intensified the heat blazing through her.

She craved this man with an insatiable hunger that she knew beyond a doubt would plague her the rest of her life.

Regardless of how long or short that life might be.

"You're trying to charm me again."

His thigh rubbed against her sensitive clit, his fingers continuing to toy with her maddeningly responsive nipple.

"Not charm," he murmured. "Truth."

Serra released a shaken breath, feeling her resistance melting.

Christ. She was already heading toward another orgasm. Already aching to feel him deep inside her as she convulsed around his thick length.

No. This wasn't sex.

This was . . . dangerous and painful and eventually heartbreaking.

Now, however, didn't seem the time to argue the point.

"We agreed this was just sex," she ridiculously tried to insist.

He parted his lips to bite the spot where her neck connected with her shoulder. It wasn't hard enough to pierce the skin, but the punishing nip sent a shocking jolt of ecstasy through her body.

"There was no agreement," he reminded her in harsh tones. "You said this was just sex, not me."

She struggled to breathe, her body trembling with need. "I don't want you to think—"

"Good," he interrupted, using his tongue to soothe the tender skin of her neck. "Because right now thinking is the last thing I want to do."

She tried to focus on the expensive Picasso prints framed on the far wall.

Trying desperately not to lose herself in the complex combination of sensations that surged through her.

There was lust. Hell, she was a few good strokes away from climax.

But there was also tenderness, and affection, and a dangerous yearning for more.

Was she really willing to put herself in a position to have this man destroy her again?

"I can guess what you want to do," she said in husky tones.

Fane gave a low groan, pressing his lips to the pulse beating at the base of her throat.

"There's no need to guess," he rasped, "I'm quite willing to show you."

"Generous of you."

Slowly he pulled her leg higher on his thigh, allowing the tip of his cock to brush down her ass before he was between her legs and pressing the massive crown into her wet entrance.

"I intend to be generous as often as you'll allow me."

She hissed in need as he allowed just the tip to dip inside her channel.

Dammit. Was he deliberately trying to torment her?

"Can you be generous any faster?"

He spread hungry kisses up the length of her exposed neck. "No."

"That's it?" She tried to wiggle lower. Just the few inches needed to impale herself on all that Sentinel yumminess. "Just no?"

His hand gripped her hip, holding her immobile. "I like it slow."

She scowled, glimpsing the ruthless warrior who needed control.

"And I like it . . ." Her complaint ended on a sharp moan of exquisite pleasure as he slid inside her with one deliberate, ruthless thrust. Yes. God, yes. She struggled to form the words. "Oh, just like that."

His lips nibbled over her nape, one hand stroking over her lower stomach while the other continued to tug at her nipple.

"I told you slow was good."

"Did you?"

"You need to trust me, Serra," he murmured. "I'll never hurt you."

She squeezed her eyes shut. How could he say that? He'd already hurt her time after time.

But the reminder of just how bad an idea this was shattered as he withdrew until he was once again posed at her entrance before surging upward with enough force to make her moan in pleasure.

Her mind fogged with bliss her hand slipping over his side to dig her nails into his hard ass.

"I trust you know what you're doing in bed."

"It's a start."

She intended to remind him about the whole this-is-only-sex thing, but all thought evaporated as he sank deep inside her, joining them until it felt as if they had become one.

It was hokey, and stupidly romantic, but it was dangerously true.

"Fane," she breathed, feeling oddly vulnerable as he buried his face in the curve of her neck and his hands began a slow, delectable exploration of her exposed body. "I need—"

"What do you need?" He moved his hand to caress her

neglected breast while his other hand blazed a sizzling path down the damp skin of her stomach. "This?"

A groan was wrenched from her throat and her head dropped back to his shoulder as his fingers stroked boldly over her eager clit.

"Yes," she rasped in approval.

He pressed heated kisses down the curve of her cheek as he rocked his hips forward and back, creating a delicious friction. She hissed in pleasure, her arms lifting over her head to wrap around his neck.

"Slow and sweet," he said against her shoulder, his lips lightly caressing her flushed skin. "We have to enjoy the solitude while we have it."

Serra didn't intend to argue. Her eyes slid closed as she concentrated on the sensation of his cock penetrating her with slow, steady thrusts. It felt so good. So . . . she groaned, already sensing the looming climax.

"I suppose you have a point," she moaned, her nails scraping his nape.

She savored the scorching heat from his large body pressed behind her, her body bowing with a coiled tension as he caught the tip of her breast between his finger and thumb.

"You will soon discover I'm always right," he assured her with outrageous arrogance.

She tried to make a sound of disgust, only to have it come out as a shaken moan. "Is that so?"

"Absolutely."

As if to prove the truth of his words, Fane picked up his pace, slamming into her until her entire body shuddered with satisfaction.

"God, you feel as if you were made for me," he rasped.

"Or maybe you were made for me," she muttered, shaken by the intensity of their lovemaking.

And it was lovemaking.

Not sex.

Not a casual hookup that would be forgotten the minute she crawled out of bed.

Females would sacrifice everything to hold on to this sort of feeling.

"I don't have any doubt at all," he groaned, pumping into her with a swift, magical pace. "Just you."

"Fane—"

"Shh," he said, halting her protest, kissing a path of destruction up the side of her neck. "Just let me pleasure you."

Serra shoved aside the warning voice in the back of her mind.

What did it matter?

She would deal with the emotional fallout later.

After she'd found Molly.

And the toxin was removed from her body.

And she'd killed that bastard Bas.

"Yes," she breathed, forgetting everything but the explosive pleasure.

Serra took one last glance in the mirror.

Any other night she would have appreciated the Chanel silver lamé gown.

A skimpy sheath with spaghetti straps, it skimmed her lush curves before ending several inches above her knees. The short style combined with her three-inch Jimmy Choo shoes gave the illusion her legs went on forever, while her upswept hair emphasized the slender length of her neck.

It was shimmery and flirty and designed to drive men crazy.

Exactly what an expensive gown was supposed to do.

But this wasn't any night, and she was far more interested in disguising the pallor of her skin with a light coat of powder and emphasizing her lips in a brilliant shade of red.

She grimaced.

Just an hour ago she'd been flushed and disheveled, her eyes smoldering with the pleasure from her most recent orgasms.

She forced her lethargic, delectably sated body into the shower. The knowledge that Bas would soon be arriving had stripped away the lingering haze of passion, brutally reminding her that this wasn't a magical holiday with the man of her dreams.

This was life or death.

And not just for her.

Tucking the ribbon from Molly's stuffed hippo along with the picture of the heart-wrenchingly vulnerable girl into a tiny silver clutch purse, Serra sucked in a calming breath and forced her feet to carry her to the sitting room.

Her lips twitched as Fane slowly turned to her from the windows where he was watching the spectacular sunset, his massive body covered in the elegant black tux that had been delivered just before she stepped into the shower.

Only a Sentinel could be dressed in a thousand-dollar suit and still manage to look completely feral.

His dark gaze searched her face, easily noticing the pallor beneath her carefully applied makeup.

"Ready?"

She grimaced, her mouth dry and her stomach clenched with nerves.

"As ready as I'm going to be."

He stepped forward, grasping her hand in the heat of his. "You won't be alone."

The urge to melt against the solid strength of his chest was so overwhelming Serra actually caught herself swaying forward.

Dammit, this was exactly what she'd been scared of.

This instinctive desire to depend on a man who was only here because she was in danger.

With a muttered curse, she was yanking her hand from his comforting grip.

"Fane."

He scowled, his jaw clenching as she stepped back. "What's wrong?"

"Are you serious?" She forced a stiff smile to her lips. "What isn't wrong?"

"Fine, let me be more specific." His expression was tight, his fingers twitching as if they were longing to grab her shoulders and give her a good shake. "Why are you putting walls between us?"

She tilted her chin. "I wasn't the one who put them there."

"So this is my punishment?"

His dark, accusing gaze flayed over her skin, but she resisted the impulse to turn away. She'd given in to temptation. No, she hadn't *given in*. She'd leaped headfirst into temptation and then wallowed in it. But that didn't mean she had completely given in to insanity.

Not when she still carried the wounds of loving him.

"It's survival."

Heat filled the air as his temper threatened to combust, then with a visible effort, he regained his stoic Sentinel composure.

"You're right."

She studied him in suspicion. "I am?"

"You need to concentrate on finding the child." He held

her wary gaze, his voice soft. "Just know that I'm here for you. Whatever you need."

She frowned. Damn, the aggravating man.

She was all braced for a battle of the wills. One she was determined to win.

Instead he slid past her fragile defenses, touching her where she didn't want to be touched.

Lost for words, she was almost relieved when Fane turned toward the door, his acute hearing picking up the sound of Bas's arrival before he ever knocked.

Moving to open the door, Fane reached into the pocket of his jacket, no doubt palming a handgun.

He had a hundred different methods to kill, many of them with his hands and feet, but Sentinels were trained to use the most effective tool for the job.

Sometimes a bullet to the head was the most effective.

Stepping into the room, Bas ignored both the gun and the massive Sentinel who was poised to kill.

It was a deliberate insult, as was his smooth stride that brought him directly in front of her so he could lift her hand to his lips.

Serra rolled her eyes. The bastard looked indecently handsome, of course. Dressed in a Gucci tux, he hadn't bothered with an illusion to disguise his astonishing bronze eyes, or the dark hair smoothed from his pale, breathtakingly handsome face.

It was a damned shame he was a sociopath.

"My lovely Serra," he purred, his low voice filled with a sensuous promise. "I understand why you hover at her side like a rabid pit bull."

Fane snorted, refusing to rise to the bait. "Serra doesn't need my protection."

"True. A dangerous female." The bronze gaze swept

downward, lingering on the tantalizing hemline of her dress. "In more ways than one."

Serra yanked her fingers free, not in the mood for his games. "The clock is ticking."

"So it is." He waved a slender hand toward the still-open door. "Shall we?"

Serra deliberately moved to stand beside Fane as they left the suite in silence. Then, entering the elevator, Bas used a key card to punch in a secret code. They traveled downward, and it was no surprise when the elevator opened to reveal the underground parking lot that was off limits to the public. What did startle her was the fact that it was suspiciously dark, as if someone had shut off several lights.

Prepared to step off the elevator, Serra was halted as Bas held an arm across the opening, waiting until the uniformed driver climbed out of a black stretch limo and gave a nod.

Obviously that was the all-clear signal, although Serra didn't know what they were all-clear from, as Bas lowered his arm and led them toward the car.

All very James Bond, she wryly acknowledged, her heels clicking on the cement floor.

The driver moved to open the back door, the light from the interior outlining the stark male profile.

Kaede.

Serra rolled her eyes as she slid into the butter-soft seat. That's all she needed. Three male alphas trapped in one small space.

As if to prove her point, she was abruptly squished between two male bodies that smothered her in a searing heat. Sweat trickled down her spine and she struggled to breathe as the overabundance of testosterone seemed to suck the oxygen from the air.

Kaede slid into the driver's seat, adding to the smoldering

tension, as he shifted the car into gear and they headed toward the north.

Serra clutched her tiny purse, resisting the urge to slam her elbows into the ribs of her two companions, telling them to tamp down the heat before they fried her to a crisp.

They were all on edge. She could bitch all she wanted, nothing was going to ease the tension.

Her only hope was directing all that male aggression in a constructive direction. "Where are we going?"

Bas adjusted his starched, diamond-studded cuff, which glittered in the passing streetlights.

"A local socialite is hosting a ball to raise funds for one of her pet charities."

Well, that explained the tuxes.

And her own drop-dead gorgeous dress.

"The socialite was a client?" she asked.

"No, but the owner of the home directly behind her estate was," Bas explained. "We can slip away once the dancing starts to see if you can sense Molly."

Serra nodded, resisting the urge to fan herself. Christ, it had to be a hundred degrees.

Her sideways glare toward Bas was predictably ignored, as was the more direct glare she sent at Fane's rigid profile. Even Kaede managed to elude her silent chastisement as he split his attention between the road and the mannequinlike passengers in the backseat.

Eventually the car slowed and they pulled into a narrow side street. Serra grimaced as she realized they were headed into one of those fancy-assed communities that were stuffed with the rich and overprivileged.

It was even gated to keep out the riff-raff.

Stuck-up prigs.

Of course, there was some satisfaction in watching the guard wave them through the gates with a wide smile.

The idiot had just invited in three lethal killers and a psychic who could crush his mind without batting an eye.

And all it'd taken was a limo and a pretense of sophistication.

"Nice neighborhood," she muttered.

Bas deliberately rubbed his knee against hers, the bronze eyes shimmering in the darkness.

"I would be willing to purchase you a home in the area if you wanted to come and work for me."

"Work for you?" Serra sent him a glare filled with loathing. "You've infected me with a toxin, threatened to kill me if I don't perform a miracle, and you think I would ever willingly work for you?"

"It's not personal, Serra." A flicker of emotion tightened his expression. Something she might have suspected was regret if she hadn't known just what a cold-blooded bastard he was. Whatever. It was swiftly replaced by a mocking smile. "I've done what was necessary to earn your cooperation, but that doesn't mean we couldn't have a profitable alliance in the future."

"Go screw yourself."

He softly chuckled. "Sex is negotiated in a separate contract."

There was a blur of movement as Fane reached over Serra to grasp Bas's knee, his grip hard enough to make the assassin grunt in pain.

"There are few things in life I'm going to enjoy more than watching you die," he said, the flat certainty in Fane's voice disturbingly chilling.

Serra froze, the violence in the air hammering at her psychic senses.

Shit. This could get really bad, really quick.

Then, with an experience that spoke of years dealing

with pissed-off Sentinels, Kaede was pulling the limo to a halt and turning to send his boss a warning glance.

"Show time."

Fane slowly released his punishing grip and settled back in his seat. The threat of bloodshed remained, but it had returned to the slow simmer that allowed Serra to draw in a shaky breath.

Bas muttered something beneath his breath, then, closing his eyes, he focused on weaving his magical disguise.

At his side, Serra watched as the illusion altered his hair to a sandy blond that was slightly thinning, his face becoming even leaner. The magic worked lower, making his body appear shorter, softer.

She shook her head. She would have been fascinated by such a talent if it wasn't being performed by a homicidal jackass.

"Who are you tonight?"

"Sir John Baxter."

She snorted. Even his voice had changed, becoming higher with a distinct English accent.

"Royalty?"

He held up a slender hand, using his powers to create a gold ring stamped with the Baxter family suit of arms.

"A minor barony."

"Arrogant."

"A title opens doors." He shrugged, climbing out of the limo as Kaede pulled open the door. "Especially when I also happen to be generous with my donations."

Serra slid out behind him, barely managing to enjoy being out of the inferno before Fane was at her side, his arm possessively curved around her waist.

She didn't try to pull away. She could feel the coiled

tension of his muscles and the heat that still rolled off his body like a furnace.

He was hanging on by a thread.

Instead she turned her attention to the imposing red brick structure with large windows framed by white shutters and a large columned portico. It was large enough to house a football team, with all the warmth of a locker room.

She far preferred her parents' cabin hidden in the woods less than two hours away. It was a quarter of the size, and probably cost less to build than the four-car garage, but it was filled with the light and warmth of a home well loved.

The thought had barely formed when the double doors opened and a slender, middle-aged woman with perfectly coiffed auburn hair stepped onto the flagstone porch, clearly eager to welcome her newest guest.

"Sir Baxter, welcome," she called, holding out her hand for Bas to kiss.

Serra arched a brow. Was the woman for real?

She looked and acted like a damned Stepford Wife.

With an elegance that should have warned anyone with a brain that he wasn't entirely human, Bas moved to obediently place his lips against her fingers, before straightening and glancing toward Serra.

"I hope you do not mind if I brought friends with me?"

She batted her lashes that were as false as her too-rounded tits.

"Certainly not. Any friend of yours is a friend of mine." Latching on to Bas as if she feared he might escape before she could display him like a rare artifact to her friends, the woman herded him over the threshold. "I have someone you absolutely must meet."

Forgotten, Serra exchanged a resigned glance with Fane.

Christ. She just wanted to be done with this horrible nightmare and back at Valhalla where she belonged.

Safe with her friends and family.

And Fane . . .

Shit.

She sharply slammed the door on her treacherous thoughts.

She could be impetuous. Even reckless.

She wasn't about to repeat her self-destructive pattern over and over, hoping for a different result.

That was insane.

Chapter Twelve

Fane stood next to Serra as the string quartet hidden in a far corner struck up a waltz.

Instantly the guests crowded into the formal sitting room that had been converted into a dance floor.

Standing at an angle to block Serra from bay windows that offered a perfect opportunity for a sniper, Fane allowed his gaze to scan the room.

He ignored the pampered humans who twirled beneath the chandelier, their fine plumage and sparkling jewels designed to attract attention. The strutting peacocks were all norms, many already impaired by alcohol or drugs. They posed no immediate danger.

Instead he concentrated on the shallow alcoves that held imitation Greek statues and a distant door that led to a back hallway.

He didn't actually think anyone was about to attack. Certainly not in such a highly visible area.

But he was nothing if not thorough when it came to his guardian duties.

Especially when he was guarding the female who was the reason his heart beat.

His senses tingled with the warning of an approaching

high-blood and he turned to watch Bas stroll toward them with a narrowed glare.

The jackass stood just close enough to Serra to make Fane's teeth clench, adjusting his cuff as he spoke in low tones that wouldn't carry.

"Wait ten minutes, then meet me on the back terrace."

His command delivered, Bas moved to join a buxom blonde who he soon had clinging to his arm as he coaxed her into leaving the room.

"Someday," he muttered.

Serra clicked her tongue, pale green eyes flashing fury. "You're presuming I won't kill him first."

Fane felt his heart slam into his ribs at the sight of her.

God, but she was magnificent.

Even surrounded by females who spent a fortune to look beautiful she stood out from the crowd.

The pale perfect features. The satin gloss of her dark hair.

The lush body with its sultry sensuality that was a challenge to every man who caught sight of her.

The unapologetic confidence in her own worth.

It all combined to make her a formidable female.

And that was before you added in her lethal psychic abilities.

"He was right about one thing," he said, his voice edged with pride.

This amazing creature was his. All his.

Whether she was ready to accept the truth or not.

"What's that?"

He stepped close enough that his breath would brush over the bare skin of her exposed neck. "You are dangerous."

She trembled, a pulse leaping at the base of her throat. "Are you flirting with me?"

The hint of disbelief in her voice hit him like a body blow.

Shit.

His self-righteous attempts at nobility had done even more damage than he'd ever allow himself to acknowledge.

To both of them.

"Better late than never," he said gruffly.

Her eyes darkened, before she was hastily turning to scan the crowd. "Where'd that waiter go with the champagne?"

Sensing her walls coming up, Fane slid an arm around her waist and hauled her against his chest.

He had ten minutes.

He wasn't going to waste them.

"Do you want to dance?"

She blinked in shock, but she didn't try to pull away.

Or punch him in the face.

He'd take that as a win.

"You dance?"

"Is that surprising?"

"I suppose it shouldn't be," she said, smiling as she delivered her insult. "After all, bears can dance."

"I think I can do better than a bear."

With a tug, he had her in his arms and was swirling around the dance floor with a confidence that managed to catch her off guard.

Her eyes widened, her steps easily following his fluid movements and Fane hid a smile. He wasn't about to confess that all Sentinels were forced to take dance lessons to help with their balance and flexibility. Let her wonder how many other secrets he was hiding.

Twirling her in a complicated pattern, Fane watched the flush of pleasure touch her cheek. Not that she was about to admit she might enjoy being in his arms, he wryly conceded. She was determined to pretend that they could be lovers while she kept her emotions locked safely away.

Silly female.

She belonged to him.

Including her messy, unpredictable, glorious emotions.

Soon the crowd on the dance floor began to thin as the humans stopped to gape at their elegant movements, the women's faces tight with envy while the men were all but panting with lust.

"Fane," she whispered into his ear. "People are staring."

He pressed a fleeting kiss to her temple. "Of course they're staring. You're stunning."

"Oh . . ." She hissed in exasperation, pulling back to meet his steady gaze. "Dammit. You're the most aggravating male to ever walk the face of the earth."

He allowed a rare smile to curve his lips, his hand splayed on her lower back urging her closer.

"I always try to be the best at everything."

"You succeeded," she muttered, even as she allowed herself to melt against him.

He pressed his cheek to the top of her head, savoring the rich scent of chamomile and warm, wicked woman.

God. She fit perfectly against him. Her head snuggled into the hollow of his shoulder, her arm wrapped around his waist, and her fingers warm in his hands.

He craved her with the force of an addiction. To hold her, to please her. To know she was safe and that he could whisk her back to Valhalla and spend the rest of his very long life adoring her.

Instead he led her off the dance floor as the music came to a flourishing end, holding her tight against his side as he halted in the shadows at the back of the room.

Lowering his head, he whispered directly into her ear. "Ready to disappear?"

"Yes."

"Stay close."

She nodded, understanding he intended to use his powers to allow them to slip away unnoticed.

A Sentinel couldn't make himself invisible, but he could *encourage* people to look the other way.

Waiting until the music started up and the crowd was rushing to fill the dance floor, Fane urged Serra out the side door and into the narrow hallway that led toward the back of the house. He halted once, searching the shadows for unseen enemies before continuing in the direction of Bas's scent.

They entered a long, informal living room that was shrouded in shadows, discovering the assassin waiting for them next to the French windows that overlooked a sunken rose garden.

Fane released Serra, wanting his hands free as Bas turned to glare at them. "Took you long enough."

Serra shrugged. "Where's the blonde?"

Bas allowed his gaze to sweep down her slender body. "Jealous?"

Serra made a sound of disgust. "Making sure her body isn't stuffed behind the curtains."

The assassin chuckled. "She's eagerly waiting for me in the library."

Serra shuddered. "Bleck."

Bas's amusement was abruptly wiped away as he turned to point through the French doors.

"The estate I want you to search is just beyond the hedge."

Fane stepped forward, judging the distance. "Who lives there?"

Bas made a sound of impatience. "Does it matter?"

Fane shot him a warning glare. "It does if you expect me to allow Serra anywhere close to the place."

The assassin shrugged. "A harmless businessman who asked me to search for his missing wife."

"That sounds like a job for the police or a private detective," Serra said, pointing out the obvious.

"Not when she took off with $6 million in cash and the secret recipe for his barbecue sauce," Bas said.

Serra frowned. "Barbecue sauce?"

The assassin nodded. "It's sold around the world and has made him a billionaire several times over."

"Did you find her?"

"Of course."

"Is she alive?"

"She was when I sent her location to my client. After that . . ." Bas gave a dismissive wave of his hand. "Not my business."

Serra grimaced. "Nice."

Bas leaned to push open the nearest French door, pointing toward the center of the garden. "If you follow the path past the ugly-ass excuse for a fountain you'll see a narrow opening in the hedges that connects to the adjoining estate," he said. "You'll have to use your powers to disarm the security system."

Fane moved past Serra to step onto the wide terrace. "Are there guards?"

"One outside. One inside."

Serra joined Fane, turning her head to study Bas who remained in the house. "You aren't going with us?"

"No." Bas shook his head. "I'll keep our hostess distracted so your absence won't be noticed."

Serra rolled her eyes. "Convenient."

"Not really," Bas countered. "She can't seem to keep her hands out of my pants."

Serra marched down the shallow steps. "Let's go."

Fane was swiftly at her side, reaching into the pocket of his tux to pull out a small handgun.

His gaze searched the rigidly organized flower beds and mandatory marble fountain that sprayed water into the moonlight. There was nowhere for an attacker to hide. So why did the back of his neck prickle and his finger tighten on the trigger of his gun?

They circled the fountain and moved toward the small gardener's shed at the very back of the property. Darkness wrapped around them, the sounds from the party muted to a distant murmur. Fane should have felt relieved. They were out of sight of the guests and far enough from the main street not to be spotted by stray passersby.

But he wasn't relieved.

Instead his instincts were on full alert.

Finding the narrow opening in the hedge, Fane shoved his large body through the prickly branches, indifferent to the damage to his expensive tux. As far as he was concerned any male attire that required a tie and cufflinks should be banned for all eternity.

Then turning, he held the branches apart for Serra to join him.

Once through, she paused to yank off her impossibly high heels and tossed them aside. He stood at her side, inspecting the massive Tudor-style mansion that blazed with lights. There was a large back patio and the predictable pool with an attached pool house. Closer to them was a ring of large oaks that blocked the view of the house from its neighbors.

Fane grimaced as he realized there were way too many places an enemy could be lurking.

"I don't like this," he muttered.

Serra pressed close to his side, her profile tense. "I don't either."

"Do you sense something?"

She shook her head in frustration. "It's all too muddled to pinpoint specific thoughts, but there's a—" Her words broke with a shudder.

"Malevolence?" he finished for her, feeling the same creepy vibe.

"Yes."

His teeth clenched, his instincts were screaming to toss Serra over his shoulder and get the hell out of there.

"How close do you need to get?" he managed to choke out.

She hesitated, her eyes closing as she tried to search for a specific mind among the masses.

"The pool house should be close enough," she at last announced.

Grasping her hand, Fane slowly led her forward. When she was concentrating on her search for Molly she was completely vulnerable.

"Hold on tight," he commanded, releasing a short burst of power that would disable any surveillance equipment.

Holding the gun in one hand, he passed through the trees and angled toward the pool house. He resisted the urge to hurry, knowing that Serra needed time to search through the thoughts that were bombarding her.

But, as they reached the edge of the cement that surrounded the pool, she came to a sharp halt.

"Stop."

Fane was instantly on alert. "Is it Molly?"

Serra opened her eyes, her face pale with strain. "No, she's not here."

"Then what is it?"

"We're being . . ." She struggled for the proper word.

"Serra?"

"Hunted," she at last breathed.

Fane's reaction was instantaneous. "Shit." With one movement he had Serra scooped off her feet and pressed against his chest. Then, calculating the nearest escape route, he headed toward the high hedge at top speed. "Hold on."

He managed to make it past the pool when he heard the barely audible *click* and then felt the blow to the back of his upper shoulder.

A man less experienced might have assumed that someone had slugged him with a baseball bat. But he'd been shot enough times to know he'd been hit by a large-caliber bullet.

Gritting his teeth against the pain, he continued running forward, ignoring the warm wetness that was already spreading down his back.

They needed to get past the hedge before he tried to stem the bleeding.

There was another faint sound, but it didn't sound like a trigger. Still, Fane tensed, preparing for another blow. Instead it was Serra who cried out in pain.

Fuck.

"Serra," he rasped. "Are you hurt?"

"I've been mind-stunned," she said between clenched teeth.

Fane hissed in disbelief. A mind-stunner was a weapon developed by the human scientists when they discovered the true power of psychics. Idiotically they'd feared the high-bloods could take command of the leaders of government and force them to obey like mindless robots.

Once it was obvious that such a covert overthrow of the political system wasn't possible, the weapons had been confiscated by the Army and supposedly locked away for safekeeping.

So who the hell was toting one around?

Continuing forward, Fane was abruptly halted as a man leaped off the roof of the pool house and landed directly in front of them, a gun pointed at the female in his arms.

With a speed that was too swift for the human to follow, Fane was turning to block Serra with his large body.

Intending to sprint in the opposite direction, he was stymied by the sight of another male approaching

"Fane," Serra cried out, easily realizing they were caught between a rock and a hard place.

Thank God she didn't realize he'd been wounded and was losing blood at an alarming rate.

"I've got them," he soothed, setting her down before he surged into action with a blinding speed.

Serra instinctively fell to her knees and curled into a small ball.

Her brain was still scrambled from the mind-stunner, the pain so intense she could barely breathe. Even worse, her powers were temporarily offline.

Dammit.

Which meant that she was nothing more than a liability to Fane.

The best thing she could do was stay out of the line of fire so the Sentinel didn't have to worry about her.

Cautiously lifting her head, she felt her breath tangle in her throat as she watched Fane in glorious action.

Despite having seen him in training, she still marveled at his sheer beauty as he leaped forward to wrench the gun from the nearest attacker's hand, using the butt to smash in the man's forehead with a sickening thud.

He was raw power, liquid speed, and ruthless, deadly skill.

The perfect weapon.

By then the second attacker was closing in, his gun pointed at Serra.

Once again Fane was placing himself in front of her, protecting her with his solid body. Her heart clenched as she caught the unmistakable scent of blood. He'd taken a bullet and was bleeding out.

The realization had barely crossed her mind when the second attacker fired off his shot, the bullet whizzing past her ear.

"Stay down," Fane commanded as he charged forward, ramming into the man with the force of a cement truck.

Both men hit the ground and Serra desperately tried to battle through the haze in her mind, seeking her powers.

She hated feeling helpless.

Especially when Fane was in danger.

Fane gave a soft grunt as the man slid from his grasp and managed to give him a vicious kick to the head as he jumped upright. Serra shoved a hand over her mouth to avoid drawing attention to herself. Even the smallest distraction could leave Fane open to attack.

With a blinding speed, Fane was upright, his arm raised to block the second kick aimed at his head. At the same time he landed a solid punch to the man's midsection.

The man bent over, but as Fane threw a punch toward his head, the man jerked to the side, his movements a smooth flow that made him look like he was dancing. Fane stepped back, giving himself the space to adjust to the enemy's fluid style.

The man slid a hand behind his back, yanking free a dagger he sliced toward Fane's neck. Serra swallowed a scream. Unnecessary, of course.

Fane dodged the blow, managing to wrap his fingers around the attacker's wrist. With a fierce tug he had his enemy close enough that he could grab him by the throat, lifting him three inches off the ground.

With a low growl, the man kicked out, striking Fane in the knee. It was a blow that would have busted the leg of a normal man. But Fane barely flinched as he dug his fingers into the man's throat, crushing his windpipe.

There was one more weak kick before the man went limp in Fane's grip, as dead as his companion.

Fane tossed him aside with a gesture of contempt, and Serra rose shakily to her feet, too relieved that Fane was alive to take much notice of their attackers.

Not when she already had a good idea who was responsible.

Glad she'd ditched her cumbersome high heels, Serra hurried toward the first attacker. She had to make sure he was dead. They'd managed to avoid what looked to be certain death. This wasn't any time to get sloppy.

Convinced the creep wasn't going to wake up and shoot them in the back, Serra returned her attention to Fane, her heart squeezing with fear as she watched him lean heavily against the pool house.

Shit.

Despite the darkness, she could see his face had gone pale beneath his tattoos and his broad shoulders were slumped in weariness.

The rapid loss of blood was taking its toll on the warrior.

Leaving them both dangerously vulnerable.

They had to get out of there.

Now.

Moving to his side, she slipped beneath his arm, arranging it across her shoulder. Fane muttered a protest, but, too weak to actually stand on his own, he had no choice but to allow her to help him across the wide yard and through a gate that led to a narrow pathway.

She hesitated, trying to decide the fastest means of getting Fane away from the estate without alerting Bas. The bastard could easily track them down, but she wasn't letting him near Fane until he'd managed to regain at least part of his strength.

A fine thought that barely had time to form before it was crushed by the sight of Kaede who appeared from the darkness.

The henchman frowned as he took in Fane's obvious pain and her own disheveled appearance.

"What the—"

With a speed that caught both men off guard, Serra had pulled Fane's handgun from his pocket and had it aimed directly into Kaede's face.

"Call your boss and tell him to get his ass out here."

Kaede narrowed his eyes, but with a surprising lack of protest, he had removed his cell phone and sent a quick text. Then, pretending he couldn't easily snatch the gun from Serra's hand, he nodded his head toward Fane.

"We need to get him to the car."

She wanted to tell him to go to hell. Or just shoot him in the knee.

But Fane was obviously only seconds away from collapse and there was no way in hell she was going to be able to keep him propped up.

"Fine."

Kaede held his hands up, revealing he wasn't armed. As if Serra didn't know he had at least half a dozen weapons hidden beneath his uniform, not to mention the fact he could easily snap her neck.

"Can I help?"

She glanced toward Fane, a shaft of fear piercing her

heart. God. She'd never seen him so pale. Or his face clenched with such pain.

"Fane?" she asked softly.

He gave a nod, his breathing ragged. "Yes."

Keeping the gun pointed at the man, Serra allowed him to take Fane's other arm and wrap it over his shoulder. She bore the majority of Fane's weight as they moved along the edge of the pathway to the limo that was parked at an angle to prevent them from being blocked by the other cars.

Kaede managed to pull open the back door and get Fane settled in the backseat. Serra moved to join them only to abruptly jerk to the side, the gun aimed toward the sound of approaching footsteps.

She kept it pointed as she recognized Bas swiftly approaching, his illusion of an English aristocrat fading as he reached her side.

"What happened?" he demanded.

"An ambush, you son of a bitch," she rasped.

He frowned, his outrage annoyingly sincere.

"Don't be foolish," he chided. "Why would I go to such an elaborate ruse? If I wanted you dead I'd kill you."

"And risk being hauled before the Mave for murder?"

"It wouldn't be the first time," he muttered, turning to glance in the car where Fane was sitting with his eyes closed and sweat dripping down his face.

She blinked in shock at the blunt confession. "What?"

Ignoring her question, he gestured for her to get into the car. Serra didn't hesitate. Although she knew that Fane had an astonishing ability to heal even the most grievous of wounds, it would take time. And, more importantly, plenty of rest.

Something he wouldn't be able to get until they were back at the hotel.

Sliding in beside him, she grasped his hand, relieved when he squeezed her fingers in a gesture of comfort.

Joining them, Bas closed the door of the limo then waited for Kaede to take his place behind the steering wheel and pull onto the street before leaning forward.

"Kaede, call for a healer to meet us at the office."

Fane's breath hissed between his clenched teeth. "No. Take me to the hotel."

Bas made a sound of impatience. "You want to be seen in public like this?"

Fane lifted his lashes just enough to glare at the assassin. "The hotel. And no healer."

"Stubborn bastard," Bas breathed the obvious. "Kaede, take us to the hotel." Without waiting for the driver's nod, the assassin turned in his seat to study Serra with a piercing gaze. "Tell me what happened."

She hesitated, still angered by the thought the bastard might have been involved in the attack. Then, she grimaced, lowering the weapon she'd unconsciously been pointing at Bas.

He was right.

If he wanted them dead, he could have taken care of business as soon as she arrived in St. Louis.

Hell, he could have killed her with the mysterious package she'd found outside her door and had so stupidly opened without taking precautions.

For now, she had no choice but to assume he hadn't sent them into a deathtrap.

"We were approaching the house when two men appeared from the shadows and attacked without warning."

Bas didn't bother to hide his surprise. "Only two?"

She flattened her lips in annoyance. How dare the jackass mock her? She felt guilty enough that she'd been reduced to a helpless bystander as Fane had fought off the strangers. She'd never been this long without her powers and it made her feel . . . dangerously vulnerable.

Not to mention she was battling a throbbing headache.

"They used a mind-stunner on me."

He swiftly disguised his shock at her revelation. "Interesting."

She leaned against Fane's broad chest, covertly testing his temperature. When she'd led him out of the estate, she'd been terrified by the chill of his usually hot skin. Now she was comforted by the knowledge that it was growing warmer. That had to mean he was getting better, not worse despite his ragged breathing and the sweat still dripping off his face.

She sent the assassin a sour frown. "Someone tries to kill me and you find it interesting?"

"I find it interesting that whoever tried to kill you already knew they would be dealing with a psychic."

She held Bas's gaze. "Yeah, me too."

He waved off her implication that he could have been involved. "It means that it couldn't have been my client."

"Why not?" she demanded, not nearly so convinced. "It was his property."

"He couldn't possibly have known you would be there tonight."

"Not unless you tipped him off," she pointed out. "Or someone in your merry band of misfits did."

Bas's jaw tightened as the limo swept out of the gated neighborhood and picked up speed.

Expecting an angry response to her continued implication he was somehow responsible, she felt a prickle of premonition as he gave a slow shake of his head, his expression unreadable. She didn't have a clairvoyant's ability to peek into the future, but she knew that she wasn't going to like Bas's explanation.

"No. Not one of mine," he said.

"Then who?"

"The kidnapper."

Her breath hissed through her teeth. Yep. She'd been right. She didn't like the explanation at all.

She had a lethal toxin flowing through her blood, just waiting to kill her. Like a ticking time bomb.

Now she had to worry about being stalked by a stranger who was ruthless enough to kidnap a little girl for profit?

"Why would he try to kill me?"

Bas shrugged. "I told him that I had to delay his payoff until you left St. Louis."

Of course he did. The . . . creep.

"Thanks a lot."

"It was the only way to buy time for Molly." He shrugged, blatantly lacking any hint of regret in throwing Serra into the firing line. "Obviously the kidnapper has decided to take matters into his own hands."

Fane's hand clenched her fingers, his temperature ratcheting up several more degrees in reaction to Bas's confession.

She returned the squeeze, a silent reminder to concentrate on healing his body. This was one battle she didn't need him to fight for her.

Leaning over Fane's massive chest, she sent Bas a pissed-off glare. "Just what I need. Another psychopathic lunatic trying to kill me."

Another shrug. "Unfortunate, but his ill-fated attack might be a blessing."

Her lips curved into a humorless smile. "Unless you want me to kick you in the nuts you'll stop talking."

He ignored her warning, reaching into his pocket to remove his phone. "I assume that the two attackers are dead?"

She scowled. "Yes."

"Good." He punched in a speed-dial number on his phone, waiting only seconds before he started barking orders. "I have a double stiff pickup. I'll send the coordinates. Make sure the necro is with you. Also, have a ghost keep a watch on the estate. I want to know everyone who comes in or out."

Serra watched as Bas returned the phone to his pocket, squashing a brief hope that necros would arrive in time to read the last memories of the corpses. It would bring an end to the entire situation if they could dig out the name of the kidnapper.

But a man capable of stealing Bas's child from beneath his nose wasn't stupid.

He'd make damn sure that he didn't jeopardize his ultimate goal.

"The kidnapper would have to be an idiot to hire killers who could be traced back to him," she pointed out.

Bas tapped an impatient finger on his knee. "We might get lucky."

"Yeah, because our luck has been running so great," she muttered.

He glanced out the window as the limo turned onto the street leading to the hotel. "Did you have the opportunity to search for Molly?"

Serra grimaced. She didn't need to see his tight expression to know the cost of trying to keep his voice calm.

The man might be all kinds of a villain, but he adored his daughter. And the fact that she was out there in the hands of some twisted stranger was slowly destroying him.

"She wasn't there," she softly admitted.

His tense shoulders abruptly slumped. "Shit."

Serra rested her head on Fane's chest, taking comfort in the steady beat of his heart. "For once we can agree."

Chapter Thirteen

Fane wasn't blind to his faults.

He could be stubborn. Or pigheaded, as Serra preferred to refer to his ingrained knowledge that he was always right. And he didn't take orders from anyone but Wolfe, and only then if he agreed with them.

But his determination to return to the hotel had nothing to do with stubbornness. Well, at least not everything to do with his stubbornness.

As long as he was wounded and Serra was without her powers they were utterly vulnerable.

There was no way he was going to return to the office penthouse where they could easily be imprisoned by Bas and his cohorts.

The hotel might belong to the assassin, but it was public enough that it would be difficult to keep out a horde of furious Sentinels if he sent out the signal for the cavalry to charge.

So ignoring the searing pain in his shoulder and the lingering weakness from his blood loss, he forced himself out of the limo as it came to a halt in the underground parking lot.

His one concession was allowing Serra to pull his arm

over her shoulders as she wrapped her own arm around his waist. He didn't need her to hold him upright, but she helped to stabilize his balance.

Besides, having her pressed tight against his side provided something more than strength.

It gave him the courage to put one foot in front of the other to enter the elevator, and then to ignore Bas's mocking gaze as the doors closed and they were rushing to the top floor.

The bastard was well aware that Fane was in agony. He'd been trained by monks, which meant he knew the well-guarded secret among Sentinels that healing was far more painful than the original injury.

Not only more painful, but it took a hell of a lot longer to heal.

The bullet had ripped through his shoulder in a nanosecond, but it would take hours for the muscles and tendons and skin to repair the damage. And several thousand calories to replenish the lost blood.

With a low *hiss* the elevator doors slid open and he clenched his teeth as he waited for Kaede and Bas to step into the hallway before he moved forward. At his side, Serra sent him a worried glance, her face pale.

He wasn't the only one who was in pain.

The mind-stunner didn't just disrupt mental powers. It did physical damage to her brain. She had to be suffering behind her stoic mask.

Not that she was worried about herself, he ruefully acknowledged as she sent him a smile that didn't reach her shadowed eyes.

"Hang on," she urged him softly. "Not much farther."

His fingers lightly brushed her shoulder, offering comfort. "I've got it."

Bas pulled out a key card to unlock the door, bringing a low growl from Fane. The first time Bas opened the door without being invited in while he was inside, the bastard was going to discover a boot shoved up his ass.

The assassin sent him a taunting glance, no doubt reading his mind. Then, shoving open the door, he pointed into the hotel suite.

"The healer is waiting for us."

Oh hell, no. Fane halted, literally digging in his heels. "I told you . . . no healer."

Serra frowned at his vehement refusal. "Fane."

Bas folded his arms over his chest, his gaze more curious than offended. "Do your glyphs interfere with their magic?"

Fane narrowed his gaze. "I don't trust anyone working for you."

Serra reached up to place her fingers against his cheek, her expression pleading. "Please, Fane."

He grabbed her fingers, pressing them to his lips. "I'll be fine."

"You were shot."

He lowered his head, whispering directly into her ear. "Trust me."

She gave a slow, reluctant nod of her head. "Okay."

Bas shrugged. "Vicky, it appears your talents are not required." They waited for the slender woman with red hair pulled into a braid to step out of the room. Her smile was deceptively kind and she was wearing a casual sundress that gave her the appearance of a bohemian. Bas halted the woman's departure with a hand on her shoulder, his gaze shifting to Serra. "Unless you would like her to get rid of your headache, my dear?"

"No," Fane snarled.

He had no desire for Serra to be in pain, but there were healers who could use their powers to do more harm than good, even creating diseases in the unwary. Long ago, disreputable healers would heal their client while subtly infecting them with a sickness that would force them back for further care.

The healer offered a nod, continuing toward the elevator.

Fane waited until he was certain she was gone before he allowed Serra to urge him into the suite. Then, moving toward the low couch near the window, he gratefully sank onto the cushions and pointed a finger toward Kaede as he followed Bas into the room.

"He stays outside."

The enforcer scowled. "No fucking way—"

"Kaede," Bas interrupted, giving a wave of his hand.

The man hesitated, clearly wanting to argue before he muttered a foul curse and turned to leave, closing the door with lethal softness behind him.

Serra settled at Fane's side, their hands instinctively linking as they watched their unwelcome guest move to the center of the floor. But even as Bas opened his mouth to annoy him with questions, the assassin's phone gave a shrill *chirp* and he was pulling it from his pocket with a sigh of impatience.

"What?" The bronze eyes flared with fury. "Goddammit. Have you tried a tracker? Keep searching."

"Your stiffs are missing?" Fane drawled, easily overhearing the frantic voice on the other end of the line.

Bas glowered, shoving the phone back into his pocket.

"Describe your attackers," he snapped.

"For God's sake, he's injured," Serra said, instantly leaping to his defense.

He hid a weary smile. If he asked Serra if she cared about him, she'd cut out her tongue before she'd admit the truth. But she instinctively did everything in her power to protect him.

"It's okay, Serra." He deliberately kept his gaze locked

on the assassin's too-handsome face. "We need to know who the bastards were working for."

"Agreed." Bas gave a nod of his head. "What did you notice about them?"

Fane paused, using the technique taught to him by the monks to strip away the emotions attached to his battle with the unknown enemies.

Anger, fear, excitement could all color the memories and distort vital details.

Only when he was certain that he could control the fury of how close Serra had come to being injured, or worse, did he allow the images of his attackers to form.

"They were well trained, but not high-bloods." He abruptly frowned. "Odd."

"Why odd?" Bas shrugged. "If there were other high-bloods in town I would know."

"They had a weapon that's illegal for a civilian to own," he said, referring to the mind-stunner that had disabled Serra.

The assassin lifted a brow, belatedly realizing how difficult it would be for a mere norm to get their hands on a banned weapon.

"True."

"How much does a stunner go for?" Fane demanded.

Bas folded his arms over his chest, silently calculating. "On the black market they wouldn't go for less than $2 million."

Fane nodded. That's the price he would have put on it. "That amount of funds should be easy to track."

Serra cleared her throat. "It could have been stolen, you know."

Bas and Fane shared a grimace, acknowledging she had a point.

"What else did you notice about the attackers?" Bas pressed.

Fane considered their clothing, dismissing it as too generic to give them a clue as to their identities. The same with the handguns. They could have been bought on any street corner.

Then he remembered the fluid, dance-like movements and the precise blows the attacker had struck.

Just like a chess player, a skilled fighter had a series of calculated moves that they used in battle. Moves they learned from their master or sensei.

"They were trained in Thailand."

Bas studied his stoic expression. "How do you know?"

"From their style of fighting."

The assassin made a sound of disbelief. "You can't be sure they're from Thailand just because of their fighting style."

"You're an idiot if you don't listen to him," Serra snapped, glaring at Bas.

Fane slid his fierce defender a startled glance, but Bas merely smiled with wry resignation.

"You're right."

Forcing his attention back to Bas, Fane struggled to concentrate on the conversation. As much as he wanted to toss the assassin out of the hotel suite so he could reassure himself that Serra was alive and well in the most basic way possible, he understood it was far more important that they track down the bastards who had tried to kill her.

"Did any of your clients have connections to the Far East?" he asked, the most obvious question.

"I'll need to do some research," Bas said.

"Do it quickly."

Bas sent him a narrow-eyed glare, but he turned toward the door, clearly intent on sorting through his clients.

He'd reached the door when Serra abruptly stopped him. "Wait."

He turned back, the bronze eyes shimmering with impatience. "Yes?"

"How could the corpses have disappeared so quickly?"

Fane stiffened, turning to study Serra's profile. Damn, but she never failed to amaze him.

Not just her intelligence. But her rare ability to see right to the heart of the matter.

"They must have had companions close enough to retrieve them," Bas muttered.

Fane shook his head, anger slicing through him.

Goddammit. How had he been so blind?

He should have suspected the truth from the minute the attackers appeared.

"Or they were spelled," he ground out.

"Yes," Serra breathed. "That would explain the sense of evil."

Fane nodded. A wise person who wanted to hire a professional killer would pay the astronomical fee to have that killer wrapped in a magic spell that would be triggered if they were to die performing their mission.

The spell would rapidly destroy the bodies, leaving behind no evidence.

If they'd lingered only a few more minutes they would no doubt have seen the spell in action.

Of course, he should have suspected the truth from the minute they caught a whiff of the foul stench. Black magic always carried an unpleasant odor. The darker the magic, the worse the smell.

"Shit," Bas snarled. "That would mean the kidnapper has access to a witch."

"Have you considered the possibility the kidnapper

might be a witch?" Fane asked. "Or some other kind of high-blood?"

Fane's logic made the assassin growl in growing frustration, the air heating with the force of his suppressed emotions.

"Then it might not be a former client at all."

They all sucked in a deep breath, mutually terrified that they'd been on a wild goose chase.

Every tick of the clock brought them closer to death.

Not only for Molly. But Serra as well.

Both unacceptable losses.

In the back of Fane's mind he began to solidify his various backup plans if things went to hell.

"What about a former colleague?" he asked.

Bas scowled. "I told you, I had my people questioned."

Fane gave a lift of his shoulder, relieved to discover he could move it without difficulty. That meant there hadn't been any damage to his bone.

"There must be a few who no longer work for you."

"A very few."

Fane held his gaze. "Maybe you should give them a call."

Bas stiffened, anger flashing through his eyes. He was a man who gave orders. He didn't take them. Not even when they clearly were in his best interest.

Stubborn bastard.

Before he could open his mouth, however, the door to the suite was shoved open and Kaede stuck his head into the room.

"We have trouble."

"Christ." Bas moved to join his enforcer, his body rigid with the need to strike out. "What now?"

Kaede stepped into the room to speak directly in Bas's ear, his voice pitched low, thankfully unaware that Fane's hearing was enhanced enough to catch the merest whisper.

"I have to go," Bas growled, moving to follow Kaede as he headed into the hallway.

Serra abruptly surged to her feet, her hands clenched. "What about me?"

Bas sent her a dismissive frown. "I'll be in touch."

Absently dodging the vase that Serra threw at his retreating back, the assassin slipped out of the room and firmly closed the door.

Serra watched the vase splinter against the wall with a sense of satisfaction.

She'd only wished it'd smashed against Bas's bloated, arrogant head.

He'd be in touch?

That was it?

She was hours from death and he'd be in touch?

The jackass.

"Woodward," Fane murmured, still seated on the sofa with his legs outstretched and his head leaning against the cushions.

Her breath was squeezed from her lungs as she noticed his lingering pallor and the shadows beneath his dark eyes.

God, she'd come so close to losing him.

Too close.

The knowledge was like an open wound in the center of her heart.

Momentarily forgetting her fury toward Bas, Serra turned to give Fane her full attention.

"What?"

"That's what Kaede whispered to Bas."

She didn't bother to ask how he could possibly have overheard Kaede. The man had the hearing of a freaking bat.

"Woodward?" She wrinkled her nose. "A person?"

"Impossible to say."

Struck by a sudden thought, she leaned down to grab her tiny purse. It had been sheer instinct that had kept her clutching the thing through the crazy-ass night, but now she was glad she had.

Opening the purse she removed her cell phone and pulled up the Internet, swiftly typing in the name.

"Maybe not impossible," she murmured, scrolling through the links.

A ski resort . . . a reporter . . . a handful of small businesses . . .

"Anything?"

She frowned, returning to the top story. "A citywide blackout hits Woodward, Oklahoma."

"Is there a reason given why?"

She clicked on the link, swiftly scanning the story.

"Not yet. It's being investigated, but at last report the blackout is spreading."

"It's a possibility." Fane pulled his own phone from his pocket, punching in a short message that was no doubt heavily coded. "I'll have Wolfe investigate. Anything else?"

She shook her head. "Nothing that jumps out at me."

With an effort to disguise his lingering weakness, Fane rose to his feet.

"Let me know if you find anything."

She stepped forward, pressing a hand on his chest as he swayed.

"What are you doing?"

"I'm going to shower and change out of these ridiculous clothes."

It was the innocence of his expression that set off alarm bells.

Fane was many things, but innocent wasn't one of them.

"And then?"

He hesitated, almost as if he was considering a lie. Then realizing not even he could lie to a trained psychic, he heaved a resigned sigh.

"I want to do some investigating—"

"No."

He arched a brow. "No?"

"No." She planted her fists on her hips, determined to stand her ground. "You know what Bas will do if he finds out you're sneaking around behind his back."

He sucked in an outraged breath. "You think I'm incapable of slipping past Bas's surveillance?"

Damn. She grimaced. She'd just broken the cardinal rule when dealing with a man. She'd pricked his delicate male ego.

Which was a certain way to make him dig in his heels.

Time for a change of tactics.

Softening her expression, she stepped forward so she could place a hand on his chest.

"I think you're wounded and tired and the only place you're going is to bed."

The dark gaze lowered to her lips, his lips twitching. "Is that an invitation?"

Serra resisted the urge to slide her hand over the hard muscles of his chest, exploring his physical perfection.

His skin was warm beneath her palm, but it wasn't the blaze of heat she'd come to expect when he was aroused. And even with his magical glyphs she could sense the pain throbbing through his body.

He was far from recovered from his injuries. Besides, she didn't believe for a second he'd been distracted from his foolish desire to charge into the night looking for a way to break Bas's hold over her.

"It's an order," she said in stern tones.

His brows drew together. "Serra."

"I know," she said. "The clock is running down, but you're in no condition to try to creep around the city." She pressed her fingers to his lips when they parted in protest. "Don't even try to lie. You're leaking."

He grimaced. "Leaking?"

"A few hours' rest isn't going to change anything."

His jaw tightened, then, reading the unwavering resolve etched onto her face, he conceded defeat with a slow, heart-melting smile.

"Very well, but I might need help getting out of my clothes."

She hid her surge of relief. "I think that can be arranged."

Taking his hand, she silently led him into the bedroom and across the carpet to the attached bathroom. Flipping on the overhead light, she turned to tug at his bow tie.

He watched her from beneath half-lowered lashes as she tossed aside the tie and slid her hands beneath the tailored jacket to help him shrug it off his shoulders and down his massive arms.

Unprepared for what was hidden beneath, she sucked in a sharp breath at the sight of the blood that stained the purity of his white shirt. Christ. The whole left side was painted in red.

"Oh, Fane," she breathed, her mouth dry with the realization that the wound was even worse than she had suspected.

Grasping the front of his ruined shirt, Fane ripped it off his body, using it to wipe away the blood coating his skin.

"It's nearly healed."

She studied the ragged hole in his shoulder that continued to ooze blood, not nearly as convinced as he was pretending to be.

"What about the bullet?"

He kicked off his shoes, unbuckling his belt so he could allow the silk pants to slide to the floor.

"Through and through," he assured her, yanking off his socks to leave him standing in front of her in all his naked glory.

And it was glorious.

Her stomach clenched, sparks of excitement racing through her blood as her gaze traveled downward.

The broad shoulders, the wide, sculpted chest, the narrow waist that flared only slightly at his hips. The muscular legs that ended at surprisingly narrow feet.

And all that delectable manhood was covered in dazzling, exquisitely inked tattoos that made her fingers itch to explore.

She forcibly kept her hands clenched at her side, returning her attention to his injury.

She would have time later to indulge her seemingly insatiable need for this man.

"Why didn't you allow the healer to help?"

He held her concerned gaze, his expression somber. "The only woman allowed to touch me is you."

Oh. Hell.

A huge crack formed in the wall she was so desperately trying to build between them.

"Dammit. You're not supposed to be charming me," she growled, even as she stripped off her itty-bitty dress and stepped into the shower.

Indifferent to the damage to her silken panties and matching bra, she turned on the water, adjusting it until it was just a degree below scalding.

"You're joining me?" Fane demanded, stepping beneath the hot spray of water with obvious pleasure.

"You're always taking care of me," she said, reaching for the soap. Pouring a small dollop in her hand, she began to spread it over his shoulders and down his chest, careful to avoid his wound. "It's my turn to take care of you."

"It's my job to protect you," he murmured, his voice suddenly husky with emotion. "And my honor."

She leaned forward to press a tender kiss directly over his heart.

"Tonight, it's my honor."

Chapter Fourteen

Bas remained silent as they'd reached his safe house north of town. The onetime government lab had proved to be a perfect place to set up his St. Louis headquarters.

Not only was the building heavily reinforced, it also had a built-in security system and several levels constructed underground, including one that had once been used as a bomb shelter.

Once he'd taken over the property he'd only increased the layers of protection around the building, using both magic and technology to turn it into an impregnable fortress.

Or at least he thought it was impregnable before Molly was stolen from him.

Struggling against the tidal wave of frustration that threatened to sweep him into madness, Bas headed through the sterile hallways painted institutional white with linoleum floors to the private elevator that led to the top floor.

Kaede remained closely at his side, monitoring his phone for incoming messages.

The warrior understood that Bas was waiting to ensure they had absolute privacy before discussing the latest fuck-up in a long list of fuck-ups.

The elevator doors slid open and they stepped into a long room filled with top-notch computer systems, monitors, and a steel vault on the far side that was filled with special-force-grade weapons.

Two trained Sentinels rose to their feet at his unexpected entrance, but waving them back to the security cameras they were monitoring, he headed directly into the back office.

Placing his hand on the scanner, he waited for the door to slide open. He motioned Kaede to enter ahead of him, his brutal training refusing to allow him to have anyone at his back, even his most trusted warrior.

With a last glance over his shoulders at the monitor that displayed the front gate to ensure they hadn't been followed, he stepped into the office and closed the door behind him.

Unlike his office at the Cavrilo International Building, this room was erected for comfort with glossy wooden floors and walls painted a soft ivory. There were built-in bookcases on either side of the window with a cushioned window seat built between them to look out the window at the wooded area at the back.

The perfect size for a young girl to sprawl on while she was looking through her picture books or playing with her dolls.

His breath was jerked from his lungs with a pain so fierce it nearly drove him to his knees.

With a grim determination, he forced his feet to carry him toward the large desk that dominated the center of the room, perching on the corner. Only when he was able to regain his composure did he meet Kaede's knowing gaze.

"How widespread is the damage?" He got straight to the heart of their current trouble, his voice cold.

The only way to get through this was to lock away his emotions.

Kaede grimaced. "Extensive enough to attract media attention."

Bas narrowed his eyes, sensing that was just the tip of the iceberg.

"What aren't you telling me?"

He turned around his phone to display the image of a smoldering pile of tangled metal.

"A small plane crashed just a few miles from town."

"Shit." He pressed the palm of his hand against his right eye. Stress was making him feel like someone was driving a railroad spike through his head. "That means government officials sniffing around."

"They're already arriving."

Of course they were. The spike drove even deeper.

"What about Anna?"

"Already moved to a more isolated location."

"She's still in stasis?"

"Yes, but her powers—"

Bas sliced his hand through the air, silencing his companion's protest.

"That can't be helped for now."

Kaede gave a reluctant nod. "I'll tell Stella to keep her locked down as tight as she can."

"Good." Bas didn't need to be reminded it was a risky solution. He was walking a tightrope with no net, but there wasn't a damned thing he could do about it. Not unless he could track down the kidnapper. "I need you to do something for me."

Kaede didn't hesitate. "Anything."

"I want you to make a list of any former colleague and their current location."

"Okay." The younger man didn't try to hide his confusion. "That's going to be a short list."

Bas dropped his hand, giving a weary nod of his head. When high-bloods joined his organization it was with the understanding that the only way out was death. He had way too many secrets to risk having dozens of employees coming and going.

Besides, it was the one certain way to protect his people from the wrath of Valhalla.

No policy, however, was foolproof and there had been a few stragglers who'd been allowed to slip away.

"Then I'll expect it by the end of the night," he said.

Kaede was headed toward the door. "I always deliver."

Bas waited for the door to close behind Kaede before he allowed his furious resentment to boil over.

Goddammit. Shoving away from the desk, he paced from one end of the office to the other.

This is what came from trying to play the good guy.

He should have sent Anna to the designated location without hesitation.

What did it matter to him if the kidnapper was some sort of terrorist nut job who intended to use Anna's abilities to destroy whole civilizations? Or more likely, a greedy bastard who wanted to force cities or even governments to fork over millions of dollars to halt the electronic dead zones that Anna created.

As long as he had Molly back home, the rest of the world could go to hell.

Rounding the desk, he sat in the leather seat and clicked on his computer, opening his only connection to the kidnapper.

He tapped an impatient finger on the arm of his chair, smoothing his face into an expressionless mask.

Once again he was acutely aware of the risk he was

taking by contacting the bastard who held his daughter, but he also understood that every time he had the opportunity to get a glimpse of the kidnapper, even when he was disguised, it offered him more clues to his identity.

Besides, it would be strange if he wasn't concerned that Serra had been attacked and this risked attracting the attention of Valhalla. The kidnapper would instantly realize that he must be plotting behind his back.

Abruptly the monitor flickered and the shadowed form of the kidnapper appeared on the screen.

"Are you deliberately trying to piss me off?" the distorted voice demanded.

He leaned forward, pressing his hands flat on the desk. "The psychic was attacked tonight."

The figure gave a faint shrug that Bas closely studied. Once Kaede had names to offer him it might trigger a memory.

"And?" the stranger prompted.

Bas allowed a portion of his seething frustration to tighten his features.

"And Valhalla will be sending Sentinels to investigate."

"I warned you to get rid of her."

"You also said I had four days."

Another shrug. Always with the right shoulder. And his head tilted to the side without any disturbance in the shadows that would indicate long hair.

"She's an unwelcome distraction from our game."

Bas stilled, shock jolting through him at the offhand words. "You think this is a game?"

"Of course." Even with the voice distorted, Bas could detect the mockery. "Two masters of strategy battling to the death. What could be more thrilling?"

Fuck. Bas forced himself to lean back in his seat, barely containing the fury that blasted through him.

A game?

The son of a bitch thought this was a game?

"Masters don't use little girls as pawns," he rasped.

The pause was less than a heartbeat, but it was enough to tell Bas his accusation had struck a nerve.

"She was necessary."

"For what? If you're such a skilled player then meet me in a face-to-face challenge." Bas twisted his lips into a sneer. "Don't hide behind a child."

He heard the hiss of an annoyed breath. "You don't get it, do you?"

"Get what?"

"Molly isn't the pawn." A deliberate pause. "You are."

The ground shifted beneath Bas.

He'd considered a dozen different reasons for Molly's kidnapping.

But not once had he considered the hideous possibility that it was personal.

"Me?"

There was a low laugh, made all the more chilling by the distortion.

"The infamous Bas Cavrilo. The mercenary who lives his life in shades of gray," the stranger taunted. "What better way to test your claim to moral ambiguity than to place you in a position where a choice has to be made?"

Bile clogged Bas's throat, nearly choking him. Goddammit. Who the hell was this bastard? And what had he done to inspire such rabid hatred?

"A choice between the lives of hundreds or thousands—"

"Millions," the kidnapper smoothly interjected.

"Or my own daughter?" Bas continued between clenched teeth.

"Exactly."

Christ. The man truly was a lunatic.

Bas clutched the arms of his chair, his knuckles white as

he battled back the urge to grab the monitor and toss it across the room.

"Have you considered the possibility that the use of Anna as a weapon will spark a war between high-bloods and norms?"

"Of course I have."

"And it doesn't bother you?"

"If there is a war, there is no one to blame but yourself." Bas didn't have to hear the gloating in his voice to know it was there. "You could keep Anna locked in her cell, and the world would never learn of her and her apocalyptic powers."

"This isn't a game, it's revenge," Bas rasped. "What have I done to you?"

"You offend me simply by being alive," the man fired back without hesitation.

Anger. Bitterness. A feral need for payback.

Could Bas somehow use the man's seething emotions against him?

"Then come out from the shadows and fight me like a man," he taunted. "Or are you like all cowards who talk a big game but never have the balls to stand up to a superior opponent?"

The shadow twitched, as if Bas's words had landed a physical blow.

Which meant he might be a high-blood, but he hadn't been trained by monks.

"Careful, Bas." With a jerk of his arm, the man reached to press something in front of him. "Have you forgotten what's at stake?"

Bas's lips flattened. "I haven't forgotten."

"Perhaps you need a reminder."

There was a flicker on the corner of his monitor as a second screen was opened.

Bas frowned, studying the darkened room in confusion. Then the overhead light was flipped on and he could see the camera was focused on a narrow bed with a tiny child covered by a pink blanket.

The ruthless control that had been hammered into Bas during his training threatened to shatter.

Christ. *He* threatened to shatter.

His sweet, innocent baby.

What kind of monster snatched a child from everything that made her feel safe, just because he wanted to punish Bas?

It was only the knowledge that the kidnapper was still watching him, eager to see him break down, that kept him from laying his head on the desk and howling out the bleak agony that filled his soul.

Instead he reached an unsteady hand to touch the monitor as the light woke the slumbering child and she slowly sat up, rubbing her eyes in confusion.

He swallowed his tears at the sight of her unruly mop of silver-blond curls and the round cheeks that were pink from sleep.

"Molly," he breathed.

Astonishingly, she abruptly turned toward the camera, her eyes the same unique bronzed shade as his, widening with hope.

"Daddy?"

Oh, hell. She could hear him.

He leaned forward, his nose nearly touching the screen. "I'm here, sweetheart."

She perched on her knees, her arms wrapping around her thin body that was covered in a pink nightgown. Bas's jaws clenched until they nearly crushed his molars.

Molly hated pink.

"Are you coming to get me?" she demanded, her voice low, as if she was afraid of attracting unwanted attention.

Which meant there must be a guard on the other side of the door he could just catch a glimpse of them at the corner of the screen.

Other than that there was nothing to indicate her location. White walls, a kiddy bed that could be bought at any discount store. No windows. Cheap carpeting.

Shit.

There was no way in hell he was going to risk asking Molly if she could offer him any information about where she was or who had kidnapped her. The bastard holding her captive thought this was a game. A twisted, sick game. If he didn't play by the rules, there would be no hesitation in snuffing out the life of this precious child.

"Soon." He used his magic to lace his voice with a soothing spell that would ease her fear. "I promise. I just need you to be patient for a little longer."

She nodded, but her lower lip trembled. "I miss Daisy."

Bas bit his lip until he could taste the blood. The battered stuffed hippo was now on his bed, a reminder of the child who utterly trusted that he would protect her.

"She's here waiting for you," he assured her, keeping his voice light. "Just like I am."

She managed a tiny nod. "I'm being a good girl."

His heart twisted at the soft promise. Molly had always been a child too old for her years.

As if she'd been born with a wisdom that she would one day share with the world.

"I know you are, sweetie," he softly assured her. "I'm so proud of you."

Without warning the connection was broken and the

monitor was consumed with the shadowed form of the kidnapper.

"That's enough," the man announced. "Decide. Send me my prize or she dies."

Bas busted the arm of his chair as he desperately sought to hide his desperation.

"The psychic—"

"Will be taken care of."

The monitor went black. The connection severed.

"Shit."

Wolfe was standing in central command, the very heart of Valhalla despite the fact it was nine levels below ground.

Surrounded by three of his most trusted Sentinels, Niko, Arel, and Gideon, he was going over his final instructions when the air was abruptly sucked from the room.

His lips twisted into a wry smile as he turned toward the open door of his office. No surprise the Mave was standing next to his desk, her dark beauty emphasized by the sleeveless yellow sweater she'd matched with a pair of white capris.

With her glossy hair pulled into a braid and her feet encased in a pair of casual sandals, she looked young and deceptively harmless.

An image that had no doubt fooled any number of idiots into underestimating her.

Wolfe wasn't one of them.

"Gentlemen, if you'll excuse me?"

With a haste that made Wolfe smile with wry amusement, the massive warriors scrambled to find some task that would take them to the other side of the long room.

Shoving a weary hand through his hair that he'd left unbound to brush his shoulders, Wolfe walked past the long bank of surveillance equipment. He'd been working nonstop since receiving Fane's coded message, assigning his duties to his Sentinels to make sure everything ran smoothly during his absence.

Now it was well past midnight and he had less than an hour to finish up his preparation and meet the guardian Sentinel in the chapel so he could be transported by portal.

"Mave," he murmured, stepping into his office and closing the door behind him.

Instantly he was wrapped in the cool wash of magic and intoxicating female power.

His pulse kicked into overdrive, everything male inside him stirred to full attention.

Including parts that had no business being stirred when they weren't going to get any satisfaction.

At least not with this woman.

"Do you have a minute to speak with me?"

He hid his grimace. Like it was a choice?

"Of course." He leaned against the door, folding his arms over his chest covered by a black T-shirt that matched his black jeans and black combat boots. Hey, he was a warrior. He bought clothes that were comfortable, not fashionable. "What do you need?"

"I received your message that you were leaving Valhalla."

"I shouldn't be gone for long." He gave a lift of his shoulder. "A few days at the most."

"Where are you going?"

He frowned, pulling out his cell phone to reread Fane's text.

"Woodward, Oklahoma."

"Is this Sentinel business?"

Wolfe nodded, shoving the phone back in his pocket.

"Fane asked me to investigate a series of power outages there."

The gray eyes narrowed in confusion. The same confusion Wolfe had felt since receiving the message.

"Why would he be interested in power outages hundreds of miles away?"

"That's what I'm going to find out."

Her lips parted, but even as he waited for her predictable command to keep her informed, her lips were snapping together and she was pacing toward the glass display case that held his prized samurai swords.

"I think I should come with you," she at last said.

"No."

The word escaped his lips before he could call it back. Well, hell. He really was tired, he acknowledged, bracing as his companion turned to glare at him in full Mave-mode.

"You are becoming far too fond of that word."

He held up a hand, trying to minimize the damage. The last thing he wanted was to provoke her pride.

Like any good leader, Lana was always willing to listen to suggestions from her various advisors. But she didn't take commands. Not from anyone.

"We don't know what danger we might be walking into."

"I'm capable of taking care of myself."

She was.

She was, indisputably, the most dangerous woman on the face of the earth.

But she'd already hinted at a past connection to the man they believed responsible for Serra's disappearance from Valhalla. He didn't want her conflicted emotions compromising her when they didn't know just how dangerous the mission might be.

He gave a tiny shake of his head, his lips twisting into a self-derisive smile.

All very noble.

Or it would have been if there wasn't a tiny voice of honesty whispering in the back of his mind that he didn't want this woman anywhere near Bas Cavrilo.

"I have never doubted that. Not ever," he said, the sincerity in his voice unmistakable. "But there's an unknown threat out there and someone needs to be in charge of Valhalla."

The anger prickling in the air eased, but her determination remained.

"I understand my duty, but on this occasion I believe my talents will be necessary."

Wolfe frowned. Okay. This was more than mere curiosity about an old flame.

Lana would always put the safety of Valhalla and her people first.

If she was demanding to travel with him then she believed there was a threat only she could eliminate.

He straightened from the door, his weariness abruptly replaced by a swelling sense of unease.

"What do you know?"

She turned back to the display case, effectively hiding her expression.

"Nothing more than rumors."

"Are you going to share?" He stepped forward, lightly touching her shoulder. "Lana, talk to me."

There was a long pause before she at last turned to meet his searching gaze.

"It was a difficult time when Valhalla was being formed and the high-bloods were exposing their presence to the world."

Wolfe frowned. He didn't know what he'd been expecting, but it sure as hell wasn't that.

"I have a vague memory, but I was still in my training

behind the walls of the monastery," he said. "There was little contact with the outside world."

Long before the first Mave had started her crusade to convince the high-bloods to come out of the shadows and band together, the monks had already formed their monasteries to train Sentinels. Actually, if the recent information that'd been uncovered in the depths of the Middle East was to be believed, the monasteries might have been around since the original high-bloods had been driven underground by infuriated humans who'd once worshipped them as gods.

Whatever the truth, the Sentinels had been tracked down by the monks and separated from the world for as long as even the eldest warrior could remember.

Valhalla had been well established before they'd agreed to become a part of the community.

"The founders of Valhalla tried to present a unified front. They realized that the humans' fear of them could escalate into violence with the least provocation," Lana continued.

He glanced toward his desk where a file folder was growing thicker every passing day with information they were gathering on the Brotherhood. A secret society of humans that considered high-bloods their enemies.

"Things haven't changed that much."

Lana absently lifted a hand to touch the witch mark just above the curve of her lush breast.

At one time that tiny mark would have been a death sentence.

"I hope we've gained some trust."

"Some." Wolfe's mouth went dry as he forced his gaze away from the temptation of her low neckline. Humans might be terrified of the emerald birthmark, but for him it was a tantalizing invitation. Sentinels rarely mixed with humans. They were simply too fragile. A powerful man needed a powerful woman. He cleared his throat. "But it's human nature to destroy what they don't understand, just as it's the nature of high-bloods to consider themselves superior to mere norms."

"True." She grimaced. "As I said, we gave the image of a united front."

Wolfe searched her pale face, sensing the tumultuous emotions that she kept sternly trapped behind her calm composure.

The creation of Valhalla wasn't just a history lesson for her. It had been a personal journey.

"But you weren't so united?"

"No. There were factions who were horrified by the thought of revealing ourselves to the humans."

Wolfe shrugged, well aware that even today there were high-bloods who remained in the shadows.

He'd never understood the desire to fit in with norms. Why be another sheep when you could be the wolf? A philosophy that had earned him his name.

"It wasn't as if they hadn't realized there were people who were different," he pointed out.

"Yes, but so long as they were allowed to pretend those people were nothing more than charlatans then they didn't have to accept that their neighbor could actually read their mind. Or that their son's little playmate was able to set things on fire with a stray thought."

"True." Another shrug. "But if they wanted to hide their gifts then I assume they weren't forcibly outed?"

"No, but that didn't keep them from doing everything in their power to undermine the Mave." Her eyes darkened to charcoal, as if remembering a long buried pain. "And there were other factions."

He folded his arms over his chest. It was that or doing something stupid. Like stroking his fingers over her satin-soft cheek. Or worse, pulling her into his arms to offer her comfort.

"Tell me."

"The original Mave was a brilliant, eloquent leader who also happened to be a powerful psychic," she continued, her voice flat. "She had the ability to sway large numbers of people to follow her lead."

"A dangerous gift," Wolfe murmured.

He'd never personally met the original Mave, but he'd heard enough rumors to know that she could be a hard-ass tyrant with a bloated belief in her own greatness.

Of course, it usually took an egomaniac to believe they could change the world.

"It can be." The beauty of her eyes was abruptly hidden beneath the downward sweep of thick lashes. "Especially when you happen to have a ruthless belief in your own destiny."

"The creation of Valhalla?"

She gave a slow nod, her eyes still hidden.

Shit. Whatever was coming had to be bad. Lana's composure was the stuff of legend.

If she was struggling to maintain it . . .

Yeah. Bad.

"She believed it was the only solution to avoiding an inevitable war."

"She was probably right."

"Yes." A tense pause. "Unfortunately."

Wolfe waited for her to continue, his brows drawing together as she became lost in her thoughts.

"Lana?" he eventually prompted. "Why unfortunately?"

She gave a faint shake of her head, as if trying to dismiss her dark memories.

"There were high-bloods who believed in the Mave's vision, but not her methods for achieving her goals."

Wolfe frowned. The stories that talked about the birth of Valhalla didn't mention the use of violence, but that didn't mean it hadn't been a part of the Mave's rise to power.

History had a way of rewriting itself.

"Did her methods include Sentinels?" he demanded.

"Assassins."

Wolfe sucked in a startled breath. There was only one reason she would have needed assassins.

"She had her enemies eliminated."

Lana slowly tilted back her head to meet his disgusted gaze, an ancient grief making his heart squeeze in fear.

"Not her enemies."

"I'm afraid to ask."

And that was the pure truth.

Wolfe had been around long enough to know that sometimes ignorance truly was bliss.

"She believed the norms would never accept Valhalla as long as there were high-bloods that were a danger to them," Lana said.

Wolfe frowned, not entirely sure where the conversation was going.

"We're all a danger to them."

"But there are some who are a danger by their very existence."

Wolfe couldn't argue. That was the primary reason the hunter Sentinels had been formed.

The mutations that created high-bloods weren't always a blessing.

Sometimes they were a curse that had to be contained.

"We've always kept them properly isolated."

"Not always." Her beautiful features tightened with regret. "And their very existence gave humans a reason to claim they would never be safe as long as high-bloods existed. For the Mave there was only one obvious solution."

Realization slammed into him, making his gut clench with horror.

Oh hell. It was bad.

Fucking hideously bad.

"She used the assassins to kill her own people?" he rasped.

"Yes."

"Christ."

Her eyes darkened to a stormy gray. "When her secret plans were uncovered a small group of dissenters banded together and tried to save the people targeted by the assassins."

A tightness in Wolfe's chest eased at the low words. He would never judge Lana. They all had made dark choices in their lives.

But he understood that she would never have forgiven herself for sacrificing an innocent. Not even if it meant achieving security for all high-bloods.

"You were a dissenter?"

She nodded. "Along with Bas."

Chapter Fifteen

The man she'd supposedly killed?

Wolfe swallowed a primitive growl. Goddammit. The sound of the man's name on her lips made him want to punch something.

Hard.

It didn't make sense. But it didn't have to.

"You worked together?" he asked, his voice hard.

"In the beginning," she admitted. "Bas would track the high-bloods marked for death and I would use my magic to hide his trail so he could disappear with the target."

"A rebel."

She frowned. "You don't have to mock."

"I'm not, I swear." With an effort he forced a wry smile to his lips. "But I have to admit I find it difficult to imagine you as part of an insurrection."

She shrugged. "I believed in Valhalla, but I wasn't going to build it with the blood of innocents on my hands."

"No." His hand was moving before he could stop his instinct to brush his fingers lightly down the slender column of her throat. His breath was jerked from his lungs by the tiny sparks of pleasure that raced through his body at the feel of warm woman and tingling magic. "I don't doubt you would always fight to the death to protect the weak and vulnerable."

Instantly she stepped from his touch, her face carefully devoid of expression.

"Thankfully my martyrdom wasn't necessary."

Wolfe waited for the pang of regret. It was a familiar cycle. He stepped over the boundaries. She shut him down. He felt like an ass.

This time, any regret was overridden by the sizzling awareness that jolted through his body.

Hell.

It felt like he'd been struck by lightning.

In a good way.

The gray eyes narrowed in warning and Wolfe resisted any urge to press his luck.

This wasn't the time or place.

Besides, she could shrivel his balls to the size of marbles if he truly pissed her off.

"What happened?"

"Eventually the Mave realized she was losing the trust of her people and altered her policy," she said, clearly skimming over the dangerous years of being an outlaw.

A role that would have made her miserable.

"Altered them how?"

"She began containing the high-bloods that were unstable or could hurt others by accident," she said. "It wasn't a perfect solution, but it halted the executions."

"That would explain the dungeons," Wolfe said, referring to the cells buried deep beneath his feet.

He had no moral objection to them. Hell, he'd used them for those high-bloods determined to cause harm to themselves or others.

Lana nodded. "Exactly."

"So your rebellion came to an end and you became an advocate for a united Valhalla?"

"Yes."

A faint smile touched his lips. He could easily see her returning to the first Mave, her chin held high despite the fact that she'd been considered a traitor. Her courage could never be questioned. Hell, it gave him nightmares.

Then the image shifted to include a handsome assassin who stood at her side.

The man who'd shared more than just a passing relationship with her.

"And Bas?" he pressed.

She lifted her brow at the edge in his voice. "The Mave disbanded the assassins."

Hmm. So that was the reason the assassins had been absorbed back into the Sentinels. Or at least, that was the command given to the monks.

In truth, most of them simply disappeared until Wolfe had started the difficult task of tracking them down.

"I doubt Bas was pleased with that decision."

"No, he disappeared." There was a long pause. "I eventually tracked him down to bring the high-bloods he was hiding to Valhalla."

"He wasn't as eager to forgive and forget?"

She trembled, wrapping her arms around her waist. "It was worse than that."

Wolfe studied her pale face, caught off guard by her rare display of emotion.

"Lana?"

"I discovered that instead of protecting the people in his care, he was using them."

"How?"

"He'd become a mercenary, selling his services and the services of those who depended on him for their safety."

"The bastard." Wolfe's gut twisted with revulsion. He fully backed this female's decision to put an end to high-bloods selling their services. Their gifts weren't meant to be used for profit. And he sure as hell wouldn't endure a high-blood pimping out his own people for money. "No wonder you killed him."

"He wasn't condemned to death because he was a mercenary."

"Then why?"

Her lips tightened as she was forced to dredge up unwelcome memories.

"Because he killed two Sentinels when he tried to escape from me."

Wolfe already knew he was going to kill the assassin. Not only because he was somehow responsible for Serra's disappearance from Valhalla, but also because he'd betrayed Lana's trust in him to care for the high-bloods he'd been given to protect.

Now he knew he was going to make him suffer.

A lot.

Heat prickled in the air. "Did he try to harm you?"

"I thought so at the time." She hesitated, as if shuffling through her memories, before giving a shake of her head. "Now I wonder if it was a ruse so I would think my spell killed him and stop any attempt to track him down."

"Assassins would have the magic to feign their own death," Wolfe agreed.

The trained warriors could not only slow their breathing until it was undetectable, but they could place themselves in a deep trance that would cool their skin and mask their heartbeat.

Like a damned vampire.

She lowered her arms, squaring her shoulders as she mentally slammed the door on her past.

"And Bas has more magic than most."

Wolfe narrowed his eyes, suddenly realizing the point of her story.

"Is that why you want to travel to Woodward? You think he's there?"

With an abrupt movement she was pacing toward his desk, the scent of warm vanilla and annoyed woman teasing at his nose. He was the only one who dared question her decisions.

"No, I want to go because one of the high-bloods in his care was a woman whose power interferes with electrical currents."

Ah. That might explain why Fane had texted him to check it out.

"You think that she could be responsible for the blackout?"

"Yes." Lana turned back to face him. "If it's her, I need to track her down as fast as possible."

The urgency in her voice sent a jolt of alarm down his spine.

"Is there something else I should know?"

She frowned in puzzlement. "What do you mean?"

"I realize that being without electricity is a nuisance—"

"It's not a nuisance," she interrupted, her expression grim. "It's life or death. This isn't just a transformer blowing. As long as the high-blood is in the area there's no electricity, period." She made a slashing motion with her hand. "None. That means the backup generators at the police stations and hospitals are worthless. Nothing will keep vital technology working. Even airplanes flying in the area will be affected."

Wolfe grimaced, beginning to realize the difference between a typical blackout and an electrical dead zone.

"Shit."

"Banks are left vulnerable, computers are wiped of memory," she continued to hammer home the point. "Not even cars will run."

He lifted his hand to halt her list of troubles. "I got it." And he did. "Armageddon."

"Yes."

He pulled out his phone, contacting the Valhalla chapel to have a guardian Sentinel waiting for him at the portal.

"Are you packed?"

Bas was standing in front of the window seat, absently running his fingers over a cushy, zebra print pillow that still held Molly's sweet scent.

How many hours had she sat on this narrow seat, blissfully lost in her own world as Bas had worked at his desk?

So tiny and vulnerable and yet filled with such incandescent joy.

An aching emptiness exploded through his chest, crashing over the barriers he'd built around his emotions.

Like a flood bursting through a dam.

Oh . . . Molly.

Pain, cruel and ruthless, surged through him, threatening to send him to his knees.

He wasn't sure how long he had stood there before the door to the office was pushed open and Kaede entered.

There was the sound of approaching footsteps that halted in the center of the room. The warrior was well trained not to interrupt. Even if Bas was doing nothing more than staring at his daughter's favorite pillow.

Taking a beat to wipe the grief from his face, Bas slowly turned to confront his companion.

He wouldn't show weakness. Not even in front of Kaede.

"A change of plans," he abruptly announced.

Kaede stilled, on full alert as he took note of Bas's grim expression.

"What do you mean?"

"I want Anna prepared to continue her journey."

"What about the psychic?" The younger man held up the file folder in his hand. "I thought you wanted to give her time to search for Molly?"

"I intend to keep searching, but in the meantime, I want Anna taken to the location we were given."

Shock rippled over Kaede's face. "Give in to the kidnapper?"

"Yes, dammit," Bas snapped. "If that's what it takes to get my daughter home."

Kaede lowered the file, his gaze searching Bas's stark expression.

"Did something happen?"

Bas clenched his teeth. He didn't want to share his precious moments with his daughter. Not when his emotions were still so raw.

But he understood that if he was going to depend on Kaede to have his back, the warrior needed to know exactly what was happening.

"I spoke with Molly."

Kaede sucked in a startled breath. "How?"

Bas nodded toward the computer. "The kidnapper allowed me a short conversation."

"She's okay?"

The image of Molly kneeling in the middle of the pink bed seared through his brain, his heart squeezing with merciless regret.

"She's scared, but putting on a brave face so I don't worry about her."

"That's our little trooper," Kaede murmured, a hint of pride in his voice.

"I don't want her to have to be brave, I want her home," Bas snarled, pointing toward the window seat. "I want her in here sitting behind me while I work, giggling because she's snacking on peanut butter cookies she stole from my private stash."

Kaede flinched. The younger man was as devoted as Bas to the little girl. Hell, who hadn't tumbled in love with the charming minx?

She had that kind of effect on people.

"She'll be here," the warrior swore in fierce tones. "Even if we have to tear apart the world."

Bas slowly shook his head. They were the exact words he would have used just days ago. Before he realized that he wasn't nearly as invulnerable as he once believed.

"It's that attitude that got Molly kidnapped in the first place."

Kaede scowled in confusion. "What?"

"I've spent the past century making enemies." Bas paced toward his desk, his gaze lingering on the stack of potential clients. He'd spent over a hundred years crafting a power basc built on money, intimidation, and blackmail. He thought it made him strong. Too late he realized he'd instead created a seething volcano that was destined to explode in his face. "Sooner or later one of them was bound to seek revenge. I just never thought that Molly would pay the price for my sins."

"Since when did you become a believer in karma?" Kaede demanded.

"Since it bit me in the ass."

The warrior shrugged. He was still young enough to believe he could control his future.

"Everyone makes enemies."

"Not everyone chooses to live without a conscience."

There was a hesitation as Kaede sought a diplomatic means of assuring Bas that his years of being an immoral bastard weren't a mistake.

"You have to make tough choices when you're the leader."

"A nice excuse." His lips twisted into a humorless smile. "We both know my decisions were based on the bottom line, not what was best for my people."

"That's not entirely true," Kaede protested.

"True enough." Bas grimaced. This wasn't a bout of self-pity. Just a long overdue examination of his life. "I've hurt too many."

There was a long silence as Kaede came to terms with Bas's unfamiliar guilt.

Then, clearing his throat, the young man asked the question that had no doubt been plaguing him for the past four years.

"You never discuss Molly's mother."

Bas smoothly turned, as if he was gazing out the window. He was emotionally compromised, and the last thing he wanted was for anyone to realize that Myst had ever been more than a meaningless coupling.

Myst.

A familiar sense of exasperation raced through his blood.

The tiny woman with a pale, perfect face that was dominated by a large pair of velvet brown eyes and long, silvery-blond color so pale it didn't look real had slammed into his life with the force of a mini-tornado and then simply disappeared.

Poof.

Gone.

And the fact that he'd secretly spent the past four years searching for her annoyed the hell out of him.

"There's nothing to discuss," he said, the words clipped. "She was a clairvoyant with only minor abilities. She asked to work for me, but to be honest she seemed more a liability than an asset."

"So you took her to your bed instead?" Kaede pressed.

Bas glanced toward the hand-carved wooden cabinet that concealed a top-of-the-line media center.

Four years ago there had been a leather couch there that was long enough for him to stretch out for an hour nap when he was working around the clock.

A common occurrence.

But after Molly had arrived, he'd had the office completely redecorated.

He told himself that it only made sense to make the room as kid-friendly as possible.

But a part of him knew that he'd commanded the change because he found himself unable to walk by the couch without catching the faint scent of cinnamon that had clung to Myst's skin or seeing her spread beneath him, her pale face flushed with pleasure.

Shit.

Bas gave an abrupt shake of his head.

"She was upset so I poured us both a drink," he said, giving a dismissive lift of his shoulder. "And then another. Eventually we ended up on the couch. One hour later she was gone."

Kaede gave a short laugh. "Left or was escorted out?"

Bas had a brief urge to allow his companion to believe he'd had her tossed from the building. After all, it wasn't as if he hadn't had to use force to remove an overly persistent lover on any number of times.

But he swiftly dismissed the cowardly impulse.

He might resent Myst's ability to walk away as if he was just another fuck, but she was Molly's mother. He wasn't going to allow anyone to disrespect her.

"I asked her to stay," he admitted, turning back to face his companion. "I felt—"

"What?"

"I felt peace when she was in my arms."

Kacde lifted a brow, but he wasn't stupid enough to press the issue.

"Then how did she disappear?" he asked instead.

Now that was a good question.

One that had nagged at him for four years.

"I got up to answer the phone and when I turned around she was gone."

"That must have been a first for you." Kaede didn't bother to hide his surprise. "Did you look for her?"

Bas gave a warning frown. He was willing to admit he'd enjoyed sex with Myst. And even that he'd wanted more.

But there was no way he was going to share that he'd been paying a fortune to the best private detectives in the world trying to find her.

"What the hell does it matter?"

"I hear regret in your voice."

"You hear annoyance," he corrected. Which was true enough. Myst was a mystery that refused to be solved. What could be more annoying to a man who used information as a bargaining tool? "The woman disappeared and nine months later left a baby in my private rooms with a note attached saying that she belonged to me."

It was a story that Bas shared with no one, so he was fully prepared for Kaede's sudden suspicion.

"You didn't speak with her?"

"She obviously didn't feel the need to explain why she was abandoning her child, and since she had a rare talent for sneaking past my security I didn't have the opportunity to question her decision."

Kaede wasn't satisfied. "Did you have a DNA sample of the baby taken?"

"No."

"Shit, Bas, how do you know the child is yours?" Kaede stared at him as if he was looking at a stranger. "Or for that matter, if the woman you slept with is the biological mother?"

He shrugged. "Molly is a tiny replica of her. Except for her eyes."

Kaede snorted. "That doesn't make you the father."

Bas wondered how the younger man would explain the color of Molly's eyes. He'd never seen anyone beyond himself with that particular color of bronze.

Still, it wasn't the color of eyes or hair or the tiny nose tilted at the very end that made Molly his daughter.

"It doesn't matter."

"It doesn't?"

"The second I held Molly in my arms she belonged to me," Bas said with a quiet sincerity. "End of story."

Kaede's distrustful expression abruptly melted, revealing a tenderness that would shock most people.

Who would believe the man referred to as "Bas's Blade" had a heart?

Molly had changed them all.

"She belongs to all of us," Kaede said.

Which only made it all the more vital that he get her back, Bas acknowledged. His people depended on her bright spirit to lighten the darkness of their souls.

Deliberately, he forced his thoughts away from Molly. Instead, he concentrated on the vicious pleasure of getting his hands on her kidnapper, allowing a hum of anticipation to override his debilitating pain.

It was the only way to keep his sanity.

"Did you discover anything?"

Kaede snapped into his role of executive assistant, flipping open the file folder.

"Names," he said, handing over a stack of papers. "But no known addresses."

"Let me see." Bas scanned the top page. "Stephan Reyes?" He glanced up in surprise. The Sentinel had been his right hand man before he'd gotten into a drunken fight with another Sentinel over a woman. "Isn't he dead?"

Kaede shrugged. "We never found his body."

"Good point." Bas tossed the paper aside. "But Stephan was trained by the monks. The kidnapper wasn't." He scanned the next paper. "Russell Harvey?"

"He was the healer who we caught experimenting on norms."

Bas wrinkled his nose. The man had been a true genius, but he'd been lacking any sort of ethics when it came to his medical experiments. Bas had drawn the line when he'd discovered the healer infecting young women with increasingly lethal diseases to see if he could discover the power to cure them.

They still had no idea how many he'd killed before they caught him and ordered him to leave.

It was only because he truly had a gift for healing that Bas hadn't destroyed him on the spot.

"I'd nearly forgotten about that SOB." His lips curled in disgust. "This is exactly the sort of sick game he would enjoy playing."

Kaede nodded. "Agreed. But I don't think we should assume anything until we have all the facts."

Bas sent his companion a wry glance. "Logic from you, Kaede?"

Kaede flashed a smile, pretending he didn't exist on the edge of violence. "One of us has to keep his head."

With a shake of his head, Bas took out the last sheet of paper.

"Lee Sandoval?" He frowned. "The name isn't familiar."

"He was Jael's lover."

Jael. Abruptly he recalled the pretty, quick-tempered witch who had an unfortunate habit of trying to lure him into her bed. A pain in the ass.

The only reason he'd kept her around was because she had a talent for creating unbearable pain. A skill that had made Bas a fortune from human dictators who wanted to torture a prisoner.

It took longer to remember the awkward, unsociable male who'd been her lover.

"The computer geek," he at last said.

"He was also a psychic, although he rarely used his powers," Kaede said. "We assumed it was because they were embarrassingly weak. Now I wonder if he wanted to keep them hidden so we would underestimate him."

Bas frowned. "Why?"

"He was the sort who liked to fly under the radar," the warrior said, his voice filled with disdain. "There were a few rumors that he was using his computer skills to skim money and transferring it to a secret account."

A thief in his house?

Bas stiffened in outrage.

"Why wasn't I told?"

"It was all just nasty gossip, I couldn't find any proof," Kaede said, excusing his decision not to turn the bastard over to Bas. "Still, when Jael was killed and he announced he was leaving I decided to let him go. It was the best solution to a messy problem."

Bas felt a momentary pang of regret.

Jael had been in Bangkok when she'd been ambushed by a gang of humans who'd tied her to a stake and burned her alive.

Bas suspected the norms had belonged to the Brotherhood, but there hadn't been any direct links to the cult and he'd had to content himself with tracking down two of the bastards responsible and killing them as slowly and painfully as possible.

After the tragedy he hadn't considered Jael's lover, or what had happened to him.

Now he had to wonder if Sandoval had used his inside knowledge of Bas's operation to slip in and steal Molly.

"He would know about Anna and the price that cities would pay to get rid of her," he said slowly. "But it's a risky plan and there's easier ways to make money than kidnapping or blackmail. Especially for a psychic."

Kaede shook his head. "This isn't about money."

Bas met the warrior's steady gaze. "Then what?"

"Sandoval blames you for Jael's death."

Chapter Sixteen

Fane slowly opened his eyes, astonished to discover that he'd slept for over four hours.

He could have chalked up the rare occurrence to the heavy toll healing his wounds took on his body. Or even the large meal he'd eaten after his shower to replace his lost blood.

But he knew that the explanation was the warm, lush woman tucked tightly in his arms.

Remaining utterly motionless, Fane savored the rare moment.

Soft silken skin. Lush, womanly curves. Chamomile and moonlight.

Was there anything more intoxicating?

With a soft sigh, Serra turned in his arms, wiggling her perfect ass until it was pressed against his cock.

A cock that was already fully aroused and eager to seek out the moist heat of Serra's body.

With a low groan, Fane forced himself to loosen his grip on the luscious female and slip silently from the bed.

As much as he wanted to remain in bed, kissing a path down the curve of her spine until she spread her legs in invitation, he had been awakened by a distinctive *chirp* of his cell phone.

It was a text from Marco, one of the Sentinels Wolfe had sent to St. Louis.

Pulling on a pair of cargo pants that had been sent at the same time as the tux along with a pile of clothing he hadn't bothered to pull out of the bags, he glanced at his phone.

Heaven

He leaned down to press a soft kiss to the top of Serra's tousled hair before moving out of the bedroom and across the dark sitting room. He paused at the door, punching a series of numbers into his phone to trigger the tiny device he'd planted when he'd paid a visit to the spy in the hotel suite across the hall.

The device would release an odorless gas that would knock out anyone in the room for a short period of time.

He counted to one hundred, then slowly opened the door, allowing his powers to disrupt any nearby surveillance equipment as he headed toward the back of the hall to the fire escape.

Another burst of power disabled the alarm on the door and he was in the stairwell, heading toward the roof.

Marco's message HEAVEN had indicated he was waiting for Fane on top of the building.

Pushing open the door that led to the helicopter pad, Fane stepped out of the building. He halted as the warm breeze wrapped around him, absorbing the various scents. He never walked into an unfamiliar place without assuming it was a trap.

Confident that there were no hidden dangers, he walked forward, already prepared when the tall, broad-shouldered male dressed in faded jeans and a black T-shirt stepped out of the shadows.

Even without the tattoos there was no mistake what Marco was.

Hunter.

Predator.

His face was lean with the high, chiseled cheekbones of his Slavic ancestors and a narrow blade of a nose. His black hair was ruthlessly pulled into a braid that hung past his shoulders. His eyes were ice blue and rimmed with indigo, shimmering with a disturbing intelligence in the security lights.

A dragon tattoo circled his neck, hiding the scars from his battle with a crazed group of humans who'd managed to capture him on his way back to his monastery. The bastards had hung Marco from a tree and left him to die. It was rumored it'd taken him over a week to get free.

The fact that the scars had never faded revealed just how close he'd hovered near death.

That kind of experience changed a man.

Made him harder. Grimmer. Unpredictable.

It also made Marco one of the most lethal hunters in Valhalla.

Which was no doubt why Wolfe had sent him.

"You have information?" Fane asked, not bothering with chitchat.

Leaving Serra alone for even a few minutes was scraping against his raw nerves. Besides, Marco wasn't a chitchat kind of guy.

Marco nodded, shoving a picture of a building into Fane's hand.

"I followed the secretary from Hull Insurance to this location."

Fane studied the plain brick structure surrounded by a high fence. He frowned as he read the sign at the front of the building.

"A lab?"

"Doubtful." Marco shoved another photo into his hand. Fane grimaced as he recognized Bas and Kaede stepping out of the stretch limo. "These men arrived there a few hours ago."

"Bas." The name came out as a low growl. "This must be where he keeps his people."

"I've spotted five high-bloods plus these two," Marco said, his voice low and as rough as gravel. A result of his injuries. "My guess is that there are several more inside."

"How close did you get?"

"Not close enough." Marco gave a frustrated shake of his head. "The place is wired like the damned Pentagon. One wrong step and I would have triggered a dozen alarms."

"Don't take any chances," Fane commanded. "I don't want the bastard knowing we've found his bat-cave."

Marco nodded, planting his hands on his hips. "I want to take Serra out of here."

Fane grimaced. "Not right now."

The older man scowled. "Dammit, Fane, she's obviously in danger. I could sneak her—"

"No," Fane said, sharply shutting down the suggestion. He didn't want any of his brothers making the mistake that they could solve the situation by "rescuing" Serra or killing Bas. "She's been poisoned by the assassin. Only he can remove the toxin."

The ice-blue eyes narrowed in shock. "Assassin? God-dammit. This is bad."

"No shit."

"What can I do?"

"We were attacked earlier tonight by two humans that we suspect had been spelled to decompose on death." Fane's voice was flat. A sure indication he was battling a tidal wave of emotions.

"A witch?"

Fane shrugged. "Perhaps. They also had a mind-stunner. So obviously money is no object. Whoever it is could have paid the witch to perform the spell."

"Or they could be hired guns who placed the spell on themselves for added security," Marco suggested. "A client would be more likely to hire assassins who couldn't be traced."

Fane nodded. "Good point. Do you have any contacts that would know about professional hit men?"

Hunter Sentinels usually had a network of spies they could tap when they needed info that they couldn't get by more formal resources.

Like a street cop with confidential informants.

"I have a few I can tap," Marco assured him. "Anything else?"

"Have the Sentinels scout around the lab," Fane said, pushing the photos back into Marco's hand. "If things go to hell we'll need to be able to get in and use those inside as leverage." Fane didn't have to spell out that he didn't care what methods they had to use to gain that leverage. He was willing to sacrifice anyone and everything to protect his woman. "The bastard is going to remove the poison from Serra one way or another."

Marco nodded without hesitation. "We'll be waiting for your signal." He reached into his pocket and pulled out a burner phone and gave it to Fane. "My number is already programmed in. Call me when you want us to move."

"You got it."

Marco narrowed his eyes. "Keep her safe, Fane," the hunter warned. "You aren't the only one who loves her."

"I'll protect her with my life," Fane assured his fellow Sentinel before turning to head back into the hotel.

He'd left Serra unguarded too long.

He thought he heard Marco warn him to be careful, but he was already focused on making his way back to the hotel suite. Bas's spy wouldn't stay asleep for long. The last thing he wanted was the bastard realizing that Fane had the ability to slip in and out when he wanted.

Moving with a stealth that marked him as a Sentinel, he used his key card to unlock the door to his hotel suite and stepped inside. He had closed it silently behind him when a fist connected with his upper arm.

"Damn you," Serra growled, rearing back her fist for another punch.

Fane gently grasped her hand, pressing it to his lips. She hadn't hurt him, but he was afraid she might have bruised her knuckles.

"I missed you too," he murmured.

"How would you like it if I snuck out while you were sleeping?"

He grimaced, his gaze sweeping over her flushed cheeks and the pale green eyes that sparkled with anger. Her hair was disheveled and her lush body covered by a plain hotel robe, but she'd never looked more beautiful.

"You're right. I'm sorry." His thumb brushed her inner wrist, a renegade surge of satisfaction racing through him when he felt her pulse leap at the small caress. "I thought I would return before you woke up."

She was far from appeased. "So your theory is what I don't know won't hurt me?"

Hmm. He hesitated.

"I sense a trap."

"No more sneaking out."

"I promise." He pressed a kiss to her lips. This was exactly why he'd always dreaded becoming involved with this female. His job would always put him in danger. Which meant Serra would spend her life constantly in fear. "I didn't mean for you to worry."

She stilled, her anger abruptly melting as she realized that she'd reminded him exactly why he'd kept his distance from her.

"There's always going to be times when I'm worried," she said softly. "It's an unavoidable part of life."

"Serra—"

"No." She pressed her fingers against his lips, halting his instinctive concern. "Have you been worried about me?"

Fane frowned at the ridiculous question.

"Christ, of course I'm worried." His fingers tightened on her wrist, the heat from his body filling the air. "I've never been so fucking scared in my life."

Her fingers gently traced his lips. "Would it be better for you if I pushed you away so you didn't have to go through the pain of knowing I'm in danger?"

He hissed as she threw his logic back in his face, the mere thought of being denied the right to protect this female enough to make his blood run cold.

Oh hell, no.

No matter what the fear or pain or even grief he was forced to endure, nothing could be worse than not having a place in her life.

"Don't," he muttered.

"Then don't push me away."

"I'm trying, *milaya moya,* but I'm a male. It takes me a while to accept I might be wrong."

She rolled her eyes, but she didn't press. He hoped it was because she understood he was truly doing the best he could, but he was betting it was because she wanted to punch him in the face.

"Where did you go?" she asked, her steady gaze daring him to refuse to answer.

Yeah. That wasn't a dare he was taking.

He'd already reached his quota of dumb-ass decisions for one night.

"I met Marco on the roof."

"And?"

"And they managed to locate at least one of Bas's secret lairs."

She lifted a brow. "Lairs?"

"He's a villain," Fane said with a shrug. "Don't they have lairs?"

There was a startled beat before Serra gave a choked laugh. "Oh my God. Was that a joke?"

His expression remained bland. "I have my moments."

Without warning, she went onto the tips of her toes to press a teasing kiss to his lips.

"Yes, you do."

His reaction was explosive. One second he was counting his blessings she hadn't been waiting at the door with a baseball bat, and the next his body was humming with a darkly erotic anticipation.

"How are you feeling?" he asked, his voice suddenly rough with need.

A slow smile of temptation curled her lips. "The headache is all gone."

He brushed his fingers over her still pale cheek. "Your powers are back?"

"Yes, thank God." There was no missing the sincerity in her voice. "I'm not used to feeling completely vulnerable. I don't know how norms can stand it."

His gaze lowered to the plump temptation of her lips, he was not particularly interested in humans or their petty problems.

"I assume it's their sense of vulnerability that provokes

their prejudice against high-bloods," he said, his distraction obvious.

"Yes." Her eyes darkened to emerald, the rich scent of chamomile filling the air. "How do you feel?"

He lowered her hand to press it over his thundering heart, peering deep into her wide eyes.

"You tell me."

Her lips twitched. "I was asking if you've recovered."

"All healed. But—"

"But what?"

Using his speed to his advantage, he scooped her off her feet and headed toward the bedroom.

"I should probably return to bed to make sure I'm fully rested."

"I don't think you intend to rest," she accused, the sparkle in her eyes assuring him that she wasn't opposed to delaying sleep.

"I might." He lowered her onto the bed, swiftly ridding himself of his cargo pants. "Eventually."

Holding his darkened gaze, Serra tugged on the belt of her robe. Slowly the terry cloth fabric parted and then fell aside, revealing her naked body.

He choked back a groan as his cock hardened in response to the beautiful vision below him.

He wanted to kiss every inch of her pale, ivory skin. To sink between her thighs and taste of her heat. To watch her eyes squeeze closed with pleasure as he entered her and pounded them both into mindless bliss.

Placing a knee on the edge of the bed, he leaned down to slide the robe off her shoulders and down her arms, allowing her beauty to be fully exposed.

Now the only question was where to touch first.

He settled on the delicate curve of her throat, brushing his fingers down to the pulse racing at the base of her neck.

He smiled, savoring the sensation of her soft skin beneath his fingertips.

"I thought you would still be asleep," he murmured.

She studied him from beneath half-lowered lids. "You have the temperature down to sixty degrees. I was cold without you wrapped around me like a human heater."

Fane gave a soft chuckle. "I promise to warm you up."

Her eyes sparkled as a smile of wicked temptation curved her lips.

"I don't know." Her gaze traced the tattoos on his bare chest. "I'm awfully cold."

Without hesitation, Fane joined her on the wide bed. The warm scent of chamomile and woman wrapped around him, arousing the hunter that always lurked just beneath the surface.

Growling in anticipation, Fane pulled her into his arms and performed a smooth roll. She gave a tiny gasp of surprise as he anchored her on top of his aching body with her legs straddling his hips.

He smiled into her startled eyes, his hands gripping her hips.

"*Milaya,* I'm going to have you burning before I'm done."

She planted her hands on his chest as his fingers skimmed around the curve of her hips to cup her ass, pressing her firmly against his throbbing shaft.

"Promises, promises" she breathed.

Fane chuckled as he lifted his head to nibble at the base of her throat.

"I'm more than willing to turn my promises into reality."

"I . . ." Her head tilted to the side, her hair tumbling over her shoulder as he gave her a small nip. At the same time her hips moved backward and forward in silent encouragement. "Oh."

Fane groaned. Her skin fascinated him. Like ivory satin.

He licked a hungry path to her breast.

A part of him longed to simply thrust deep inside her and find his release. What male didn't enjoy a swift, sweaty orgasm?

But a greater part was determined to relish a slow, heated bout of lovemaking.

And it was *lovemaking* with Serra.

Not mindless coupling.

Not a quick fuck.

A beautiful joining that could feel right to the center of his soul.

Delighting in the sweet taste of her, Fane circled her tightening nipple with the tip of his tongue. With light strokes he teased her until her nails dug into the flesh of his chest.

"More," she whispered.

"Like this?" he demanded, closing his lips around the peak to suckle her with gentle urgency.

"Yes."

A sigh of pleasure tumbled from her lips, her legs spreading until she could rub herself against the length of his cock.

Fane closed his eyes at the staggering shock of pleasure that jolted through him. Damn. He was on the brink of an orgasm and he wasn't even inside her.

The heat from his body warmed the air, adding to the erotic sensations. He arched his hips upward, his hands stroking up the curve of her spine. Aimlessly, he traced patterns on her soft skin, simply enjoying the freedom to touch her.

Christ. He'd deliberately denied himself this heaven.

How stupid could a man be?

Still teasing the puckered nipple, he slid his hands down

to grasp her thighs. Giving them a gentle tug, he trailed a finger between her soft folds.

"Fane," she moaned.

He kissed a path to her neglected breast, using his teeth on the sensitive tip even as his finger slipped into her sleek heat.

Serra breathed out a rough sigh, her hands exploring the hard muscles of his chest. He lowered his head to the mattress to watch the flush of arousal darken the skin over her cheekbones.

God almighty, but she was magnificent. A powerful, exotic female who could have any man in the world. And yet had chosen him.

At least for tonight.

With a slow expertise he stroked his finger deep within her. At the same time he used his thumb to caress her tiny nub of pleasure.

"I'll never have enough of you," he muttered, his tongue flicking over her tightly budded nipple. "Never."

"Don't stop," she gasped.

Fane gave a choked groan. "Not a chance in hell."

Serra allowed her hands to smooth up the length of his neck and over the muscles of his shoulders. Her touch was light but a trail of fire followed in the wake of her fingers.

Bolts of pleasure shot through his body. Oh hell. His cock twitched, anxious to surge into the tight heat of her body.

He hadn't been entirely celibate over the years.

There'd been occasional females who'd shared his physical needs without emotional complications.

Now he realized just how meaningless those exchanges had been.

There'd been no soft, lingering touches.

No delicious foreplay that made him tremble with bone-deep need.

As if sensing his vulnerability, Serra lowered her head to press her lips to the center of his chest. With open-mouthed kisses she moved to tease his sensitive nipple, her hands roaming down the washboard muscles of his stomach.

"Christ, *milaya*," he groaned as she boldly reached down to grasp his straining erection in a firm grip.

"Maybe you're not the only one who can create heat, Sentinel," she teased as she stroked him from top to bottom and back again.

Fane hissed at the brutal pleasure that seared through him. Heat? Oh, hell no. Her touch was burning him alive.

His hips instinctively rocked upward to thrust his cock in her grip. Damn. It felt so good.

Too good.

Gritting his teeth against the looming climax, Fane focused his attention on her flushed face as he slid his finger in and out of her body, quickening his strokes as she gave a low moan.

"Come for me, Serra," he commanded softly.

Her breath hissed between her teeth. "Fane . . ."

"Yes," he encouraged, using his thumb to bring her to the edge.

Bewitched by the pleasure that softened her features and parted her lips as her breath came out in soft pants, Fane was unprepared when she suddenly reached down to grab his wrist.

"Serra?" he questioned softly.

Her smile widened as she tugged his hand to one side and used her other hand to place his aching cock at the entrance to her moist heat.

The world halted as he stared into mesmerizing eyes, and he knew that this moment would be engraved on his memory for all of eternity.

Slowly, deliberately, she impaled herself on his rigid shaft.

"You were right. I'm starting to get warm," she murmured with a gleam in her eyes. "Burning hot, in fact."

Fane groaned as she tossed his teasing words back into his face.

Oh yes.

They were going up in flames.

To both their satisfaction.

He gave another groan as he pressed himself into her welcoming body. At the same time she ground her hips down to meet his thrust.

Damn.

She was surely going to be the death of him.

Chapter Seventeen

Serra struggled to breathe as Fane placed a gentle kiss on her forehead and rolled off her quivering body.

"God almighty," she muttered, not entirely sure she hadn't briefly blacked out during the last orgasm.

She'd always known sex with Fane would be fantastic. The minute he walked into a room she was hot and bothered. And those small, accidental touches over the years had nearly made her self-combust.

So, yeah.

She'd expected good.

But this . . .

This was mind-blowing, I'm-not-sure-I-can-ever-walk-again sex.

Nuzzling his lips down the curve of her cheek, Fane tugged her liquid body tight against his chest.

"Is that good or bad?"

She shook her head. "Don't try to fish for compliments. You don't need me to feed your outrageous ego."

"Ego?" Fane lifted his head to study her with a faux expression of outrage. "I'm a Sentinel. We are trained to be humble."

Serra felt her heart melt to another level of mush.

She'd thought she knew everything there was to know about Fane. After all, she'd been obsessed with him for years. But who the hell could ever have suspected that beneath his grim demeanor was a secret, mischievous man who loved to tease?

The tangible sensation of just how vulnerable she remained to the man she swore would never hurt her again had Serra instinctively scrambling to repair her defenses.

Great sex was great sex.

But offering up her heart to have it stomped on was a level of self-masochism she wasn't prepared to suffer through.

Not again.

"You really are hysterical," she murmured.

His dark gaze studied her suddenly guarded expression. "You can ask the monks if you don't believe me."

"I believe they tried to teach you humility, but I've yet to meet a Sentinel who isn't impossibly arrogant." She lowered her lashes to cover her expressive eyes. "Except for Arel. He has more charm and less ego than most."

She'd deliberately used the name of the one Sentinel she knew got under Fane's skin.

Anything to shatter this dangerous sense of intimacy.

She just hadn't expected his reaction to be quite so . . . epic.

With a low growl he was perched above her, his fists by her head and his knees on either side of her hips.

A rational part of her brain understood he was caging her without using any force that might make her feel trapped. Fane would die before he used his strength against her. But a less rational part understood that she might have struck a nerve that was better to avoid.

His expression was stark as he glared down at her wide eyes.

"Don't say his name again."

She met his fierce gaze, ignoring the ruthless beauty of his face. It'd been petty to mention Arel, but dammit, he kept slipping beneath the walls of her defense.

"You pushed me into his arms."

His jaw tightened, a blast of heat from his body searing over her naked body.

"Do you think that it didn't destroy something deep inside me every time I saw you together?"

"You made me feel unwanted."

He sucked in a harsh breath at the low words that were wrenched from her heart.

"Never again," he swore, lowering his head to seal his pledge with a tender kiss. "Trust me."

And that was the problem in a nutshell, she silently acknowledged, readily parting her mouth to deepen the kiss.

She trusted this man with her body and with her very life.

But her heart . . .

As if sensing her reluctance, Fane gave her bottom lip a punishing nip before soothing it with the tip of his tongue.

Serra moaned, a ready heat spreading through her body. Christ. One kiss and her legs were parting in open need for his possession.

But even as Fane lowered his body to press his stiffening cock against her lower stomach, his head was jerking toward the side.

She blinked, her body protesting as he leaped off the bed and pulled on a pair of camo pants.

"Fane?"

"Bas is coming down the hall."

Serra heaved a resigned sigh, heading to the bathroom for a quick shower before dressing in a pair of jeans and scooped stretchy top in a cheery shade of yellow. She added a pair of tennis shoes and pulled her hair into a high ponytail. God only knew where the bastard intended to drag them today.

She entered the sitting room in time to watch Fane pull open the door. He'd added a white muscle shirt to his camos and a heavy pair of boots, but his expression remained grimly unwelcoming.

Not that the too-handsome assassin seemed to care as he stepped into the room, a mocking smile curving his lips as he took in Fane's barely contained frustration.

"Am I interrupting?"

Serra moved forward, assuming Bas had a death wish. Why else would you taunt a Sentinel on the edge of a meltdown?

"What do you want?" she demanded.

Bas shrugged. "Kaede managed to discover three potential candidates."

Fane folded his arms over his chest. "Have you tried to contact them?"

"Why would I attempt something so pathetically simple as trying to contact them?" Bas asked, once again tempting death.

Fane took a step forward, the heat from his body blasting through the air.

"Don't press me."

Bas lifted a hand, his own composure so brittle Serra sensed it would take very little to shatter it into a million pieces.

Shit.

This could get real bad, real quick.

Reaching beneath the jacket of his smoke gray Armani suit that he'd matched with a pristine white shirt and cranberry silk tie, Bas pulled out a folded sheet of paper.

"I have my computer experts running searches on them and Kaede is out trying to track down any friends or family they might have in this area," he said, shoving the paper into Fane's hand.

The Sentinel unfolded the sheet with a frown. "What's this?"

"The addresses I want you to check out."

Fane muttered a curse, lifting his head to glare at the assassin.

"There's over twenty of them."

Twenty? Serra moved to glance at the paper in Fane's hand, her heart sinking.

Shit. She'd hoped when Bas had realized it might be a former colleague he would be able to pare down the list to one or two.

"Most we'll be able to search by just driving by," Bas assured them.

Serra stepped away from Fane. When she stood too close to the Sentinel her senses were consumed with the heat and scent and sheer power of him.

Nice when they were in bed.

But right now she wanted to concentrate on Bas.

Something had happened.

Something that had him so on edge he couldn't maintain his magical barriers.

"And the others?" she prompted.

The bronze eyes were carefully guarded. "They will be more difficult to investigate."

Fane narrowed his gaze. He didn't have her own psychic abilities, but he was a predator who studied how to read his prey.

He had to be able to sense that Bas was hiding something from them.

"How dangerous are the high-bloods we're tracking?" he asked.

"A dead Sentinel, although I have serious doubts

about him," Bas readily said. "A mediocre psychic. And a psychotic healer."

Serra studied the handsome face, wondering if he was trying to be funny.

"A dead Sentinel?"

"We never found the body," Bas said. "But the man who has contacted me wasn't trained by monks."

Fane didn't miss the small revelation. "You're sure it's a male?"

Bas gave a grudging nod. "Yes."

Serra continued to study the assassin, her senses searching for the cause of his tension.

"Which are you leaning toward?"

His lips twisted with an unmistakable bitterness. "I'm trying to keep an open mind."

Okay. Enough trying to be subtle.

If there was trouble, she needed to be prepared.

"Something happened."

The bronze eyes narrowed at the flat certainty in her voice.

"You can read me?"

"I don't have to. You're leaking."

Genuine indignation touched the lean face. "Leaking?"

Fane snorted. "You really have to stop using that word, *milaya*."

She rolled her eyes. Good God. She hated the word as much as anyone, but right now she didn't give a shit about political correctness.

"Your emotions aren't fully shielded," she clarified. "I can sense you're upset." She hesitated, hit by a sudden surge of emotion from the assassin. A chill inched down her spine. "And frightened."

Fury flared through his eyes. But it wasn't directed at Serra. At least not this time.

"I was allowed a brief conversation with my daughter."

Serra's heart missed a beat. "Was she hurt?"

"No. But the warning was clear. Time is running out," he said, his voice coated in ice. Not that it disguised the emotions stewing just below the surface. Abruptly, he turned back toward the door. "We have to go."

"Not yet." Fane stepped next to Serra. "Serra needs breakfast."

She lightly touched his arm. "It doesn't matter, Fane."

"It does." He sent her an impatient glance. "You haven't eaten in hours."

Bas turned back, the air sizzling with the emotions he could no longer contain.

"Have you forgotten I'm not the only one on the clock?" he rasped. "Serra—"

His taunt was cut short as Fane had him slammed against the wall, pressing an arm against the assassin's throat.

"Remind me again and I'll slice out your tongue."

The bronze eyes shimmered, as if the idiot was happy that he'd at last provoked Fane into a physical retaliation.

"Careful, Sentinel," he mocked. "You need me alive."

Fane's face was stripped of emotion, his body poised for violence.

"You're a fool if you believe I won't destroy you and everything you value to protect her."

Bas shoved at Fane's chest. "Do you think I feel any different about my daughter?"

Serra hissed in annoyance, not sure who was pissing her off more.

Bas for being a jerkwad. Or Fane for rising to the bait.

"Can you men measure the size of your dicks later?" she snapped, moving to glare into Fane's startled gaze. "There's a little girl out there who's depending on us to rescue her."

Both men grimaced, but it was Bas who answered. "She's right."

"Of course I'm right." She stepped back, her chin high. "I'm a woman."

Slowly Fane lowered his arm, allowing Bas to straighten from the wall.

The assassin carefully straightened his thousand dollar suit, at the same time reconstructing his shields.

Once they were in place he sucked in a deep breath and squared his shoulders.

"I know a place that serves the best chicken and waffles in town. It's on our way to the first location." He sent Fane a tight smile. "Satisfied?"

Fane planted his hands on his hips. "Not even close."

"Oh, for God's sake." Brushing past the assassin, Serra grabbed the purse she'd left on the table next to the door and headed into the hallway. "Let's go."

She had reached the elevator when the men caught up with her, stepping into the small interior as soon as the doors opened.

The two men entered behind her, Bas leaning over her shoulder to press his key card into the console and punched in his security code.

"Serra," he murmured softly.

"What?"

He spoke directly into her ear. "When we do have the time to measure our dicks, mine will be the biggest."

She closed her eyes, giving a weary shake of her head.

"Christ, this is going to be a long day."

It took Wolfe a minute to regain his balance as they arrived at the monastery in western Oklahoma.

Traveling by portal was always the fastest way to get

from point A to point B. Unfortunately, it usually left his stomach queasy and his knees weak.

In an effort to disguise his momentary weakness, Wolfe studied the exquisite hieroglyphs carved into the stone walls of the chapel. The same hieroglyphs that were tattooed on the guardian Sentinel who stood next to the copper post in the center of the floor.

Guardians were the only Sentinels that had the necessary magic to travel by portal, and only from monastery to monastery.

Who had created the magical pathways had been lost in time, although they'd recently discovered an ancient temple that was revealing the truth of the high-bloods beginnings. The scholars were busy trying to decipher the hidden glyphs.

Wolfe was sure it was all very fascinating. But he was a man who looked to the future, not the past.

With a grimace his gaze slid past the dark-haired Sentinel to the female who stood at his side with a cool composure.

She was still dressed in her casual jeans with a pair of running shoes and a jade sleeveless sweater. Her hair was pulled into a tight knot at the base of her neck, and her pale face was devoid of makeup.

There was nothing to draw attention to her, but she had only to walk into a room to take center stage. It was more than her compelling beauty and the power of her magic that sizzled around her. It was a calm confidence that made people follow her without question.

She could be dressed in rags and sitting in a gutter and she'd still look like a queen.

With a shake of his head, Wolfe turned toward the young man dressed in a rough brown robe who entered the chapel. The boy's lean face and recently shaved head marked him as a Sentinel in training, although he was still too young to have the tattooing of a guardian.

Smiling with a faint air of boredom, the novice met Wolfe's piercing gaze, his eyes widening as he caught the distinct streak of white that stood out like a banner on Wolfe's glossy black hair.

A flush stained the cheeks that still didn't need a razor as he cleared his throat.

"Tagos." He used the formal title, a hint of hero-worship in his voice. "Welcome to our abbey."

"I need a vehicle."

"Of course. And . . ." If the youth had been impressed by the sight of Wolfe, he was completely overwhelmed as he realized who was traveling with him. "Oh." With a smooth motion he dropped to his knees, his head bowed. "Mave. We weren't warned of your visit."

"It wasn't planned," she said, sending Wolfe a wry glance. "On your feet, son."

As hoped, the boy instinctively obeyed the command in Wolfe's voice, rising to his feet although his expression remained dazed.

"How can I be of service?"

Wolfe resisted the urge to roll his eyes. Novices.

"The car?"

"Oh . . . yes." He backed toward the door, his gaze remaining locked on the Mave as if she were some myth that had magically appeared in the quiet abbey. "Right away."

Lana held up a hand, her smile kind. "First I would like to speak with Father Valdez, if he's not too busy?"

"No . . . I mean . . . he's not too busy." The boy turned to bolt toward the opening. "Follow me."

Wolfe paused to hand over his bag along with Lana's to the guardian Sentinel, commanding him to have them taken to the garage so they could be loaded in the vehicle they would use while in Oklahoma. After that the Sentinel would find rooms and wait for them to return.

Then, with long strides he caught up with Lana as she followed the novice out of the chapel and down a narrow corridor lined with a stone colonnade. They at last came to a large bay that was decorated with fine frescos and silver candelabras shimmering in the early morning sunlight peeking through high arched windows.

"If you'll wait here I'll tell the abbot you're here," the novice offered.

"Thank you." Lana offered a small smile. "I didn't catch your name."

The smooth cheeks reddened, the poor schmuck falling beneath Lana's potent spell.

"Landon."

"Thank you, Landon."

With an awkward bow, the novice turned and disappeared through a medieval archway.

"I hope he doesn't trip on his tongue," Wolfe said wryly.

Lana shrugged, moving to study a fresco depicting a row of scribes bent over their desks to write on scrolls with their feather quills.

"He's young."

"You have that effect on every male, no matter what their age."

She turned to study him with an unreadable expression. "Do you have a point?"

Did he?

Not really.

Time for a change of subject.

See? He wasn't entirely stupid.

"Why do you want to speak with Father Valdez?"

"He's been the abbot of this monastery for many years,

he'll have a better knowledge of the area," she explained. "Hopefully he'll be able to help us pinpoint the epicenter of the blackout."

Wolfe nodded. It made sense.

"Do you know the high-blood responsible?"

She frowned. "It's still just a theory."

"Fine. Do you know the high-blood you suspect might be responsible?"

Lana paced toward the fresco on a far wall. This one had golden fields and what looked like angels dancing in the sky.

Wolfe didn't believe for a minute she was truly interested in the faded picture, but it conveniently kept him from reading her expression.

"Her name is Anna," Lana finally offered. "She was born in a time when her disruptive powers could be easily hidden by leaving her in remote locations."

Wolfe folded his arms over his chest. "She probably had no idea how quickly electricity would spread."

"Or that the invention of air travel would make it impossible to find a home even in the most isolated area where she wasn't at risk for causing destruction."

Wolfe felt a pang of sympathy for the high-blood. "What did you do?"

"As the world became more and more dependent on electricity we had to surround her with a stasis spell to mute her powers. Even then she has to remain in a special cell or the area becomes saturated with her magic."

"So someone removed her from the cell and then broke through the stasis spell."

Lana turned to face him. "No. She must still be in stasis. Otherwise the entire state would be feeling the effects."

Wolfe frowned, struck by a sudden thought. "How could they be moving her if she knocks out electricity?"

"I would suspect they're traveling the old-fashioned way," she said. "Horse and carriage."

Wolfe cursed, slowly beginning to realize the depths of the danger. God. If the female could cause blackouts and plane crashes while she was still wrapped in a stasis spell, what the hell would happen if she were walking around with no protective barrier?

Apocalypse.

"A perfect weapon for a mercenary," he rasped.

Lana gave a dip of her head. "That's what I fear."

Wolfe shoved his fingers through his hair. "Damn. What a mess."

"For everyone." Lana's expression tightened with regret. "Poor Anna. The healers tried to help, but they couldn't do more than put her in a deep sleep so she doesn't suffer."

"Mave." A tall, gray-haired man entered the bay, his still powerful body covered by a simple brown robe and his lined face wreathed with a pleased smile. "Welcome."

Moving forward with an innate grace, Lana held out her hands.

"Father Valdez."

The abbot took her hands, pulling her forward to press a kiss to her forehead.

"Michal," he insisted in gentle tones.

She returned his broad smile. "Michal."

Wolfe frowned. There was a familiarity between the two he hadn't been expecting. It wasn't the usual dazed appreciation of a man stunned by a beautiful woman.

This was more . . . friendly.

Almost like father and daughter.

"You know one another?" he asked.

Lana never allowed her gaze to waver from the older man. "Michal saved my life."

The abbot clicked his tongue. "Nothing so dramatic."

"What happened?" Wolfe demanded.

It was Lana who answered. "When I was just a child he took me into his abbey after my parents were killed."

"It was hardly a burden," Michal protested, his voice fond. "My brothers squabbled over the privilege of caring for her."

Wolfe's lips twisted into a wry smile. "Nothing has changed."

Lana ignored him as she concentrated on the abbot. "I need your help."

He gave her hands a last squeeze before dropping them and stepping back.

"You know you have only to ask."

"I'm afraid the Woodward blackout might be caused by a high-blood."

The older man looked startled. Obviously the same thought hadn't crossed his mind.

"Sabotage?"

Lana shrugged. "The high-blood would be unaware of the damage, but those holding her might be deliberately causing the damage. It's impossible to know at this point."

Turning, Michal pointed toward the novice who hovered in the doorway.

"Landon, bring us the latest satellite images."

"At once."

The boy disappeared and the abbot reached into the pocket of his robe to pull out a small electronic pad.

"I've been monitoring the situation, although I never suspected it might be the result of one of ours," he said, flicking his finger over the screen of his pad, no doubt searching through the latest news and police reports. He abruptly stiffened, lifting his head in surprise. "Oh."

Lana looked concerned. "Has it grown worse?"

"No. The opposite, in fact."

Wolfe wanted to believe that was good news, but the tension in the air only thickened.

"What does that mean?" he at last asked.

"The electricity has been restored to a few neighborhoods in Woodward," the abbot explained.

Wolfe met Lana's troubled gaze, immediately realizing what had happened.

"She's on the move," Lana breathed.

Chapter Eighteen

Serra shifted on the leather seat. After two hours of driving around the city of St. Louis her ass had fallen asleep. And worse, her brain was fried from the tidal wave of thoughts and emotions that had been bombarding her since leaving the hotel.

Thankfully, Fane had been seated beside her in the backseat of the black Mercedes with Bas in front driving. The Sentinel's ability to help her block out the background noise was the only reason she wasn't a babbling idiot by now.

Lifting a hand to rub her aching temple, Serra frowned as Bas turned off the main road and headed into an abandoned industrial complex. Then, pointing his phone toward an approaching warehouse, Bas slowed the car as a large steel door slowly lifted so they could pull inside.

They came to a halt in the center of the empty building.

"Why are we stopping?" Serra demanded.

She just wanted to be done so she could return to the hotel. Or even better, drive far enough from the city that she could find some peace.

"The other addresses you'll have to enter to fully search," Bas explained, shoving open the door of the car and stepping out. "I can't be seen with you without alerting the kidnapper that we're working together."

Exchanging a resigned glance with Fane, Serra opened the car door and stepped out. A swift mental sweep revealed they were alone. Unless, of course, there was an unseen enemy able to cloak their minds from her powers.

After last night a very real possibility.

"Why can't you use one of your illusions?" she demanded as Fane moved to her side, his arms folded over his massive chest.

Bas touched the knot of his silk tie before smoothing back his dark hair. Serra sensed it was a ritual he performed to soothe his inner demons.

"That was fine when I assumed we were dealing with a former client," he explained. "None of them are aware of my little talent. Anyone who worked for me would know that I can disguise my appearance."

Serra frowned. "So what do you intend to do?"

Bas glanced at his Rolex. "I told Kaede to wait half an hour before picking me up. Just in case we're being followed."

"And then?" she pressed.

"I have a friend in the illegal arms business." Bas smiled at her look of disgust. "He might be able to tell us who recently purchased a mind-stunner."

"Fine." Fane opened the door of the front passenger seat for her, his gaze moving toward the still-open warehouse door. "But tell your goons in the black Civic to keep their distance."

Bas made a sound of annoyance while Serra craned her neck to locate the car that was parked in the shadows of a nearby building.

"They're there for your protection," the assassin ground out.

Serra studied the lean face, taking note of Bas's tightly clenched teeth. Had he actually thought he could have them tailed without Fane spotting them?

"I thought you just said you wanted to avoid any connection to us?" she pointed out.

"The kidnapper would expect me to be keeping tabs on you," Bas said without apology.

Fane touched the handgun holstered at his side. "Warn them to stay away."

"Have you forgotten that the kidnapper has already tried to kill Serra once?"

"Exactly." Fane's voice assured Bas he wasn't screwing around. "Which means that anyone who gets too close is considered the enemy. Make no mistake, I'll kill first and ask questions later."

Bas stiffened. Serra wondered how many people ever dared to stand up to him.

She was going with zero.

Until now.

"They have no reason to get close unless you're being attacked," the assassin snapped, his gaze shifting toward Serra. "Or trying to do something stupid."

She arched a brow. "Something stupid?"

"Trying to contact Valhalla," Bas said. "Running away."

"Yeah right." Serra gave a disgusted shake of her head. "Where would I go?"

Bas shrugged, clearly at a breaking point despite his grim composure.

"Just being cautious."

Fane pointed a finger at the assassin. "Warn them to stay back or prepare for their funeral."

Bas carefully adjusted his cuffs, speaking to Serra. "I don't know how you stand spending so much time with him, my dear. He's barely housetrained."

Serra smiled. "He grows on you."

"Like fungus?" Bas smoothly suggested.

Fane rounded the car, his body rigid with the desire to hit someone.

"Shut up before I cut off your nuts," he warned Bas as he slid into the driver's seat and slammed shut the door.

Bas stepped back, his hands lifted in surrender. "He's all yours."

Serra slid into the passenger seat and closed the door before turning to study Fane's perfectly chiseled profile.

"All mine," she murmured, her heart giving a treacherous flutter.

"No doubt about it."

He sent her a smoldering glance before he shifted the car into gear and gunned the motor.

They turned in a tight circle and headed out of the warehouse at a speed that no doubt had their tails cursing.

Serra ignored the manly temper tantrum, instead concentrating on typing in the addresses they still had to search into the GPS system.

Once the voice began offering monotone directions to the first location, Serra settled back in her seat, trying to hide the pain stabbing into her brain.

Fane was just looking for an excuse to snap. Serra preferred to avoid bloodshed until they'd found Molly.

"Do you still intend to travel to Tibet?" she asked, hoping to soothe the Sentinel's seething frustration.

Fane slowed the car to a reasonable speed, following the directions to a residential neighborhood.

He sent her a brooding glance. "I think I've proven that I'll travel wherever you are."

She shook her head. There never had been any doubt he would rush to her rescue.

He would have done it for anyone.

"I mean after I'm no longer in danger."

"Exactly."

Her heart missed a strategic beat. Was he saying . . .

She gave a sharp shake of her head. This wasn't the fairy tale she'd created over the years.

It was real life that was messy and disappointing and didn't always end up with Prince Charming riding off with the heroine.

"You can't give up your future just to be with me."

His hands tightened on the driving wheel, his knuckles white with the strain.

"It's the only future I ever wanted," he said, his voice so low she barely caught the words. "I just never dreamed it would be possible."

Well . . . crap.

A rueful laugh was wrenched from her throat.

"For a man who spent years barely speaking more than two words, you're remarkably talented in saying just what I want to hear," she muttered.

He sent her a searching glance as they turned onto a narrow street that led to an increasingly grungy neighborhood.

"Is that a bad thing?"

In truth, she didn't know what it was.

And it didn't seem particularly wise to try and figure it out when she was smack-dab in the middle of a life and death situation.

"I was all prepared to spend the rest of my life as a tragic martyr," she said, trying to lighten the suddenly tense mood.

Fane paused, as if wanting to demand that she believe his sincerity. Then, with a twist of his lips, he reluctantly followed her lead.

"You'd make a terrible martyr," he informed her.

"Are you kidding me?" She sniffed, pretending to be offended. "If I put my mind to it, I could have poets writing epic poems to immortalize my tragicness."

"Tragicness?" He turned the car into a parking lot. "Is that a word?"

"If it's not, it should be."

Pulling into a fire lane, Fane put the car in park and turned off the engine. Only then did he glance in her direction.

"It doesn't matter since there's no way in hell you're ever getting rid of me."

A hot flash blasted through her. She wanted to blame it on Fane's damned ability to heat the air with his emotions. Or menopause.

She didn't want to think she was the kind of woman who responded to the "caveman" approach.

That was just . . . pathetic.

"You should try to make it sound more like a promise and less like a threat," she informed him with a sniff.

His lips twitched, as if aware of her renegade reaction. The annoying, oversized, tattooed brute.

"I'll work on it," he assured her, nodding toward the building in front of them. "This is the place."

Serra grimaced. The faded brick structure with a flat roof and industrial windows was one of three structures that made up the apartment complex. It looked like any other low-rent, going-nowhere housing unit to be found in every city in America. The sort of place that was on your downward slide to the gutter.

"Why can't it ever be a shopping mall?" she muttered.

Fane shuddered. An honest to God shudder at the mention of a lovely, sparkling, fashionista playground.

"I'd rather search through the sewers."

"Hmm." She gave a disapproving click of her tongue. "You're going to need a lot of training."

The dark eyes smoldered with a sudden heat as his gaze drifted down to the low scoop of her neckline.

"There's some training I enjoy more than others."

"So I've noticed." With a roll of her eyes she shoved open the car door. "Let's get this over with."

Fane quickly joined Serra as she exited the car, shooting a brief glance over his shoulder.

The black Civic didn't bother to be subtle as it slid to a halt at the far edge of the parking lot, the two Sentinels smart enough to keep their asses in the car.

With a cold glare, Fane turned his attention toward the building in front of them, searching for any hint of danger.

Not easy in an area where humans lived piled so closely together. His nose curled at the stench of rotting garbage from a nearby Dumpster, his attempt to catch the sound of movement blocked by the screech of a child being hauled toward the building by a frustrated mother.

He gave a shake of his head, glancing down at the paper in his hand. There was no way to adequately scout for potential enemies. The best he could do was get Serra in and out as quickly as possible.

"The apartment number is 512," he said, grudgingly headed up the crumbling sidewalk toward the nearest door.

"I think we should start at the top and work our way to the basement," Serra said, easily keeping pace. "That way we don't miss any janitor closets or empty apartments where a child could be hidden."

Reaching the building, he turned to study Serra's pale

face and the bruises that marred the delicate skin beneath her eyes.

She tried hard to disguise the toll this search was taking on her, but he wasn't fooled.

He could feel her pain as if it were his own.

Lifting his hand, he brushed his fingers lightly down the curve of her throat.

For high-bloods it was a gesture of affection.

"Do you have to search each floor?"

"Yes." She gave a decisive nod. "There are too many thoughts interfering for me to pick out just one from a distance."

Fane bit back a curse. "I was afraid of that."

She frowned, watching as he easily broke the lock and tugged open the door.

"Is something wrong?"

He nodded toward the long, narrow hallway lined by closed doors.

If an attacker suddenly jumped from one of the apartments there would be no room to fight. And he'd bet his left nut everyone in the building had a weapon. If the bullets started flying the humans wouldn't hesitate to join in the gunfight.

"It's a perfect location for an ambush."

She offered that special smile that sliced straight through his heart.

"I trust you to protect me."

"With my life," he pledged, holding out his hand. "Will it help you to have me mute the voices?"

She started to grab his offered hand before giving a regretful shake of her head.

"I can touch your back if it becomes too unbearable," she promised. "I know you prefer to keep your hands free."

His lips abruptly twisted as he recalled the hours he had spent with his hands filled with lush, female curves.

"Under most circumstances," he murmured.

She gave a choked laugh, eyeing him in surprise. "You are proving to be a man with many layers, Fane."

"You have no idea, Serra Vetrov." He leaned forward to steal a brief, but fiercely possessive kiss. Then straightening, he held her pain-darkened eyes. "Tell me when you're ready."

She sucked in a deep breath before giving a nod of her head.

"Ready."

Taking the lead, Fane headed toward the nearby stairs to the top floor.

Inside the building wasn't any better than its outside.

The stairway smelled of marijuana smoke and stale piss, the blare of TVs echoing through the stairwell. The once white walls were now yellowed and covered by graffiti while the windows were covered by chicken wire that blocked most of the late morning sunlight.

A depressing, bleak place that would suck the hope from the most optimistic person.

Finally reaching the top floor, Fane jerked open the thick fireproof door and moved down the long hallway. He kept his pace deliberately slow, knowing Serra needed time to process the various minds that were slamming into her.

He hated putting her through the relentless torture, but until he found a way to get rid of the toxin pumping through her bloodstream, he didn't have an option.

Dammit.

They reached the end of the hall before he glanced over his shoulder to study her pale face.

"Anything?"

She shook her head. "Not yet."

With a grimace, Fane pulled open the door to the opposite stairwell. They headed down to the fourth floor, entering the hallway that was an exact, depressing duplicate of the top floor.

"God," Serra breathed, placing her hand flat on his back.

"What's wrong?" He remained on high alert even as he allowed his powers to help her mute the overwhelming surge of human emotions.

"I'm beginning to appreciate your decision to travel to Tibet," she muttered. "Although I prefer a remote mountaintop instead of the monastery."

A lifetime with Serra on a remote Tibetan mountaintop? Hell yeah. Sign him up.

"Wherever you want," he assured her.

They finished the sweep of the floor and headed down the stairs. Entering the hallway, Fane had taken fewer than a dozen steps when the door beside him opened and a large male norm stepped out of his apartment.

The man was middle-aged with greasy black hair and a flabby body. His heavy face was ruddy from years of alcoholism and his eyes yellowed from liver damage. Dressed in a filthy muscle shirt and saggy sweatpants he could have been the poster child for "A Life Wasted."

Still, while he might be a pathetic specimen, even for a norm, Fane wasn't stupid enough to underestimate the man.

Despite the early hour he was clearly drunk and looking for trouble.

The bleary gaze landed on Serra, a mean smile curving his lips.

"Well, well," he slurred, hiking up the sagging sweatpants. "What a fine piece of ass."

Fane shifted to stand between the drunk and Serra. "Step back in your apartment."

The man appeared stupidly unaware he was staring death in the face. Or maybe he just didn't give a shit. Life had clearly been a long series of disappointments.

"Who the hell are you?" The jaundiced eyes narrowed. "The cops?"

"I won't tell you again," Fane warned. "Return to your apartment."

"Give me the bitch and I'll . . ." The idiot gave a high scream as Fane pulled his handgun and clipped his upper shoulder with a bullet. Slamming his hand over the small but painful wound, he flicked a shocked gaze over Fane's massive form. A belated fear made his thick jowls quiver. "What the fuck? Are you one of those freaks?"

Fane pointed the gun dead center at the man's chest. "Last chance."

"Shit." The man stumbled backward, the sharp stench of fresh piss assaulting Fane's nose. "I'm going."

The door slammed shut and Fane calmly returned his weapon to the holster.

"I could have dealt with him," Serra said, a hint of disappointment in her voice that she hadn't been allowed to screw with the man's mind.

The drunk truly had no idea how lucky he'd been. Fane gave him a flesh wound. Serra could have given him nightmares that would have haunted him for weeks.

"I know. I like to flex my muscles." Placing a hand on Serra's lower back, he urged her toward the distant door. "We need to pick up the pace."

"The idiot just pissed his pants," Serra said, shuddering in revulsion. "I doubt he's going to bother us."

"No, but he might have called the cops."

She grimaced. "Good point."

Gathering speed, she returned her attention to the various thoughts and emotions that assaulted her from the apartments.

They had nearly reached the end of the hall when she came to a sharp halt.

"Serra?" Fane studied the distracted frown that pulled her brows together. "Is it Molly?"

She remained silent, her eyes closed as she shifted through the mental noise only she could hear.

"No," she at last said, her eyes opening. "But there's someone following us."

Fuck. He glanced over his shoulder.

"One of Bas's goons?"

"I don't think so." She bit her bottom lip, unease abruptly darkening her eyes. "This feels like the men who attacked us last night."

"Shit."

Chapter Nineteen

Serra slammed down her mental barriers, focusing on the vague sense of menace that was growing stronger with every beat of her heart.

At her side, Fane moved several steps away, giving himself plenty of room to fight.

"How many?"

"Just one." She struggled to pinpoint the mind that was causing her growing unease. "A male."

"Which direction?"

"Below us."

Fane reached for her hand. "This way." He tugged her toward the door to the stairwell, only to come to an abrupt halt. "Wait."

"Why?"

"I don't want our tails to spot us leaving the building."

Serra stared at him in confusion. "You think Bas's Sentinels are working with the kidnapper?"

"Doubtful." He shrugged, moving to lean his head against the door of the nearest apartment. When he was convinced it was empty he straightened and with one shove of his shoulder he had the door swinging open, the frame shattering beneath the impact. "But I want to have a little talk with our stalker," he continued, leading her into the empty apartment. "Alone."

Serra made a sound of disbelief as they crossed the puke yellow carpet and entered the back bedroom.

Less than twelve hours ago she'd watched Fane take a bullet. It wasn't an experience she was anxious to repeat.

"Are you crazy?" she snapped. "The last time they got close to us we nearly died."

He moved directly to the window, snapping the lock as he shoved it open.

"They caught us by surprise." He leaned out the window to scan the back lot. There wasn't much to see. A row of Dumpsters, an overgrown lot that was framed by a chain link fence, and a rusty tin shed. "This time we'll have the upper hand."

Upper hand? Yeah, right.

They hadn't had the upper hand since leaving Valhalla.

"What's the plan?" she grudgingly demanded.

"We lead our shadow into an isolated location and ask him a few questions."

She glanced at his grim profile, knowing there wasn't a chance in hell she could convince him not to take the risk. Not when he believed it might help her.

"Why not include Bas's Sentinels?" she suggested, willing to play nice with their unwanted tails. Anything to keep Fane from being injured again. "They'd provide extra muscle."

He gave a shake of his head. "I want Molly in our hands before Bas realizes we have a lead."

She studied his tense expression. There was something he wasn't telling her.

Something that wasn't going to make her happy.

She hesitated before demanding an answer.

As a woman who could read the thoughts of others, she

thoroughly approved of the old saying that ignorance was bliss.

Unfortunately, she had a terrible premonition that on this occasion sticking her head in the sand wasn't going to be an option.

Gripping the sill of the window, she forced the question past her stiff lips.

"Why?"

He turned to meet her searching gaze. "We have no guarantee Bas will remove the toxin after he has Molly back," he said, reluctantly sharing his fear. "In fact, it makes more sense to kill both of us and make our bodies disappear."

The breath was jerked from her lungs. "He wouldn't."

Fane studied her in disbelief, as if he couldn't believe she was so gullible.

"He's a mercenary without honor or ethics," he growled. "There's no way in hell he'll let us return to Valhalla and reveal his crimes."

"God." She felt dizzy. Maybe she was gullible. Of all the things she'd been stressing over, the fact that Bas might betray her hadn't even entered her mind. Shit. "I never considered the possibility he wouldn't remove the spell."

Fane's eyes hardened until they looked like polished ebony.

"Oh, he's going to remove it. One way or another." The lethal promise in his voice made Serra shiver, but before she could make him swear he wouldn't put himself in danger, he was pointing toward the rusty shed. "Can you sense if the shed is empty?"

She gave a shake of her head, trying to clear her thoughts. She didn't have time to panic.

First they had to survive the encounter with the unknown stalker.

"I think so."

"Good."

The word had barely fallen from her lips when Fane was grasping the edges of the sill and with one smooth motion was leaping through the open window.

"Shit."

Serra thrust her head through the opening, watching as Fane hit the ground. Despite the thirty-foot drop, he landed as light as a cat, swiftly straightening to hold out his arms.

"I'll catch you." He frowned as she hesitated. "Trust me."

"It's not you I don't trust," she muttered, awkwardly putting one leg over the sill. "It's gravity."

"Just close your eyes and jump."

Her lips twisted at his command. He seemed to be asking her to do that a lot lately.

Of course, leaping through the window was a lot safer than leaping with her vulnerable heart.

Wiggling her second leg through the opening, she didn't give herself time to hesitate, leaning forward until she was flying through the air.

She barely had time to process the air brushing over her cheeks or her heart crashing against her ribs before she was landing in a pair of rock-hard arms.

"See," he whispered in her ear, pressing her close to his chest. "I'm not going to drop you. Not ever."

She forced open her eyes, meeting his steady gaze. "I'll admit you're useful on occasion."

He smiled with resigned amusement, then slowly he lowered her to the ground, careful to make sure she had her balance before removing his arms.

"Stay near the edge of the building," he commanded, leading her toward the end of the apartment complex.

He halted when they ran out of sidewalk, peering around

the corner. Only when he was sure the coast was clear did he jog toward the shed.

Serra followed behind him, rounding the building to discover him yanking the padlock off the door as if it were made of plastic.

But instead of entering the building, he gave a jerk of his head toward a nearby Dumpster.

"I want you to wait over there."

Serra grimaced in horror. "You can't be serious?"

He leaned down to press a swift kiss to her mouth. "Hurry."

"Fine, but if you get hurt—"

He cut off her warning with another fierce, way-too-short kiss, then with a firm push he had her headed toward the Dumpster.

She muttered a curse beneath her breath, but reluctantly obeyed his command.

When it came to the psychic world, she was in charge. When it came to the physical world, Fane was in charge.

He was bigger, stronger, faster, and far better trained as a warrior.

Besides, if she was stubborn enough to refuse to follow his lead, there was a good chance she was going to get him hurt.

Ducking behind the Dumpster, she slapped a hand over her mouth and nose, struggling not to heave up the chicken and waffles she'd consumed for breakfast.

How was she supposed to concentrate when she was being drowned in the stench of week-old garbage?

With an effort, she shut down her physical senses, and instead concentrated on her mental ability.

She easily picked up the void that surrounded Fane. She could monitor his physical presence, but his tattoos prevented any psychic intrusion.

Only a few minutes later, she could detect the mind of their stalker. Just as on the previous night, she was aware of the sense of approaching malevolence. A dark malice that was almost tangible.

He was close. Really close.

On the point of trying to penetrate into the stranger's mind it abruptly went dark, along with the weird evil vibe.

With a frown, she shifted to peek around the edge of the trash, not surprised to discover Fane reaching down to grab an unconscious man and toss him over his shoulder.

The warrior had obviously concealed himself on the roof and dropped onto the unsuspecting man when he passed beneath him. That would be enough to knock anyone's brain offline.

Serra could only hope that it came back on.

And soon.

Leaving her hiding spot, Serra joined Fane as he reached the door and pulled it open. She frowned as she studied the unconscious man draped down his back.

He looked surprisingly young. Under thirty, with black hair cut short and a body that was whipcord lean. His features were pale, revealing he spent little time in the sun. Of course, a killer would feel more comfortable creeping around in the dark, wouldn't he?

Or maybe he was pale because he was dead.

"You didn't kill him, did you?"

"He'll live," Fane muttered, not particularly concerned with the man's impression of a wet noodle.

Together they entered the shed, Fane pulling the door behind him before dropping the stalker's limp body on the dust-covered floor. Then, with brisk steps he was taking a quick inventory of the shadowed interior, shoving aside oilcans, rakes, shovels, and long neglected lawn mowers.

Once he was certain they were alone, he turned to toss a small object toward her.

Serra instinctively caught the weapon that was the size of her hand and shaped like a Taser. A closer inspection revealed the electrical impulses were designed to fill the air, not to press against someone's body.

She grimaced. "Is this the mind-stunner?"

"Yep." Fane knelt beside the stalker, removing a thin wire from his pocket and slipping it around the man's neck.

One yank and the wire would slice off a head.

Serra ignored his efficient movements. She was far more concerned with the nasty device in her hand.

With a sound of disgust, she dropped the mind-stunner on the ground and began crushing it with her heel. Over and over, she stomped on the weapon, not halting until it was beyond any hope of repair.

Glancing up, she discovered Fane watching her with a faint smile.

"Feel better?"

She shrugged. "Yes."

"You know, that might have come in handy."

With a hiss, Serra kicked away the broken pieces. "I would never use a nasty device like that on one of our people."

He studied the stubborn line of her jaw. "You can't always be so noble when it comes to war."

She knew that he spoke the truth. Hell, they'd barely survived the attack by the necromancer.

She still felt no regret for the destruction of the weapon.

"Maybe not, but I won't become my enemy," she said, her chin lifting to a defensive angle.

"And that's why I love you," Fane murmured, his voice so soft she barely heard him.

She caught her breath in disbelief.

Holy crap. Did he just say what she thought he said?

She licked her suddenly dry lips, studying the stark beauty of his face.

"Did you just say the 'L' word?"

His gaze slid down to linger on her damp lips. "That's probably a discussion we should postpone to a more appropriate time and setting."

Her heart fluttered. Just as if she were one of those girly-girls.

But she didn't care.

She'd waited to hear those words for so long.

An eternity.

She cleared her throat. "What kind of setting would you prefer?"

He kept his voice low. "Music, candles, wine."

She lifted a teasing brow. "Flowers?"

"White lilies," he answered without hesitation.

Oh hell. He knew.

White lilies had always been her favorite.

"You're right," she said with a shaky sigh. "This isn't the place."

In the blink of an eye, he was back into Sentinel mode, his face as hard as granite.

"You can wait outside and keep watch."

She scowled. "No. Way."

He sent her a dark glare. "Serra, this guy isn't going to give up info without . . . encouragement."

He didn't have to explain what he meant by encouragement.

"I'm not completely naive," she assured him.

"It's not that." He held her gaze. "I don't want you to see."

"Trust me, I don't want to see either," she said. Not because watching Fane beat the shit out of the stranger would change her opinion of him. Nothing on this earth could do that. She simply refused to allow him to take the risk. "Have you considered the possibility this man might be spelled like the others?"

"I don't intend to kill him."

"That doesn't mean he won't have a trigger to kill himself."

He narrowed his eyes. "What do you suggest?"

"Let me tranq him."

Fane barely managed to battle back his instinct to shut down the suggestion. In fact, the "oh hell no" was on the tip of his tongue before he managed to swallow the words.

It wasn't just because he knew that it would fracture the fragile trust she was slowly beginning to offer. Serra would never tolerate a man who tried to interfere with her talents. Not if she thought they could help.

But because he was well trained enough to realize when it was better to use cunning than brute strength.

He could torture the man until he would admit to anything Fane wanted to hear.

By going into his mind there was the very real possibility they could discover the identity of the kidnapper.

"Okay," he grudgingly muttered. "Just don't go too deep. He could have a mental trap waiting for a psychic."

She sent him a wry glance. "You concentrate on keeping him from escaping and let me do my job, big boy."

He studied her with a faint smile. "Big boy?"

Her gaze made a slow inventory of his broad shoulders before moving to take in his chest.

"You are big." Her gaze slid lower. "In all the right places."

His cock hardened in instant reaction to her soft words.

As if hoping to prove just how big it really could be.

Shit. It seemed entirely unfair that she had such complete control over his body.

Giving a resigned shake of his head, Fane returned his attention to the stalker sprawled on the ground. His hand tightened on the thin wire that was wrapped around the man's neck as he caught the sound of a low moan.

"He's starting to wake up." The warning had barely left his lips when Serra was moving forward to kneel beside the stranger, her hand reaching to press against his cheek. Fane clenched his teeth, his body vibrating with the intense need to yank her away from the man. Who knew how dangerous he might be? "What are you doing?" he rasped.

"It helps if I'm touching him."

Fane was distracted as the man's eyes snapped open and he was shoving himself to a seated position.

Pulling on the wire, Fane stopped just short of cutting through the man's flesh. One more jerk and the head would be flying across the shed. But the man wasn't even aware he was in danger. Not when Serra was leaning forward to capture his confused gaze, her soft voice compelling him to obey.

"Shh. Easy," she murmured, holding his face in her hands. "That's it. Just relax."

Fane watched as the man's face went slack. He wasn't entirely certain what Serra was doing, but he knew that she was able to put him in a state of deep relaxation, making it impossible for him to conjure magic or to fight against her intrusion.

Or that was the theory. On this occasion, the stalker remained limp, but his pale eyes flashed with a mocking amusement.

"You can't . . . get in," he slurred.

Fane frowned in concern. "Serra?"

"He's right," she admitted through gritted teeth. "There's a barrier."

Shit. Of course there was. "Magical?"

"Yes." She glanced up with an expression of frustration. "I can't force my way past it without killing him."

Fane shrugged, a smile of anticipation curling his lips. "Then we do it the old-fashioned way."

Serra reached up to touch his hand, keeping him from tightening the noose.

"Hold on."

"What?"

"I can't get in, but I can read what comes out," she said.

Read what comes out? He shook his head in confusion.

"Was that supposed to make sense?"

She returned her attention to the stranger, keeping her hands pressed to the sides of his head.

"Just ask a question."

Okay. Clearly she had a plan.

Giving a quick glance through the window of the shed to make sure no one was trying to sneak up on them, Fane concentrated on the information they needed from this man.

"Why are you following us?" he demanded.

The pale eyes held the cold indifference of a true psychopath.

"Fuck you."

Serra sucked in a sharp breath. "Check his back pocket."

Fane didn't hesitate, bending down to pull out the thin, disc-shaped object that was clearly designed to be strapped around a hand with the disc pressed against the palm.

"Dammit," Fane growled, shoving the object into the front pocket of his camos. "Do they have a treasure chest of banned weapons?"

"What is it?" Serra kept her gaze locked on the stranger,

clearly prepared to capture any thought that slipped past the barrier.

"A disrupter."

"What does it do?"

Fane shuddered, all too easily able to visualize the man sneaking up behind Serra and placing the weapon against her back.

"At close range it would stop your heart," he said, his voice harsh. "To the world it would have looked as if you'd died of a heart attack."

She grimaced, but her courage never faltered.

He wished he could say the same.

Goddammit. He was tired of people wanting this woman dead. He'd give everything he possessed to grab her in his arms and flee as fast and as far as possible.

"Ask another question," she commanded.

Fane waited until the icy blue gaze turned in his direction.

"Who are you?"

"A soldier." A cold smile. "Like you."

Fane curled his lips. "You're nothing like me."

"Release me and let's see who is the better fighter."

"Who hired you?"

"I don't know his name."

"Wrong answer," Fane retorted, pulling the wire just hard enough to slice through the first layers of skin.

"Wait, Fane." Serra halted his fun. "He really doesn't know."

Fane instantly sensed the tension in her voice. "What do you see?"

"He was contacted by a third party."

"Name?"

Her brows drew together, as if she were struggling to get a clear image.

"The Dark Side."

"That's a name?" Fane asked in confusion.

"A place," she corrected. "An empty factory . . . I think." She abruptly stiffened, her breath hissing between her teeth. "Damn."

"What's wrong?"

"He was blindfolded when he was picked up from his apartment," Serra explained her annoyance. "He has no idea where it is."

Fane muttered a curse, but he refused to be outsmarted by some mysterious kidnapper. There had to be a way to get to the person responsible for taking Molly.

"How were you contacted?" he abruptly demanded.

"There was a man," the stalker said. Then, without warning a smile curved the man's lips as his eyes rolled back in his head and he fell backward, dead as a fucking doornail.

"Shit," he rasped, kneeling beside the startled Serra.

She yanked back her hands, her expression baffled. "What happened?"

"The trigger we were worried about wasn't magical," he admitted, furious at his stupid oversight. Reaching down, he shoved the man's mouth open, his nose curling at the foul stench. "He had poison hidden in a false tooth," he said in disgust, giving a shake of his head.

"Poison?" She sent him a startled glance. "Who does that besides cheesy characters from action movies?"

"Obviously this guy," Fane muttered. He couldn't have known the man had a suicide tooth. But that didn't keep him from being pissed the man was dead. "He must have taken the poison as soon as he realized he wasn't going to escape."

Serra's expression became distracted as her mind picked up an approaching danger.

"Someone's coming," she whispered.

Fane rose to his feet, picking up the unmistakable vibe of high-bloods approaching from the parking lot.

"Sentinels," he said, knowing it had to be the two goons sent by Bas. They must have realized they'd left the apartment building and had come looking for them. The last thing he wanted was to get caught with the stalker. Bas would know exactly what they'd been up to. "Let's get out of here."

"What about the . . ." Serra's words broke off as she straightened and waved a hand toward the corpse.

"He's no doubt triggered to self-destruct," Fane reminded her.

She shuddered, heading toward the door. "Convenient."

Fane gave a last glare at the idiot hit man who'd denied him the knowledge he needed to protect Serra.

"Not really."

Chapter Twenty

Bas's neck ached from the afternoon spent at his computer.

He was familiar with the big names in illegal arms, and the businesses they used to whitewash their ill-gotten gains. Still, he'd nearly missed the bank transfers to a particularly nasty dealer south of the border. They'd been shifted through more than one business and labeled as payment for medical supplies. It was only because the name of the corporation caught his eye that he pulled up the account for closer inspection.

"What the hell?" he muttered, clicking through the bank accounts as Kaede crossed the floor of his office to glance over his shoulder.

"Have you found something?"

"I've tracked all these bank transfers to one account in Kansas City."

"Kansas City?"

"Girard Import and Export." Bas frowned. "Where have I heard that name?"

"It is familiar," Kaede agreed.

Bas pulled up the information on the corporation, his

breathing hissing between clenched teeth at the list of stockholders.

"Damn."

Kaede instinctively reached to palm the handgun holstered at his lower back.

"What's wrong?"

"The Brotherhood," he rasped, his voice laced with disgust.

Kaede made a sound of surprise. "Do you think it's possible?"

Bas frowned in confusion.

Did he?

Nearly fifty years ago, he'd stumbled across the secret organization.

It wasn't the usual hate group filled with norms who needed someone to blame for their shitty lives. Or the unstable high-bloods who hated the fact they were mutants.

This organization was well funded, dangerously armed, and, most disturbing of all, they seemed to have the means to actually sense high-bloods.

A toxic combination.

Bas kept informal tabs on those he'd identified as part of the group, but since they seemed more interested in their own nasty politics within the organization, he'd done nothing to alert Valhalla to their presence.

If they ever became too dangerous, he'd decided to take care of them on his own.

Now he had to wonder if they'd grown tired of their infighting and decided to strike against him and his people.

"They've made a pledge to destroy high-bloods, but I assumed their tactics would be far less subtle," he said slowly.

Kaede shrugged. "I agree. When I investigated them

they seemed more interested in sweeping genocide rather than guerrilla warfare. Still, they're one of the few groups crazy enough to sacrifice an innocent child."

True. Bas had the sense that they were twisted enough to sacrifice their own mothers if they thought it would serve their greater purpose.

Morons.

Still, he remained unconvinced.

"But what would be the gain?"

Kaede considered for a long minute. "If they had control of Anna then they could prove to the world just how dangerous high-bloods are," he at last suggested. "It could spark a civil war."

Bas tapped a finger on his desk. "Maybe."

"What?" Kaede prompted, clearly sensing Bas's distraction.

"It doesn't feel right."

"Then maybe one of their members decided to go rogue," Kaede offered.

"That's a possibility," Bas conceded. Greed was at the core of most atrocities committed by both norms and high-bloods. "Fanaticism might feed the soul, but it doesn't buy you a Maserati." Not a bad theory. So why did the doubt remain lodged in the center of his gut? He eventually hit on the obvious flaw. "But how would they know of Molly?"

Kaede straightened with a grimace. "A good question."

There was a light tap on the door, interrupting their conversation.

Bas shut down the computer before pressing a button on the desk that released the lock.

"Enter," he commanded.

The door was shoved open to reveal two Sentinels. The first to step into the room was Aldo, a large, bulky man with blond hair buzzed next to his skull and pale eyes that sparkled with more enthusiasm than intelligence. The second man, Damis, was Aldo's exact opposite. A small man with a slender body and dark narrow face, he had black hair smoothed into a tail, and deep brown eyes that glowed with a ruthless intelligence.

They were both dressed in the standard uniform of jeans and T-shirts, but Damis had a diamond stud in one ear and a spider-web tat on the side of his neck.

"Well?" Bas demanded, rising to his feet.

"The psychic and her guardian have returned to the hotel," Damis said.

Bas studied his warriors, knowing they wouldn't have bothered to check in unless they had something to report.

"Did they discover anything?"

Damis spoke for both of them. Aldo wasn't much for conversations. Not if they had to include more than grunts.

"They claim they didn't."

Bas moved around the desk. "But you suspect otherwise?"

"When we arrived at the first apartment building they disappeared for longer than it should have taken to search the place."

Bas was instantly alert. Had they been meeting with someone from Valhalla?

"Did you follow them?"

"Of course." Damis's lips thinned. "We'd just tracked them to an abandoned shed when they took off in your car."

"What happened?"

"We followed them until they'd searched the rest of the addresses and returned to the hotel."

Bas wasn't impressed. He paid his employees an obscene

salary because he demanded complete loyalty and because they were very, very good at what they did.

"That's it?" he demanded.

"No, we returned to the shed to see if we could find any clue as to why they'd been in there."

Ah. Now they were getting somewhere.

"Did you find anything?"

The Sentinel reached into his back pocket to remove a shattered Taser.

"This."

Bas held out his hand, allowing Damis to dump the pieces of plastic and electronics into his palm.

"What the hell?" He frowned as he realized his first impression had been wrong. This wasn't a Taser. It was far, far more dangerous. He lifted his head to meet Damis's dark gaze. "It's a broken mind-stunner. How did it get in the shed?"

"We think the guardian and psychic must have followed someone in there and overpowered them," Damis answered, although Aldo managed a nod of agreement. "Probably a hit man."

"But why . . ." Bas snapped his teeth together. Shit. He didn't have to ask why Fane would have wanted to get his hands on the hit man. And why he hadn't wanted Bas to know that he'd spoken with the enemy. "That son of a bitch," he growled, headed for the door. "Kaede, get the car."

It hadn't been Wolfe's best day.

Driving a Jeep with the windows down along the dusty road in one hundred plus degree temperatures would be at the bottom of anyone's list of fun things to do.

Add in his acute awareness that he had the safety of the

leader of all high-bloods in his hands, and it wasn't any wonder his head was beginning to ache.

Then again, it wasn't his worst day.

He'd once spent an entire afternoon being skinned by his uncle who believed he had a demon inside him.

Hard to top that.

They'd traveled several hours in silence when Wolfe brought the vehicle to a halt, his senses on full alert.

"Here," he murmured.

Lana peered out the open window, searching the flat, desolate ground with occasional corn fields and even more occasional groves of trees for some sign of danger.

"Do you sense something?"

Wolfe put the Jeep in park, then, leaning back in his seat, he closed his eyes and breathed deeply of the hot breeze swirling through the vehicle.

He ignored the familiar scents of dry grass and choking dust and the less familiar stench of a distant oil well. And even the occasional whiff of horse dung. Despite the fact it was the twenty-first century, there were still a surprising amount of local ranchers who not only bred and raised horses, but used them as their preferred form of transportation.

It was less difficult to ignore the intoxicating hint of vanilla that teased at his senses.

He had an almost irresistible urge to lean sideways so he could bury his face in the curve of his companion's neck and suck in the delicate scent.

Thankfully, he wasn't in the mood to be hit by some nasty spell that might give him boils in sensitive places or make him think he was the Queen of England.

Two things quite possible when you ticked off a witch.

Finally locating the scent that had first caught his attention, he concentrated on the swiftly fading clues.

"There was more than one high-blood in this area."

"How do you know?" Lana demanded.

He opened his eyes, glancing at her with his usual arrogance.

"I'm a Sentinel."

"Hmm." She rolled her eyes. "Do you want to get out?"

"Yes."

Together they climbed out of the Jeep, Wolfe following the footprints toward a circle of rocks while the Mave studied the hazy horizon. Her natural telepathy allowed her to detect if there were any human minds within a mile or two radius.

She was better than any scout he could have brought with him, although he'd be damned if he'd admit it.

Confident when she remained silent that there weren't any hidden enemies, Wolfe concentrated on the distinct signs of recent activities.

Circling the rocks, he squatted down to touch the scorched earth.

"There was someone camped here."

Lana made one last mental sweep of the empty landscape before turning to join him.

"How recent?"

"Within hours."

She nodded, her brows pulling together as she held up a hand. Wolfe straightened, sensing her sudden tension.

"What is it?"

A faint shiver shook her body. "Magic."

Wolfe pulled his gun. Not that it would do a damn thing against magic. But he felt better with it in his hands.

"A trap?" he asked.

"No." She lowered her hand, but the frown remained. "Residue."

Wolfe had heard that there were a few spells that contained

enough magic to linger long after the caster had released them. The thought had always sent a chill down his spine.

"And you can still feel it?"

She nodded. "It was a powerful spell."

Wolfe straightened, glancing around the remote area. There couldn't be many reasons for a group of high-bloods to be here. And even fewer reasons for a witch to waste her energy on a spell that was powerful enough it could linger for hours.

"Can you recognize what it was?"

"A binding spell."

Wolfe studied her pale, beautiful face in confusion. "To hold someone against their will?"

"Or to keep them in stasis."

Ah. That made sense if Anna had been with them.

"You believe it might be the high-blood we're searching for?" he asked.

She grimaced. "I'm afraid it might be."

Wolfe swallowed a sigh of resignation. Of course the blackout had to be caused by a high-blood who had the potential to destroy the entire electrical grid.

It couldn't possibly have been the result of a squirrel getting into the transformer.

He shoved away the inane thought. Nothing mattered now but locating Anna and halting whatever nefarious scheme Bas had going.

"Why would they come to this location?"

Lana glanced in his direction, but her expression remained distracted.

"What do you mean?"

Wolfe waved a hand toward the emptiness that surrounded them. There was an unmistakable beauty in the stark landscape, but it wasn't prime terrorist territory.

"There's no nuclear power plants in the area," he said. "No multimillion-dollar bank. No large airport. What would be the target?"

"I don't know."

Wolfe paced toward the edge of the road, feeling oddly restless. Was it the lingering spell? Or just an unwanted premonition of bad things to come?

"If Bas is behind this he has to have a reason for bringing Anna here," he pointed out.

Lana made a sound of disgust. "The only thing that motivates him is power."

Okay. So what the hell would a megalomaniac gain by bringing a potential time bomb to this place at this time?

He was shifting through the various possibilities while his gaze studied the footprints that remained clearly outlined in the loose dust.

Abruptly he realized that there had been more people at the campsite than he'd originally suspected. As well as a heavy wagon being pulled by at least two horses.

"There are at least four separate footprints here," he muttered, wondering if there was more to Anna's reappearance in the world after so many years of being hidden. "Is it possible she was stolen from Bas?"

"I suppose so." The Mave sounded even less convinced by his suggestion than he felt.

Wolfe grimaced, trying to imagine himself as the kidnapper with a priceless treasure he'd just stolen. It wasn't hard. He'd been one of the most feared criminals in the Middle East before he'd been taken in by the monks.

It didn't take long to pinpoint a major flaw in his theory.

"But if they're on the run, why would they expose their location by knocking out the power for a fifty-mile radius?"

"It could have been accidental."

Caught off guard by Lana's soft words, he turned to face her. "Accidental?"

"They must have been stopped here for several hours if I can feel the residue of the spell," she explained. "Without a stable cell around Anna, she would have swiftly started causing damage."

He met her steady gaze. "So this particular spot might just have been a pit stop?"

"Yes."

Which meant they weren't any closer to knowing who had Anna or why she was being used to black out small towns in the middle of nowhere.

"Great."

Lana remained as cool and unflappable as ever, but the pale green eyes held a concern she couldn't entirely disguise.

"Can you track them?"

If anyone else had asked the question Wolfe would have slugged them for doubting his skills. He was one of the finest trackers in the world.

Lana, however, wasn't insulting his talent as a Sentinel.

She was asking if he was willing to take the responsibility for finding a high-blood who had the potential to create utter chaos.

"I can, but it will have to be on foot," he informed her.

Now that he had a visual on the wagon tracks, he was not going to risk losing it.

"Fine," Lana said, surprising him by her ready agreement. "They won't be able to move very fast. Not only because they're traveling by wagon, but it will drain the energy of the witches to keep Anna's powers contained."

"Good. You stay with the vehicle and I'll—"

"No."

Wolfe hissed in frustration. Of course it couldn't be that easy.

"Lana."

She rested her hands on her hips, her spine stiff. "This isn't up for debate."

He stepped toward her, ignoring the edge of frigid authority in her voice.

"You know I have the power to shut down this hunt the minute I believe it's too dangerous."

She narrowed her eyes. "Are you claiming it's too dangerous?"

"I'm saying that the Mave isn't going to get killed on my watch," he growled.

Her lips parted to remind him who gave the orders. She hadn't reached her position by allowing anyone to tell her what to do.

But, neither had he.

And they both knew that he had the right to protect her if he thought it necessary.

With an effort, she forced herself to use logic instead of brute force to make her point.

"Wolfe, we both know this danger is bigger than both of us." Her voice was soft, but unyielding. "If Anna isn't contained her powers will eventually create enough havoc to start a nationwide panic. Once that happens then the humans will begin to look for someone to blame." She didn't have to spell out that Valhalla would be the focus of the humans' hatred. The norms had wanted an excuse to attack them since the high-bloods had gone public. "I've worked too long for peace to allow anything or anyone to threaten my efforts." She deliberately paused, holding his gaze. "Either you're working with me or against me."

Shit.

He couldn't argue against her reasoning.

The man inside him might rebel, but he was also the Tagos, leader of the Sentinels.

He had to use whatever weapon necessary to eliminate the threat to his people. And however he might want to deny the truth, Lana was his most powerful of weapons.

"Stubborn female," he breathed.

Wise enough not to gloat, Lana moved toward the Jeep to grab a leather satchel and a large bottle of water.

"We should get going," she said as she settled the strap of the satchel over her shoulder. "The sooner we have Anna in our custody the better."

He grimaced, collecting his own gear. Ammo clips, a dagger he sheathed at his hip, and a second handgun.

The essentials.

Then he pulled his cell phone from his pocket. "We're going to need backup," he muttered, waiting for the guardian Sentinel that had brought them to the monastery to pick up.

Giving him concise commands to collect three more warriors and follow the direction of the GPS signal connected to Wolfe's phone, he ended the call and studied the dusty road that stretched before them.

"It would help if we knew where they're going," he muttered, not particularly happy at the thought of walking several miles in the fierce heat.

"Or what they intend to do when they get there," Lana responded.

Wolfe grabbed the last bottle of water and started down the road.

"No shit."

Chapter Twenty-One

Fane led Serra from the elegant restaurant just off the lobby of the hotel. The aggravating female had squawked when he'd insisted she sit down and eat a decent meal, claiming they had no time to waste on food. So he'd simply tugged her into the restaurant and forced her into a seat, ordering enough food to feed a dozen Sentinels.

He'd never realized just how ready she was to ignore the needs of her body when she was concentrating on her work. Probably a good thing since it would have made him nuts not to be able to care for her.

Now he wasn't going to tolerate her indifference. If she wouldn't take care of herself, he damned well would.

Period.

She wasn't happy with his insistence, but she did manage to clear an entire plate of chicken parmesan and half a loaf of bread.

A bottle of wine later and she'd mellowed enough to allow him to lead her to the elevator without kicking him in the ass.

He was taking that as a win.

Entering the elevator, Fane went rigid, catching the unmistakable scent of a high-blood. On the point of shoving

Serra out of the small cubicle, he abruptly recognized the scent.

Pressing the doors closed, he used his powers to disable the cameras and stood back as the elevator smoothly headed upward. Within seconds a panel in the roof was tugged aside and Marco was dropping through the opening to land lightly on the carpeted floor.

He was dressed in black jeans and a black tee that revealed the dragon tattoo around his neck. His lean face was grim as he turned to study Serra with his ice blue eyes.

Unprepared for his abrupt arrival, Serra gave a small gasp of shock. "Good God, Marco," she rasped, pressing a hand to her heart. "You scared me."

The Sentinel gave a lift of his dark brows. As a hunter, Marco didn't have the same magical protection as Fane. Serra should have picked up his presence the minute she stepped into the elevator.

"You didn't sense me?" the older man chided. "Sloppy, Serra. Very sloppy."

Serra sent him a sour glare, even as a hint of affection softened her pale green eyes.

Fane might have been jealous if he hadn't known Marco had trained Serra in self-defense.

All high-bloods were taught to protect themselves, not only with weapons, but also with their bodies. A witch or psychic, no matter how powerful, could have their talents disabled. They needed to know they could do basic hand to hand combat.

The bond between a Sentinel and his pupil often lasted the rest of their lives.

"I'm a little distracted," she informed her former trainer.

Marco reached to place his fingers against her throat, his expression fierce.

"I know, little one."

Fane reached to knock aside his fellow Sentinel's hand. He was willing to accept a familiarity between the two, but he had his limits.

"There's no need to touch."

Marco flashed him a mocking smile. "Feeling possessive, amigo?"

Fane didn't bother answering the ridiculous question.

"I assume you risked being discovered because you have information for me?" he demanded.

"Some." Marco reached to hit the STOP button on the elevator. There was a tiny jerk as the elevator halted on floor ten. "First I traced the weapons."

Reaching behind his back, Marco pulled out a folded piece of paper from his pocket.

Fane unfolded it, his brows drawing together at the familiar name.

"Girard. Shit," he muttered. They had discovered Jacques Girard and his band of idiots during their battle with the necromancer. Supposedly they were an ancient society determined to rid the world of high-bloods. "The Brotherhood?"

"That was my thought as well," Marco growled.

"Have you contacted Wolfe?"

Marco shook his head. "Not yet."

Fane glanced up in surprise. Marco was nothing if not ruthlessly efficient.

"Why not?"

"My contact said that there's . . ." He searched for the right word. "Chatter."

"Within the Brotherhood?"

"Yes," Marco said. "It seems that several weeks ago they lost a cache of weapons."

"Lost?" Serra asked the obvious question.

"It was in transit from Mexico to Kansas City." Marco shrugged. "It simply disappeared."

"So anyone could have stolen it," Fane ground out, his hands clenched in frustration.

He'd hoped the illegal weapons would lead them to the location of the kidnapper.

Now it was just another dead end in a long line of dead ends.

"Yep," Marco agreed, his own expression bleak.

"Shit. What about the Dark Side?"

Marco shook his head. "You're not going to be any happier."

"Tell me."

"It's a fight club."

Fane paused, wondering why the hell the name wasn't triggering an alarm. Wolfe had zero tolerance for his Sentinels making a little extra cash in unsanctioned fights. Perhaps because he'd been forced to fight when he was young. He kept close track of fight clubs and often sent one of his men to check them out. Any Sentinel caught in a club was looking at some face time with the Tagos. Something no one wanted.

That meant the club was new or so underground that it hadn't hit Wolfe's radar.

"Where?" he asked.

"That's the problem," Marco admitted. "It changes location every night."

"Like a rave?" Serra asked.

"Something like that." Marco sent her a rueful grimace. "Only with a lot more blood and broken bones."

"Shit." Fane barely resisted the impulse to slam his fist into the steel wall of the elevator. "We're running out of time."

Marco's tight expression revealed he was struggling against his own desire for violence.

"I've got my contacts searching for tonight's location, but it's going to be hard without someone with direct access to the group who runs the club."

Fane nodded. There wasn't a doubt in his mind that the Sentinel was doing everything in his power to track down the information.

"Keep on it," he muttered.

"Of course." Marco pushed the button to open the elevator doors.

"You're prepared?" Fane demanded as the Sentinel stepped out of the cubicle.

Marco paused to give him a nod. "Just give the word."

The doors slid closed and the elevator resumed its swift climb to the top floor.

Fane avoided Serra's steady gaze. The fact that her life remained in danger was like a hot dagger slicing through his heart.

And each second that ticked by only dug the dagger deeper.

Christ. He had to do something.

But what?

The elevator halted and the doors slid open. Instinctively taking the lead, Fane scouted for any hidden traps before allowing her to follow him into the hotel room. Once there he closed the door and did a swift sweep of the rooms, releasing small bursts of power to destroy any hidden bugs that might have been installed during their absence.

Once confident they were alone, he returned to the main room to find Serra staring out the wall of windows.

He halted in the middle of the floor, sensing she had something on her mind.

It took a few minutes, but finally she turned to face him, her chin tilted to an angle that warned he wasn't going to like what she had to say.

"We have to tell Bas what we learned," she abruptly said.

His brows snapped together. Nope. He didn't like it one damned bit.

"Why?"

"He has far better resources in St. Louis than we do to track down tonight's location," she said, her expression stubborn.

"There's no guarantee," he growled.

It would be a cold day in hell when he shared any info with the bastard.

"Do you have a better suggestion?"

"No."

His flat tone must have warned her that he wasn't in the mood to discuss a partnership with the ass who'd poisoned her. Her lips thinned before she gave an annoyed shake of her head. Then with unerring accuracy, she managed to pounce on the only subject he wanted to discuss less than Bas.

"Why did you ask Marco if he was prepared?"

He kept his face devoid of expression. "If things go south he'll have to get the Sentinels pulled out of the city before Bas or his people track them down."

It was a perfectly reasonable explanation she didn't buy for a second.

"Nice try."

She gave a faint toss of her head, the movement releasing the dark silk of her hair to spill over her shoulders. The sunlight tangled in the glossy strands, picking up hints of fire.

Fane's breath was jerked from his lungs as he studied her, arrested by her sheer beauty.

It didn't matter how long he'd known her. Or how many times he'd seen her across a room.

She still captivated him.

Barely aware he was moving, he halted directly in front of her, his hand lifting to brush through her soft curtain of hair.

"It doesn't matter."

Her lips parted as his heat surrounded her, revealing his stirring arousal.

"Fane," she breathed.

His fingers moved to stroke down her throat, deliberately replacing Marco's lingering scent with his own.

Territorial?

Hell yeah.

"We have more important things to discuss."

She laid her hand on his chest, directly over the steady beat of his heart.

"We do?"

He smiled in slow invitation, grabbing her wrist so he could press her hand to his lips.

"Or we don't have to talk at all . . ." Debating between tossing her over his shoulder and heading for the bedroom or simply tumbling her onto the thick carpet, Fane suddenly stiffened. "Dammit."

Stepping back, she studied his furious expression with a rueful grimace.

"Let me guess. Bas?"

Fane ground his teeth together, trying to battle back his bloodthirsty desire to break the man's neck.

"He is truly wearing on my last nerve."

She wrinkled her nose. "The sooner we're done with this mess the sooner we can go home."

Home.

The simple word helped to soothe his homicidal lust.

Okay. Maybe it didn't soothe him. But it helped him maintain his composure as he ran a light finger down Serra's pale cheek.

"I hope you're serious about that mountaintop in Tibet," he said in a husky voice. "I want you to myself for the next century or so."

Serra stilled, her gaze warily searching his face.

"What about your duties?"

His finger moved to trace her lush lower lip. "You are my duty."

"Duty?" She trembled beneath his soft caress, but the wariness remained. "That's not very romantic."

He swallowed a sigh, realizing she was deliberately twisting his words. Which was precisely why he preferred to communicate in a more . . . basic way.

A damned shame he didn't have time to prove just how romantic he could be. Not when Bas the Bastard was nearly at the suite.

Muttering a low curse, he was just pressing a frustrated kiss to Serra's stubborn lips when the sound of a heavy thud, followed by the splintering of wood, had him spinning around, his fighting instincts on full alert.

The door flew open, hanging at a drunken angle as Bas stormed into the room, closely followed by the faithful Kaede.

A dark, murderous fury lashed through Fane at the sight of the assassin. What the hell was going on?

He'd warned the son of a bitch what would happen if he entered uninvited, hadn't he?

Now he was going to beat the ever-living shit out of him.

Serra watched in horror as Fane charged forward. She knew what was going to happen before Fane grabbed Bas by the front of his silk shirt and tossed him into the wall.

For God's sake. What sort of idiot burst into the room of a fully trained Sentinel?

Obviously the sort who picked himself up off the floor and launched himself into a battle where he was going to get his ass kicked.

"I told you not to barge in here," Fane snarled.

Bas bared his teeth. "Fuck you, Sentinel."

With a roar, the assassin was ramming into Fane's chest, barely flinching when Fane's massive fist hit him on the side of his face. Instead he used his own fist to pound into Fane's rock-hard abs. Then, without warning, Bas slammed his head forward to smash Fane's nose.

Serra gave a choked cry, moving to try to separate the two warriors.

Dammit. If Fane killed Bas then she was screwed. And if Bas killed . . .

No. Her mind couldn't even go there.

She'd taken a step forward when fingers wrapped around her upper arm, bringing her to a sharp halt.

"No." Kaede spoke directly in her ear. "Don't interfere."

Her gaze remained locked on the two men who stumbled into the couch, both holding on to each other with a death grip as they sought to gain an upper hand.

"I don't understand." She flinched as Bas jabbed his knee into Fane's upper thigh. "What's going on?"

Fane slammed Bas's head against a side table, splitting the wood in half.

Already the scent of blood and violence filled the air.

"It's been brewing a long time," Kaede said, clearly unconcerned that his boss might be ripped apart limb by limb. "You might as well let them get it out of their system."

Serra frowned. Of course the two men wanted to kill each other. And not just because Bas had kidnapped and poisoned her. They were too alpha not to feel the need to flex their muscles when they were in the same room.

Men.

But until this moment they'd both understood that they had to work together. At least until Molly was home.

"Did something happen?" she demanded.

Kaede snorted, his fingers biting into the flesh of her upper arm, but it was Bas who answered, his gaze briefly flicking in her direction.

"You thought you could meet with my enemy and not have me discover your betrayal?"

Serra disguised her grimace. He had to be referring to the hit man they'd confronted in the shed. But how the hell had he found out?

Had the two Sentinels following them been spying?

She gave a mental shrug. Who cared how he knew? All that mattered was that he didn't use it as a reason to hurt Fane.

"My betrayal? Are you really going to go there?" She pointed a finger at his bloody face. "I have toxin flowing through my blood, you bastard. Don't talk to me about betrayal."

The assassin's head jerked back as Fane clipped him on the chin with a right hook, sending him flying over the back of the couch.

Climbing back to his feet, Bas grabbed a heavy ceramic lamp, throwing it at Fane's head.

"I warned you what would happen," he snarled, still speaking to her despite the bloodthirsty Sentinel charging in his direction. "Do you think I won't kill you?"

The two men collided once again. Bas was clearly a trained fighter, but he was no true match for Fane. No one was except Wolfe, the Tagos of the Sentinels.

Still, Serra knew that Fane was at a disadvantage because he couldn't strike a killing blow.

Not so long as Bas was the only one who could remove the toxin from her body.

She had to end this before Bas managed to truly injure her guardian.

Shaking off Kaede's hand, she moved in a wide circle. She didn't want to wade directly into the battle. She just wanted to capture Fane's attention.

Halting near the window, she shifted until she was in Fane's line of sight without being close enough to get caught up in the violence.

"Fane." She wrinkled her nose as he glanced in her direction and Bas used his distraction to land a punch just below his left ear.

"I'm a little busy," he rasped, blood dripping from his nose and a large lump already forming on his temple.

"I need to speak with Bas." She took a deliberate step forward, knowing it would horrify her guardian to have her within striking distance. "Please."

The dark eyes smoldered with a fevered heat, a testosterone enjoyment at being allowed to release his pent up fury obvious in his tight smile.

"Can't it wait?"

She rolled her eyes. "No."

He cursed, shoving Bas against the wall before stepping back and folding his arms across his chest.

There was a tense silence as the two men glared at one another. The smallest twitch would send them back to flying fists and crunching bones.

Then, with a mocking smile, Bas glanced in her direction. Serra squared her shoulders, studying the man's lean face. Despite his smile, the assassin had lost his familiar smooth sophistication.

Her lips twisted. No, it was more than a lack of sophistication. He looked like he'd been in a drunken brawl.

His dark hair was ruffled and there was blood trickling from the side of his mouth. Not even his clothing had survived unscathed. The white silk shirt was stained red and the black slacks ripped.

"Say what you have to say," he commanded, as bossy as ever.

Jackass.

She met his accusing gaze without flinching. "We didn't betray you, whatever the hell that's supposed to mean."

The bronze eyes narrowed. "You didn't have a secret meeting?"

"No. Fane realized we were being stalked so we set a trap to catch him."

"And?" Bas prompted.

It was Fane who smoothly answered. "He took poison and killed himself."

Bas snorted. "That's it?"

Fane met the man's derision with stoic indifference. "That's it."

Bas remained unconvinced. "You learned nothing?"

"Maybe," Serra murmured.

Fane scowled, taking a step toward her. "Serra."

She refused to be intimidated. "You said it, Fane, we're running out of time."

The dark eyes were hard with warning. "I don't trust him."

Like she did? God almighty. The man had kidnapped her. Hell, he'd *poisoned* her.

She'd sooner trust a rattlesnake.

But she understood that she was between a rock and a hard place.

"We don't have any choice," she stubbornly insisted.

He shot Bas a venomous glare. "I always make sure I have choices."

Bas ignored the bristling Sentinel, taking a step toward Serra. "Tell me what you discovered."

Well aware of Fane's disapproval, Serra kept her focus trained on Bas's lean face, noticing the shadows beneath his eyes that had nothing to do with his recent battle with Fane.

Inanely she wondered how long it'd been since he'd actually slept.

"The man's thoughts were blocked by a barrier, but we managed to discover he'd been hired by a third party," she confessed.

His features might have been carved from stone, but he couldn't disguise the flare of hope in his bronze eyes.

"Who?"

"We didn't get his name."

Bas clenched his hands. "Liar."

Fane made a low, dangerous sound as he moved to stand at her side.

"Careful, assassin."

Serra kept her gaze on Bas. "He was taken blindfolded to an underground fight club."

Bas blinked, as if caught by surprise. "Fight club?"

"Yes." Serra nodded. "He called it the Dark Side."

"I've never heard of it," Bas muttered.

Serra grimaced. Well, crap. She'd been desperately hoping the name would mean something to Bas.

So much for her grand plan.

Then Kaede stepped forward, speaking directly to his employer.

"It's a very exclusive club. Only the fighters who've earned a reputation at other clubs are issued an invitation."

Attention turned toward the younger man.

"You fought there?" Fane asked.

Kaede nodded. "Once."

Bas sucked in an audible breath, the fragile hope returning to his eyes.

"Where?"

"It was in an abandoned factory," Kaede said. "But it never stays in the same place."

Bas's expression hardened. "How do we find it?"

Kaede gave a lift of his shoulder. "I was contacted by a friend."

"Call your friend and get the location for tonight."

"I can try." Kaede pulled his phone from his pocket. "We didn't part on the best of terms."

Fane watched Kaede in narrow-eyed suspicion, no doubt assuming this was some sort of trap.

"Why?"

Kaede flashed the Sentinel a taunting smile. "I took his title of champion."

Bas made a sound of impatience. "Just call him."

Chapter Twenty-Two

Bas grimly glanced toward Fane, his expression rigidly composed despite the violent emotions that continued to churn just below the surface.

Fear. Fury. Hope.

And threaded through it all a vicious, throbbing pain from his cracked ribs.

"You stay here," he commanded, turning to head stiffly toward the door. There was no way he was going to reveal his growing weakness in front of the Sentinel. "I'll call when I need you."

"No fucking way," Fane growled.

Sensing the Sentinel following behind him, Bas forced himself to turn and glare at the interfering ass.

"Don't for a second think you can give me orders, Sentinel," he snarled.

"And don't think I'm going to allow you to confront the kidnapper without me." Fane met his warning with the cold confidence of a warrior certain he could kick the ass of anyone in the room.

Unfortunately, he was probably right.

Even if Bas hadn't been nursing at least three cracked ribs.

Thankfully there was nothing wrong with his pride. It allowed him to meet the dark, lethal gaze with an expression of disdain.

"This has nothing to do with you."

"It does if you decide to get yourself killed by charging after the kidnappers without a plan," Fane informed him, his chin jutted to a stubborn angle.

Bas snorted. "You make one ugly-ass mother hen."

"We've been through this before. If you die, Serra dies," he growled. "I can guarantee you that's not going to happen."

Bas wasn't particularly happy with the edge of certainty in the man's voice. Like he had a plan already set in place. Something that might have troubled him if he didn't have a dozen far more important problems to consume his thoughts.

"I have plenty of muscle," he bit out.

Fane folded his arms over his massive chest, his tattooed face stripped of emotion.

"Not as good as me."

Not boasting, a simple statement of fact.

Before Bas could respond, Kaede was moving to stand at his side.

"He's right," the younger man said with a grimace.

Bas snapped his lips together. He *was* right.

He might hate the bastard, but Fane's reputation as a fighter was the stuff of legends.

His pride was no match for his desperate need to find Molly.

"Fine." He held Fane's gaze, allowing the Sentinel to see his ruthless determination. He didn't want to kill the psychic, but he would. "But you both come. If we track down the kidnapper she might be able to pull Molly's location from his mind."

He turned back toward the door where Fane was abruptly standing in front of him.

"Where are you going?"

Bas narrowed his gaze, his fingers twitching with the urge to wrap them around Fane's thick throat and squeeze . . .

Instead he was forced to content himself with a glare as a stabbing pain shot through his side.

Soon.

"I need to prepare my people so they're ready when Kaede has a location."

Fane shook his head. "How do I know you'll share the location with me?"

Bas's lips twisted into a sardonic smile. "You'll have to trust me."

"Like hell," Fane rasped.

Feeling sweat begin to drip down his spine, Bas stepped around the looming Sentinel and out of the suite.

He walked steadily toward the elevator, knowing Kaede was directly behind him, ensuring that Fane didn't do anything stupid.

He maintained his pretense of composure until the doors slid shut. Only then did he lean heavily against the side of the steel compartment, a low moan wrenched from his lips.

Kaede used his key card to send the elevator directly to the parking lot beneath the hotel before moving to stand next to Bas, clearly prepared to catch him if he collapsed.

Not an unreasonable fear.

"How badly are you injured?" Kaede asked.

Bas's lips twisted. "A quick visit to Vicky and I'll be as good as new." He gave a humorless laugh. "Or as good as a man can be at my age."

Kaede sent him a questioning glance. "There's no shame in being injured by a worthy opponent."

"Thanks," Bas said dryly. Fantastic. He hadn't felt shame. Anger, yes. A desire to return and finish kicking Fane's ass. But no shame. At least not until his companion had mentioned the word. "Don't you have some calls to make?"

Kaede lifted his cell phone, clearly sensing Bas wasn't in the mood for conversation.

The silence lasted as they left the hotel and made their way to the lab that served as Bas's current home.

Reluctantly Bas allowed Kaede to help him from the car and into his office, the pain becoming almost unbearable by the time he was lowered into the leather chair behind his desk.

"Have Vicky sent to me," he ground out, sweat dripping down his face.

Kaede gave a swift nod, heading toward the door. "Of course."

"And let me know the second you hear anything," Bas called out.

"You got it."

Kaede disappeared and Bas leaned his head against the back of his chair, closing his eyes as he released a weary breath.

Christ, he was tired.

He couldn't remember the last time he'd slept. Or ate. Or did anything that didn't include trying to retrieve his daughter.

Logically he knew he was close to the edge of complete collapse, but he refused to give in to the weakness of his body.

Not when they had a potential lead.

Or at least what he hoped was a lead.

Groaning softly, he pressed a hand to his ribs, trying to think through the pain.

The Dark Side meant nothing to him, but a fight club

made sense. What better way to discover humans capable of becoming adequate hit men?

And while it wasn't necessary for the kidnapper to actually be at the fight, he had to have his people there to manage the club. People who could be convinced to give Bas the information he needed to find Molly.

Of course he first had to depend on Kaede to find the location of the club.

Dammit.

He caught the scent of violets before the door to the office was pushed open and Vicky was crossing the room in obvious concern.

Wearing a dress that floated around her slender figure and her red hair left loose to frame her features, she looked young and enticingly fresh. Like a sensuous elf.

With a graceful movement, she sank to her knees beside his chair, her green eyes doing a swift survey of his less than pristine appearance.

"Vicky," he murmured. "Thanks for coming so quickly."

"You know you only have to ask for me to be at your side," she said, lifting her hands. "May I?"

He nodded, grimacing as much from the husky invitation in the healer's voice as from the gentle press of her hands as they ran over his shoulder and down his arms before moving to his chest.

He'd been fending off Vicky's flirtations for the past twenty years.

"You've been a good friend," he assured her, grunting as she located the source of his pain.

"Friend?" She grimaced, holding her palm over his ribs as she glanced up at him with open regret. "Not exactly what a girl wants to hear."

"It's all I can offer."

Expecting her to drop the subject as usual, Bas ground his teeth as she continued to study his tense expression.

"Because of Molly?"

The unwelcome vision of a silver-haired beauty with velvet brown eyes flared through his mind. Myst. Instantly he slammed the door on the aggravating memories.

"In part," he said between gritted teeth.

"And the other part?"

"I don't have any interest in a relationship." The icy edge in his voice warned the healer that this conversation was done. "Are they broken?"

Vicky lowered her head, accepting that Bas wasn't going to change his mind.

"Fractured," she said, pressing her hands against his side. "This is going to hurt."

"Just do it." The words had barely left his mouth when the heat of Vicky's power slammed into him. "Shit."

He gripped the arms of the chair, the sensation of his bones knitting back together even more painful than the blow that had fractured them in the first place.

Next a searing heat ran through the muscle and cartilage, repairing the damage.

By the time the healer removed her hands and slowly straightened, Bas was panting as if he'd just run a marathon at full speed, his body shivering with shock.

God. Damn.

This was why he only used a healer when he had no other choice.

"You need to eat and then rest for a few hours," Vicky said, her face pale from the amount of energy she'd drained healing him.

"Thanks."

She smiled ruefully at the sincerity in his voice. "It seems to be all I can offer."

Walking across the room, the healer turned to send him a wry glance.

"Bas."

"What?"

"Don't get yourself killed."

With a toss of her red hair, Vicky turned to leave the office, closing the door behind her.

"Amazing how many people suddenly want me alive," Bas muttered, easily dismissing the healer from his thoughts as he closed his eyes.

He intended to concentrate on putting together a plan once Kaede found the location of the fight. Or at least consider his next step if the place couldn't be found.

Instead his exhaustion washed over him like a tidal wave, dragging him into a deep, dreamless sleep.

He was unaware of the passage of time until the sharp knock on the door echoed through the office. Then he snapped open his eyes to discover that dusk had filled the office with shadows.

Shit.

With a faint groan he forced his stiff muscles into action as he pushed himself out of the chair. He was relieved to discover his pain was gone, but furious with himself for wasting an entire afternoon.

"Enter," he called.

Kaede pushed open the door and stepped into the office, his gaze discreetly monitoring Bas as he moved around the desk to perch on the corner.

Bas knew the younger warrior was judging whether he was fully healed. A practical precaution, but one that annoyed the hell out of Bas.

It reminded him that he'd lost control of his notorious composure and charged into the hotel room like a hot-headed novice. And worse, he'd indulged in his primitive lust for violence, allowing himself to be injured when he needed every ounce of his strength to rescue his daughter.

"You have a location?" he asked in crisp tones.

Kaede nodded, handing a scrap of paper to Bas with an address written on it.

"An abandoned warehouse on Broadway. Near the river."

Bas tossed the paper on the desk. "When?"

"It starts in two hours."

"That's not much time," Bas muttered, concentrating on what had to be taken care of immediately. They'd have to make up the plan on the fly. A method he detested. Careful preparation was the key to success. Trite but true. "Send Damis and Aldo to scout the building and have the other Sentinels begin to infiltrate the neighborhood two at a time. Make sure they stay out of sight. We don't want to spook the manager of the fights."

"On it." Kaede whipped out his phone.

Leaving Kaede to organize the troops, Bas moved to type the address of the warehouse into his laptop. He cursed as the satellite view revealed a three-storied red brick building that stretched half the block with boarded over windows and a flat roof.

"Shit."

Kaede was instantly at his side. "What's wrong?"

"There's two dozen windows and at least six doors plus the loading bays." He zoomed in for a closer look. "There's no way we can keep a watch on all of them. We'll have to go in."

"Bas, there will be a hundred people at the fight. Most of them pumped full of steroids and all of them armed," Kaede warned. "Let me do some recon and—"

"No," Bas snapped, impatience twisting his gut. They had an address. A tangible location to try to trap the kidnapper. There was no way in hell he was waiting one minute longer than necessary. "There's no time. We go tonight. Contact Fane."

He headed toward the door at the back of the office that led to his private quarters. He needed a shower and change of clothes.

Then he was heading toward the warehouse.

Hang on, Molly, he silently urged his fragile little girl. *Daddy's coming.*

Dusk was painting the sky in vivid colors of orange and violet and deep rose as Wolfe came to a halt to study the wagon tracks that were perfectly outlined by the powder-fine dust on the road.

Around them the flat landscape was giving way to low hills and prickly shrubs that clung to the dry, rocky ground.

A part of Wolfe appreciated the fact that they were at least partially hidden behind the hills and bushes. On the other hand, it made it impossible for him to see more than a few hundred yards.

Which meant he had to stay on constant guard while keeping focused on the trail they were following.

It slowed his pace, but he wasn't about to walk into an ambush.

Not when he had Lana with him.

Sucking in a deep breath, he judged the scent of horse manure in the air. It was thicker than it'd been just a few miles back.

"I think we're gaining on them," he said, a frown touching his brow as the unmistakable stench of a recently smoked cigarette captured his attention. "They must be going at a snail's pace."

"They wouldn't have any choice," the Mave said, taking a drink from her water bottle. Despite the heat that coated her pale skin with a moist sheen, and the dust clinging to her jeans, she still managed to look as cool and dignified as a queen. "Even the wagon they're using to transport Anna would have to be heavily reinforced with spells. It's complicated enough to maintain magic under the best circumstances. It's nearly impossible when you're moving."

Wolfe absently followed the acrid scent of smoke and burned tobacco, his thoughts trying to sift through the various reasons anyone would waste that amount of magic just to transport a dangerous high-blood.

"Bas must have an important reason to go to such an effort," he muttered.

"Yes," Lana swiftly agreed, following behind him as he headed toward a large rock outcropping. "He's flown below the radar for years. He wouldn't have risked exposure if it wasn't something he considered vital."

Wolfe agreed. Unfortunately anything vital to Bas, a man willing to use his own people as weapons, couldn't be good.

And quite possibly catastrophic.

He paused, struck by a sudden thought. "There's one angle we haven't considered yet."

"What?"

"How this connects to Serra."

The Mave halted next to him, her gaze scanning the horizon as she considered his words.

"Is she still in St. Louis?"

"She was just a few hours ago." Wolfe pulled out his phone to check for any new messages. "I don't have any info that she's been moved."

Lana grimaced. "I don't know whether to be relieved or terrified."

Wolfe knew which he was.

Terrified.

"Could she be psychically linked to Anna?" he asked.

She considered before giving a sharp shake of her head. "Not at such a distance."

It's exactly what Wolfe had expected, but that didn't prevent him from cursing in frustration.

"Then what the hell does she have to do with this?"

She turned to meet his smoldering gaze. "A question only Bas can answer."

Of course it was. With a shake of his head, he continued around the outcropping, coming to an abrupt halt as he caught sight of the unmistakable indentation in the ground.

Even with the stench of a recently smoked cigarette he hadn't expected this.

"Damn."

Lana was instantly at his side. "What?"

He pointed at the ground. "Tracks."

The Mave bent down to study the wide tire grooves in the dust. "A car?"

"SUV."

She straightened, her perfect, beautiful face bathed in the warmth of the sunset.

"It could be a coincidence," she said.

Wolfe used his boot to kick the small pile of cigarette butts next to the rocks.

"The SUV was behind this outcrop of rock long enough for the driver to smoke half a pack of cigarettes."

"Hunters?" she suggested. "Humans enjoy killing things."

"Possibly."

Lana didn't miss the lack of confidence in his voice.

"What do you think?"

It didn't occur to him to try and sugarcoat the truth. Lana wasn't a female who wanted to be pampered and protected.

Hell, she'd demote him to kitchen duty if he even tried.

"I think that someone waited here for Anna," he admitted. "Either to join them or shadow them."

She nodded, accepting his explanation without hesitation. Wolfe hid his wry smile at his stab of pleasure.

Idiot.

"Can you sense if they're high-bloods?"

He gave a shake of his head. If a high-blood had been in the area they would have left behind an electric charge in the air that would linger for hours.

"Norms."

Lana sent him a startled glance. "Then it's very unlikely they work for Bas."

"He's prejudiced against humans?" It wasn't an uncommon flaw among high-bloods.

Many felt their special talents made them superior to mere humans.

Not Wolfe. That sort of belief allowed a man to underestimate his opponent. Something Wolfe was never stupid enough to do.

"Bas has no interest in anyone who doesn't have a power he can exploit," the Mave said, her voice edged with disgust. "He's always considered humans beneath his notice."

"Charming guy."

She pretended not to hear his sarcastic remark.

"Unless he's changed over the years then the people in the SUV weren't working for him."

That made it simple.

If the SUV full of norms wasn't part of Bas's crew, then they'd been waiting behind the rocks for one purpose.

"Then they're following Anna," he said grimly, pointing toward the tracks that ran parallel to the road.

Lana didn't bother to disguise her fear. "We have to get to her first."

Chapter Twenty-Three

Fane peered around the corner, staring at the abandoned warehouse across the street.

The plain brick building was shrouded in darkness, but it'd clearly seen better days. Several of the windows were boarded over and the front façade was spray painted with human graffiti.

Still, it appeared structurally sound and in a neighborhood that was deserted after the sun set.

The perfect location for illegal cage matches.

He glanced toward the assassin who stood next to him. They'd parked several blocks away and made their way to the neighborhood through several back alleys that had made him gag in disgust. Nothing like piles of rotting garbage and human feces to make a man regret his heightened senses.

Now Fane was anxious to be on the hunt. Dammit. Each tick of the clock was a brutal reminder that time was running out.

It wasn't going to take much for him to explode.

Quite an admission for a man who'd once considered his rigid control to be indestructible.

"You have your people in place?" he asked of the assassin standing at his side.

Bas pointed upward. "I have two Sentinels on the roof and the rest spread through the neighborhood," he explained. "Kaede is inside."

Silently Fane added Marco and one other Sentinel loyal to him in hiding in the shadows. He'd sent a quick text to Marco as soon as he'd learned the address of the fight.

If things went to hell he wanted to make sure he had someone he could depend on to get Serra out of danger.

Not that their hidden presence made him any happier to have Serra walking into the potential trap.

He grimaced, acutely aware of the female pressed against his back. He'd had a moment of insanity earlier, attempting to convince her to stay in the car while they investigated the club. He might as well have tried to ram his head through a brick wall.

Stubborn female.

"Did you find any info on the club?" he demanded of Bas.

Bas shrugged, his attention locked on the warehouse. He was standing so close Fane could feel the tension that hummed off the man's tightly coiled body.

Fane wasn't the only one on the edge of self-combustion.

"From what Kaede could discover it's a group of norms who make money betting on the fights, selling drugs, and pimping females in a back room."

A typical fight club.

Which told him nothing.

"No connection to a high-blood?" he pressed.

Bas appeared equally annoyed with the lack of information. "Not that he could uncover."

"Which means that the kidnapper might have chosen to

meet his potential hit men at the last fight club because it was a convenient cover," he rasped. "He might not have any connection at all to the fights."

Bas smiled with lethal intent. "I'm about to find out."

Fane returned his attention to the warehouse. From the front it appeared deserted, but he easily spotted the two men leaning near the double doors in the center of the building. He didn't doubt there were several more sentries posted around the place.

It wouldn't be easy to slip in unnoticed.

"Did you get us invitations?" he demanded.

"Better." Bas reached into the pocket of his slacks to remove an old-fashioned key chain. As always the assassin was attired in a white silk shirt and black chinos that looked ridiculously out of place in the decaying neighborhood. Obviously he had more vanity than sense. Fane had on his usual camo and tee. "I have the key."

He scowled with impatience. "What are you waiting for?"

"Kaede is scouting the interior of the building to make sure there are no hidden surprises."

A reasonable precaution, but Fane was in no mood to be reasonable.

"How long can it take?" he snapped.

"I prefer that he's thorough, not fast."

Fane sent the assassin an irritated glare. "I can be both.

"We're trying to be discreet," Bas muttered.

"I can be discreet."

The bronze eyes widened at his simple claim. "Is that supposed to be funny?"

Fane met the mocking disbelief with a stoic expression. He often used his menacing appearance to intimidate others. He preferred to avoid actual confrontation whenever possible. But he was a trained Sentinel who could become virtually invisible when he needed to fly beneath the radar.

"I could get all the info we need without anyone knowing I was there."

Bas's lips twisted at his arrogant confidence, but before he could retort, there was a soft *beep* from Bas's phone.

"That's Kaede's signal," Bas muttered, returning the phone to his pocket and nodding toward the far side of the warehouse. "We'll go through the north door."

The assassin whirled around to head toward the back of the building they were standing beside. The crumbling mechanic's garage would shield them from the guards out front.

Fane turned, grasping Serra by the shoulders. "Serra—"

"Don't start," she warned, going on tiptoe to place an all too brief kiss on his lips before she was hurrying to follow Bas.

For a minute Fane watched her retreat, his gaze locked on her slender body dressed in casual jeans and a black sweater. Her raven hair was pulled into a sensible braid and she wore a pair of flat running shoes.

He grimaced, a jagged pain ripping through him.

Serra wasn't meant to be slinking through dark, filthy streets with a lethal toxin pumping through her bloodstream.

She was meant to be safely hidden behind the walls of Valhalla, dressed in leather pants and halter tops that made men forget to breathe when she sashayed past in three-inch heels. That was why he'd fought so hard to deny his attraction to her.

His world was never safe. Now he had to accept that no place was entirely without risk.

The only true way to keep her safe was to be at her side. Always.

Pulling his handgun from the holster strapped over his

chest, Fane swiftly caught up with Bas and Serra. Together they moved in silence, pausing as they reached the edge of the garage.

Bas glanced up, waiting for a hand signal from one of the Sentinels on top of the warehouse roof before he darted across the street and into the loading bay at the end of the building.

There was a tense second as they paused to listen for any sound of alarm. Only when Bas was certain they hadn't been spotted did he unlock the side door and lead them into the vast open space that made up the first floor.

Fane slid ahead of the assassin, making a quick search of the shadowed room to ensure that nobody was hiding behind the cement columns that ran the length of the warehouse.

He returned to Serra's side, giving Bas a short nod. The assassin pointed toward the back of the room before he was jogging forward. He ignored the massive open elevator that was the obvious means of transportation to the upper floors, instead heading toward the narrow metal staircase attached to the wall.

They traveled to the top floor, at last stepping onto the narrow catwalk that framed the upper level, allowing them to have a clear view of the action one floor below.

It looked like any other fight club, Fane decided. A large, chain metal cage set in the center of the dusty floor. A crowd of loud, testosterone-driven men screaming at the two fighters who were attempting to beat each other senseless. A handful of prostitutes leaning against a back wall to service the spectators, or perhaps offer comfort to the losers. And a few hired guns to keep the event running smoothly.

There was nothing to indicate this was set up by the kidnapper.

Halting in the deepest shadows, Fane felt Serra press close against his side.

"How can they stand it being so loud?" she muttered, her face pale with the strain of being surrounded by such a large crowd.

Fane grimaced, realizing that she was being assaulted by the violent thoughts and emotions that seethed among the crowd. He reached to grasp her hand, using his powers to blunt the worst of the psychic energy.

"Norms don't have our hearing," he reminded her.

"And they're too drunk to notice their ears are bleeding," Bas muttered, turning his head as Kaede appeared from the shadows. "Have you noticed anything out of the ordinary?" he demanded.

The younger warrior shook his head. "No." He gestured toward a heavyset man with dark hair slicked back from his face seated at a makeshift table. "The man in the corner is dealing coke." Kaede moved his finger toward the girls. "The far door leads to a storage room where the pros are plying their trade."

Fane ignored the petty criminals, his focus trained on a steel door that was set in a shallow alcove.

No doubt at one time it'd been a private office.

"What about that door?" he asked.

Kaede shook his head. "It hasn't opened and no one has gone near it."

Bas moved further down the catwalk, his concentration centered on the cage where the two norms continued to battle one another with astonishing skill.

"Those fighters are trained," the assassin muttered.

Fane arched a brow as the smaller of the two performed

a butterfly kick that caught his opponent directly on the chin.

Maybe there was more to the fight club than he originally suspected.

"Well trained," he growled.

Bas nodded. "This would be the perfect method of auditioning soldiers, bodyguards or—"

"Hit men for kidnappers," Fane completed the obvious conclusion.

"Yes." Bas glanced toward Kaede. "Were you approached after the fights?"

The warrior shrugged. "I'm always approached after I fight."

Fane didn't doubt him. Kaede had the calm confidence that came from rigid training and natural skill.

If he hadn't been a damned traitor, Fane would have tried to convince him to join the Sentinels at Valhalla.

Bas held his warrior's gaze. "Do you remember anything in particular?"

"The usual offer to meet with the upper management," Kaede said in offhand tones.

There was a hint of surprise on Bas's lean face, as if he hadn't considered the possibility the younger man had been offered alternative employment.

"You turned them down?"

Kaede shrugged. "I already have a job."

"Good answer," Bas retorted wryly.

Fane scowled. Good answer? The hell it was. If Kaede had at least agreed to meet with the owners of the fight club they might have some idea if they were high-bloods.

Clenching his teeth, he allowed his gaze to scan the catwalk. If he wanted to watch the fights without being seen, he'd have a camera mounted from this angle.

"Do you sense something?" Bas demanded, picking up on his distraction.

"They have to be monitoring the fights," he said. A grim smile touched his lips as he caught sight of the tiny devices tucked beneath the narrow catwalk that crossed the middle of the room. "There."

Bas leaned forward, studying the equipment with a knowledgeable eye.

"Cameras." The assassin abruptly straightened, a tight smile curving his lips. "Closed-circuit cameras."

Anticipation hummed through Fane, the air heating around him as he prepared to hunt down the kidnapper. He'd rip apart the warehouse with his bare hands if necessary.

"I'm guessing the upper management is near," he murmured.

Bas nodded. "Probably behind door number one."

Fane studied the open space in front of the door. It was too brightly lit and too distant from the crowd to simply stroll up to the alcove without attracting attention.

Even for him.

"The question is how we get a peek without attracting attention."

Bas tapped a slender finger on the railing of the catwalk. "We need a distraction."

Serra laid her hand on Fane's arm. "I can—"

Both men spoke as one. "No."

Serra scowled, but before she could insist on putting herself in danger, Kaede took command.

"I'll take care of it," he said, leaping over the railing of the catwalk to drop to the floor below.

Fane frowned as the younger man disappeared among the shadows. There was no predicting what sort of distraction he was plotting.

He could only hope it didn't include anything too flamboyant. The last thing they needed was human authorities showing up to raid the place.

One minute, then two ticked past. Fane ground his teeth. Dammit, what the hell was the enforcer waiting for?

Then, just when he'd reached the end of his limited patience, the throbbing music came to an abrupt end.

The silence was shocking, and as one, the entire crowd turned to glare at Kaede who stood at the edge of the warehouse, an unplugged electric cord dangling in his hand.

"Listen up you bunch of bitches," he called out, dropping the cord so he could stroll toward the cage. "If you want a real fight, I'll give a thousand dollars to the first man who can knock me out." He held up a hand as a roar of fury shook the crowd. "But first you have to catch me."

Tossing out his challenge, Kaede turned and swiftly headed toward the distant door, a hundred infuriated norms charging after him.

"Shit," Bas muttered. "Let's go."

Bas leaped over the railing, closely followed by Fane and Serra.

Although a few stragglers remained, those too drunk to realize the party had moved, or too smart to fall into a potential police sting, they crossed directly toward the door.

With a concentrated burst of energy, Fane knocked out the cameras. Whoever was monitoring the fights was now blind.

Which meant they had to come out of their hidey hole to find out what was going on.

On cue the mystery door was shoved open and a large man with a shaved head and bulging muscles stepped out of the inner room.

Fane felt a familiar prickle of energy.

The man was a Sentinel.

A hunter, not a guardian, which meant he didn't have any magic, but that didn't make him any less dangerous.

Thankfully, the man's attention was locked on the fleeing crowd as he moved forward. A foolish mistake that he paid for when Bas stepped forward and laid a hand against the back of his neck.

Instantly the Sentinel crumpled to the floor, knocked unconscious by Bas's magic.

Without hesitation, they stepped over the slumbering Sentinel's body, Bas taking the lead as they entered a small office.

It was a barren room with the windows boarded over and the walls stripped bare. The wooden floor was covered in dust, and cobwebs drifted through the air. The few pieces of furniture were battered from use, but the computer system set up on the desk was top of the line and worth a small fortune.

At their entrance a man glanced up from the computer screen, his expression of annoyance altering to sheer terror as Bas stepped forward.

"Hello, Lee Sandoval. It looks like our game is at an end," the assassin drawled. "I win."

Wolfe caught the scent of tobacco smoke long before they were close enough to sense the presence of the norms, or even the high-bloods hidden in the old-fashioned covered wagon.

He shook his head in disbelief.

Did humans not realize how far the smell of a cigarette could travel?

Cautiously he crept toward the crest of a nearby hill,

stretching out on his stomach as he scanned the shallow valley directly below.

Night had fallen, but he was able to make out the wagon covered by a black canvas top that blended into the shadows. It was halted in the center of the dusty path, the two horses that pulled the vehicle standing with stoic patience.

There was no way to see inside the wagon, so instead he closed his eyes, seeking the tell-tale tingle that revealed the presence of high-bloods in the van.

There were at least four, he swiftly decided. Witches. And . . . something else.

Something he couldn't recognize.

He opened his eyes to study the area surrounding the wagon. There wasn't much to see beyond dirt and shrubs and a few large boulders sticking out of the ground. Then, glancing directly below the small ledge he was lying on, he caught sight of the heavy SUV that was hidden in the shadows of the hill.

He was briefly baffled, wondering why they hadn't driven straight to the wagon after it'd become disabled. The heavy steel wouldn't offer complete protection from magic, but it was better than nothing.

Then abruptly he realized that the vehicle must have been stalled by Anna's powers.

"Lana," he breathed softly.

Silently she moved to lie beside him, the scent of warm cinnamon filling his senses.

"I see them," she murmured softly. "There are four," she said, counting the male norms crouched behind the SUV before her attention turned toward the wagon. There was a pause as she concentrated on the fragile vehicle. Abruptly she turned to send him a concerned glance. "They have Anna inside."

Wolfe nodded. "I don't know whether to be terrified

your suspicion was right or relieved we managed to track them down."

"Terrified," Lana promptly answered, her tone distracted. "Why don't they just keep moving?"

"The wagon axle is broken," he said, nodding toward the undercarriage.

"So they're helpless."

Wolfe gave a lift of his brows. He'd never heard the words "witches" and "helpless" in the same sentence.

"Not really," he said wryly. "There are at least four highbloods inside the wagon."

"It would take three of the witches just to keep Anna contained," she said. "They no doubt rotate so one is able to concentrate on controlling the horses while the others maintain the spell."

Three witches just to hold one spell? Wolfe grimaced. It was hard for him to wrap his brain around the fact that one mere girl could be as dangerous as a weapon of mass destruction.

"What happens when the morons below us go in for the attack?" he asked.

"They either drop the protective shield around Anna to fight back or they die," she said bluntly. "My bet is they drop the shield."

"Mine too."

She held his gaze. "We have to stop this before that happens."

Wolfe turned to the side so he could pull out his phone and call the Sentinels who were following their trail. He grimaced when he realized the electronics had been fried.

"My phone's dead," he said, his voice pitched so it wouldn't carry. He returned his attention to the men behind the SUV. Although they remained crouched out of sight of the wagon, they were beginning to shift with a growing restlessness that warned they were swiftly reaching the limit of their patience. Very soon they would manage to goad each other into attacking. When that happened all hell was going to break loose. "They won't get here in time."

"Then we have to take care of the situation," Lana said, her voice soft, but edged with a steely determination that made his heart twist with dread.

This was the Mave.

The woman who commanded an entire race of dangerous high-bloods.

And the woman who would happily sacrifice her life to protect them.

He frowned. "We don't know who the good guys are." He tried to play for time.

"It doesn't matter." She fluidly rose to her feet, her decision made. "We need the witches to keep Anna contained."

Shit. Wolfe pushed upright, shoving his fingers through his hair that was tangled from the night breeze.

"I can handle the norms," he assured her. "You stay here."

"They're armed," she protested.

He glanced down at the various weapons strapped to his body. "So am I."

She studied his stubborn expression, then without warning she was heading toward the small trail that led down the hill.

"I'm coming and that's final."

"What the hell . . ." Swearing in frustration, Wolfe watched her walk away. "Jesus Christ, woman, are you trying to drive me into an early grave?"

Chapter Twenty-Four

Bas studied the bastard he hadn't seen for over three years. Lee Sandoval.

He supposed the man looked the same, although he could barely recall him.

He was scrawny and dressed in wrinkled khakis and a polo shirt. His hair was a dirty blond that needed to be combed and he had a narrow face with a weak chin. His pale eyes were set too close together and his teeth were too large for his mouth.

Christ. He looked like a math teacher, not an evil mastermind.

As if to prove Bas's point, the man leaped to his feet, awkwardly grabbing a handgun off the desk to point it in their direction.

"Stay back," he warned, an unexpected hint of fear in his voice.

Bas frowned, taking a deliberate step forward. His frown deepened when the man took an answering step back.

This was the man who'd outwitted him?

The man who'd devised a Machiavellian plot to kidnap

Molly and trade her for a high-blood capable of destroying society?

Granted, he was obviously intelligent. And it was far easier to be brave when you were hiding behind a camera.

No doubt he treated it like a computer game where he could play the grand chess master without worrying about getting beat to a bloody pulp.

But still . . .

Bas gave a sharp shake of his head. Right now all that mattered was the gun pointed in his direction.

An untrained idiot was far more dangerous with a firearm than a trained professional. And while he would probably survive being shot, it would disable him.

Something he couldn't afford. Not when Molly needed him.

"It's done, Sandoval," he said through clenched teeth.

"No." The man gave a frantic shake of his head. "I still have Molly. If you want her to remain alive you'll turn around and leave this office."

Pure, undiluted fury seared through Bas. How dare the bastard even speak his daughter's name?

"You'll tell me where Molly is or I'll have it forcibly removed from your brain," he said, his voice edged with the power of his magic. "Not a pleasant experience or so I hear."

Surprisingly Serra stepped forward, her beautiful face set in an icy expression.

"I can do it."

The man obviously believed her, his hand shaking so bad he could barely hold the gun.

"Try it and Molly is dead."

Bas growled low in his throat. Dammit. The man had enough high-blood in him to make him immune to Bas's compulsion. Granted, he had the magic and the training to torture the truth out of even the most obstinate enemy, but his control was on a razor's edge. He couldn't be confident he wouldn't accidentally kill the son of a bitch during his "interrogation."

"Not before I snap your neck."

The man took another step backward. "If I'm dead you'll never find her."

"One of your henchmen will be happy to share any info they have." Bas's lips twisted into a humorless smile. "Well, maybe not happy. But they'll share."

The man shot a quick glance toward the door where Fane was standing guard, as if hoping his Sentinel would return to save him.

"They know nothing."

Bas swallowed a curse. The man was speaking the truth. Or the truth as he believed it to be.

The men with Sandoval didn't know where Molly was.

Which meant he had to keep this pathetic, soulless worm alive.

For now.

"I have to admit I'm surprised," he said, covertly shifting forward.

A few more steps and he could knock the gun away. Until then he had to keep him distracted.

The man licked his lips. "Surprised by what?"

"You seemed so . . . competent." Bas flicked a dismissive glance over the man's wrinkled khakis and the hand that continued to shake. "Even cunning."

The man compressed his lips, his pride pricked by Bas's mocking tone.

"I was cunning enough to steal Molly from beneath your nose."

Bas gave a taunting shake of his head, moving a foot closer.

"Now you're the same spineless computer geek who used to cower when I walked by."

Sandoval made a valiant effort to steady the gun in his hand.

"Take another step and I'll shoot you."

Bas held up his hand, pretending to be intimidated by the man's warning.

He wanted Sandoval distracted, not goaded into putting a bullet through his heart.

"Tell me how you did it," he commanded.

The geek glanced toward the door, then the computer screen that remained blank from Fane's little trick. He was clearly hoping for help.

Help that wasn't coming.

"Did what?" he at last demanded.

"Kidnapped Molly."

Hate filled the pale eyes. A festering loathing that stemmed from the jealousy of a weak man in the constant shadow of a more powerful male.

"You always did underestimate me," the younger man accused.

"Doubtful," Bas sneered.

The man's finger tightened on the trigger. "And you wonder why people want to see you suffer?"

Bas instantly latched on to the revealing word. "People? Who?"

Sandoval paled, as if realizing he'd revealed more than he should have.

"Me," he snapped. "That's why I took Molly."

Bas's gut twisted with a rising sense of dread. There was no way in hell this man was any sort of mastermind.

"You haven't explained how you got her," he rasped.

"I . . ." Again with the lip licking. "I walked in and took her."

"A lie." He blatantly stepped forward. "Tell me."

Sandoval wiped the sweat from his brow. "What does it matter?"

Without warning, Fane was standing at Bas's side, clearly running out of patience.

"Dammit, assassin, you're wasting time."

He sent the Sentinel a warning glare. The geek might be a coward, but he was also a psychic, which meant that it would take time for Serra to bust past his shields. He had to get Molly's location by more . . . old-fashioned means.

"I want to know," he snarled, returning his attention to Sandoval. "Tell me."

"I helped write the code for your security system," Sandoval grudgingly confessed. "It was easy to override it. Once I was in I used my psychic powers to disable the cameras."

Shit. That was why Bas didn't allow his ex-employees to walk away alive.

They always came back to bite him in the ass.

"That explains the tech, but there's no way in hell your psychic skills got you past the spells I have woven around the property," he said between gritted teeth.

"Why do you care?" Sandoval's voice was laced with a growing desperation. "I have your daughter—"

Bas took another step forward, indifferent to the gun pointed at his heart. Goddammit. He was done with games.

He was getting his daughter back.

Period.

Before he could move, however, Serra was laying a restraining hand on his arm.

"Don't."

He ignored her warning, concentrating on the man who was now drenched in sweat.

"Who is it, you piece of shit?"

The man shook his head, his breath coming in rapid pants. "No."

Serra squeezed his arm. "Bas . . . stop."

"Not now, psychic," Bas growled, trying to shake her off. His attention remained focused on Sandoval. The geek was ready to crack. He could *feel* it. "Tell me who you're working for."

Serra dug her nails into his arm, determined to gain his attention.

"Don't press him."

"Are you fucking kidding me? He has Molly," Bas grated, yanking his arm free. "I'm getting answers." He moved forward, his gaze locked on Sandoval's wide eyes. "One way or another."

Sandoval gave a wild wave of his gun. "I've told you, stay back."

Bas continued forward. "Shoot me."

"Bas!" Serra cried out.

For a second Bas wondered why the psychic was trying to interfere. Hell, she had more reason than anyone to want Molly found.

Then the realization hit as Sandoval glared at him in bleak resignation.

"You arrogant fool," the man muttered, turning the gun and pressing it against his forehead.

"Shit." Bas leaped forward even as the man squeezed the trigger.

Sandoval had obviously been spelled to kill himself if cornered.

A spell that Serra had sensed, but he'd been too caught up in his desperation to notice.

The man collapsed in a bloody heap on the floor, the hole in the side of his head warning that his lack of skill with a weapon hadn't prevented him from managing a killing shot.

Dropping to his knees, Bas reached to grab Sandoval's shoulders, giving him a shake.

"Don't you die on me, you bastard," he growled, his heart squeezing as the pale eyes stared blankly at the ceiling. He could physically feel the life draining from the man. Terror dried out his mouth, his heart refusing to beat as he turned toward the female who had knelt beside him. "Search his thoughts," he commanded.

She grimaced. "His mind is blocked."

What the hell. The man was a breath from being stone-cold dead and he was maintaining his shields?

"Still?"

"It's not a psychic block," she said, her face tight with frustration. "It's magic."

"Tell me where Molly is." He gave the man a shake, indifferent to blood splattering his white shirt. "Tell me."

Serra made a choked sound, as if unnerved by the sight of the dying man.

"He can't," she managed to force out.

He turned to glare at her pale face. "Do something."

In less than a heartbeat Fane was at Serra's side, wrapping a protective arm around her shoulders.

"No."

Bas used his only true leverage over the female psychic. "Molly needs you."

"I can't."

Anguish darkened her eyes, then without warning she was arching backward, a scream ripped from her lips as Fane pulled her tight against his chest.

She gave one more scream before her eyes rolled to

the back of her head and she slumped unconscious in the Sentinel's arms.

Fane lifted his head to stab him with a lethal glare, the heat of his anger sizzling through the air.

"You're a dead man," he promised in flat tones.

Instead of following the Mave down the narrow track that offered a gentle angle down the hill, Wolfe headed directly over the top and down the steep slope, leaping the last six feet to land directly behind the squatting norms.

He wanted to take care of the band of idiots before Lana could get herself shot.

Silently stepping within striking distance of the first norm, Wolfe folded his arms over his chest.

"Put your guns down," he said, his voice filled with authority.

In unison the men surged upright, spinning to eye Wolfe with expressions varying from shock to outright fear.

The ones with fear were the smart ones. They might actually survive the encounter.

"What the hell?" the nearest idiot muttered, a gun in his hand. "Who are you?"

Wolfe allowed his gaze to drift down the line of men, judging the character of each of them by the way they held themselves.

They were all in their mid to late twenties and dressed in the usual jeans and black T-shirts. All had tats in an effort to make them look badass and a few had piercings on various parts of their bodies.

Ridiculous, of course. Such markings only made it easier for them to be identified.

The one closest to him was clearly the leader while the one at the far end looked like he was about to piss his pants.

The second in line was calculating, no doubt willing to kill, but preferring to do it without risk to his own skin. The fourth was a wild card.

"I gave you a command," he reminded them, conspicuously leaving his own weapons in their holsters.

This close he could kill quicker with his hands.

The leader spit directly toward Wolfe's heavy boots.

"We don't take commands from you."

His smile had chilled the blood of trained assassins.

"Then you're a fool."

The man remained defiant, but Wolfe could smell his rising fear.

"No, you are," he tried to bluff. "We're here on the orders of the new leader of the high-bloods."

"Strange," a female voice floated from the back of the SUV. "I didn't realize I'd been deposed."

Wolfe muttered a string of foul words beneath his breath as the men jerked around to watch the dark haired beauty step into view.

Had the aggravating woman run down the hill at full speed?

There was a moment of stunned appreciation before the leader recognized the emerald birthmark on her upper breast that shimmered in the moonlight.

"Fuck," a man in the middle breathed, awe tingeing his voice. "You're—"

"The Mave, current leader of the high-bloods," Lana offered as the man's words faltered. Her gaze shifted toward the man nearest Wolfe, the power of her presence making the air sizzle. "Or at least I was the last time I checked."

The leader gave the man next to him a shove in the back. "Shoot her."

The norm stiffened, glancing over his shoulder in horror. "Are you out of your mind? I can't kill her."

"Fine." The leader aimed his gun. "Then I will."

Wolfe moved with lightning speed, grabbing the man by the head and giving it a sharp twist. His neck snapped like a twig, his body limp as Wolfe tossed him to the side.

In the same motion he reached for the second man, wrapped his arm around his throat, and pulled until the man's back was pressed against his chest. The idiot made the perfect shield.

Waiting for the bad guy's inevitable reaction, Wolfe was prepared when he jerked his gun up in an attempt to shoot him. If the moron had any sense he would have shot through his own body in an attempt to kill Wolfe. Or at least he should have rid himself of the weapon so it couldn't be used against him.

Grabbing the man's wrist with enough strength to crack the bones, he forced the hand down, aiming the gun at the remaining norms.

"I gave you an order," he said, squeezing the man's wrist to make him cry out in pain. There was nothing like a grown man screaming to make people nervous. "Put down your guns."

There was a flicker of movement from the man on the end as he tossed his gun to the side, and just as swiftly reached behind his back. He'd just managed to get his hidden gun pulled and pointed toward Wolfe when Wolfe shot him directly between his eyes.

The man stood for a half second, blood dripping down his nose. Then, with a harsh sigh, he toppled to the side, hitting the ground with a sickening thud.

Hissing in fear, the man in the middle dropped his gun, pressing himself against the SUV as if he could make himself invisible.

The man that Wolfe still held tight against his chest shivered, the stench of his fear making him grimace.

"What do you want?" the norm rasped.

With a jerk of his hand, Wolfe forced the man to drop the weapon. Then, he shoved him next to his friend, waiting until both of them were staring at him with open terror.

"That's the question I was about to ask you," he drawled.

It was the man with the crushed wrist who answered, his wary gaze darting between Wolfe and the Mave.

"We were hired to follow the wagon."

"And that's all?" Wolfe prompted.

He gave a jerky nod. "Yes."

"Do you want me to tell you what I do to liars?" he drawled in soft, lethal tones. "Or maybe I'll just show you."

The second man gave a squeak of alarm. "No. Wait."

"Tell me."

"We were hired to track down the wagon and to kill the witches, but to keep the female who would be sleeping in the back of the vehicle alive."

Wolfe flashed a grim glance toward Lana. If they were hired to kill the witches, then whoever had done the hiring wanted Anna's destructive power unleashed on the world.

But why?

He returned his gaze to the men. "And then?"

"And then we were supposed to contact a specific number and say the deed was done."

Lana strolled forward, her eyes breathtakingly beautiful as they caught and reflected the silver moonlight.

"Who hired you?"

"I don't know." The man fell to his knees, his hands pressed together in a pleading motion. The Mave tended to have that effect on people. "I swear. We were hired by some dude who found us at a fight club. He said he worked for the new leader of the high-bloods and that we could expect some serious cash if we were willing to eliminate her enemies."

"Name?" Wolfe snapped.

"He didn't give it." The man sent him a wary glance. "And before you ask, he didn't give us his boss's name either, but I'd bet my left nut that she's a witch."

The revelation caught Wolfe off guard.

He'd somehow leapt to the conclusion that the men had been hired by another norm.

Why would a high-blood hire humans? Unless these men were mere cannon fodder?

And why would a high-blood be willing to release such dangerous powers on the world?

He gave a frustrated shake of his head. More questions without answers.

"Why are you so certain the leader is a witch?"

"I spoke to another . . . employee who said he was taken to a dark room and a female came in and put some sort of spell on him," the norm said. "He swore she was in charge."

Lana studied the two men with a searching intensity. "But she didn't put a spell on you." Her gaze moved to the dead men lying on the ground. "Or any of the others."

"Hell, no." The man gave a shudder of revulsion. "I ain't letting any freak screw with me."

Wolfe choked back a laugh as Lana narrowed her gaze. Had the idiot forgotten that he was speaking to the most powerful witch in the world?

Clearly he wasn't the brightest crayon in the box.

Which was no doubt the reason he was chosen for what could easily have turned out to be a suicide mission.

Wolfe yanked his dagger from the sheath at his lower back, moving toward the moron with a lethal smile.

"I'm going to do more than screw with you."

With a fluid motion, Lana was abruptly standing next to him, her hand resting on his forearm.

"Wolfe."

He sent her a questioning glance. "Shall I kill them?"

She shook her head. "I prefer to take them to Valhalla to stand trial for attempted murder of high-bloods."

Both men gave low groans, the one on his knees trying to reach for Wolfe.

"No, please," he begged. "Just kill me."

Wolfe kicked away the man's hand, offering Lana a wry smile.

"Your reputation terrifies even norms."

"Enough." With a rare display of her stunning power, the Mave lifted her hand and spoke a soft word of command.

An instant later both men were sprawled face first on the ground, knocked unconscious by her spell.

Wolfe sheathed his dagger, studying his companion's tense expression.

"I could have taken care of them."

"We don't have time to play."

With a swift movement she was heading toward the end of the SUV, her gaze locked on the nearby wagon.

Wolfe was on instant alert. "What's going on?"

"The spell is fracturing."

Chapter Twenty-Five

Serra struggled to regain consciousness, feeling like she was drowning in molasses as she forced her heavy lids to lift.

It took a minute for her eyes to focus and she felt panic threaten to explode within her. She could tell she was lying on a hard surface and that she wasn't in Valhalla. There was a stench of must and mildew the Mave would never tolerate.

So where the hell was she?

And what happened to her?

Then her eyes slowly settled on a stark, beautiful male face hovering mere inches above her and her panic immediately receded.

Fane.

If he were near then nothing could hurt her.

Her hand lifted to touch his clenched jaw, but Fane grabbed her fingers and pressed them to his lips.

"Don't move," he urged.

Concentrating on the concern in his dark eyes, Serra flinched in surprise when a lean male face shoved itself next to Fane.

She grimaced, recognizing the astonishing bronze eyes.

Bas.

As the name tumbled through her brain, so did the recent events that led up to her current presence on the floor with Fane's arms wrapped tightly around her.

She shivered. They were in the abandoned warehouse and the male psychic had just shot himself in the head.

And her brain felt as if it had been pierced by a hot poker.

"What happened?" the assassin demanded, his voice lacking any concern for her welfare.

The jerkwad.

"It was the psychic," she said, wincing when her voice came out as a thready whisper.

There was nothing she hated worse than revealing weakness.

Especially when Bas was watching her like a vulture.

"Did he attack you?" he pressed.

"No." Ignoring Fane's grunt of disapproval, Serra forced herself to a seated position, keeping her gaze firmly averted from the dead psychic. Not that she could entirely block out the presence of a corpse only a few feet away. There was the acrid smell of gunpowder that lingered in the air along with the unmistakable scent of blood. A *lot* of blood. She gave another shudder. "He mentally shoved through my shields."

Fane tightened his arms around her. "Why?"

"To give me a name."

Both men stiffened at her revelation, their combined heat washing over Serra to sear away the lingering chill.

"What name?" Fane asked, his fingers trailing a comforting path up and down her arm.

"Jael," she said, repeating the name that had been so roughly shoved past her mental barriers.

Bas abruptly surged upright, his expression shocked. "Shit."

Serra tilted back her head to watch as the assassin paced jerkily across the office. The name had obviously disturbed him.

"Does the name mean something to you?" she asked.

"She was one of my witches," he explained, waving a hand toward the dead man. "And the psychic's lover."

Serra frowned. If the witch was a lover to the psychic, why the shock?

Unless he was arrogant enough to assume anyone who'd ever worked for him maintained complete loyalty to him.

"Did you fire her?"

Bas halted his pacing to send her an impatient glance. "I thought she was dead."

Serra gave a confused shake of her head. "You killed her?"

"Not me." His gaze moved to the dead man on the floor. "But it's possible that Sandoval held me responsible for her death."

Serra rigidly kept her gaze from Sandoval. Unlike her friend Callie, she wasn't used to being around dead bodies. Fane, however, moved to investigate the corpse with swift efficiency.

Ruthless, but necessary. The man might very well have a vital piece of evidence in his pocket.

"So you think he kidnapped your daughter for revenge?" Fane demanded.

"It's possible," Bas said, his tone unconvinced.

"No." Serra gave an emphatic shake of her head that made her wince in pain. Her connection to Sandoval had been brief, but it had given her a glimpse into his tortured mind. "When he spoke her name it was filled with . . . anger. Betrayal. He wasn't naming his dead lover," she said. "He was revealing his accomplice."

Bas returned to his pacing, his expression troubled. "He was saying she's the kidnapper? How the hell is that possible?"

Fane straightened, holding what looked to be a small cocktail napkin in one hand while covertly tucking a small scrap of paper into his pocket with the other.

"We know there has to be a witch involved to spell the men who attacked us," the Sentinel reminded the assassin. "I don't believe in coincidences."

Bas turned to face her, his eyes narrowed with suspicion. As if she would lie about something that could lead them to his daughter.

"If it is Jael, then why didn't Sandoval just tell me?"

She glared at the assassin in exasperation. If it weren't imperative that they concentrate on discovering Sandoval's accomplice, she would have punched him in the throat.

She was only here because the ass had forced her to try to track his daughter.

Now he wanted to question her psychic skills?

"Because he was spelled. He couldn't physically say her name or give details about her plans, but she wasn't clever enough to include his psychic abilities," she said between clenched teeth. "Once he realized he was going to die he used the last of his powers to try to bypass my shields. They're strong enough that all he could get through was the name."

Fane moved to her side, wise enough to accept her claim without hesitation.

"Do you have a way to track Jael?"

Bas hesitated, then, grudgingly accepting that Serra wasn't plotting some mysterious trap, he shoved impatient fingers through his hair.

"She lived at the lab with the rest of us so she didn't have an apartment in town," he said, his brow furrowed with concentration.

"Any family?" Fane pressed.

"No."

Fane held up the napkin he'd taken off Sandoval and unfolded it to reveal that it was emblazoned with gold.

"Does the name The Emerald Lounge mean anything to you?"

Bas sucked in a startled breath, his lean face beginning to show the strain of the past days. The shadows beneath his eyes had darkened to bruises and the high cheekbones were more prominent, as if he'd lost several pounds.

"There was a club she used to visit whenever she was off-duty called The Emerald Lounge," the assassin said. "The woman who ran it was a close friend."

Fane placed an arm around her waist, no doubt sensing she was barely keeping herself upright.

"Do you know where it is?" he asked the assassin.

"Yes. Jael took me there one night." Bas grimaced at the memory. "She hoped that I would have sex with her and her friend."

Serra wrinkled her nose. She didn't judge people for what they did behind closed doors. But she knew if Fane asked her to allow another woman into their bed there would be knives and the removing of balls included in her response.

"Did you?" she asked.

Bas scowled, as if offended she would even ask such a question.

"No."

She snorted at his outrage. "It couldn't have been your morals that stopped you."

"I don't consider sex a spectator sport," he growled, pulling his phone from his pocket and pushing the speed dial. Within seconds they could hear a male voice through the speaker.

"Tell me you found her," Kaede breathed, no doubt hiding from the norms who all wanted the opportunity to knock him out.

"Lose your groupies and meet us at the car," Bas commanded, heading toward the door with decisive movements.

Serra turned to follow him, only to be halted as Fane stepped in front of her, his hands gently cupping her face as he studied her with a stark concern.

"Are you all right?" His thumb brushed her pale cheek.

"Yes." She managed a smile, knowing he was already trying to find a way to keep her from continuing the search for Molly. "He just stunned me."

The dark gaze searched her upturned face for any hint she was still in pain, the heat of his skin almost scorching. A sure sign of his agitation despite his grim composure.

"I don't suppose you'd return to the hotel?"

She hid a smile at his resigned tone. He was learning.

"No, we're too close now."

"We don't know that for certain," he muttered.

"I feel it," she said. They weren't empty words. She could feel a strange buzz that made her adrenaline rush through her body. Of course, it could be the toxin beginning its destructive path to her ultimate death, she wryly acknowledged. "Besides, I want to keep Bas in my sights until he's removed his freaking spell."

He pressed his forehead to hers, his body tense with frustration.

"Fine, but—"

"Don't get killed." She stroked her fingers down the line of his clenched jaw. "I get it."

He swooped down to kiss her with a fierce urgency. Then, just as she was swaying against the solid wall of his chest, he was gently pulling away and reaching for his phone.

She frowned as he tapped in a short message and hit SEND. Nervously, she glanced toward Bas as he left the room.

"What are you doing?"

"Texting Marco to return to the lab," he murmured so softly Serra barely caught the words.

"Why?"

"I intend to make sure the assassin keeps his promise."

She grabbed his arm, remembering Bas's conversation with Sandoval.

"Bas said there were spells—"

"There are guardians with him who can get past any magic," Fane assured her, referring to the tattooed Sentinels like him who were immune to most magic.

"What about the alarms?" she pressed. It was ridiculous to worry about Marco. He was a trained warrior who'd been charging into danger for over a century, but that didn't keep her from being concerned. "Bas won't have left it unguarded."

He sent her a tight smile as he reached into his pocket to pull out the small piece of paper he'd found on Sandoval.

"I have the codes." Swiftly he typed them into his phone. Then, with a smooth motion he was shoving the paper and his phone back into his pocket, pressing a finger to her lips. "Shh."

At that precise minute Bas stuck his head back into the room, his expression tight with impatience.

"Are you coming or what?"

Wolfe followed the Mave as she moved to stand near the wagon, taking a position at her side.

This time he was happy to allow her to take the lead.

He could fight any norm and most high-bloods, but magic . . .

That was Lana's area of expertise.

A young female climbed out the back of the wagon, her pale face surrounded by a mop of reddish curls making her appear ridiculously young.

"Stay back," she called out, her voice not quite steady.

Lana stepped forward, her face calm as she confronted the nervous witch.

"I can help."

The girl shook her head. "No."

"Your spell is fracturing."

"We will repair it after you leave."

"It's beyond your ability." Lana took another step closer, pretending she didn't hear Wolfe warn her to stay back. "You need my help."

The young woman licked her lips, her gaze flickering toward Lana's brilliant emerald witch mark. Even from a distance the female would have to sense Lana's power.

"Who are you?"

"Your Mave," Lana said, using a trickle of magic to ensure that her voice carried to the other high-bloods hidden in the wagon.

The girl gave a sharp shake of her head. "Not mine. We don't accept your authority."

Wolfe moved until he was once again at Lana's side. "That seems to be going around," he murmured.

She sent him a chiding glance before returning her attention to the wagon.

"I assume you're referring to the fact that you've given your loyalty to Bas?"

The young witch gave a small gasp of shock. "How did you know?"

"I have my spies everywhere," Lana murmured, digging her elbow into Wolfe's side when he gave a low snort. "We have to get Anna to a stable location."

"No." The woman remained stubborn despite the fear she couldn't disguise.

Lana curled her hands in fists of annoyance. Clearly she hoped to avoid any further violence, but time was running out on returning the dangerous high-blood to a safe location.

"Do you understand the disruptions she's already creating?"

"Better than you," the witch muttered.

"Then you know eventually the humans will come searching for the cause," Lana retorted, edging her voice with a powerful compulsion. Even Wolfe felt the urge to bow at her feet. "When they find you they'll kill you."

The woman gave a small whimper, her hands clenched so tightly her knuckles turned white.

Still she struggled to fight against her Mave's authority.

"All we need is an hour to rest and a new wagon."

"Don't be a fool," Lana snapped. "You can't believe I will allow you to leave here."

The girl glanced to the side, as if seeking strength from her fellow traitors.

"I'll do whatever I have to do to finish my job."

Lana exchanged a frustrated glance with Wolfe, both of them baffled by the girl's refusal to accept that she was trapped in a disabled wagon with a high-blood that would soon cause massive chaos.

"Why?" Lana demanded. "Does your employer demand that you give your life to his cause?"

The witch shook her head, her face ashen in the moonlight as she struggled against Lana's magic.

"I'm not risking my life for Bas," she hissed. "It's for Molly."

"Who?" Lana asked in puzzlement.

"His daughter," the witch explained. "She was taken from us and the kidnapper demanded Anna in return for keeping her alive." Genuine grief twisted the youthful features. "She's only four."

Well, shit. Wolfe ground his teeth together.

This was a complication they didn't need.

"Dear God," Lana breathed, predictably moved by the thought of a little girl in danger. "Who would do such a thing?"

The witch shook her head. "We don't know."

Wolfe placed a hand on Lana's shoulder, speaking directly to her although he allowed his words to carry.

He wanted the witches to know he was running out of patience.

"It doesn't matter why they have Anna out here. People are going to start to die."

Lana nodded, shifting her gaze back to the young witch. "He's right. Let me help."

"Molly—"

"I swear on my honor that I will do everything in my power and in the power of Valhalla to rescue Molly," Lana interrupted the protest, her composed authority giving the nervous young witch more assurance than any amount of pleading. "May I approach?"

The female glanced over her shoulder, clearly seeking guidance before turning back to Lana and giving a slow nod of her head.

"Yes."

Chapter Twenty-Six

Serra climbed out of the car and studied the discreet three-storied brick building with a black awning over the front door. There were neatly trimmed shrubs beneath the tinted windows and near the curb stood a doorman along with several young valets, all dressed in black and gold uniforms.

It looked more like a posh hotel than a club.

"This is the place?" she demanded as Bas and Fane joined her.

Bas answered. "Yes."

She glanced up and down the block situated in an expensive suburb west of the city. They'd driven to the location in record time, all of them aware that the witch would soon discover her partner-in-crime was dead.

If that happened before they could corner her, she might very well disappear.

"Not much of a crowd," she muttered.

"It's a private club," Bas explained, his gaze taking a cautious survey of their surroundings. "Invitation only."

Fane nodded, as if familiar with such establishments. A subject they would discuss in private. At length.

Serra frowned, realizing she could hear crickets.

Even a private club should have some sign of life, shouldn't it?

"I don't understand." She glanced toward Bas. "Is it a brothel?"

"It's a sex club."

She lifted a brow. "What's the difference?"

"There aren't any pros here," Bas explained. "It's a place where willing participants come to explore their fantasies."

Serra wrinkled her nose. Public sex with strangers was . . . yeah, not her thing.

"Isn't that what a bedroom is for?" she muttered.

Bas sent Fane a mocking smile. "Lucky man."

Fane kept his attention locked on the club, no doubt already having located every hidden guard and surveillance camera placed around the building.

"Is the witch in there?" he demanded.

"Yes." Bas gave a sharp nod, concentrating on his former employee. "She hasn't sensed me yet, but it's only a matter of time."

"How are you going to get us in?" he demanded of Bas.

The assassin pointed toward the side lot where several expensive cars were parked.

"Jael took me through an employee entrance at the back. We should be able to sneak in unnoticed."

Serra barely heard Bas's words, her entire body going rigid as her mind-sweep touched on the small, terrified mind she'd been desperate to find.

She held her breath, concentrating on the fragile connection as she reached into her pocket to pull out the tiny ribbon she'd been carrying.

Yes. The child was sleeping, but there was no mistaking it was Molly.

About to release her breath, Serra was baffled by the odd sense of another mind reaching out to the child.

Shit. She yanked her mind away. Was the child being watched by a high-blood who was monitoring her on a psychic level? There hadn't been any hint of malevolence in the mind. Actually, it'd seemed more . . . protective.

Still, she might have given away the fact that they were searching for the child.

"She's here," she breathed softly.

Bas glanced at her in confusion. "Jael?"

"Molly."

The assassin made a choked sound, grabbing the door of the black Mercedes that Kaede had parked at the corner of the block before jogging off to search the neighborhood.

"She's alive?" he rasped, his skin paling to a pasty gray.

Serra gave a swift nod. "Yes. She's sleeping."

He released a shaky breath. "Where?"

There was the soft sound of footsteps as Kaede returned, but no one spared him a glance. The men kept their gazes focused on Serra as she closed her eyes and concentrated on her fragile bond with the child.

"I can't pinpoint her exactly," she said softly, slowly opening her eyes. "But she's in that building." She gestured toward the small brick structure at the back of the parking lot that looked as if it'd been renovated into a private residence.

She'd barely gotten out the words before Bas was shoving away from the car and heading down the street.

"Let's go."

Fane moved with blurring speed to stand directly in the assassin's path, one hand pressed to the middle of Bas's chest.

"Wait."

The bronze eyes narrowed. "Release me, Sentinel, or—"

"You can't rush in there without a plan," Fane interrupted,

his expression carved from granite. "Not unless you want your daughter to die."

Snapping his fingers around Fane's wrist, Bas trembled with the need to battle his way past the large Sentinel. Then, with a visible effort, he swore beneath his breath.

"Christ." Bas released Fane's wrist to shove his fingers through his hair. "There's no way for me to approach without Jael sensing me."

Serra turned to glance at the club. It was a large structure, but once Bas entered any high-blood in the building would recognize his presence.

"She'll be expecting you and Kaede," she said slowly, thinking out loud. "But she won't be expecting us."

Bas jerked his head to send her a suspicious frown. "What are you suggesting?"

"You and Kaede go through the employee entrance and track down Jael," she said. "That's what she'll be anticipating."

"And you?" Bas pressed.

"I'll find Molly."

The bronze eyes narrowed, the air vibrating with his tension. "How can I trust you?"

Serra shrugged. "Because you have no choice."

Fane abruptly stepped to stand at her side. "She's right."

Bas pressed his lips into a flat line, his hands clenched into tight fists.

"Molly . . . is an innocent."

Serra stepped forward, her face flushed with annoyance. "For God's sake, there's nothing in this world that could make me harm a child," she snapped, pointing a finger in Bas's face. "Not even you. Now go."

Without warning Kaede placed a hand on Bas's shoulder, his manner deliberately calm.

"She's right. We have to go before Jael realizes we're here and they lock down the club."

Bas closed his eyes, sucking in a deep breath to regain his shaky composure. At last he lifted his lids to stab Serra with a fierce glare.

"Get her out and keep her safe."

Bas sent her one last warning glare before jogging silently across the street and becoming lost in the shadows of the night.

Fane waited until the two men had time to round the building before lightly touching her arm.

"Ready?"

She nodded, following his silent path down the sidewalk to approach the back building from the side drive that led to the parking lot.

They both halted beneath the branches of a large oak tree, studying the building in silence. It looked empty. The square windows were dark, and the front gate heavily locked.

But Serra easily picked up the buzz of at least three human brains nearby.

Fane leaned down to speak directly in her ear. "Wait here until I scout for guards."

"But—"

He pressed a finger to his lips. "This isn't up for debate."

She heaved a resigned sigh. "Stubborn."

"Cautious," he corrected.

Stepping back, he disappeared in the darkness. Serra gave a small shake of her head. She logically knew a Sentinel couldn't make himself physically vanish, but their ability to convince people not to notice them never failed to amaze her.

The healers had studied the strange phenomenon for

years without being able to decide how they were capable of achieving the mental illusion.

Serra leaned against the rough tree trunk, still not fully recovered from Sandoval's intrusion into her brain.

She might be happy that he'd revealed the name so they could track down the witch, but he'd left her with a headache that was going to last for days.

Five minutes passed before Fane silently appeared at the gate, giving it a sharp jerk to break the thick chain that was held together by a padlock.

No doubt the residents had been confident they were safe behind the wrought iron fence.

They were about to discover they were mistaken.

Fane gestured for her to join him, taking her hand as she passed through the open gate.

"Did you find anything?" she murmured in a hushed voice, not surprised he was leading her toward a side entrance.

"I took care of the two guards and disabled the alarms, but there's a high-blood upstairs with the girl," he murmured.

They climbed a shallow set of stairs that led to the double French doors.

"A witch?" she asked.

"No." Fane halted, glancing in her direction. "A norm."

"Strange," she said before she abruptly realized that maybe it wasn't so strange. The witch and psychic had both been high-bloods, but they had shown a preference for hiring norms to do their dirty work. Which would make their job easier. "Are you ready?" she demanded as Fane hesitated.

The Sentinel reached for the door handle, keeping his gaze on her pale face.

"There's no need for you to go in," he said.

She went on the tips of her toes to press a swift kiss to his mouth.

"I love you, but you're terrifying," she pointed out. "Molly would scream bloody murder if you try to get close. I prefer not to alert everyone in the neighborhood we're sneaking away with a child."

Fane reached to grasp her hand, tugging her until she was pressed against the blazing heat of his body.

"You love me?" The dark gaze seared over her face, lingering on the soft curve of her lips.

Her hand lifted to trace the tattoos that circled his throat.

"Was there ever any doubt, you big lug?"

He traced the line of her jaw with the tip of his finger.

"And you claim I have no romance?"

Bas and Kaede moved through the storage room and into the elegant salon that had been decorated to resemble an old speakeasy.

The ceilings were low with heavy wooden beams and there was a long bar that ran along the side of the room. There were several dark alcoves with wide leather benches and low tables for those who enjoyed sharing their sexual fantasies in public, as well as a small stage where two middle-aged women were giggling while doing an awkward striptease for two men Bas assumed were their husbands.

He headed directly for the stairs that led toward the private rooms upstairs. A slender young hostess in a microscopic black dress hurried to intercept him only to stumble to a halt as he sent her a fierce glare. He hadn't bothered with an illusion to disguise his eyes that revealed him as something other than "human."

Reaching the stairs, Bas motioned for his companion to halt.

"I can sense Jael above us," he said. "But she might try to double back and escape out the front door. Stay here and keep a watch."

Kaede nodded, moving to lean against the carved balustrade with his arms folded over his chest.

Nothing was getting past the onetime Sentinel.

Taking the steps two at a time, Bas swiftly reached the third floor of the club. He bypassed the closed doors, heading down the hall.

He'd just reached the end when the last door was yanked open and Jael stepped out of the room.

She was a small woman dressed in a low-cut red dress and wearing black fuck-me-now shoes. Her long, light brown hair was left free to frame her pixie face and her brown eyes remained hard even when she smiled.

Those cold eyes were the only hint that she was a female who possessed a sick love for giving pain to others.

"Going somewhere, witch?" he drawled.

"Bas." She stretched her lips into a humorless smile. "What an unpleasant surprise."

Lifting his hand, Bas shoved the witch back into the lavish black and gold bedroom, shutting the door behind him. He glanced around the room that was designed with whips and shackles on the walls instead of artwork and a table in one corner with a pile of sex toys.

No visible weapons or lurking companions.

He returned his attention to the female who was eyeing him with a defiant expression that didn't entirely hide the terror that pulsed just below the surface.

The bitch hadn't expected him to track her down.

Which only made this moment sweeter.

"I see the rumors of your death were greatly exaggerated," he said.

Without warning, Jael dropped the illusion she'd wrapped around herself to reveal that one side of her face was deeply scarred. The silvery spiderweb of damage could only have been caused by a deep, near lethal burn.

"Believe me, I spent weeks wishing I had died." A vicious hatred abruptly smoldered in the dark eyes. "Not that you cared. Or even bothered to search for me."

If Bas were a better man he might have felt sympathy. But he wasn't, and all he felt was a cold, brutal fury that this woman had nearly destroyed his life.

"Your death was witnessed by a dozen people," he said, not bothering to hide his indifference. "I had no reason to doubt their claim."

Her face twisted with a bitterness that came from the very soul.

"Just admit the truth," she spat out. "You didn't care if I was dead or alive. As far as you're concerned your 'people' are just tools you use to gain power."

He couldn't deny her accusation.

Hell, he didn't *want* to deny her accusation.

He did his best to protect his people and make certain they all shared in the wealth. He even had a rare few he considered friends.

But his ultimate goal was always power.

No matter who he had to use to gain it.

"How did you survive?" he instead demanded.

Her hand lifted to touch the scars, the festering fury in her eyes tinged with madness.

"The Brotherhood captured me in my hotel room and set me on fire in the alley, but I had enough magic to survive the initial blaze."

He grimaced. Being burned alive was a nasty way to die.

It had to have been an even worse hell to survive.

"But you escaped?" he asked, not because he actually wanted to know, but because he had to keep her distracted until Serra could find Molly.

"No. I was still tied to the stake, barely clinging to life, when one of the Brotherhood had the bright idea they could use me as a weapon." She curled her lips as she flicked a practiced gaze of derision over him. She'd obviously spent a great deal of time considering what she would say to him if they were ever face-to-face. "You have a lot in common with them."

He shrugged. "They held you hostage?"

"Yes." She tilted her head so her hair slipped over her scarred face. "In the beginning I was too weak to try to escape. It took me months to heal. Then I remained because they had something I wanted."

Bas frowned in confusion. Was she saying that she'd become a member of the Brotherhood?

"You became a traitor to your people?"

She gave a sharp, near hysterical laugh. "You of all people dare to call me a traitor? That would be amusing if it weren't so predictable." Her features twisted with a soul-deep loathing. "You really are the most arrogant son of a bitch I've ever met."

Bas silently breathed a spell as the female spiraled toward a complete meltdown.

He didn't have the magic of a true witch, but he had a few stun spells that could disable her long enough for him to snap her neck.

"What did you do for the Brotherhood?"

She glanced toward the whips that lined the walls. "The same thing I did for you. Pain, terror . . . torture."

Bas grimaced. It offended him to think of her sharing her high-blood talents with a bunch of idiots who hoped to destroy them.

"Did you tell them about Anna?" he snapped.

She scowled. "Of course not."

"Then they aren't behind Molly's kidnapping?"

"The Brotherhood?" She studied him as if he'd lost his

mind. "They're a bunch of bumbling idiots. They couldn't plan their way out of their own asses."

He agreed. But that didn't answer his question.

"Then why did you stay with them?"

"Because they have excellent taste in illegal weapons."

Ah. That explained where the weapons had come from, and why they'd traced back to the Brotherhood.

"You stole them."

"Yes." She trailed a red-lacquered fingernail along the edge of her plunging neckline. "I knew a large supply was coming in from Mexico so I waited until I had the exact dates and times. In the meantime I had Lee gathering us a small army of norms."

"And kidnapped my daughter?"

She tilted her head to an aggressive angle. "Yes."

He leaned down, the heat of his fury blasting through the air.

This twisted, bitter female had stolen a mere babe from her bed and used her as a bargaining chip.

That was nothing less than evil.

"Why?"

The madness in her eyes glittered in the muted light. "Because I'm done with being at the mercy of asshole men who think they can use and abandon me without consequences." Tingles of magic began to fill the air as the woman teetered on the edge of sanity. "From now on I'm in charge."

Bas's gaze lowered to her neck, imagining the pleasure of wrapping his fingers around the slender length and squeezing.

"Being in charge means kidnapping innocent little girls from their beds?" he mocked in disgust.

"How else could I have gotten my hands on Anna?"

He narrowed his gaze. "Any number of ways."

"True." A malicious smile curved her lips. "I wanted to

punish you and I knew that nothing would hurt you as much as losing your precious Molly."

"Because I didn't realize you hadn't died in a fire?"

"For that." She glanced toward the nearby bed. "And because you humiliated me in front of my friend. No man turns down the opportunity to become my lover."

He clenched his teeth as her magic sliced wildly through the air, striking against his skin like a whip. He restrained his own power. He would only have one chance to strike before she could conjure a spell that might very well disable him.

"You've terrorized a mere baby because I pricked your vanity?"

The bitch had the nerve to look offended. "Molly is fine."

He waved aside her assurance. In just a few minutes he intended to discover for himself if Molly was fine or not.

Surely Serra had to be getting close?

"What do you want with Anna?" he asked, abruptly changing the subject.

Once he had Molly safe he would have to find a way to return the dangerous high-blood to her protected cell.

Jael shrugged. "I want her to be who she was meant to be."

"Is that supposed to make sense?"

The witch took a covert step toward the center of the room.

Bas frowned. Why?

Did she have some hidden trap she was trying to lure him into?

"You've tormented the poor woman long enough," Jael said, taking another step.

Realization abruptly hit Bas. The witch was trying to inch her way toward the nearby table where a collection of bottles was lined against the wall. He'd bet among the oils and perfumes was at least one lethal potion.

"I've done nothing but protect her," he said, shifting so he was blocking her path to the table.

Jael stiffened, but her brittle composure never faltered. "She's been held in stasis for endless years," she accused. As if she gave a shit about Anna or the limited life she was forced to endure. "Like Sleeping Beauty with no prince to waken her. Can you imagine the horror of that existence?"

Bas offered a taunting smile. "And you intend to waken her?"

The witch reached into the small handbag she was carrying, unaware that Bas had reached behind his back for his gun. She was a powerful high-blood so a bullet probably wouldn't kill her, but it would hurt like a bitch.

"It's already in process," she said, pulling out a cell phone.

Bas frowned. "What do you mean?"

"My men called just an hour ago." She gave a wave of the phone. "The wagon carrying Anna has broken down. I gave the word to start killing your witches."

A chill inched down Bas's spine. He might not be a hero. Hell, he was probably a villain. But the thought of the four young witches being butchered made him sick.

Not to mention the fact that Anna's powers might even now be spreading through the land . . .

It was enough to make him wish the evil bitch had died on the stake.

"You're going to release her powers?"

A feverish anticipation flared through the dark eyes. Just another glimpse of the madness seething just below the surface.

"She deserves to be free."

"You don't give a shit about Anna," he said. "What do you hope to gain?"

She paused, as if considering a lie. Then, with a shrug, she gave him the blunt truth.

"Chaos. War. Destruction."

Even expecting her answer, Bas was shocked. "Why?"

She stepped toward him, a snarl on her ravaged face. "Because I've discovered that I don't particularly like this world," she ground out. "I was abandoned by my own people and burned at the stake by norms. All of you deserve to suffer."

Bas shook his head. He'd always known Jael wasn't entirely stable. Not just because of her love for delivering pain, but her unpredictable mood swings.

Now it seemed she had also been harboring delusions of grandeur.

"And after the destruction?" he pressed.

"Then I rebuild. I'll reconstruct a world where I'm in charge." She said it with the blithe confidence of a true narcissist. "So I killed two birds with one stone. I kidnapped Molly to force you to bring Anna out of her hibernation—"

"Why did you have me take her across the country?" he interrupted.

"There's the chance that the spreading devastation might be traced back to Anna," she admitted. "If that happened I didn't want any connection to the high-blood."

Bas shook his head in self-disgust. He'd jumped through rings to try to protect his daughter, and it'd all been nothing but a game to stroke this woman's damaged ego.

"You were never going to release Molly, were you?" he growled.

"Not as long as I was enjoying our game." With a taunting smile she lifted her phone and swiftly pressed in a number. "But now you've violated the rules. It's time to move to the next level."

Molly. His heart stuttered to an agonizing halt.

"What are you doing?"

"Calling my men to make sure they've gained control of Anna."

Bas nearly went to his knees as relief blasted through him. Shit. He couldn't stand much more.

He had to get rid of this crazy-ass female and get to his daughter.

Watching the growing frown on her face, he inwardly prepared to launch his spell.

"A problem?" he demanded as she shut her phone off with an angry stab of her finger.

Something that might have been fear briefly replaced the madness in her eyes.

"They're in the middle of nowhere," she muttered, trying to convince herself her egotistical scheme wasn't falling apart. "They probably lost service."

"More likely my witches killed them. Unlike you, I choose my employees with care." He allowed his gaze to move up and down her body in a blatant insult. "Or at least, most of them."

She shook her head, taking a step backward. "No. It's not possible."

She was going to crack. It was a matter of seconds.

He had to pray that Molly was safe.

"Now what, Jacl?" His body tingled as he allowed his magic to race through his blood. "Your men are dead. Sandoval is dead. Do you have another game to play?"

She licked her lips. "I still have your daughter."

"Are you so sure?"

Her eyes widened at his soft words. "What have you done?"

His smile was as cold as the Arctic. "You don't think I was actually interested in your pathetic dreams of grandeur, do you?" he mocked. "I was keeping you distracted while my associates were retrieving my daughter."

"Kaede is downstairs . . ." she began, only to have her words trail away as the realization that she'd been tricked slowly tightened her damaged features. "The psychic," she breathed. "She was working with you."

Bas lifted his hand, his magic sparking on the tips of his fingers.

"You're not nearly so clever as you think you are."

Manic hatred flashed through the dark eyes as she made a frantic leap toward the potions on the nearby table.

"I'm clever enough to make sure that I don't die alone."

Bas released his stun spell, knocking her to her knees. "You of all people, Jael, should know I never lose."

"No."

Thwarted of her potions, Jael raised her hand, preparing to launch a counter-spell.

Bas didn't give her the opportunity. Ignoring the weapons strapped to his body, he grabbed the potion she'd intended for him and tossed it directly into her face.

She screamed, her back arching as that magic ravaged through her.

It was a particularly nasty potion. One brewed to destroy the internal organs.

Bas, however, didn't stay to savor the destruction of his enemy.

The bitch would soon be dead.

All he cared about was wrapping his arms around his daughter.

Chapter Twenty-Seven

Serra stared at the paneled wall with a frown of impatience.

"She's behind this wall," she muttered, clearly able to sense Molly just a few feet away.

They'd managed to search through the dark house without incident. Fane had taken care of any guards and the witch was clearly still occupied with Bas.

Or, if they had any luck at all, she was already dead.

Foolishly she'd started to hope that this would be a quick in and out.

Find Molly. Grab her. Leave.

Easy peasy.

Of course it couldn't be easy. Or peasy.

She glared at the blank wall, tired of playing games with the damned kidnappers.

"There has to be a hidden door," Fane said, slowly running his hands over the paneling.

Squashing her seething impatience, Serra moved to place her hands on the wall of the hallway. Fane was right. There had to be a way to get into a secret room.

"I'll search this side," she said. Not that she knew what the hell she was searching for. All she could do was hope she could trip some lever and a hidden door would slide open. "I think—"

Her words came to an abrupt halt as there was a draft of air to her side and the muzzle of a gun was pressed to her temple.

"Don't move," a female voice commanded. "One twitch and I pull the trigger."

Shit. Too late Serra realized a hidden door had indeed slid open. Only she hadn't found a hidden lever.

The female norm had managed to catch her off guard.

Dammit.

Fane took a smooth step toward them, his expression stoic and his body relaxed.

At a glance it would be easy to believe he wasn't particularly concerned that some strange woman was pressing a gun to Serra's head.

Serra, however, was well aware that he'd retreated into warrior mode.

He was a predator poised to strike, patiently waiting for an opening that would allow him to kill with lightning speed.

Serra might have felt sorry for the woman who was about to die if the bitch wasn't currently threatening to blow her brains out.

"Release her," Fane commanded, his cold, flat tone more terrifying than any amount of shouting.

"I don't think so."

The woman moved closer to Serra. As if realizing the only reason she wasn't dead was because Fane didn't have a clear shot. Glancing covertly to her side Serra caught sight of a slender woman with shoulder-length hair dyed a deep black and pale, pale features. Her dark eyes that were framed by fake lashes were currently watching Fane with barely concealed terror.

"Who are you and what do you want?" the norm demanded.

Fane briefly allowed his attention to shift to Serra, his gaze silently asking her if she could use her psychic abilities to disable her enemy.

Serra paused, allowing her mind to gently touch the female at her side. She had naturally stronger shields than most norms, and perhaps a trace of magic, which no doubt had attracted the attention of Jael, but she was no match for Serra's powers.

She gave a discreet nod.

Fane stepped forward, deliberately holding the female's attention as Serra prepared to attack.

"We're here for Molly," he said.

The woman's breath hissed through her clenched teeth. "You work for Bas?"

Fane's lips twisted at the implication he would work for the assassin.

"We are . . . reluctant allies," he grudgingly admitted. "Give us the girl and we'll leave. No one has to get hurt."

The gun was pressed even harder against Serra's temple. "You don't get to give the orders here," the woman said, her voice shrill. "This is how it's going to happen. You turn around and leave. Once I know you're off the property I'll release your woman."

His woman?

Serra rolled her eyes, continuing to probe at the edges of the female's mind. Once she found the weakest point she would strike.

Fane shook his head. "I can kill you before you squeeze the trigger."

"I don't believe you," the woman rasped. "Besides, there's a spell around Molly. If you try to take her from the room she'll die."

Fane arched a brow. Obviously the woman didn't realize that a guardian Sentinel was capable of breaking through all but the most lethal spells.

"I know it's a cliché, but I'm going to give you to the count of five to release her." Fane lifted a fist, straightening his index finger in a slow motion. "One."

The woman made a sound of desperation. "You can't get Molly."

Another finger straightened. "Two."

"Jael will kill you," she stammered. "She's a powerful witch."

Another finger. "Three."

"Wait, I . . . argg."

The woman's words turned into a shocked scream of pain as Serra released a psychic burst of power, slamming into the woman's brain with enough force to shatter her consciousness.

With a heavy thud the female hit the ground, the gun skittering harmlessly across the wood floor.

Serra barely had time to catch her breath before strong arms were wrapped around her and she was being hauled against an unyielding chest.

"A little premature," Fane growled in her ear, his voice not entirely steady. "I hadn't reached five."

It was a struggle to breathe as Fane's arms tightened around her, but Serra didn't protest.

She needed this moment as much as Fane.

"I always did have trouble with math," she murmured, savoring the heat and strength that cocooned her in a sense of well-being.

When she was in this man's arms, she would always feel safe.

"Will she survive?" he asked, running a comforting hand up and down her spine.

Reluctantly pulling away, Serra turned to send a dismissive glance toward the woman collapsed on the floor. She could sense a faint pulse, but it was erratic.

"Maybe," she said, giving a shrug. The woman had worked with Jael to kidnap an innocent child. Serra didn't give a shit what happened to her. "We have to get Molly."

With a nod, Fane stepped over the woman and through the hidden door that remained open. Serra followed closely behind him, using her mind to sweep for any hidden guards.

She couldn't detect another mind in the house, but she remained on guard.

There was always the off chance that there could be a guardian Sentinel like Fane in the area. They could slip beneath her psychic radar.

In front of her, Fane crossed directly toward the narrow bed where a tiny child slept beneath a pink blanket.

Her breath caught at the sight of her mussed mop of silver-blond curls that were spread across the pillowcase and the little rounded face.

God almighty.

Who could ever have threatened this sweet, innocent child?

Kneeling on the cheap carpeting, Fane held out his hand, his eyes closing as he tested the magic wrapped around the bed.

Serra took a cautious step forward. "Can you break the spell?" she asked softly.

"Yes." Fane opened his eyes and glanced over his shoulder. "Make sure we're not interrupted."

"Yes, sir." She rolled her eyes at his sharp command, but obediently moved to the door to keep watch on the hallway.

Minutes passed, then she heard Fane give a deep, shuddering sigh.

"Serra."

Whirling around, Serra headed swiftly back to his side. Dammit. Had Jael left a trap that would somehow harm the child?

"Is something wrong?" she breathed.

"The spell is broken." He nodded toward the stirring form beneath the blanket. "I think she's about to awaken."

Relief flooded through Serra as she perched on the edge of the mattress, offering a smile as the child opened her eyes that were the same startling shade of bronze as her father.

"Hi, Molly," she said softly.

Sitting up, Molly glanced warily around the room, inching toward Serra as she caught sight of Fane's massive form.

"Where's my daddy?"

Serra tucked a silver curl behind Molly's ear. "I'm going to take you to him, muffin."

With a heartbreaking trust the child climbed into her lap and rested her head over Serra's heart.

"Is he mad at me?"

Serra wrapped the tiny body in her arms, resting her cheek on top of the soft curls.

"Never," she insisted in fierce tones. Whatever Bas's faults, and they were numerous, he was a devoted father. "He loves you."

The small body shivered. "He didn't come."

"I'm here, pet," a dark male voice said from the doorway.

Serra gave a tiny jerk of surprise as Bas stepped into the

room. She'd been too distracted with the child to notice his arrival.

Fane, however, had already shifted to stand between the assassin and the bed. Clearly he hadn't been caught off guard.

"Daddy!" Molly called out, her expression one of pure joy.

"Not yet," Fane warned as Bas stepped forward. "Where is Jael?"

"Gone," the assassin muttered, his gaze locked on Molly. "For good."

"You're certain she was the mastermind?" Fane pressed.

"Yes." Bas sent Fane a lethal glare. "Now step aside or die."

Fane folded his arms over his chest. "Not until you've removed the spell from Serra."

Bas touched the dagger at his side, his hair tousled and his face looking distinctly haggard.

"Let me have my daughter," he snarled. "Once she's in my arms I'll remove the spell."

Fane stood in front of Serra. An unmovable force.

"Not a chance in hell."

Molly squirmed in Serra's lap. "Daddy?"

Fane stepped forward, his body rigid with the effort to leash his fury.

"Look in my eyes and know that I will do whatever is necessary to protect Serra," he said, his voice a ruthless warning.

Heat filled the room as the two warriors squared off, the threat of violence making Serra shiver.

"And you know what will happen if you do anything to harm Molly," Bas countered, his hand stroking over the handle of his dagger.

Serra made a sound of impatience.

Men.

"Oh for God's sake, remove the spell so you can comfort your daughter," she snapped, glaring at the assassin as she stroked her hand over Molly's satin-soft curls. "She needs you."

There was a tense minute as the two men hovered on the brink of battle. Then, glancing toward the tiny girl dressed in a frilly nightgown tucked in Serra's lap, Bas gave a sharp nod.

"Fine."

The assassin stepped forward, only to be jerked to a halt by a suspicious Fane.

"What are you doing?"

"It will be easier if I touch her."

"No—"

"Fane, it's okay," Serra interrupted.

She didn't trust Bas any more than Fane did, but what choice did they have?

Without him removing the spell, she was going to die.

Shaking off Fane's hand, Bas moved forward, his gaze locked on his daughter even as he knelt beside Serra and placed his hand on the side of her neck.

Fane growled as he moved forward, but Bas was already whispering low words. Icy tingles began to flow through her blood, the sudden chill making her shiver.

"Serra," Fane rasped in concern.

Serra glanced up to meet his searching gaze. "I felt something, but I have no idea if it was the removal of the toxin."

"The spell was removed," Bas corrected, reaching into the pocket of his slacks to remove a slender gold box. It looked like an old-fashioned cigarette case, but when he flicked it open it revealed several small vials of potions. "This is the antidote for the toxin," he said, handing over one of the vials to Serra.

Without giving herself time to wonder if this was a trick Serra lifted the vial and downed the contents.

She gagged at the bitter taste, struggling to keep herself from heaving the antidote back up as it hit her empty stomach like a small nuclear explosion.

When she at last was confident she was going to keep the potion down, she glanced up to see Bas reaching for the child in her arms.

"Give me my daughter."

Serra allowed Molly to be scooped into Bas's arms, even smiling as the child threw her thin arms around his neck and buried her face against his chest.

"Daddy," she said in sleepy satisfaction.

Bas stepped back with Molly cradled in his arms, his gaze on Fane.

"Now what?"

Fane shrugged. "Now we take you to Valhalla."

"I don't think so."

Without warning, Bas tossed the golden case in Serra's direction. Instantly Fane leaped to knock her to the side, covering her with his large body as an explosion rocked the entire building.

Serra coughed as dust from the crumbling ceiling lodged in her throat, her body bruised.

Slowly, Fane lifted his head, shaking off the debris that had threatened to bury them.

"Are you okay?" he rasped.

She nodded, allowing Fane to pull her to her feet as they both tried to slap the dust off their bodies.

The explosion had only done cosmetic damage, but it'd given Bas the opportunity to escape.

"Yes, but he's getting away," she said.

Fane gently plucked a piece of plaster from her hair, his gaze remaining locked on her upturned face.

"Let him run."

She blinked at his surprising lack of interest in the fleeing assassin.

"I thought you were so determined to kill him?"

"I will . . . eventually." His thumb brushed a smudge of dirt from her cheek. "Now all that matters is getting you back to Valhalla. I want the healers to check you out."

Serra released a shaky breath, still trying to wrap her brain around the fact that the hideous days of constant fear and danger were in the past.

Really, truly in the past.

"Is it over?" She needed to be reassured. To know that this wasn't some dream.

"The toxin is gone." He leaned down to place a tender, lingering kiss on her lips. "Molly is safe, the majority of the mercenaries are being held at the lab, and there's nowhere Bas can run where I can't find him," he assured her softly.

Her lips parted as she was struck by a sudden thought. "What about Anna?"

"I received a text while I was scouting the building from Wolfe," he assured her. "The Mave managed to transport her to Valhalla. She's safe in a magically enhanced room."

She released a shaky breath. "We're going home?"

He pressed another kiss to her lips. "Together."

Fane stood in Wolfe's office, his arms folded over his chest as the Tagos studied him with a furious expression.

"What the hell do you mean you're leaving?"

Fane shrugged. It'd been nearly two weeks since they'd returned to Valhalla.

Since then Serra had been taken to the clinic so she could be thoroughly checked out by the healers. From there she went to her foster family who'd fussed over her before her biological parents had rushed to Valhalla to lavish their daughter with endless attention.

Eventually she'd returned to her private apartments, but she hadn't been left alone for a minute as her friends, ex-boyfriends, and assorted high-bloods who'd insisted they needed to spend time in her company crowded into her home.

Fane had frankly come to the end of his patience.

He wanted to be with the woman he loved.

Alone.

This morning he'd awakened and set into motion the one certain way to have Serra to himself.

"Serra's been given a clean bill of health," he said with a shrug. "We want some time together."

"Then take a weekend at Vegas," Wolfe snapped. "There's no need to travel to Tibet to be together."

Fane studied the Tagos with a lift of his brow. The man was always aggressive. Hell, he had enough testosterone for three men. But, over the past two weeks he'd been prowling through Valhalla like a man looking for a fight.

Not surprising, the residents had swiftly learned to flee when he stepped into view.

"Is there a particular reason you're so reluctant for us to go?" Fane demanded.

"Let me see." Wolfe leaned on the edge of his desk. "I have a high-blood in stasis who's a potential time bomb just waiting to happen. I have a dungeon full of traitorous high-bloods who are waiting for their trial. Bas is on the run. The Brotherhood is obviously becoming a threat," he growled. "Do you need any more reasons?"

Fane studied his companion. Wolfe was dressed in the same casual style as Fane. Jeans, T-shirt, and combat boots. But there was an unmistakable tension etched into the lean face.

"Just the real one."

Wolfe shoved his fingers through his dark hair. "I've had word from the scholars who've been translating the hieroglyphs on the ancient temple."

Fane frowned before realizing Wolfe was referring to the temple in the deserts of the Middle East that had been revealed by the necromancer.

"And?"

"And some of them imply a destined time of trouble for our people."

Fane rolled his eyes. "Prophets always claim there is going to be some future disaster. It keeps them in business."

Wolfe held his gaze. "I agree that most of the time it's foolishness."

"But?"

"But the clairvoyants have begun to see blood in the future."

"Blood?" Fane repeated, not particularly impressed. Was there something else going on with Wolfe? Something that could explain his restless tension besides a vague threat of future trouble?

"That's all they can give me." Wolfe waved a hand toward the stack of files on his desk. "But several have had the same vision. That alone is highly unusual."

"Fine," Fane grudgingly conceded. Dammit, all he wanted was to take Serra to a remote Tibetan mountaintop and live out his life in peace. Was that so much to ask? "If this mysterious trouble reveals itself I'll return. Until then I intend to enjoy my beautiful woman."

Turning to head to the door, Fane was halted as Wolfe straightened from the desk.

"So when are you two going to tie the knot?"

Fane heaved a resigned sigh, already having had a tiny

taste of the massive, chaotic, nerve-wracking project that would eventually lead to a wedding.

"Apparently it takes no less than a year to prepare for the big day," he admitted with a shudder. "If it was up to me we would already be wed. I'm not taking the chance of ever letting her escape me again."

Wolfe grimaced. "No wonder you're so anxious to get to Tibet." Stepping forward, the Tagos clapped Fane on the shoulder. "Enjoy yourself."

Fane smiled, heading out the door. He fully intended to enjoy Serra.

As often and as thoroughly as she would allow him to.

Stepping into the hall his heart slammed against his chest as he caught sight of Serra leaning against the wall, her lush body shown to perfection in her leather pants, red halter top, and four-inch boots.

Christ . . . he went up in flames just looking at her.

With a small, wicked smile that revealed the clever psychic knew her exact effect on him, she pushed from the wall and moved to wrap her arms around his neck.

"Well?"

Fane studied the exquisite face of the woman he loved.

He'd fought it for so long.

Too long.

Now he just wanted to savor each and every minute with her.

"Are you packed?" he asked, his voice rough.

She tilted her head to the side, studying his face with the knowledge of a woman who knew him better than anyone in the world.

"He wasn't pleased was he?" she asked.

He shrugged. "Wolfe thinks every Sentinel should live and breathe for their jobs."

"And what do you think?"

"I think my life is yours, *milaya*." His low voice was filled with promise. "For now and all eternity."

She framed his face in her hands, her eyes shimmering with love.

"Now that was romantic."

He lowered his head, burying his face in the curve of her neck.

"I'm just getting started."

Epilogue

Bas was studying the skyline from his penthouse suite of the luxury hotel.

His first impulse after fleeing from St. Louis was to go underground. Keeping a low profile was easy for a man capable of altering his appearance.

But after only a few days in a squalid house in the middle of nowhere, he'd realized he couldn't possibly drag Molly from one location to another.

She needed stability in her young life.

Not to mention three meals a day and a warm bed complete with her stuffed hippo, Daisy.

All things impossible to ensure when he was on the run.

Instead he'd headed to this hotel that was owned by his corporation.

Eventually the Mave would track him down, but he was confident he had a few weeks before she unraveled his complicated accounts and numerous false names to connect him to this hotel.

Until then he intended to plot his future in comfort.

Sipping his brandy, he watched as the sun dipped low in

the sky, lost in his thoughts until he heard the pitter-patter of tiny feet.

Slowly turning, he watched as Molly entered the salon, Daisy clutched in her arms.

"Daddy?"

"Hey, sweetie." Crouching down, he studied his daughter's sleep-flushed face surrounded by her silvery curls, an undiluted joy piercing his heart. Christ, he still got up a dozen times a night to make sure she was safely tucked in her bed. Molly, on the other hand, barely seemed to remember her time with the witch. Thank God. "What are you doing up? Did you have a bad dream?"

Her sweet smile lit up the shadowed room. "Mama called me."

Bas froze. Molly often spoke of her mother. Almost as if Myst were a constant companion.

He'd always assumed it was her childish way of coping without a mother.

"Called you?" He gave a tug on a silvery curl, his expression teasing. "On the phone?"

She giggled, a dimple appearing beside her mouth. "No, silly. In my head."

"It was a dream," he gently assured her.

The bronze eyes widened. "No. It was real."

"Molly."

"She talks to me all the time."

He bit back his impulse to inform the child that her mother had walked out on him without a backward glance. Molly was innocent of Myst's callous lack of concern for her daughter. Or the man who had created a child with her.

And if Molly needed to create fantasies about her mother then he would have to play along.

"Okay," he murmured. "What does she say?"

"That she has something she has to do, but she misses me," Molly promptly shared. "And that soon we'll be together again."

He tenderly smoothed her silken curls. "I don't want you to be disappointed if she can't come," he said gently. "You have me. And I'm never going away."

"But she is coming." She flashed her dimpled smile at the sound of the door to the suite being opened. "Now."

Bas surged to his feet, his hand reaching for the gun holstered at the small of his back.

How the hell had the intruder gotten past his locks?

"Molly, go to your room."

The little girl sent him a puzzled glance. "But it's Mommy."

On cue a female stepped into the salon, dressed in a yellow sundress. Bas hissed, feeling as if he'd been punched in the gut.

She was just as beautiful as ever.

Her pale, perfect face was dominated by a large pair of velvet brown eyes. Her hair was pulled into a long braid that fell to her waist, the silvery-blond color shimmering in the muted light.

"Myst," he breathed in disbelief.

She regarded him with a somber expression. "Hello, Bas."

He gave a shake of his head, trying desperately to dismiss his potent, intoxicating response to the sight of her.

"What the hell are you doing here?"

Her gaze shifted to the tiny girl standing beside him, a luminous smile lighting her fragile features.

"I've come for my daughter."

Please turn the page for an exciting sneak peek of

Alexandra Ivy's

WHEN DARKNESS ENDS,

the final installment in her
Guardians of Eternity series,

coming in June 2015!

Prologue

Laigin (Ireland), 1014 AD

The man woke with a blinding headache, stripped of his clothing as well as his memories.

With a groan, he sat up, shoving his tangled hair out of his face. It was immediately obvious he was in a damp cave. A strange place to awaken. But not nearly as strange as the abrupt realization that something was terrifyingly wrong with him.

Despite the darkness he was able to see the limestone walls that had been chiseled by the water dripping from the low ceiling as clear as if it were day. And it was not only his sight that was unbearably acute.

He could smell the distant salt of the sea. And hear the faint scramble of a bug crossing the stone floor. He could even detect the warmth of two creatures that were rapidly approaching the cave.

What madness was this?

No man should have the senses of a god. Not unless he was a monster.

The dark thoughts barely had time to form before they were interrupted by a hunger that thundered through him.

He groaned. It was as if he hadn't eaten in weeks. Months. But it wasn't the thought of food that made his stomach cramp, he realized with a flare of horror.

It was . . . blood.

His mouth watered, the pain of his fangs ripping through his gums startling him as the image of the red, intoxicatingly rich substance filled his mind.

He had to feed.

Aye. That was what he needed.

Disgusted with the knowledge he slowly rose to his feet, a virile strength running through his massive body even as his head remained thick with confusion.

His instincts urged him to leave the cave, to hunt down his prey and bury his fangs deep in their throats, but the tantalizing scent of fresh strawberries kept him frozen in place.

It appeared that his prey was willingly coming to him.

And they smelled . . . delectable.

Like an animal, he warily shuffled to the deepest shadows. From his vantage point, he silently watched the two slender creatures enter the cave. His eyes widened at the sheer beauty of the strangers. The male had hair the color of rust with bold green eyes set in a lean face, while the female possessed long tawny hair with eyes the shade of spring grass.

They looked like angels.

His fangs ached, his muscles tensing as he prepared to strike.

Angels or not, they were about to become dinner.

But before he could charge, the male held up a slender hand, the scent of strawberries becoming overpowering.

"Hold, berserker," he commanded, a tingle of magic in the air.

He frowned. "I am a berserker?"

"You were."

The confusion only deepened. "Were?"

"Two nights ago you were attacked by a clan of vampires."

He shook his head, his hand instinctively lifting to touch his neck.

"I survived?"

The pretty female grimaced. "Not as a human. The local villagers left you in this cave to see if you would rise as a vampire. Even now they are on their way to either see your corpse or slaughter you." She held out a slender hand. "Come with us in peace and we will harbor you until you are able to care for yourself."

Vampire . . .

He went to his knees in shock.

Holy shite.

Chapter One

Ireland, Present Day

Cyn, clan chief of Ireland and former berserker, moaned as he slowly regained consciousness. His brain was fuzzy, which meant it took a full minute to realize he was lying butt-naked on the cold stone floor of a cave.

Bloody hell. It had been a millennium since he'd awakened in this precise cave, naked and disoriented. He didn't like it any better today than he had a thousand years ago.

What'd happened?

With a groan he forced himself to a sitting position, his body hardening at the intoxicating scent that teased at his nose.

Champagne?

A fine, crisp vintage that made his entire body tingle with anticipation.

For a blissful minute he allowed the fragrance to swirl around him. It was oddly familiar. And, surprisingly, it stirred a complex mixture of emotions.

Arousal. Wariness. Frustration.

It was the frustration that abruptly forced him to recall why the scent was so familiar.

Muttering a curse, Cyn had a searing memory of following a beautiful fairy through a portal. No . . . not a fairy, he wryly corrected himself. A Chatri. The ancient pure-bloods of the fey world who'd retreated to their homeland centuries before.

He'd been there to help Roke locate his mate, but Princess Fallon had shoved him out of the throne room when it was obvious that Roke and Sally needed time to work out their differences, insisting that he leave them in peace.

He'd only been vaguely annoyed at first. He didn't trust the cunning Chatri as far as he could throw them, especially not their king, Sariel. But, he wanted Roke to work out his troubles with his mate.

Besides, he was male enough to appreciate being in the company of a beautiful woman.

Or in the case of Fallon . . . a breathtakingly exquisite woman.

Her hair was a glorious tumble of rich gold brushed with hints of pale rose. The sort of hair that begged a man to bury his face in the silken mass. Her eyes were polished amber with flecks of emerald and framed by the thickest, longest lashes Cyn had ever seen. And her ivory features . . . gods almighty, they were so perfect they didn't look real.

He might be suspicious of Fallon, but that didn't mean he couldn't enjoy fantasizing about having her tossed on the nearby chaise longue while he peeled the gown off her slender body, he'd assured himself.

So he'd allowed himself to be distracted by the lovely female as he sipped the potent fey wine, not realizing the danger until his head began to spin and the world went dark.

Idiot.

He should have known that they were plotting something.

He might have a fondness for the fey, but that didn't mean he wasn't well aware of their mercurial natures.

And their love for luring the unwary into their clever traps.

With a low growl he turned his head, easily spotting the female who was sprawled naked on the ground, her golden hair shimmering even in the darkness.

He wanted to know how the hell she'd managed to bring them to the caves beneath his private lair. And he wanted to know now.

Cyn moved to bend beside her slumbering form, pretending that he wasn't acutely aware of the enticing temptation of her long, slender body and the fragile beauty of her pale face.

Sleeping beauty . . .

A scowl marred his forehead. Aye. She was a beauty. She was also a powerful fey princess who'd managed to catch him off guard once.

It wasn't going to happen again.

"Fallon?" Cyn murmured, his voice deep and laced with an accent that hadn't been heard in this world for centuries. She heaved a sigh at the sound of his voice, but she remained stubbornly asleep. Cyn knelt at her side, knowing better than to touch her. The feel of that satin skin beneath his fingertips was guaranteed to make him forget he was pissed as hell at her little trick. "Fallon," he growled, his voice a command. "Wake up."

She gave a small jerk, her lashes fluttering upward to reveal the striking amber eyes with the shimmering flecks of emerald.

For a long moment she studied him in stunned confusion.

Understandable.

Most people found Cyn . . . intimidating.

At six foot three he had a powerful chest and thick muscles that marked him as a warrior. His mane of dark blond hair hung halfway down his back except for the front strands that he kept woven into tight braids that framed his face.

His features were chiseled along blunt lines with a square jaw and high cheekbones. His brow was wide and his jade green eyes heavily lashed. Females seemed to find him handsome enough, but there was never any mistake that he was a ruthless killer.

She sucked in a shaky breath as her gaze lowered to the barbaric Tuatha Dé Danann tattoos that curled and swirled in a narrow green pattern around his upper arms, emphasizing the perfect alabaster of his skin.

His lips twisted, as he wondered what she would think of the golden dragon tattoo with crimson wings that was currently hidden beneath the thick mane of his hair.

He'd earned the mark of CuChulainn that was branded onto his right shoulder blade after he'd survived the battles of Durotriges.

It marked him as a clan chief.

"Vampire," she muttered, as if having difficulty remembering who he was.

He narrowed his gaze, wondering what game she was playing. "Cyn."

"Yes . . . Cyn." Her confusion was replaced with a horror as if she were suddenly remembering who he was. A horror that only intensified when she belatedly realized they were both butt-naked. "Dear goddess." She shoved herself to a sitting position, curling her arms around her knees as she glared at him with angry accusation. "What have you done to me?"

"Me?" He made a sound of disbelief, unconsciously

reaching to push a strand of golden hair off her flushed cheek.

"No . . ." With a flare of panic she was scrambling backward, a genuine fear flaring through the amber eyes. "Stay away."

Cyn muttered a low curse. Her pretense of confusion was annoying the hell out of him, but he didn't like the thought she was afraid of him.

Strange when he had devoted several centuries to terrifying his enemies.

"Settle down, princess," he murmured softly.

"Settle down?" A flush stained her beautiful face. "I wake up naked in the company of a strange vampire far away from my home and you want me to settle down?" She bit her bottom lip, her flush deepening to crimson. "Did you—"

"What?"

"Violate me?"

What the hell? Cyn surged upright. Six foot three of quivering, offended, naked male.

"No, I didn't damn well violate you," he rasped. "And if I had I can assure you that you would not only remember, but you'd be on your knees thanking me for the privilege."

Her fear was replaced by a more familiar disdain. As if he was a bug that needed to be squashed beneath her royal heel.

"Why you arrogant . . . leech."

He folded his arms over his massive chest. "At least I'm not a stuck-up prig of a fairy."

"If you didn't violate me why are we naked?" she demanded, careful to keep her gaze locked on his face. Was she afraid his bare body might strike her blind? "And how did we get here?"

He snorted. "That's a question I should be asking you."

"I beg your pardon?"

"I'm a vampire."

Her lips thinned in annoyance, her chin tilted as she continued her ridiculous charade of innocence.

"Yes, I had managed to figure that out."

"Then you know that I can't create portals," he snapped, deliberately allowing his gaze to skim downward. Unlike the aggravating female, he had no problem enjoying a naked body. Especially one so appetizing. "Only the fey can do that."

She frowned, belatedly realizing she couldn't try to pin the blame of their abrupt teleportation on him.

Odd, she hadn't struck him as stupid.

Just the opposite, in fact.

"Fey aren't the only creatures who can create portals," she tried to hedge.

"Well I obviously didn't do it."

"Neither did I."

He made a sound of impatience. Why was she continuing with this game?

"You expect me to believe you?"

The flecks of emerald shimmered in her eyes. "My father has forbidden his people to leave our homeland."

"Oh aye, and a daughter has never dared to disobey her father."

She cast a condemning glance around the barren cave. "Trust me, if I did decide to defy my father I wouldn't choose to travel to this dump."

His low growl filled the air. He was a true hedonist. A vampire who reveled in rare books, fine wine, and beautiful women.

And in turn, women adored him.

All women.

But this female . . .

She wasn't the warm, willing bundle of pleasure he was accustomed to. She was rude and prickly and downright dangerous.

"Watch your tongue, princess," he snarled. "This dump happens to be a part of my private lair."

"There." She pointed an accusing finger toward him. "I knew it. You kidnapped me."

Cyn rolled his eyes. Could this farce get any more ridiculous?

"The only one kidnapped was me."

"Why would I kidnap an oversized, ego-bloated vampire?"

Yeah. Why would she? It took him a minute to shuffle through his still fuzzy thoughts.

"To keep me from protecting my friend," he at last concluded.

Hadn't she pulled him out of the throne room leaving Roke at the mercy of her father, Sariel? And then she'd plied him with some wicked fey brew that had knocked him unconscious.

Aye. It made perfect sense that it was a nefarious plot to separate him from his friend.

At least it did until she glared at him in outraged disbelief.

"Are you completely mental? Your friend was exactly where he wanted to be."

Okay. She had a point.

Roke hadn't looked like he needed Cyn's services. In fact, the last he'd seen of his fellow vampire he was wrapping his mate in his arms, his expression one of besotted devotion.

Bleck.

"Then perhaps you simply wanted to be alone with me." He flashed a smile that revealed his snowy white fangs.

One way or another he was getting answers. "You wouldn't be the first female to use magic to get me into her bed."

She muttered something distinctly unladylike beneath her breath.

"I am a fairy princess."

"And?"

"And I don't share my bed with—"

He planted his hands on his hips, his expression daring her to finish the sentence.

"With?"

Her lips parted to complete her insult, but before she could speak there was a sizzle of power in the air. Cyn turned toward the center of the cave, his muscles coiled to attack as there was a faint *pop* and then a tiny demon dressed in a long white gown appeared out of thin air.

Cyn gave a startled hiss, his eyes widening at the creature who could easily pass as a young girl with her small stature and long silver braid that nearly brushed the floor. Cyn, however, wasn't fooled. He recognized the strange oblong eyes that were a solid black and the sharp, pointed teeth.

This was no harmless juvenile.

She had enough power to crush him and his entire clan.

Even worse, she was an Oracle. One of the rare demons who sat on the Commission, the ultimate rulers of the demon world.

"Enough squabbling, children," she chided, folding her hands together as she studied them with an unnerving intensity.

"Holy shite." Cyn offered a belated bow. "Siljar."

Fallon crouched on the ground, her arms wrapped around her knees in a futile effort at modesty.

"You know this person?"

"Not person," Cyn corrected, shivering as Siljar's energy sizzled over his skin. "Oracle."

The amber eyes widened. "Oh."

"Forgive me." Siljar gave an absent wave of her hand and Cyn made a strangled sound of shock as he found himself covered by a plain white robe that hit him just below the knees. The Oracle gave another wave of her hand and Fallon was covered in a matching robe. "I haven't created a portal into the fairy homeland for a number of centuries."

Cyn scowled, ignoring Fallon's I-told-you-so glare. "You brought us here?" he demanded.

Siljar gave a nod of her head. "I did."

"Why?"

"Because I have need of you."

His acute hearing picked up Fallon's soft sigh of relief as she rose to her feet and brushed her hands down the satin robe.

"You need the vampire?"

"I have a name," he reminded the princess with a snap.

Siljar clicked her tongue, her gaze shifting from Fallon to Cyn.

"I need both of you."

Cyn stiffened. It was never, ever a good thing when an Oracle had need of him.

"Why?"

There was the unmistakable scent of sulfur as Siljar's expression tightened with anger.

"I fear the Commission is being tampered with."

Cyn arched a brow. Hadn't Styx sent word that they'd uncovered the plot by the strange demons who'd been holding Fallon's father captive?

"Aye, we know the Nebule planted a spy to pose as an Oracle," he said.

Siljar shrugged. "He has been destroyed."

Oh. Cyn grimaced. "You suspect there's another traitor?"

"That was my first thought," Siljar admitted. "But I believe that on this occasion the Oracles are being manipulated without their knowledge."

That seemed . . . unlikely.

"Why are you suspicious?" he demanded.

Siljar hesitated a second before revealing what was troubling her.

"Over the past few weeks I've found myself awakening as if from a trance to discover I'm seated in the Council Room," she at last said.

Cyn blinked in confusion. That was it? He'd been kidnapped and dropped naked in these caves because the old gal was becoming forgetful?

He forced himself to consider his idea. Only an idiot implied that an Oracle might be going a bit batty.

"The past year has been stressful, especially for the Commission," he murmured.

"It has. And if I was the only Oracle to experience the strange phenomenon then I would assume that your implication that I'm suffering from some sort of mental decay was right." Her lips twitched as he flinched at her blunt words. "I am, after all, quite old and it wouldn't be entirely unlikely that I would accidentally transport myself to a familiar location without realizing what I'm doing."

Cyn ignored Fallon's barely hidden amusement at his discomfort.

"But?"

"More than once I discovered I wasn't alone."

Cyn grimaced even as he heard Fallon suck in a startled breath.

Having Siljar suffering from an occasional blackout

was one thing. To think of the entire Commission being controlled by some unseen force . . . bloody hell.

"The other Oracles didn't know how they got there either?" he rasped.

Siljar gave a somber shake of her head. "No."

When Fallon had opened her eyes to discover herself far removed from her fairy homeland she'd been more annoyed than frightened.

Strange considering that it was the first time in her life she'd ever awakened in a dark cave, stark naked, and in the company of an equally naked vampire.

Hell, it was the first time she'd ever been away from her father's vast palace.

She should have been freaking out.

Shouldn't she?

But while she'd tried to convince herself that he must be some sort of deranged beast who'd stolen her from her home for God only knew what sort of perverted reason, she couldn't truly make herself believe he was intending her harm.

She hadn't spent much time with Cyn, but while the massive clan chief was obviously a terrifying predator, she'd easily sensed he posed no danger.

No, that wasn't true, she wryly conceded.

He posed all sorts of dangers, not the least of which was the unwelcome excitement that sizzled through her whenever he happened to glance in her direction.

But she didn't for a second believe he would physically hurt her.

Not unless he believed she was a threat to his people.

The tiny demon in front of her, however, had just sent a chill of terror straight down her spine.

She knew of the Commission, of course.

Unlike most Chatri, the pure-blooded ancestors of the fey, Fallon had never been content with her secluded existence. Others might be happy in her father's royal palace, surrounded by lush gardens and meadows that were drenched in perpetual sunshine, but for her it was all too . . . flawlessly monotonous.

There was only so much perfection a woman could endure before she became bored out of her mind. Which meant that Fallon had been driven to develop a secret life just to keep her sanity.

No one among her people knew that she'd created a hidden chamber where she honed her skill at scrying until she could not only peer into other dimensions, but she could also maintain several images at once.

Over the years she'd spent endless hours studying this world, fascinated by the rapidly changing cultures while her own life remained stagnant. She'd even kept up on the current fads and speech patterns, telling herself that she might have the opportunity to visit this world, even when she'd known deep in her heart that her father would never allow her to leave their homeland.

Now she wondered if she'd been mistaken in her belief that the powerful Oracles were both wise and fair leaders for the demon world.

"What would be the point of trancing you?" she demanded in confusion.

Siljar regarded her with an unblinking gaze. It was . . . creepy.

"My guess would be that they want us in the Council Room," she said.

She forced herself not to wilt beneath that basilisk stare. "Why?"

"It's the place we gather to share information, and to

settle disputes between demons," Siljar explained, abruptly pacing across the cave with jerky movements. As if she was trying to contain her emotions. "And in extreme cases it's where we share our power."

"Do you think it could be a demon who is trying to influence you to judge in his favor?" Cyn abruptly demanded.

"It is possible. We are currently negotiating a land treaty between the mountain ogres and the woodland sprites." Siljar gave a sharp shake of her head. Swish. Swish. Her white robe brushed the uneven floor. "But in truth, I fear the plot is far more nefarious."

"Nefarious?" Cyn demanded.

Siljar nodded. "I think someone is trying to force the Commission to combine their powers to cast a spell."

Cyn grimaced. "Who or what could have the necessary strength to influence the entire Commission?"

Siljar halted her pacing, regaining her composure to turn and meet the vampire's troubled frown.

"That's what I need you to discover."

"You want me to spy on the Oracles?" Cyn rasped.

"Of course not," Siljar chided. "I want Fallon to spy on them."

Fallon's mouth dropped open, her blood running cold. "Me?"

Siljar lifted a brow. "You are a master at scrying, are you not?"

Oh . . . damn.

"How did you—"

"I know many things, my dear," Siljar smoothly interrupted.

Fallon shuffled beneath the dark, steady gaze. What else did the tiny demon know about her? Not that Fallon had an exciting enough life to hoard many secrets, but still . . .

Cyn sent her a searching glance, as if surprised that she might have an actual skill.

Jerk.

"What does a master of scrying mean?"

Siljar answered. "Fallon can keep track of the Oracles, even when they travel between dimensions."

He didn't look particularly impressed. "How will that help?"

"She can see if there is anyone in particular who has contact with all of the Oracles," Siljar explained. "Or if there is someplace they travel where they could be manipulated."

"How close does she have to be to scry?" Cyn demanded of the Oracle.

Fallon muttered a low curse. Had she suddenly become invisible?

"Distance doesn't matter," she informed the vampire, not about to be treated as if she couldn't speak for herself. She'd had enough of that at her father's court. "The only thing I need is a location to start."

Without warning, Siljar was moving to stand directly in front of Fallon, her hand reaching to press against her cheek.

"There," the demon said, searing the image of a vast complex of caves into Fallon's mind. "You can track them?"

Fallon hissed in shock as the location locked in her mind and she realized just what was expected of her.

Crap. What was wrong with her? She should have told Siljar she couldn't scry. That she'd made some sort of mistake.

Instead she'd practically boasted about her skill.

As if she was trying to impress . . .

No. She locked out the disturbing thought.

Cyn was an arrogant lug with an oversized ego. Okay, he

was gorgeous. And sexy. And his hard, warrior body was lickably delicious. But she certainly wasn't going to waste her time trying to impress him.

Siljar cleared her throat. "My dear, can you track them?" she repeated her question.

Fallon swallowed a sigh. It was too late to get out of her unwelcome duty.

Besides, if her talent would help, then she surely had a duty to do whatever she could to prevent the portals from being closed.

"I think so," she said.

"Good." Cyn folded his arms over his chest. "Then she can return to fairyland?"

Fallon's mouth dropped open at his blunt words. "Why you rude—"

Siljar held up a hand. "No."

Cyn's jade green eyes narrowed. "Why not?"

"Although it has been several weeks since you left Fallon's homeland—"

"Several weeks?" Fallon forgot her annoyance with Cyn as she sucked in a shocked breath. How was that possible? It felt as if it'd been a matter of minutes since she was standing in the small reception room in her father's palace.

Siljar gave a lift of her hands. "Traveling through dimensions can often create temporal fluctuations."

She was lying. Oh, it was true that traveling through dimensions could screw with time, but Fallon suspected that the cunning Oracle had deliberately altered time for her own purpose.

With a low growl Cyn clenched his hands in frustration, clearly more pissed than suspicious.

"What's the date?" he demanded.

"The middle of January."

The vampire's icy powers pulsed through the air, making Fallon shiver.

"Shit," he rasped.

Siljar calmly smoothed her hands down her robe, pretending there wasn't a massive vampire filling the cave with enough power to make it collapse on their heads.

"As I was saying, I brought you here so Fallon could concentrate on her task without the interference of her father and her fiancé who are both searching for her."

Fallon sucked in a shocked breath. It made sense that her father would come in search of her. But her fiancé?

The prince barely remembered she was alive most of the time.

"Magnus is here?"

"Fiancé?" Cyn muttered, sending Fallon an oddly angry glare before turning his attention to Siljar. "You can't expect me to be her babysitter?"

"I request that you give her your protection," Siljar spoke before Fallon could call him a jackass. "Which will be considerably easier if you remain behind the potent magic that hides your lair from prying eyes."

"And what about my people?" he snarled. "I've already been gone too long. They need their chief."

Siljar waved away his concern. "You surely have a trusted servant who can keep your presence here a secret and yet allow you to ensure the welfare of your clan?"

The chill in the air became downright frigid. "There are others more suited to taking care of a fairy."

Fallon met him glare for glare. "Amen."

Siljar reached into the pocket of her robe, pulling out a small scroll.

"But they would not be more suited to deciphering this."